Redress of Grievances

Brenda Adcock

Quest Books

Nederland, Texas

ISBN 978-1-932300-86-4
1-932300-86-4

First Printing 2007

9 8 7 6 5 4 3 2 1

Cover design by Donna Pawlowski

Published by:

Regal Crest Enterprises, LLC
4700 Highway 365, Suite A
PMB 210
Port Arthur, Texas 77642

Find us on the World Wide Web at
http://www.regalcrest.biz

Printed in the United States of America

Acknowledgments

My mother never missed a single episode of *Perry Mason* and I suppose that is why I am, and always have been, such a fan of legal dramas on television even though I have been told many times by real attorneys that most, if not all, bear little resemblance to the real thing. I confess to dreaming of one day becoming an attorney myself, but soon realized my future was not in practicing law, but in studying it. I have used it at every opportunity in my classroom and hold those brave enough to stand before a jury and argue the merits of either side in a case in the highest regard.

As always my first thanks must go to Cheryl, who makes what I do worthwhile. I have thanked them before, but the time devoted to reading this manuscript in its assorted revisions by my wonderful readers Kim Miller, Ruta Skujins, and Q cannot be stated often enough. You told me where the story was truly bad and made me think more and, hopefully, write better. My continuing thanks to my friend and editor, Susan Fabian, as well as my technical editor, Rick Reed. Donna Pawlowski came through with yet another wonderful cover. A very special thank you goes to Norma Busse for catching my legal errors and keeping me from looking like a total fool. All of you deserve the credit for the final story far more than I do.

Dedicated to the wonderful fans who read and support
all lesbian literature.

You are the reason I write.

Prologue

SHE DROPPED TO her knees behind a row of bushes on the embankment overlooking Interstate 20 near Dallas. Taking a deep breath, she watched the stream of vehicles flow by. The cool night air ruffled her hair as it was swept upward by the passing cars and trucks, and despite the wind, nervous sweat trickled down her neck and into the hollow of her spine. She pressed the barrel of the rifle against her cheek for a moment, savoring the feeling of the cold, smooth metal against her skin. She was filled with a sense of comfort as her fingers gently caressed the curves of the walnut stock. She felt as powerful as the sleek weapon itself.

This was a good place, affording her an unobstructed view of the west-bound lanes. She glanced over her shoulder at her car parked in the shadows of the underpass behind her. She shifted forward and lay on her stomach to observe the traffic a few more minutes. Yes, this was a very good place, just far enough from the city to be isolated and without the trashy gas stations and convenience stores that seemed to be everywhere. She settled into a comfortable prone position, wrapped the rifle sling around her left forearm, and positioned her elbows to form a secure tripod, the rifle stock pressed firmly in the hollow of her shoulder as she looked through the scope. Her finger tapped restlessly against the trigger guard as she waited for the perfect target to come into view. She ignored cars with a front seat passenger. Tonight the driver had to be a woman, which seemed fitting considering how a woman had humiliated her only a few hours earlier.

Oh, there she is. Alone in that smart little sportster and superior looking in her dark power suit; arrogantly talking to someone on her hands-free cell phone. She closed her finger over the trigger and squeezed it steadily until the bullet erupted from the barrel of the rifle, hitting its target no more than a hundred yards away. As the windshield shattered, she smiled and felt the tension that had been building inside begin to dissolve. You're not in control now, are you, bitch? she thought.

She saw the woman's panicked expression before rolling onto her back, hugging the rifle against her chest. She lightly, lovingly stroked its length, waiting for the climax. As she scanned the stars in the clear night sky she heard the sound of metal screaming as the sports car careened into another vehicle. Her breathing came more quickly with each sound. She smelled the scent of her own arousal as it traveled through her body, reaching its peak at the unmistakable sound of metal colliding with the concrete abutment of the nearby overpass. She felt the final shudders of release course through her as vehicles began braking to avoid the twisted wreckage.

When her breathing began returning to normal, she loosened her grip on the only lover she trusted to satisfy her. She sat up and scooted calmly down the embankment toward her car. She didn't want or need to watch the activity around the site. Even though some drivers had survived in the past, denying her the revenge she sought, she was certain the woman in the power suit had not. She laughed, knowing the next time could be even more satisfying.

Chapter
One

HARRIETT MARKHAM GLANCED briefly at the legal pad in front of her before rising. Casting a reassuring smile at the woman seated beside her, Harriett unbuttoned the single button on her navy blue blazer and moved forward. As she reached the jury box, she paused and removed her glasses, holding them loosely in one hand. "Ladies and gentlemen, you are charged with an awesome responsibility in judging the merits of this case," she began with a soft West Texas accent. "You have listened attentively to the evidence presented by both Mr. Davidson of the District Attorney's office and me, and we both appreciate the time you have given up from your jobs and families to hear this case."

In the midst of Harriett's closing remarks, the courtroom door opened, and a well-dressed woman in her mid-fifties slipped into the room and took a seat in the last row. She had heard Harriett Markham address juries many times in the past. But this was the first time in eleven years. When she saw the glasses Harriett held in her hand, she couldn't restrain a slight smile. Harriett's prop, her security blanket, had remained unchanged.

"Mr. Davidson has presented an admirable case on behalf of the State, and indeed, we should all be disturbed when a person loses his or her life before God intended. It isn't a part of the normal pattern of life for most of us. But neither is being repeatedly beaten by a person who assures you he loves you with each blow he delivers.

"The State has presented the physical evidence to you, and the facts of this case are not in dispute. Lawrence Bowers is dead. Carol Bowers shot him. Those are facts. However, the difference between what the State believes and what I believe is a matter of interpretation. My job has been to convince you that my interpretation of the events leading to the untimely death of Lawrence Bowers is the correct one.

"In all cases like this, the burden of proof lies with the State. They must prove to you, beyond a reasonable doubt, that Carol Bowers killed her husband for no other reason than that she wanted to. She thought about it, planned it, and then executed Lawrence Bowers, a defenseless six foot three, two-hundred-fifty-pound man."

Pausing for effect and turning slightly toward the prosecutor,

Harriett continued. "Remember what you have heard during the last four days. Despite what Mr. Davidson would have you believe, if you consider the testimony of witnesses presented by the defense, you will find that the attorney for the People has failed to meet his burden.

"Friends of the deceased testified to his violent temper that intensified when fueled by alcohol. Douglas Sanders testified that Mr. Bowers was, in fact, drunk and disorderly before he was physically ejected from the Longhorn Tavern on the evening of his death. Susan Castro and Dr. Hector Rivera have given testimony as to numerous occasions when Mrs. Bowers arrived at either their home or clinic for comfort or treatment due to injuries received at the hands of Lawrence Bowers. We have presented physical evidence which documented a long trail of abuse against Mrs. Bowers for at least five years."

Moving slightly away from the jury, she leaned against the wooden railing surrounding the court stenographer's desk and crossed her arms across her chest.

"I know what you're thinking, ladies and gentlemen. Carol Bowers should have left her husband five years ago, and I couldn't agree with you more. But she didn't. She stayed, for reasons none of us will probably ever understand. Why does a whipped dog stay with an abusive owner? Why do you stay at a job you hate? I don't know the answers to those questions, either. But I'm not here to delve into the psychology of abused wives, abused dogs, or abused workers. It isn't your job to determine whether Carol Bowers was abused physically by her husband. That fact is also undisputed. You're here to decide whether she had a right to stop the abuse when she became afraid that failure on her part to react this time could result in her own death. Would there be something worse about this beating than the others? Perhaps not, but did Carol Bowers believe Lawrence Bowers would kill her this time? Eventually, ladies and gentlemen, even a whipped dog will turn on its master.

"The evidence shows that Mr. Bowers was shot at extremely close range. There was gunpowder residue on his clothing at the point of contact. But gunpowder residue was also found on Mrs. Bowers' clothing at a place that would be consistent with a weapon being discharged during a struggle. The prosecution is not claiming that Mrs. Bowers lay in wait for her husband, and they concede she had been an abused spouse. What Mr. Davidson expects you to believe is that based on one or two punches or slaps, Mrs. Bowers had not yet reached the point where deadly force for the protection of her own life was necessary. How many punches or slaps would have been enough? Five? Ten? Twenty? I submit that once you have been knocked unconscious, you are no longer capable of defending yourself.

"Mr. Davidson has presented a vast array of statistics dealing with spousal abuse for you to digest. What those statistics have done is cloud the issue you are considering. The prosecutor has attempted, in essence, to throw a handful of feathers in the air, hoping a duck will fly out. The evidence and testimony do not support any contention of premeditation. This is simply a case of self-defense on Carol Bowers' part and nothing more. Lawrence Bowers is dead, and that is regrettable. But I submit to you that Lawrence Bowers' own actions were the proximate cause of his death. If Lawrence Bowers hadn't been in the habit of drinking heavily and then beating his wife, he'd be alive today, and you wouldn't be sitting in that jury box."

She pushed herself away from the railing and slipped her glasses back on. Looking into the eyes of each juror, Harriett concluded softly.

"The simple truth, ladies and gentlemen, is that once you have considered all of the evidence and the testimony of the witnesses, you have no choice but to return a verdict of not guilty to the charges against Carol Bowers. Thank you."

She returned to the seat next to her client and patted her hand as she sat back and waited for the prosecutor to present his closing argument to the jury. In the back of the courtroom, the woman left as quietly as she had entered.

NINETY MINUTES LATER, Harriett walked through the beveled glass front door of Markham and Lazslo. She had spent the early part of her career in a towering glass office building and had hated the impersonal atmosphere. Eleven years earlier, she had purchased an older home in Austin and spent six months refurbishing it to house her new private legal practice. For the first few years, it had served double duty as her office and home. But six years later, she had taken on a partner, and that coupled with a steadily growing clientele, had finally forced her to live elsewhere.

Waving at her receptionist briefly, she continued past a small, homey waiting area and down the carpeted hallway toward her office. Phyllis Schaeffer, her secretary for the last eleven years, was at a large file cabinet near her desk. Harriett opened her briefcase and dropped a thick manila folder on Phyllis's desk. "Any messages, Phyllis?" she asked.

"A couple," Phyllis answered over her shoulder. "Strike another blow for the underdog?"

Harriett glanced through her messages. "Hope so. By the way, I appreciate the overtime you've put in on the Bowers case. Why don't you take off early, and treat your husband to dinner on me? Put it on the office credit card, and I'll authorize it."

"I was just doing my job, Ms. Markham."

"Never turn down free food, Phyllis. Nick in?"

"I don't think he's back from lunch yet."

Harriett performed the same ritual every time she won a case in court or felt confidant of a win. Entering the bathroom that connected to her office, she looked in the mirror and winked at herself. "Way to go, kiddo," she said to her reflection in the mirror.

Following the greeting to herself, she undressed, changing from the business suit, heels and pantyhose she hated into comfortable gray slacks and a loose fitting black, gray, and white striped man-tailored shirt. Rolling her shirtsleeves up, she ran warm water in the sink and washed her face, removing most of the makeup she had worn for court. She patted her face dry and reapplied only a thin line of eyeliner and a light coating of lipstick before running a brush through her hair. Gazing at herself in the mirror once again, she smiled. "Much better."

There were a number of advantages to having an office in a house, not the least of which was the kitchen. A side door from her office led into a small kitchen area with a well-stocked refrigerator. She rummaged around and a few minutes later returned to her office with a sandwich and a glass of iced tea. Propping her feet up on an overstuffed hassock, she leaned back on an early American couch and bit into a delicious sandwich. She was relieved to have finally reached closure on the Bowers case.

Her thoughts and sandwich were interrupted by the buzz of her intercom. "Could you pick up, Ms. Markham?" Phyllis asked.

Barefoot, she dragged herself up from the couch and went to her desk. She placed her sandwich on a piece of paper and finished swallowing her last bite as she sat and picked up the sleek beige receiver. "What's up, Phyllis?" she asked, looking longingly at her sandwich.

"You have a visitor, Ms. Markham. She says she's an old friend."

"Does she have a name?"

"Alexis Dunne."

For a moment, Harriett was speechless trying to imagine why her former lover would be in Austin and wanting to see her. Memories flooded her mind, not all of them pleasant.

"Ms. Markham?"

"Uh, I'm sorry, Phyllis. Could you ask Ms. Dunne to wait a few minutes and then show her in?"

Replacing the receiver on its cradle, she looked around her office but didn't know what she was looking for. In what seemed more like a few seconds than a few minutes, there was a knock at her office door.

Phyllis opened the door, and Harriett stood as Alexis Dunne entered the office. A tall, slender woman, she seemed to glide effortlessly into the room.

"Is there anything you need, Ms. Markham?" Phyllis asked.

"No, thank you, Phyllis, unless Ms. Dunne would like something to drink?"

"I wouldn't mind a cup of coffee, if it's not too much trouble." Alexis smiled at Phyllis. If anything, Alexis was more stunning than Harriett remembered. After eleven years, the only difference in her appearance was a slight graying at the temples of her short, dark hair, giving her a decidedly distinguished appearance. Even her hair was styled the same way Harriett remembered, sweeping across her forehead, tapered along her neckline and cut over her ears to reveal small gold hoop earrings. She was casually dressed in tan corduroy slacks and a brown sweater.

"How do you take your coffee, Ms. Dunne?" Phyllis asked.

"One teaspoon of sugar and plenty of cream," Harriett answered before Alexis could reply.

Phyllis looked questioningly at her employer as she left the office. Alexis waited until the door was closed before turning her head toward Harriett.

"Nice office," she smiled. "Very homey. Very you."

"It meets my needs."

"May I?" Alexis asked, pointing to a chair across from Harriett's desk.

"Of course."

Leaning back in the chair, Alexis crossed her legs and glanced around the office.

"What can I do for you, Alex?" Harriett asked.

"I have a case I'd like to refer to you."

"Really?"

"It's a criminal case, and I know you're the right attorney to handle it."

"Have you given up criminal practice?"

"No, but I can't take this one." Alex shrugged. "Conflict of interest."

"So why am I the lucky attorney you want to palm it off on? Winston and Dunne must have a dozen excellent criminal associates."

"This client needs your particular expertise, Harriett. It's a very delicate case. However, Winston and Dunne is prepared to provide whatever support you might need."

Their conversation was interrupted as Phyllis returned with a mug of coffee and set it on a small table next to Alex's chair. Smiling the smile that Harriett had seen many times, Alex picked up the cup and took a sip.

"Perfect," she purred, looking at Phyllis.

As soon as Phyllis left the office, Harriett leaned forward slightly.

"I'm afraid I wouldn't be interested in taking on a case that would take me away from Austin, Alex. I have too many cases pending here."

"I'm prepared to offer you the use of our corporate jet, which would allow you to move more easily between Austin and Dallas."

"This must be some case," Harriett said as she pushed light brown hair back from her face and took a deep breath.

"It is. What I'd like to propose, Harriett, is that you meet this evening with the client's brother. He has suggested dinner where you would be able to ask him whatever questions you need to about the case."

"I'd really like to help you out, Alex, but–"

"Don't turn the case down before you talk to the gentleman tonight."

"Is he the conflict of interest you mentioned?"

"Yes. He's engaged to my sister, Paige. She's a legislative assistant to State Senator Parker Collins. They became engaged over the Thanksgiving holidays."

"And the accused is...?"

"His sister. The Senator believes she would feel more comfortable with a female attorney, and naturally, I thought of you. I agreed to contact you on behalf of the family and arrange a meeting to discuss the case."

"There are hundreds of good attorneys who would be much more delighted than I to receive a referral like this."

"He wants you, Harriett," Alex said firmly. "He's aware of your excellent reputation."

"Uh, huh. Why can't he come here?"

"He prefers to meet outside your office. I can warn you that this will probably be a very high profile case. Potentially a media circus. He doesn't want people following him around to see what he's going to do."

"It sounds like I'm preparing to make a drug buy."

"It's not quite that bad," Alex chuckled, sipping her coffee. "I'm surprised you remembered. About the coffee."

"Just one of those annoying miscellaneous pieces of trivia that seem to stick with you," Harriett frowned. "Where and when?"

"Seven at the Austin Country Club."

"I suppose that means I'll have to wear something more appropriate than this," she said looking down at her clothes.

"Only if you feel you need to. I'll send a car for you."

"I think I can find my way. Is there anything else?"

"No. You can cover everything else this evening," Alex answered, setting her cup down. "We'll see you about seven then?"

Harriett stood and walked around the desk preparing to escort Alex to the door.

Alex smiled as she glanced at Harriett's bare feet, "I seem to remember a little piece of trivia myself. You still talk to yourself in the mirror, too?"

"Sometimes," Harriett said, blushing slightly.

"I can't tell you how much I appreciate this, Harriett," Alex said as she followed her to the door. "And by the way, I saw you in court this morning. You still have a special way of connecting with juries."

Chapter
Two

NO ONE HAD ever accused Harriett of being a cheerful person. Pleasant maybe, but she personally abhorred perpetually cheerful people. Looking through her clothes, she couldn't have been any further from cheerful. Eventually, she thought what the hell, and pulled out a sapphire silk slack suit. She had already made up her mind to turn down the case but decided to hear what her potential client's brother had to say. Time had not lessened the nagging sense of loyalty she felt toward Alex and Winston and Dunne. A tap on her bedroom door interrupted her thoughts.

"Aunt Harriett?" a girl's voice said. "Can I come in?"

"Yes, you *may*," Harriett corrected as she pulled on a white blouse with a ruffled front and began buttoning it.

A teenage girl of eighteen stepped into the bedroom, her long blonde hair piled loosely on top of her head. Plopping down on her aunt's bed, she said "Great suit! Is it new?"

Harriett smiled warmly at the girl. "No, I just haven't had a chance to wear it lately."

"Hot date?" the girl smiled back.

Looking at herself in the mirror, Harriett said with a laugh, "I don't have hot dates anymore, Lacey. I'm too busy worrying about *your* hot dates."

As she caught her niece's face in the mirror, Harriett noticed the teenager's uncanny resemblance to her father when he had been her age. She couldn't help but be amazed that in what seemed like the blink of an eye, Lacey had, in fact, become an attractive young woman and was at an age that could give any parent ulcers from worrying.

"I have a game tonight," Lacey said. "Will you be able to make it?"

"What time is the game?" Harriett asked.

"Seven-thirty."

"I wish you had told me sooner, sweetheart. I'll miss the first half, but I'll eat as fast as I can. Okay?"

"Great," Lacey said as she sprang up from the bed.

"Lacey," she said as the girl reached the bedroom door.

"Yeah."

"I'm sorry I've been so busy lately."

The girl smiled at her. "I know how you are when you have a case. But you owe me an obscenely lavish shopping spree for my infinite patience," she said dramatically.

A FEW MINUTES before seven, Harriett stopped her midnight blue show truck in front of the Austin Country Club. Looking around the parking lot, she noticed there didn't seem to be an overabundance of trucks, and the parking attendant looked around the expensive wood paneled interior as if he had just been beamed aboard a flying saucer.

She had never been to the Austin Country Club and was surprised by the pleasant, understated atmosphere inside. Harriett had played golf once or twice when she was younger, but somehow the idea of smacking a little dimpled ball around and then walking after it all day had lacked an appeal for her. Too much exercise for too little gratification. Alex, dressed in a gray, subtly pinstriped business suit that showed off her well-defined, athletic body, strode across the lobby toward Harriett.

"Let me show you where we are," Alex greeted her, smiling warmly as her eyes wandered over Harriett.

"Sorry if I'm late," Harriett said.

"You're not," Alex said as she rested her hand lightly in the small of Harriett's back and escorted her toward a small room that adjoined the main dining area.

Sitting at a table near the rear of the room, a man who appeared to be in his late thirties or early forties stood as he saw Harriett and Alexis approach. Seated next to him was a young woman whom Harriett assumed was Paige Dunne. Alexis's sister had successfully blossomed from an awkward teenager into a beautiful raven-haired woman.

"Parker, allow me to introduce Harriett Markham," Alex said. "Harriett, State Senator Parker Collins."

Harriett extended her hand to the man. "Senator."

"And although she's changed just a little since the last time you saw her, I'm sure you remember my sister, Paige," Alex smiled, placing her hand gently on the young woman's shoulder.

"She's certainly changed. Much more beautiful than I remember." Harriett said as she saw a pink flush travel up Paige's neck.

"I hope you don't mind if I pre-ordered your dinner, Ms. Markham," Collins said. "Alex told me you liked prime rib, medium rare."

Another one of those annoying bits of trivia, Harriett thought as she glanced at Alex out of the corner of her eye. She said, "That's fine, Senator."

"It's not necessary to call me Senator, Ms. Markham," Collins said as she took the seat across from him. "We should be on a first name basis if we're both going to be involved in my sister's case."

"That actually hasn't been decided yet. I've only agreed to hear what you have to tell me about the case. Alex may have already told you that I'm not very enthusiastic about traveling to Dallas for a trial."

"I'm not an attorney, Harriett," Collins said casually, "but Alex believes you might be able to get a...what did you call it, Alex?"

"A change of venue," Alex said flatly as she settled in the chair to Harriett's left.

"Right," Collins smiled. "You might be able to have the case transferred here to Travis County."

An Hispanic waiter poured coffee, and Harriett waited until he left before resuming her conversation with Collins.

"Why don't you tell me a little about the case," she said, stirring creamer into her cup.

Collins took a deep breath and looked briefly at Paige for support before speaking.

"It's very difficult for me to talk about, Harriett. The whole thing seems so unreal. My sister, Sharon, has been arrested for murder."

"Whom is she accused of murdering?"

"The police claim four people."

Harriett turned her head slightly toward Alex, but her face revealed nothing.

"She was arrested by Dallas police the day before yesterday. So far, our family attorney has been representing her, but it's his opinion that she needs someone with more criminal expertise to represent her. That's when I contacted Alex, and she recommended you."

"What charge did the grand jury hand down?"

"Murder, first degree, times four," Alex said over the top of her coffee cup.

"Did your sister allegedly kill all of these people at once?"

"No. Apparently they were spread out over the last year and a half."

"Did she have any relationship with them? Co-workers? Acquaintances?"

"Total strangers. Three men and one woman."

"Do you know what evidence the police have that indicates your sister is a suspect?"

"They have a weapon. It was found at her home and the police claim her fingerprints are on it. According to our family attorney, they have some other evidence that doesn't look good for her, either."

"Sounds like a slam dunk for the prosecution. What exactly would you expect me to do for your sister?"

Leaning forward on his elbows, the look on Collins's face became more serious. "I want you to make sure she receives whatever help she needs. If you knew Sharon, you'd know she couldn't possibly have committed any of these crimes. Unless she's lost her mind."

"Do you have some reason to believe she's mentally ill?"

"If she did, in fact, kill those people, it's the only possible explanation. She's such a gentle, quiet woman that the thought of her toting a rifle around and blasting innocent people seems totally incomprehensible to me."

Harriett took a drink of her coffee and glanced at Alex. Setting her cup down, she turned to Alex and asked quietly, "Could I speak to you for a minute?"

"Of course," Alex said as she rose from her chair.

Harriett left the table first and opened the door leading into a service hallway. Alex came through the door a moment later.

"I can't believe you thought for even one moment I would consider taking this case," she seethed as she spun around to face Alex.

"I don't know another attorney who could handle it better," Alex said calmly, folding her arms across her chest.

"You know as well as I do, Alex, that this case is extremely similar to the Wilkes case."

"No, it isn't. Sharon Taggart isn't anything like Jared Wilkes. He was a sexual predator, and Sharon certainly doesn't fall into that category."

"They're both serial killers for Christ's sake! I don't handle cases like that anymore, and you damn well knew that before you contacted me." Harriett began to pace back and forth in the narrow hallway, fighting to bring her emotions under control.

"The Wilkes case was a long time ago, Harriett."

Snapping her head around to look at her, Harriett said, "And I still think about it every goddamn day. I can't go through that again. I won't. And it's not fair for you to ask me to."

"Look, Harriett, in all likelihood Sharon Taggart is going to be found guilty. What Parker and his family want is to avoid the death penalty. That's what you'd be working for, not an acquittal."

"If she killed those people then maybe she should receive the death penalty," Harriett argued.

"She deserves the best defense she and her family can afford. I believe that and so do you. I've heard you say it a thousand times. Even the most perverted criminal deserves the best effort an attorney can put forth."

"I do believe that, but if I took this case I might not be able to put forth my best."

Alexis took Harriett by the arms and waited until their eyes met. Alex's cool gray eyes hadn't lost their ability to demand Harriett's attention.

"You have to put the Wilkes case behind you, Harriett. You did your job, and the consequences turned out to be tragic, but the prosecution didn't do its job. If they had played by the rules, Jared Wilkes would never have gotten out of jail. You were not responsible for what happened."

"I'm turning this case down, Alex. One serial killer is enough for a lifetime."

"At least talk to Sharon before you decline the case. Then if you still want to turn it down, I won't try to convince you otherwise."

Harriett shook her head. "The best I can do tonight is tell Collins that I'll think about it and give him my decision in a few days. I'd like to talk to my law partner first."

"Fair enough," Alex said as she lightly squeezed Harriett's arms before releasing them.

Harriett loved prime rib, but that evening she could have been eating cardboard and wouldn't have known the difference. Dinner seemed to last forever, and she was eager to get away from Alex, Collins, and Paige. Memories suddenly dredged up about the Wilkes case, coupled with others associated with Alexis Dunne, overwhelmed her. She thought she had gotten over the past and successfully walked away from it. Nothing could have been further from the truth.

At the end of the longest evening of her life, Harriett waited for the parking valet to retrieve her vehicle.

"I wouldn't drag you into this case if I didn't think you could handle it," Alex said as she came up behind Harriett.

"I still believe you must have an associate who can handle this one."

"We've never had an associate as good as you, Harriett," Alex said warmly.

"How is Doug?"

"Doug's Doug," Alex shrugged with a smile. "You know how he is."

The thought of Douglas Winston made Harriett smile slightly. He was a bear of a man and as gentle as a puppy. Although Doug and Alexis were equal partners in their law firm, there weren't two people on the planet more different. Doug hated the social niceties required by their clients and turned anything even remotely social over to Alex. Doug preferred hunting and fishing to cocktail parties and, as far as Harriett knew, had only attended parties given for Winston and Dunne employees.

Looking down at the pavement, Harriett wasn't sure whether she wanted to ask the next question or not.

"And how is Gwen?" she finally managed to ask.

"We're not together anymore," Alex said matter-of-factly.

"I'm sorry to hear that, Alex."

Alex looked at her and the corners of her mouth turned up slightly, "No, you're not."

Harriett was grateful when she saw her truck coming toward them. The valet jumped out and held the door for Harriett as she walked around the front of her vehicle.

"This yours?" Alex laughed.

"Yes."

"What did you do with your Beemer?"

"Traded it in. It wasn't really me. I grew up in dusty, small town West Texas, remember?"

Alex opened the passenger door and looked around the inside of the truck.

"Pretty fancy," she nodded. Her eye caught Harriett's for a moment. "Maybe you've changed more than I realized," she grinned.

"And maybe you didn't know me as well as you thought you did. Do you need a ride?"

"I can take a cab."

"Get in, Alex. You might as well see how it feels to ride around in a cowboy Cadillac."

Twenty minutes later, Harriett wheeled her truck into the drive near the front entrance of the Omni Hotel in downtown Austin.

"They have a fair bar here," Alex said. "Can I buy you a drink before you go home?"

"I can't. I promised Lacey that I'd make the last half of her basketball game."

"How is Lacey?"

"Graduating from high school this year."

"She must be tall like you if she's playing basketball," Alex said. After a pause, she continued, "I'm going to be in Austin a couple of days. I'd like to see you again."

"That's probably not a good idea, Alex, but I appreciate the offer."

Alex hesitated a minute before getting out of the truck and entering the hotel. Harriett had to stop herself from following her with her eyes. It would have been a good evening for several drinks. Pulling the truck into unusually light traffic along Congress Avenue, she headed toward Interstate 35 and St. John's Prep.

Chapter
Three

TRYING TO SETTLE her mind, Harriett leaned back against a pillow on her bed and rested a legal pad against her drawn up knees. She had ten days to prepare a motion for an appeal on a pro bono case involving a homeless man who had been arrested and convicted in the death of another homeless man during a fight over squatter's rights for a piece of worthless dirt and weeds under a train trestle in southern Travis County. But no matter how hard she tried, every time she tried to concentrate on her motion, Jared Wilkes's face flashed through her mind. She was furious at Alex for helping him escape from the mental prison in which she had had him safely locked away.

Jared Wilkes had been a young man who had everything: wealthy, doting parents who had conceived him late in their lives; and the finest life had to offer someone of his social standing. And yet he had chosen to become a serial rapist and a murderer.

NEARLY TWELVE YEARS earlier, she had been preparing for a well-deserved long weekend and clearing the last of her paperwork from her desk when Alex tapped on the door and peeked into her office.

"Do you have a minute, Harriett?" she asked.

Harriett smiled when she saw her. Even if she had been busy, she would have made time for Alexis Dunne.

"Of course. I'm just finishing up some paperwork. Nothing is going to distract me from this weekend," she smiled.

Alex wasn't smiling, and Harriett became immediately apprehensive. They had planned this weekend together for so long, but the look on Alex's face told her all of their precautions and well-laid plans were circling the drain.

"No one deserves the time off more than you, Harriett."

"But," Harriett frowned.

"One of our clients has a problem, and Doug and I both think you're the right associate to handle it."

"And I don't suppose this client can wait until Monday."

"You could refuse the case. We'd certainly honor your wishes,"

Alex continued.

Sensing Alex's managerial mood, Harriett leaned back in her chair and exhaled, "What's the client's problem?"

Alex returned to Harriett's office door and opened it.

"Eleanor, please hold Ms. Markham's calls for about thirty minutes," Alex said to Harriett's secretary.

Alex depressed the lock on the office door and closed it behind her. Harriett wondered how much Eleanor knew or thought she knew about her relationship with the firm's senior partner. Alex unbuttoned the coat to her suit and sat down on the couch as Harriett rose from her chair and poured two cups of coffee from the coffeemaker on the credenza behind her desk. Handing one to Alex as she joined her on the couch, Harriett kicked her heels off, leaned back slightly and looked at Alex.

"So tell me about this case only I am qualified to handle," she said with a smile.

Alex sipped at her coffee, looking as though she was organizing thoughts in her head.

"The client is Jared Wilkes. His father is Clarence Wilkes, CEO of Wilkes Transport, one of our corporate clients. Jared was arrested this morning by Dallas PD," Alex explained.

"What's the charge?" Harriett asked.

"Rape and murder times four," Alex answered quietly.

"He's accused of raping and murdering four women?"

"Four teenage girls between the ages of sixteen and nineteen," Alex nodded.

"I see," Harriett said.

"The deaths have occurred over about a ten month period."

"Do you know what the police have in the way of evidence?"

"Nothing specific. Of course, old man Wilkes is absolutely positive his son is innocent and wants the best Winston and Dunne has to offer." Turning to look at Harriett, she said, "And that's you."

"Why aren't you handling the case, Alex? After all, you are Winston and Dunne."

"Wilkes, the son, wants a younger woman for his counsel. Thinks the jury will believe he didn't commit the rapes if a woman is presenting his case."

"He's probably right."

"He's a nothing," Alex said with a touch of anger in her voice as she leaned her head back on the couch. "Been kicked out of every prep school and college in north Texas. As far as I know, he's never done a worthwhile thing in his entire privileged life. But he's never been in any serious trouble before, either. Just the usual juvenile problems with speeding and drinking."

"Where is he now?" Harriett asked, softly brushing her fingertips lightly along Alex's temple.

"Waiting for you at police headquarters."

"I haven't agreed to take the case yet."

"Fact is, Harriett, Junior knows we handle his father's legal matters and said he'd read about one of the cases you defended last year. Clarence Wilkes didn't exactly ask us to recommend someone. He demanded we assign his son's case to you."

"So you're not really giving me the option of rejecting the case?"

"Of course we are. If you're uncomfortable with the case, or if you agree to meet with Jared and then want to turn it down, you're free to do that."

"Why do I have that uncomfortable feeling that unless I take the case, Winston and Dunne might lose Wilkes Transport as a client?"

"People like Wilkes always make threats like that. They're used to having people jump through their asses when they speak, but Winston and Dunne will never allow itself to get tangled up in being intimidated by its clients."

"I guess it can't hurt to talk to Wilkes. Who knows? Maybe he is innocent," Harriett said taking a drink from her coffee cup. "The worst that can happen is that I'll delay my weekend by a few hours. Not much anyone can do before Monday morning anyway and it isn't likely any judge is going to grant bail on a multiple homicide."

Alex looked at her, and the slow smile Harriett had come to love crossed her face. Alex outlined Harriett's face with the tips of her fingers before rising from the couch and leaving the office. Harriett picked up her shoes and went to her desk, glancing at her wristwatch before punching the intercom button.

"Yes, Ms. Markham," Eleanor's voice answered.

"Would you see if you can catch someone at the DA's office, Eleanor? If possible, whoever will be prosecuting the Jared Wilkes case," Harriett said, slipping her shoes back on. "And see if you can reach my mother."

She vaguely recalled reading an inside article noting the death of a teenage girl in Dallas, but since that wasn't a total rarity, she didn't remember much else about the article. As soon as she knew more, she would get Eleanor to research back issues of the newspaper for articles about the cases her potential client was being charged with. Her thoughts were interrupted by a buzz on her intercom.

"Yes, Eleanor."

"I have Assistant District Attorney Connor on line two, Ms. Markham," Eleanor reported.

"Thank you," Harriett said. As she picked up the receiver, she pulled off an earring and leaned back in her chair, turning to look out her office window at a sun that was swiftly setting on what was supposed to be the beginning of her perfect weekend.

"Todd? Harriett Markham. How are you?" she said.

"I'd be better if I could get the hell out of here and go home. I was

almost out the door when your secretary called. What can I do for you?"
Todd Connor asked.

"I'm calling about the Wilkes case, Todd, and..."

"Please tell me you haven't agreed to represent that pervert,
Harriett. It's a loser from start to finish."

"Can you tell me what you've got?"

"You'll get it during the pre-trial disclosure. There isn't anything
I'd care to talk about over the phone, but it should be sufficient to get
Mr. Wilkes the fatal cocktail somewhere down the line."

"You sound pretty confident."

"On this one, I am. They don't come any guiltier than this guy,
Harriett, and I'd advise you not to let the honchos at Winston and
Dunne convince you this is a career maker."

"The young man's father is a client here and has asked us to help
the kid. You know how it goes."

"Have you talked to 'the kid' yet?"

"No, I'm meeting with him in a little bit, but thought I'd check in
with your office first."

Connor laughed, "You just wanted to know who you'd be going
against if you took the case. Guess that'd be me. Don't you hate it when
you have to oppose a friend in court?"

"Yeah, but hopefully you can still remain friends when it's over."

"You got a loser here, Harriett, but my office won't hold anything
back from you. You'll get full disclosure."

"I know, and thanks for the advice, Todd. Give my best to Erica."

"If I ever get to see her again."

As soon as she hung up, Eleanor buzzed again to tell Harriett that
her mother was on hold.

"Mom," she said as she picked up the receiver again, "I just wanted
to make sure you and Lacey got home all right."

"We got in a little while ago."

"Are you sure you don't mind having her for the long weekend? I
know it's a little late to ask that, but..."

"Don't worry, sweetheart," Irene Markham laughed. "Lacey has a
full weekend planned. She's as much of an organizer as you were. Do
you want to talk to her?"

"Yeah. For just a minute. Thanks, Mom."

"Hey, Aunt Harriett!" Lacey's cheerful six-year-old voice chirped.

"Hi, baby. Grandma told me you have big plans for the weekend.
Don't you run her ragged, you hear?"

"I won't," Lacey said. Lowering her voice, the girl giggled into the
phone, "Grandma is really the one with the big plans though."

"I know," Harriett smiled. "I'll pick you up Sunday afternoon.
Have fun. I love you."

"Love you, too."

Twenty minutes later, Harriett walked out of her office carrying her briefcase. Stopping at Eleanor's desk, she placed the last of her billable hour summaries on her secretary's desk.

"I'm going to the Dallas County Jail to interview a possible client, Eleanor. After that I'll be incommunicado for a couple of days. So if you have anything for me, you'd better give it to me now. Otherwise, it will have to wait until Monday morning."

"I think I've already given you everything that was urgent, Ms. Markham, and fended off the rest until next week," Eleanor smiled. Then lowering her voice conspiratorially, she whispered, "Have a great weekend. You deserve it."

Leaning down slightly, she winked at Eleanor and whispered back, "You're right, I do."

As she moved toward the elevator, Doug Winston came down the hall from his office, stopping as he reached her.

"I assume Alex spoke to you about the Wilkes case," Doug said, running a big hand over the beginnings of beard stubble.

"I'm on my way to the jail now. I'll make a decision after I speak to the Wilkes boy and let you know Monday morning."

Taking her by the arm and pulling her slightly closer to him, Winston said, "I don't want you to feel pressured to take this case, Harriett. I've met the Wilkes kid, and he's not someone I'd personally like to spend a lot of time around."

"Let me talk to him, Doug. I think I can handle it."

"I'd never doubt that," he said. "Sorry if this has crunched your weekend."

"It's okay, I'm not going that far from Dallas and will still have plenty of time to rest up."

"Planning to sleep in and play lazy for a few days, huh?" he asked.

"Something like that." Harriett smiled wryly.

The drive from the office tower that housed Winston and Dunne to the Dallas Police Headquarters Building ordinarily took about twenty minutes, but the late Thursday afternoon traffic made the trip longer than usual. It was after five by the time she parked her metallic gray BMW in the parking lot reserved for attorneys and entered the back door in central booking that served as the attorney's entrance. Stopping in front of a female desk officer, Harriett opened her briefcase for inspection and signed in.

"Harriett Markham to see Jared Wilkes," she said.

"Interview Room Nine," the woman said pointing down the hallway. "They'll bring him down in a few minutes."

"Do you have his jacket here?" Harriett asked.

The officer looked through a short stack of file folders and produced one marked "Wilkes, Jared, Case No. 4536885."

HARRIETT SLIPPED HER glasses on and took out a legal pad and a

pen as she waited for her prospective client to join her. The folder on
Jared Wilkes gave her the basic information about the accused. Twenty-
five years old, six feet, a hundred seventy pounds, no distinguishing
scars or marks. Placed under arrest and charged with four counts of
rape and murder. Victims were listed as Lydia Marshall, age sixteen, a
high school student; another high school student, Tiffany Watson, age
seventeen; Laurie Mitchell, an eighteen-year-old high school senior; and
Carrie Margolis, a nineteen-year-old college freshman at SMU. The
investigator's report showed four nearly identical crimes, each
involving extreme brutality. Apparently the victims had been beaten
into submission and then raped. Marks on the girls' necks indicated that
each had been strangled to death. However, due to the extensive
amount of bruising on the victims' necks, the medical examiner
speculated each girl had been strangled nearly to the brink of death
during repeated rapes over an extended period of time. Furthermore, it
was possible that the rapes may have involved some form of
autoeroticism occurring as the victims lost consciousness. From the
report, it seemed to Harriett that the medical examiner had done quite a
lot of speculating.

Nearly fifteen minutes later, the door of the interview room
opened, and Jared Wilkes, handcuffed to a waist chain and wearing leg
shackles, shuffled into the room. The bright orange prisoner's coveralls
fit loosely on the young man's body, and his dark hair hung down
slightly onto his forehead. Harriett stood as Wilkes was led into the
room, accompanied by two Dallas County jailers.

"Please remove the cuffs," she instructed.

"You sure?" one of the jailers asked.

"Since you're going to be right outside the door, I doubt Mr. Wilkes
would be able to do anything very drastic," she said.

Wilkes rubbed his wrists as the cuffs were removed and smiled at
Harriett. He was an attractive young man with blue-gray eyes that
stood out under his dark hair and eyebrows. As soon as his hands were
free, he ran them through his hair. He had a quick smile and had
probably benefited at some time in his life from the services of an
excellent orthodontist. Pulling out a chair opposite Harriett and sitting
down, he took a cigarette out of his coverall pocket and stuck it between
his narrow lips.

"Got it from another prisoner, but the guards won't allow us to
have matches," he shrugged. "Go figure."

Harriett pulled a small lighter from her briefcase and shoved it
toward him.

"My name is Harriett Markham, Mr. Wilkes. Your father has
requested that my law firm represent you. But first, I need to get a little
information."

"When can I get out of here?" Wilkes asked as he lit the cigarette.

"Considering the nature of the crimes you're charged with, I wouldn't bet on any time soon."

He extended the lighter toward her, and she glanced up when she saw him move. She held her hand out, and he set it gently into the palm of her hand, allowing his index finger to run the length of her palm as he withdrew his hand. The action startled her momentarily, and her eyes met his. He seemed pleased that he had gotten a reaction from her.

"Why do the police think you're a suspect in these killings, Mr. Wilkes?"

"Bad timing, I guess," he said as he shrugged.

"The police usually have a little more than that."

"I knew the girls who were killed."

"In what capacity?"

"Just acquaintances. You know, hanging around."

"Do you usually hang around with sixteen and seventeen year olds?"

"A lot of them go to the clubs and have fake ID's, Ms. Markham. With the way girls dress and act these days, it's hard for a guy to know how old they really are."

"So you met these girls at clubs?"

"Yeah."

"Ever take any of them out?"

"I take out lots of girls. I might have asked one or two of them out."

"Did you have intercourse with any of these girls?"

"You mean the ones who were killed?"

"Yes."

"I don't believe so. I'd have to see pictures of them to know for sure. I don't always catch the names of the women I have sex with."

Harriett wrote four names on her legal pad and turned it for Wilkes to read.

"These the girls they say I killed?" Wilkes asked, glancing briefly at the pad.

"Raped and killed, yes."

Jared Wilkes eyes flashed up to Harriett's face.

"I've never had to resort to physical violence to fuck a woman, counselor. There's plenty out there who are more than willing to jump into bed and spread their legs without the slightest hesitation. Why would I need to force myself on one who didn't want it?"

"Rape isn't about sex, Mr. Wilkes. Men with seemingly normal sex lives still rape."

Wilkes leaned forward and stared at her.

"But sex is the ultimate domination, Harriett. Every time a woman slides her body under a man's, it's a sign of submission that says, 'fuck me, I want it.'"

"Is that your own interpretation?"

"Nah, I read it somewhere," he said matter-of-factly as he leaned back and exhaled cigarette smoke. "But I think it's an accurate description."

"What if, in the midst of this sexual submission, the woman changed her mind? How would you feel about that?"

"There are plenty of other willing fish in the ocean."

Wilkes took another drag on his cigarette and his eyes scanned Harriett's face.

"How would you let a man know you were ready to give it up, Harriett?" Wilkes asked.

"Do you recognize any of those names?" Harriett asked pointing at the pad, ignoring the question.

"I already told you I knew them. I just don't remember whether I slept with any of them. I might have."

"Do you use drugs or alcohol?"

"I've been known to drink more than my share, and dear old Mom and Dad stuck me in rehab once a couple of years ago."

"For drinking?"

"Coke," he answered shaking his head. "But I've kicked that now. Found a better way to get high."

"And what is that?"

"Fuckin' women," Wilkes smiled broadly. "I like women. Very intoxicating. That's a nice perfume you're wearing, by the way. What is it?"

"According to the detective's report, you were seen with each of these girls on the night they died. And they have a hair and semen type match on all four that matches your hair and semen. I assume you have an explanation for that."

"Look, I said I might have slept with them. That doesn't mean I killed them."

"You like your sex a little kinky, Jared?"

"What do you mean by kinky?" Wilkes asked looking surprised by the question.

"Come on, Jared. Into any S&M, leather, whips, that kind of thing?"

"Is that what turns you on?"

"My sex life isn't in question. Before we go any further, there's one thing you should know, Mr. Wilkes."

"Yeah? What's that?" Wilkes smiled.

"If you expect me to represent you in court, you can't bullshit me. You have to tell me the absolute truth. Nothing you tell me can ever be repeated by me to anyone. If you told me right now that you're guilty as hell, I couldn't tell anyone. So I want you to cut the crap, and tell me the truth. If you're not willing to do that, find yourself another lawyer. So far you're not impressing me, if that's what you've been trying to do. I've been a practicing adult a long time, and there's not much that shocks me anymore."

Jared finished his cigarette and crushed it out in an ashtray on the table without looking at Harriett. She saw his jaw muscle tighten and relax.

"What's it going to be, Mr. Wilkes? I have plans for the weekend and would like to get the hell out of here."

"Okay, I'll tell you the truth, Ms. Markham. I've been a pain in the ass since I was born. Always in trouble and guilty more often than not. I admit to drinking too much and using drugs on occasion, but I'm not a murderer. I knew all of those girls, and I had sex with them, but I didn't kill them. I should have gone to the police voluntarily after Lydia and Tiffany were killed, but they were both underage, and I didn't want to get slapped with a statutory charge. But I guess that would have been better than a rape and murder charge."

"Didn't you think it was unusual that four girls you'd slept with all wound up dead?"

"Of course, but there are plenty of others I scored with who are still alive to talk about it. Maybe someone followed me and killed those girls after I left them."

"Do you have an alibi for where you were after you left them?"

"Not one that anyone would believe. All I can tell you is that I didn't kill those girls."

"Okay. Let me look over what else the police have, and I'll make a decision by Monday about whether I'll take your case. Do they have you separated from the other prisoners here?"

Jared lowered his head and nodded. "I just want to get out here," he mumbled.

"Unless the police suddenly discover another suspect that probably isn't going to happen for quite a while."

Chapter
Four

BY THE TIME Harriett pointed her BMW north toward the Texas-Oklahoma border, it was almost dark. Despite the fact that it was a long weekend, traffic was light, and she made good time. Ninety minutes later, she crossed the Oklahoma border not far from Lake Texoma. For over twenty years, her father had owned a fishing cabin on the lake. When Farley Markham died, he left the cabin to her. She had accompanied her father to the cabin many times, and she had nothing but good memories of the times the two of them had spent there. Over the years, the cabin had fallen into some disrepair. Farley hadn't made many trips after Harriett left home and had let annual repairs slide. Since his death, she had expended a tidy sum to have the chimney re-bricked and the exterior of the cabin repaired and weatherproofed. In the last two or three years, she had slowly refurbished the two bedroom cabin to the point where a person could probably inhabit it year round. She thought that one day she might retire to the cabin, but for now, it was her private getaway to stabilize her hectic life. She wished she could make more than three or four trips a year.

As she turned off the main road and onto a gravel side road, she was eager to get into the safety of the cabin. Following the road along the edge of the lake, she saw lights in the cabin windows and a wisp of smoke floating lazily from the chimney. The sun was setting; and the evening sky held hints of cooler weather, and the smell of distant rain was in the air. She loved the smell of impending rain, with its promise to wash everything away and make it fresh and clean again. She let her vehicle roll to a stop on the grass in front of the cabin and got out. The lake was as smooth as glass in the moonlight. Good fishing night, she thought. A short fishing pier jutted out into the water, and in the quiet, Harriett could hear the water lapping against its pilings. As she stared out over the water and felt its calmness soothe her, a beam of light cut into the darkness from behind her. Turning her head, she saw Alex's silhouette standing on the porch, the light from inside the cabin creating a halo around her body. The idea of Alex as an angel brought a smile to Harriett's lips for nothing could have been further from the truth. The silhouette moved across the porch and down the steps toward her as she resumed gazing out over the water. A minute later she felt Alex's arms slip around her waist, pulling her closer, making her feel safe and wanted. As she turned in Alex's arms, she could make out the fine features of her lover's face.

"You're late," Alex whispered.

"It's your fault."

Running her hand along Harriett's neck, Alex kissed her gently. "I've fixed dinner," she said.

As Harriett entered the front door, she saw candles flickering on the coffee table and two place settings. Soft instrumental music flowed from the stereo. Alex carried Harriett's overnighter into the bedroom and then busied herself with putting food on plates for them. Alex enjoyed eating by candlelight and, although no one would have guessed it from her formal demeanor at the office, was a romantic at heart.

Alex and Harriett had been clandestinely seeing each other for three years and it was a relationship they both enjoyed, intellectually as well as physically. Harriett made no demands on Alex, and Alex made no promises. Alex would never leave her partner of almost twenty years, and Harriett would never ask her to. At forty-four, Alexis Dunne wasn't happy with her life but had accepted it for what it was. Harriett had thrown herself into her career after her brother and sister-in-law had been killed in an automobile accident four years before, leaving her as the sole guardian of their two-year-old daughter. The last thing she had wanted or sought was something to complicate her life.

She and Alex had grown close while handling a particularly arduous case three years earlier. Alex's partner, Gwen, had been out of town when the case concluded, and Alex and Harriett had held an impromptu celebration that ended intimately. Harriett hadn't seriously been with another woman since law school, and rearing Lacey had taken up all of her time away from the office. She had missed having someone to hold her, to love her and had been ripe for an intimate relationship. The times Harriett spent with Alex were never more than what they were, pleasurable and passionate without the worry of future complications.

After dinner, Harriett dragged a pillow from the couch and sat on the rug in front of the fireplace, watching the flames lick at the crackling logs. Alex sat in a chair behind her and leaned back, as they relaxed in the soft cocoon of firelight and music.

"Did Lacey get to your mother's all right?"

"Yes. I spoke to her before I saw Wilkes."

"What do you think about him?"

"I don't know whether I want the case, Alex," Harriett finally said.

"Then don't take it," Alex said softly. "The final choice is yours."

"He swears up and down that he's innocent, but they all say that. There's just something creepy about him, but I can't exactly put my finger on what it is."

"Creepy in what way?"

"He's got some pretty unusual ideas about sex. Finally admitted he had slept with all four girls, but claims they were alive and satisfied when he left them. It might have been someone out to get his father, but that sounds ludicrous."

"That'd be a tough sell," Alex said, leaning forward and kissing the top of Harriett's head.

Turning to look at Alex's face, Harriett asked, "Do you think I'm submissive in bed?"

Alex laughed slightly. "God! What a question, Harriett."

"Wilkes said tonight that sex was the ultimate act of submission on a woman's part. She's flat on her back, open and vulnerable, placing complete trust in her partner."

"I think it's elementary that lovers have to trust one another."

Harriett sat up and smiled at Alexis. "Why are you always so logical?"

"I'm not, or I wouldn't be here now."

"I'm glad you are."

Harriett looked back at the fire, rubbed her hands over her arms and said almost to herself, "I must have caught a chill."

Alex slid onto the floor behind her, wrapping her hands around a hot coffee mug. Setting the cup down, she ran her hands up and down Harriett's arms.

"That feels good," Harriett breathed as she closed her eyes and leaned her head back against Alex.

Alex could smell the freshness of Harriett's hair as she stared at the glowing fire and continued to stroke her arms, allowing her hands to take on a life of their own as they moved to encircle Harriett's waist.

"Warmer now?" Alex asked as she felt Harriett's body relax.

She looked up at Alex and smiled. "Almost," she answered.

THE GLOW FROM the fire danced across Harriett's back as she slept. Alex watched the smooth rise and fall of her back as she breathed evenly. Her skin had felt like new velvet wherever Alex touched it, and she longed to touch it again. She marveled at the flawless beauty of Harriett's body as she leaned down and brushed hair away from Harriett's face and neck. Smiling at the peaceful look on her lover's face, she remembered the intensity and passion in her eyes only two hours earlier. No, submissive would never be a word anyone could apply to Harriett. She gave herself freely and completely, but never as less than an equal.

Alex softly kissed Harriett's shoulders and back until she felt her body begin to awaken. When she looked at Harriett's face, eyes still closed, a smile forming on her sensuous lips, Alex said, quietly, "I didn't mean to wake you."

"Yes, you did," Harriett said as she rolled lazily onto her side, reached up and lightly stroked Alex's face with her fingertips.

WHEN HARRIETT OPENED her eyes again, the sun was shining, and she had no idea what time it was. She had refused to buy a clock for the cabin and always left her wristwatch in the car. Alex wasn't in the bedroom, and Harriett swung her legs over the side of the bed and found her robe lying next to her house shoes. Wandering slowly through the cabin, Alex was nowhere to be seen. Next to the coffeemaker, she finally found a note that read "Gone Fishing."

Smiling to herself, she poured a cup of coffee and returned to the bedroom to dress. When they had first met, Alex hadn't been fishing since she was a child. Now when they were at the cabin, she enjoyed sitting at the edge of the pier. Fish big enough to keep rarely ventured that close to shore, but it was exciting to catch the smaller ones that teased at your line and usually made off with the bait before you could hook them. Alex had probably gotten to the cabin early enough the day before to bait the area around the pier, and Harriett could picture her as she tried to coax something to take a big enough piece of her hook to make a catch.

From the porch, Harriett saw Alex casting her line. Carrying two cups of coffee, she joined Alex, bending down to kiss her.

"Catch anything?" she asked.

"A couple of minnows and a guppy," Alex grinned as she took the cup.

"Wow, the big ones. Did you save any for me?"

"A few, but I thought you'd sleep longer. It's only..." Alex began.

"Don't tell me," Harriett said holding up her hand. "I don't care what time it is until Sunday."

MID-AFTERNOON SUNDAY, Harriett walked with Alex to her car as she loaded her suitcase into the trunk.

"Too bad this wasn't a longer weekend," Harriett said.

Alex looked out at the lake and said, "Too bad Gwen will be home tonight."

Harriett wished Alex hadn't brought up her partner but knew it was simply a statement of fact.

"I wish I could stay longer, Harriett. I wish we both could," Alexis said softly still gazing at the lake.

"Next time," Harriett said patting her on the shoulder.

In one last grand sweep, Alex wrapped her arms around Harriett and drew her into a lingering, needy kiss. Alexis Dunne was a quiet woman, not given to bursts of passion or enthusiasm, but there was something so spontaneous about the kiss that it caught Harriett by surprise. As she released Harriett to get in her car, Alex touched the younger woman's face and said, "I love you, Harriett Markham."

"I love you, too, Alex," Harriett said quietly. It was all she could do to get the words out of her mouth. In three years, it was the first time Alex had spoken those words outside the bedroom.

Alex stopped with one foot in her car and smiled at Harriett.

"By the way, you're not the least bit submissive when we make love, and I thank God for that."

Harriett left the cabin two hours later.

Chapter
Five

AT SEVEN-FIFTEEN Monday morning, Harriett stepped off the elevator and walked toward her office. No matter how early she arrived at her office, Eleanor was always there first. Harriett had been tempted to stay at the office all night to see whether the nightly janitorial crew packed Eleanor in a box somewhere at night and unpacked her in the morning. Or maybe it was that Eleanor knew Harriett always arrived early on Mondays.

"Morning, Eleanor," Harriett said as she approached her secretary's desk. "See if you can get Clarence Wilkes on the phone. If we don't have the number, call Accounting. They should have it. We'll need to set up a separate file for them anyway. Then contact Todd Connor at the DA's office, and tell him Winston and Dunne has accepted the Wilkes case, and we'll send a courier over to their office in about an hour to pick up whatever they have on the case."

"Anything else, Ms. Markham?" Eleanor asked almost eagerly. To Harriett, Eleanor seemed like an old racehorse chomping at the bit to join in another race every time Harriett took on a new case.

"I want to see what the police and DA have put together first, but you might ask Wayne Graham to stop by if he has a chance."

That would make Eleanor happy, too. Harriett suspected that Eleanor had a thing for Wayne Graham, an independent investigator on retainer with Winston and Dunne. Most of his work consisted of eavesdropping on the unfaithful, but every now and then, a case that required real investigation presented itself. Wayne had left the Dallas Police Department when they refused to return him to active duty after he had been wounded apprehending a suspect, and Harriett had represented him in a lawsuit against the police department. He had used his settlement to open his own business and would do almost anything for her. Based on Harriett's recommendation, several large law firms had used his services over the last five years. She loved talking to Wayne. There was something about him that reminded her of her father, although in a much cruder version.

Coffee was already brewing in the coffeemaker when Harriett sat down behind her desk and opened her briefcase. She glanced over the notes she had taken during her brief interview with Jared Wilkes and began jotting down a series of questions she wanted to ask his parents. In the midst of her thinking, the intercom buzzed. Without looking up from her notes, Harriett reached across her desk and picked up the receiver.

"Yes, Eleanor," Harriett answered as she continued writing.

"Mr. Wilkes is here to see you," the secretary announced.

Harriett glanced at the clock on her desk. Seven forty-five.

"Show him in," she said, setting her pen down.

Clarence Wilkes strode into her office before she hung up the phone. He was a massive figure, which seemed to match what Harriett had heard about him. A former truck driver, he had grown tired of working for other people and started his own transport company, which now rivaled older, more established haulers. The key to Wilkes's success had been his treatment of the drivers who worked for him. He could be a tyrant if he caught drivers using drugs or alcohol and imposed drinking rules similar to the ones for airline pilots. Drivers for Wilkes Transport earned above scale money and were provided with an extensive benefit package. In the years since he began his operation, Clarence Wilkes had never been cited for any labor or transportation violations and was the recipient of dozens of citations from state and national organizations. His reputation was that of a straight to the core type of man who didn't tolerate obfuscation well. Within seconds of entering her office, Wilkes was ready to get down to business.

"Dunne tells me you're willing to take Jared's case. That right?"

"Yes. I've spoken to your son but won't be receiving the specifics from the police and district attorney until later today, Mr. Wilkes. After I know what they have as far as evidence is concerned, I'll determine the best course of action for Jared's defense."

"It doesn't matter what they have as evidence, Jared will be pleading not guilty."

"I'm afraid that will be up to Jared and me, Mr. Wilkes. He is the client."

"And I'm the wallet who's going to pay your fee," Wilkes snapped. "You'll be taking instructions from me."

"No, I won't, and if that's what you're expecting, then I recommend you find another attorney."

For a minute Clarence Wilkes and Harriett Markham stared at each other, each waiting for the other one to blink. Finally Wilkes smiled slightly.

"You're not from Dallas, are you?" he asked.

"Anson," she said.

"How'd someone as feisty as you get saddled with an uptight company like this one?"

Harriett began to relax a little. "Like you, Mr. Wilkes, I try to seek out the best."

Wilkes leaned back in his chair and took a deep breath. "I suppose you've already checked out my background, Ms. Markham. Same as I did yours. These big city corporate types make me nervous, but I trust you. You do whatever you think is best for Jared. Boy's always been a pain in my ass, but I can't believe he did what they're claiming he did."

"How is your relationship with Jared?"

Shrugging slightly, Wilkes replied, "He looks at me and sees a well used, bottomless wallet. I doubt he sees anything more. We've never been what you'd call close, but he is my son. My wife and I have to believe in him."

"I don't think his case will have a negative effect on your business."

"I couldn't care less. I didn't start my business to become popular, just rich. And I've done that. It won't be long before I'll be ready to hang it up anyway."

"Will Jared be taking control of your company?"

Wilkes laughed. "There's not a chance in hell that will ever happen. I've made arrangements to turn the company over to my board of directors with a recommendation for a new CEO. There is a provision that will assure the continued care of Jared and his mother, of course. But neither of them will ever have control of Wilkes Transport."

Harriett wasn't sure how to respond to what Wilkes had said and decided not to pursue it.

"My son is a nice looking kid with money. Always had the fastest car and money to do whatever he wanted. He wasn't abused or deprived in any way. We took him to church on Sundays and sent him to the best schools. My wife and I have been better than average parents, but Jared still turned out bad. The only hope I have for him now is that he will eventually grow up emotionally as well as physically and become a productive adult. Despite what I know he's done in the past, these crimes seem to be uncharacteristic, even for him."

"Does Jared have a steady girlfriend?"

"Yeah. Sylvia Jennings, but I don't know why she stays with him. She's a nice girl. Probably better than he deserves."

"I'll need to speak to her. Do you have an address or phone number for her?"

"I've got it at the office. I'll see that you get it today."

Wilkes stood up and when Harriett shook his hand, his grip was firm, yet gentle.

"I'll do the best I can for Jared, Mr. Wilkes," Harriett said.

"I appreciate that, Ms. Markham."

From that day on, Harriett didn't see Clarence Wilkes again.

Chapter
Six

SYLVIA JENNINGS WAS a pretty twenty-three year old intern with a Dallas advertising agency and had been dating Jared for nearly two years at the time of his arrest. In an effort to get a clearer picture of Jared Wilkes as a person and a man, Harriett arranged an interview with Sylvia in a conference room of Winston and Dunne. There was something wholesome looking and quiet about Sylvia when Harriett first met her, and she seemed an unlikely match for Jared.

"I appreciate your willingness to meet with me, Miss Jennings. Would you object if I called you Sylvia?"

"Of course not. I'll do whatever I can to help Jared. I went to see him yesterday and he looked so pathetic."

"Well, maybe this will all be over soon. Tell me about your relationship with Jared."

"We met a couple of years ago at a party thrown by a mutual friend, and we've been together pretty much since then."

"Are you living with him?"

"No. I have my own place, but I spend the night at his place, or he does at mine fairly often."

"Has he ever asked you to move in with him?"

"Once, but I have an office in my apartment and do a lot of my work there in the evenings. There really isn't enough room at his place for my drawing table and stuff. Plus, I can be pretty messy at times."

"How long have you and Jared been intimate?"

"Is that important?" Sylvia said, somewhat defensively.

"It's not my intention to embarrass you, Sylvia, but because of the nature of the charges against Jared, the subject of his sex life will play a significant role in his trial."

"We didn't sleep together for a while, just heavy petting, that kind of thing. A more intimate relationship developed gradually."

"Were you aware that Jared was sleeping with other women?"

Sylvia appeared to examine her hands for a moment. "I think I suspected it, but I never made an issue of it. I could have been doing the same thing, and I wouldn't have told him."

"These girls he's accused of raping were all in their teens. The youngest was only sixteen. When you were with him, did he ever demonstrate any particular interest in younger women?"

"A lot of these teenage girls go to bars with fake IDs and pass themselves off as being older."

"I know, but Jared has admitted that he had sex with each of the dead girls. Does that bother you?"

"Of course, it bothers me," Sylvia answered, her eyes flashing. Turning her eyes away from Harriett, she said, almost to herself, "It doesn't say much for my sex appeal, does it?"

"Did you know any of the girls who were killed?"

"I might have seen them, but I never formally met any of them. The clubs were usually very crowded when Jared and I went out. I didn't spend a lot of time observing the other women."

"When you and Jared were intimate, did he ever do anything that you thought was unusual?"

"You mean did he ever want me to do something kinky?"

"Kinky probably isn't the correct word. Couples do a lot of different things when they're intimate. Did he ever ask you to do anything, or did you let him do anything that seemed a little out of the ordinary or made you uncomfortable?"

Sylvia blushed and seemed to be looking for the right words. Finally, she answered in a softer voice. "He asked me to get on the floor on my hands and knees a couple of times, so he could enter me from behind."

"Did he force you to do that, or were you willing?"

"Jared never forced me to do anything. In fact, I refused the first time he mentioned it."

"How did he react to your refusal?"

Sylvia shrugged, "We just did it the regular way. He didn't say much."

"Was he unhappy?"

"He might have been disappointed, but he seemed to get over it."

"Has he ever tried to strangle you while you were making love?"

"God, no!" Sylvia said. "For the most part, Jared is a very gentle lover."

"No whips or leather?" Harriett smiled.

"That's ridiculous!" Sylvia laughed.

"Has he ever asked you to play out sexual fantasies with him?"

"Jesus! Why do you need to know things like that?"

"The prosecution will ask you the same questions if you're called as a witness, Sylvia, in an attempt to portray Jared as sexually perverted. I can't protect you unless I know the extent of your personal relationship with him. Is there anything you'd like to tell me, so I won't be surprised? Have you ever discussed your sexual encounters with Jared with a friend or co-worker?"

"I may have."

"Did you tell anyone something that would be potentially

embarrassing?"

Once again Sylvia appeared to be searching for a way to express her thoughts.

"Once I woke up in bed in Jared's apartment and couldn't remember anything that had happened. I didn't even remember how I got there. But I knew we had made love."

"Where was the last place you remember being?"

"At a club."

"Were you drunk?"

"I don't think so. I had one drink and started a second. I really don't remember anything after that except waking up the next morning."

"Did Jared get the drinks for you at the club or were they brought by a waiter?"

"Jared got them at the bar."

"How long had you been dating?"

"Maybe a month or a little less."

"And you hadn't been to bed with him yet?"

"No. He said I had been intoxicated, and he didn't want to leave me alone like that, so he took me to his place."

"So you assumed that you consented to sex when you were drunk?"

"Apparently."

"How did you feel when you woke up?"

"What do you mean?"

"Were you hurt?"

"I had never had sex until then. Maybe it was a good thing I was drunk."

"Intercourse the first time can be painful."

"I suppose, but as I said, thankfully I don't remember it."

"But you were hurt?"

"Mostly sore. I felt raw, you know."

"Did you have any bruises on your legs or thighs?"

"I found one or two on the backs of my thighs but didn't think much of it."

"I appreciate your candor, Sylvia. I know it's not easy to talk about the intimate parts of your life."

"I hope it will help."

Harriett doubted Sylvia Jennings's testimony would be helpful. A moron would be able to twist what she had just told Harriett to create a predilection for rape and violence. If Sylvia's name appeared on the prosecution witness list, Harriett knew she would have to attack the young woman's testimony.

Chapter
Seven

AS JARED ENTERED the room to meet with Harriett, he was antsy and refused to sit down, preferring to pace about the room, smoking a cigarette.

"I spoke to Sylvia yesterday, Jared."

"She's a great girl, isn't she?" Jared smiled.

"Why did you rape her?"

Jared stopped his pacing and stared at Harriett. "She tell you that?"

"Not directly. But from what she said, it seemed apparent that you slipped something into her drink and then later took advantage of her."

"She didn't fight it. She had too much to drink, and it lowered her inhibitions. That's all that happened."

"If she was too drunk to remember anything that happened after two drinks, she must have an extremely low alcohol tolerance. What did you put in her drink?"

Jared smiled slightly. "Some sedative my mother kept around the house. Worked better than I thought it would. I thought it would just relax her, not put her to sleep."

"Did you think Sylvia wouldn't get in bed with you without assistance?"

"We'd been going out a month. She told me she was a virgin, and the idea of having sex scared her. I helped her relax."

"And you enjoyed this one-sided sex?"

Jared pulled out a chair and straddled it. He blew smoke rings into the air and looked at her. She had seen the look in his eyes before, and there was something unnerving about it.

"Not being a man, Harriett, you wouldn't understand what it's like when you pop a cherry for the first time. Syl never felt a thing. Slept like a baby all night long, and every time I got hard, all I had to do was roll over and take her. She never really got wet, but with the help of a little lube, I got her five or six times real good before she woke up."

It took every ounce of energy Harriett could muster to not show her disgust and revulsion at what Wilkes had described, making a mental note to find out if any of the dead girls had also been virgins.

"I know what you're thinking, Harriett," Jared said, filling his lungs with smoke and exhaling it through his nose. "But remember that

Sylvia is still alive. Even if you think I raped her, I didn't kill her, and we're still fucking like rabbits in heat when we're together. I didn't want to hurt her then and I never have."

"If this comes out at the trial, it will hurt your case, Jared. Have you drugged other women?"

"No. Not before and not since."

"You and Sylvia ever do anything sexually that might be construed as unusual?"

"I don't think so. At least I don't consider them unusual."

"No domination, S&M, or playing out sexual fantasies?"

Jared smiled at Harriett. "No, but those sound like interesting ideas. You think those things are unusual? I mean, I'm sure you're sexually active, counselor. You do those things with your lover?"

"I haven't felt a need to make sex any more interesting than it already is," Harriett said matter-of-factly. "Anything else you think I should know?"

"I think you're an extremely attractive woman, but I guess that's not what you had in mind. Maybe when this is all over, and I walk out of here, we can get together for a drink."

"I don't socialize with my clients. Bad business and it's not likely I'd take a drink from you anyway knowing what I know."

Jared threw his head back and laughed loudly.

WHEN HARRIETT RETURNED to her office at the end of the day, she was surprised to find Wayne Graham sitting behind her desk with his feet propped up. As she walked through the door, he looked at his watch.

"I didn't think you big time attorneys worked long hours like this," Wayne smiled. "Where the hell you been, girl? I been waiting over an hour."

Harriett kicked off her shoes and fell onto the couch in her office.

"I've been to see my client, and now I need a bath. Jesus, what a pervert!" Harriett said looking at Wayne. "Why are you here?"

"Thought you'd be glad to see my handsome face."

Harriett liked Wayne Graham enormously and smiled at him. She noticed that his thick slate gray hair was beginning to show silver streaks along his temples.

"There's no one I'd rather see at the end of a long day than you," she said.

"Except maybe Alexis Dunne."

Harriett ignored his remark, knowing he didn't approve of her relationship with Alex and got up from the couch to pour a cup of coffee.

"That why you're here, Wayne, to give me another morality lecture?"

"Nope, and that ain't any of my business. But I think I'm fixin' to save you a long nasty trial. My bill's the same anyhow."

"What are you talking about?" she asked as she sipped her coffee.

"I think they're gonna have to cut your boy Wilkes loose. Have you checked out the warrant they used to toss his crib?"

"I saw it. So what?"

"Did you notice the probable cause section?"

"You mean the informant who said he saw Wilkes?"

"Yeah," Wayne said, taking his feet off the desk and sitting up. "You're gonna be able to tear this guy up quicker'n soggy Shredded fuckin' Wheat."

"The police claim he's a reliable informant they've used before."

"Come on, Harriett! I was a cop, remember? Whadda ya think they're gonna say to get a judge to sign a warrant? Well, your Honor, we got this totally unreliable schmuck who says he might have seen whatever."

"So you're saying the police lied to the judge to get the warrant."

"I did a little diggin', and their so-called informant is a dumb-ass named Raymond Carter. I busted good old Ray-Ray half a dozen times myself. He's a double duty junkie. Shoot up both arms at the same time if he could figure out how to do it. Anyhow, Ray-Ray claimed he saw Wilkes kill that last girl, what's her name, and the detectives, who were incidentally getting their chops busted to solve the murders, took Ray-Ray's word and got the warrant."

"Go on," she said cautiously.

"What if it was a bogus warrant?"

"But he knew where the rape and murder took place and a couple of other things that weren't released to the press."

Wayne looked up at her and smiled slightly.

"Well, he mighta had a little help rememberin' those things. Sort of a Henry Lee Lucas thing."

"How would he even know Jared Wilkes's name?"

"A buddy told me they were already zeroin' in on Wilkes but didn't have anything concrete. They needed the search and kept their fingers crossed."

"This is all supposition, Wayne. I can't go into the judge and claim police misconduct with this."

"How about if you can prove that Ray-Ray couldn't have been anywhere near the park where the girl was found? Think that'd do it?"

"Possibly."

Wayne reached into his jacket pocket and pulled out a folded piece of paper, extending it toward Harriett. She unfolded the paper and read over it.

"He was in jail?"

"Yep, arrested by one Officer Hugh Albertson, and please notice the time," Wayne grinned.

"This is before dark. When was he released from jail?"

"Bounced out on bond the next day. But he spent the night of the crime out of circulation. But, I suppose he could have used ESP or something."

"Does Raymond Carter even know he's listed as an informant on this warrant?"

"I haven't had a chance to track him down, but I doubt it. Ray-Ray used to be a snitch for one of the detectives who's workin' the cases, though. I think they took a shot in the dark on this one and got lucky when they found a couple of things belongin' to the dead girls at Wilkes's apartment."

"Or maybe they planted the things they found."

"I don't think I'd take it that far, kiddo. I think your guy's guilty as hell, but this was a hot case, and I'm sure the cops involved were frustrated and desperate to resort to this. I guess this is what the public calls one of those 'annoyin' legal technicalities.'"

"Maybe you shouldn't have given it to me if you think he's guilty."

"You pay me to help you get scumbags out of jail. He mighta got off anyway," Wayne shrugged as he reached for his coffee.

"The evidence isn't very convincing, no matter how repulsive Wilkes himself is. He admits he slept with the girls. I found out yesterday that with at least one woman he used a tranquilizer to get her in bed. If he pulled the same thing with the teeny-boppers, he might have left them unconscious, and they were found by a second assailant. There's probably enough reasonable doubt to carry the case. You think the DA knew about the informant?"

"If you was a cop, would you tell the DA what you did?"

"I need to talk to Todd Connor about this. Thanks, Wayne."

"No prob. Easiest money I've picked up on a case for you. Better than followin' some guy around to see who he's bangin' while his wife's away," he said as he pulled himself up from the chair and strolled toward her office door.

The following morning, Harriett took the information Wayne had uncovered to Todd Connor's office. Connor was a good prosecutor, and although he was upset by what Harriett showed him, he accompanied her as she presented a motion to suppress evidence found at Jared Wilkes's apartment. The following day Wilkes was released, and all charges against him were dropped. The detectives involved in obtaining the fraudulent warrant were suspended from duty without pay pending a hearing, and Internal Affairs launched an investigation.

NEARLY A MONTH later, Harriett had fallen back into the mundane activities of her law practice and was enjoying a leisurely lunch with Alex at a restaurant near the Winston and Dunne offices. They had finished eating and were chatting over a cup of coffee when they heard raised voices near the restaurant entrance. Harriett looked up to see Detective James Riley coming toward her. His face was red with rage, and there was a folder clamped tightly in his hand. A few feet behind him Detective Harold Wolf hurried to catch up to Riley. The manager of the restaurant was looking toward their table, holding a telephone receiver to his ear.

Riley stopped abruptly in front of Harriett and glared at her.

"Can we help you?" Alex asked coolly.

Riley opened the folder in his hand and tossed a picture on the table.

"Thought you might want to see the result of your exceptional legal work, counselor" he spat at Harriett.

She turned her eyes toward the picture, afraid to look at it, and closed them immediately.

Riley leaned down closer to her, resting a hand on the table next to her.

"Meet number five, Ashley Lawrence, age seventeen, football sweetheart. Thanks to you she won't make it to eighteen," he breathed heavily in her ear.

"What the hell are you talking about?" Alex demanded as she stood to face the detective.

"Come on, Jimmy," Wolf said, grabbing Riley by the arm. "This ain't gonna help, man."

Riley jerked his arm away from Wolf and straightened up, turning his head toward Alexis.

"They caught Jared Wilkes again last night. Unfortunately, they didn't get there in time to save Ashley Lawrence's life," the detective said. Leaning back down next to Harriett again, he lowered his voice, "He was still fuckin' her dead body when they grabbed him. They had to pull him off. But he still managed to come all over her."

Harriett couldn't look at Riley. She felt sick, but there was no place for her to go. Other customers were staring at her table, and she had to take a deep breath to clear her head. Two uniformed officers arrived at the table to escort Riley outside. As they turned to leave, Alex said, "You forgot your picture."

"She can keep it for her memory book," Riley snapped.

"Do you want to press charges, ma'am?" one of the officers asked.

Numbly, Harriett shook her head. Her hands were shaking, and suddenly her lungs couldn't take in enough air. Alex touched her arm, making her flinch. When she could finally force herself to look at Alex there were tears in her eyes.

"I have to get out of here," she managed to say.

"I'll take you home," Alex said softly.

Alex called the office from Harriett's apartment and spoke to Doug Winston, explaining what had happened. Alex helped Harriett undress and poured her a glass of straight bourbon. When she awoke, it was after dark, and she was curled up in Alex's arms.

"I'm sorry, Harriett. There was no way anyone could have known...," Alex began.

"Where's Lacey?"

"Eleanor picked her up after school. She'll bring her home in a little while."

"I need a few days off," Harriett said flatly. "Will you have Eleanor cancel my appointments for the rest of the week?"

"Of course. Do you want me to drive you up to the cabin?"

"No. Lacey has school. I just need some time alone."

"I don't think you should be alone, Harriett. Not yet."

"Don't worry. I'll be at the office in a few days."

FOUR DAYS LATER, Harriett entered the offices of Winston and Dunne, pausing for a moment before pushing the door open. No one spoke to her as she proceeded toward her office.

"Schedule a meeting with Doug and Alex for me as soon as possible, please," she said as she passed Eleanor's desk. Eleanor nodded and picked up her telephone as Harriett closed the door to her office.

In less than an hour, she was seated in Doug Winston's office facing the two senior partners.

"I've decided to tender my resignation from Winston and Dunne," she said.

Doug Winston rose from his seat and moved to where Harriett was sitting.

"I know what a disturbing business the Wilkes case has been for you, Harriett, but you can't let it ruin your life. You'd be throwing away everything you've worked for."

"I have to do this, Doug," she said firmly.

"What are you planning to do?" he asked with genuine concern in his voice.

"I'm thinking about moving and setting up my own practice. The Wilkes case will always be in my mind, but I'll be able to get over it faster if I'm not in Dallas."

"We should have never suggested the case to you," Doug said.

"It's not your fault," Harriett said with what passed for a smile. "No one forced me to take the case. It was my decision alone. Every attorney knows this can happen. They just pray it never does. "

"I think you're making a hasty decision under duress," Alex said tightly. When Harriett looked at her, there was sadness in Alex's eyes. She loved Alexis Dunne, and she loved her job, but she knew she would have to give them both up to make peace with herself and start over.

"No, Alex," Harriett said softly. "I accept that my actions resulted in the death of Ashley Lawrence. I don't like it, but I'll learn to live with it. What I can't live with is the backlash against me and possibly against this firm. I can't spend the rest of my life wondering if there will be some type of retaliation, or if someone at Lacey's school will say something to her about the case or me. I can't place her in that situation."

"You might find it interesting that Wilkes has requested you as his attorney again," Doug said. "I didn't think you'd mind if we turned the sonofabitch down on your behalf."

"Incredible," she said.

"He's retained the Snake," Alex said.

"Lewis Sullivan?" Harriett asked.

"Yeah," Doug said. "The scuttlebutt is that Sullivan is going to file an insanity plea."

Harriett shook her head. "Jared Wilkes is sick, but he's not insane."

"Well, that's out of our hands now," Doug shrugged.

"I'd like my resignation to be effective at the end of the month. I'll clear up the cases I have pending and will probably have to reassign a few of them."

"Let us know if there's anything we can do to help you, Harriett," Doug said patting her shoulder. "You know, I was looking forward to changing the sign on the door to Winston, Dunne, and Markham."

"So was I, Doug," she said as she stood to conclude the meeting.

Harriett was in the process of going through a stack of papers on her desk when Alex came into her office, instructing Eleanor to hold any calls. Going around the desk, she bent down and kissed the top of her head.

"I don't want you to leave, Harriett. I love you."

"This isn't about just you and me, Alex. There are others we have to consider."

"I'll leave Gwen and go with you if that's what you want."

Harriett stood up and walked away from her.

"What good would that do, Alex? Everyone in Dallas will still know that I freed a killer to kill again. We both know you can't leave Dallas. The firm depends on you. I have to do what's best for me and for Lacey now."

Alex pulled Harriett into her arms and held her tightly. "What will I do without you?"

"Same thing I'll be doing. Wishing our lives had taken a different road."

Harriett moved to Austin a month later, but kept up with the Wilkes case through the Dallas newspapers and began paying regular visits to a psychologist in Austin. By the time the Wilkes case was nearing its conclusion, she had begun coming to grips with something that was every attorney's nightmare. Without informing anyone, she made the decision to return to Dallas to observe the conclusion of the Wilkes case, timing her arrival to coincide with the return of the jury's verdict. Lewis Sullivan had presented an insanity plea based on the fact that Jared Wilkes suffered from multiple personality disorder. A string of expert witnesses had argued the case for weeks and now sat with their fingers crossed.

When the jury forewoman announced the verdict of "not guilty by reason of mental disease or defect" she couldn't believe it. Although she was seated in the rear of the courtroom, she could see Wilkes's face clearly. For everyone's sake, she hoped he would spend the remainder of his life in a mental institution. As Jared stood to be hugged by his mother before being led away, he spotted Harriett in the back of the courtroom. When he was sure she was looking at him, he smiled and winked at her. He had gotten away with murder and wanted her to know it. The drive back to Austin seemed to take forever as Harriett tried to put as many miles between her and Jared Wilkes as possible.

Chapter
Eight

HARRIETT COULD SEE her breath in the cold morning air as she shifted from one foot to another on the front porch of a restored two-story turn of the century house that sat on spacious grounds a few blocks from the State Capitol Building. She hadn't been able to sleep more than three or four hours the night before. Finally giving up the battle, she had quickly dressed and left her townhouse before the sun was up. She was being childish and even though she knew that, she needed to talk to Helen.

When the front door opened, Helen Mortenson, a fifty-ish woman with silver hair, blinked into the sunlight that was just making its way over the horizon. "Harriett?"

"Good morning, Helen. I'm really sorry to disturb you so early, but could we talk?" Harriett asked, clearing her throat slightly.

"Of course, my dear." Swinging the door open wider, Helen pulled the belt of her robe tighter. "You look like you haven't slept a wink."

Stepping onto the polished wooden floor of the home's foyer, Harriett looked around at the familiar surroundings. "I'm sorry if I woke you and Eric."

Wrapping a chenille-clad arm around Harriett's shoulders, Helen said, "You didn't, dear. I was just making some coffee when I heard the doorbell. You look like you could use some, and I know I can."

Harriett stood leaning against a kitchen counter, feeling a little self-conscious, as she waited for Helen to fill two large mugs with the steaming brown liquid. She had met Dr. Helen Mortenson soon after she had moved to Austin, and their friendship had been immediate. Still disturbed by her experiences in the Wilkes case, Harriett had sought help, and Helen's name had been the one her finger had landed on in the phone directory. Helen and her husband, Eric, had a successful practice in Austin and were considered two of the best psychologists in the state by their peers. Following her into her office, Harriett found the chair she had sat in many times while she had been in therapy.

For a few minutes, neither woman spoke, and just as Harriett was finding the silence uncomfortable, she glanced at Helen who smiled benignly at her and tilted her head to the side in an unspoken question.

"It's Wilkes," Harriett said softly into her mug.

"Why now? It's been a long time."

"A case from Dallas has been referred to me. I can't go into any detail about it, but the circumstances are so similar that I'm not sure I want to or even should consider taking it."

"Do you want the case?"

"What do you mean?"

"Is it a case where you can actually help the client?"

"I don't know. They're waiting for my response," Harriett said. Looking at Helen she continued, "It was referred to me by Alex Dunne."

"Ah, I see," Helen said as she set her mug on the table beside her. "That could complicate things a little. So is it the case you're reluctant to take or the idea of perhaps seeing Alex again?"

"I've already seen her. She came to my office yesterday to refer the case on behalf of the client's family."

"And how did you feel when you saw her again?"

Taking a deep breath and blowing the air from her lungs, Harriett looked up at the ceiling. "I don't know. It was almost surreal."

"That's bullshit and you know it, Harriett. How did you feel when you saw Alex?"

"She was stunning, okay? Is that what you wanted to hear?" Harriett snapped.

"I want you to be honest with yourself about your feelings."

"I'm sorry, Helen. Everything about her was almost exactly the way it was the last time I saw her. I felt...I don't know...happy, sad, regretful, angry. Maybe all of those."

"But then there's the Wilkes thing."

"Yeah, there is that. I should just turn the case down and let it all go away again."

"But then you wouldn't get to see Alex. Isn't that what this is really all about?"

"She's not with her partner any longer. They separated," Harriett answered while studying her hands.

"Then she's available."

"Yep," Harriett nodded.

"Do you want to renew your relationship with her?"

"I don't know, Helen, and that's the God's honest truth."

"If you took the case, would that mean spending more time with Alex?"

"I suppose, at least at first. It would be my case, and she wouldn't have any say in how I conducted it once I accepted."

"I think we've hashed over the Wilkes problem as much as possible eleven years ago and resolved it. Alex is the only unresolved part of your life left."

"She's never contacted me in those eleven years."

"You chose to end it. Perhaps she accepted your decision even if you didn't fully."

"I think it's been too damn long, Helen."

"I think we need to go out for a night of honky-tonkin' and dancin'," Helen laughed. "We haven't done that in ages."

"If I take this case, I'll be in Dallas for a few days for the preliminaries," Harriett said as she stood.

"Call me as soon as you get back. I'm getting that itchy foot thing, and you know how Eric is. Dynamite couldn't blast the man out of the house, bless his heart."

Harriett hugged Helen warmly as they reached the front door. "Thank you, Helen. And give my apologies to Eric."

"Not a problem. I do some of my best work early in the morning," Helen yawned.

Chapter
Nine

ARRIVING HOME FOLLOWING her early morning visit with Dr. Mortenson, Harriett dialed the number for the Omni Hotel and asked to be connected to Alexis Dunne's room. She was on the verge of hanging up after several rings when Alex picked up the phone.

"Hello," Alex answered, sounding slightly out of breath.

"Alex, this is Harriett."

"I was hoping I'd hear from you."

"I'll speak to Sharon Taggart, but I won't make any promises."

"I don't expect you to, Harriett. Listen, I was in the shower. Why don't you meet me at the airport, and I'll fly you to Dallas this morning."

"No. I have a few things to clear up at my office. Nothing big, but I need to make sure I don't leave anyone in a lurch. I think I'd rather drive to Dallas anyway."

"Shall I make a room reservation for you, or would you rather do that yourself, too?"

There was a chill in Alex's voice Harriett hadn't heard before.

"Just let my office know where you make the reservation. I'll probably be on the road by noon."

There was a pause on the line before Alex spoke again, the edge no longer in her voice. "I'm sorry, Harriett. Would you mind if I rode to Dallas with you?" she finally asked.

"Well, I...," Harriett started.

"I could acquaint you with a little more about the case."

"I suppose that would be all right," Harriett said hesitantly. "I'll call you when I'm ready to leave my office."

"I'll meet you at your office after I check out."

Harriett dressed in tan jeans and Ropers, pulled on a lightweight sweater, and packed enough clothes for a couple of days.

Carrying her suitcase downstairs, she set it down in the front hallway before joining her niece in the kitchen. Lacey was reading the sports section of the newspaper as Harriett poured a cup of coffee.

"Anything about your game in the paper?" she asked.

Turning the paper toward her aunt, Lacey pointed to an article as she chewed a mouthful of cereal.

"Better keep this for your scrapbook," Harriett smiled. "I have to go out of town for a couple days, Lace."

"A case?"

"In Dallas," she nodded as she sipped her coffee. "I might not take it but promised to speak to the defendant. Will you be okay here alone, or do you want me to call Grandma?"

"I think I can handle a little alone time."

"Remember the house rules, Lacey."

"Can Devon come over while you're gone?"

"I'm not real comfortable with that, honey."

"You can trust me, Aunt Harriett. After all, I am eighteen now. An adult according to the law."

"I do trust you. I'm just not as trusting of your boyfriend yet." Harriett smiled.

As she looked at her niece, the thought of her growing up so fast saddened her.

"If you need anything call Nick or Phyllis."

"You're *not* going to ask them to drop by unexpectedly, are you?"

Harriett laughed. "I've taught you right from wrong already. Now that you are an adult, at least in the eyes of the law, it's up to you to practice what I've been preaching all these years."

Lacey carried her bowl to the sink and rinsed it out, stopping on her way out of the kitchen to kiss Harriett.

"Have a good trip, and call so I know you got there in one piece, okay? I love you."

AS SOON AS she was in her office, Phyllis came in carrying a mug of coffee and set it in front of her.

"I'm going to Dallas for a couple of days, Phyllis. See if there's anything on my calendar that can't be pushed back until I return."

"A case?"

"Maybe. I'm conducting a preliminary interview to decide whether to take it."

"Is it a big fat hairy one?"

Harriett smiled at Phyllis. "The fattest and the hairiest."

She spent the next hour and a half putting the finishing touches on a few briefs and the motion for a new trial for her homeless client and took them to Phyllis to be typed.

"Make sure this motion reaches the Appeals Court by Monday," Harriett instructed Phyllis.

"This the train trestle guy?"

"Yeah. Kinda makes you glad you can afford to pay rent, doesn't it?"

The front door opened, and Alexis Dunne walked in carrying a small suitcase.

"I'll be with you in a moment, Alex," Harriett said. "Did Nick call in before he went to court this morning?" Harriett asked Phyllis.

"Yes. His case is going to the jury this afternoon. Does he know you'll be out of town?"

"I left a note on his desk. What about my appointments?"

"I rescheduled them for next week. Let me know if I need to push them back further."

"That shouldn't be necessary, but I'll call later to let you know where I'm staying."

"She'll be at the Hyatt," Alex said. Taking a piece of paper from her pocket, she handed it to Phyllis. "That's the number for the hotel and the suite number."

Phyllis smiled as she took the paper from Alex.

"Well, I guess that's everything," Harriett said. "I told Lacey to call you or Nick if she needs anything."

"Have a safe trip," Phyllis said.

As Harriett climbed into the cab of her truck, she wasn't particularly looking forward to spending three or four hours in the truck with Alex. It wasn't that she hadn't thought about her former lover over the years. She simply wasn't sure what they would have to talk about.

HARRIETT ACCELERATED ONTO Interstate 35 North and felt the truck shift smoothly into a higher gear. Glancing at the clock on the dashboard, she slid a CD into the truck stereo system. As she watched the traffic around her, she adjusted the volume control. Instrumental jazz flowed through the rear speakers, and she settled down in her captain's seat. The sun was shining brightly, and she pulled a pair of sunglasses from a case on her visor even though the tinting on the truck windows filtered out most of the road glare. The weather was warm for mid-February, and the air coming through the vents kept the truck cab comfortable. Between Austin and Georgetown, traffic was heavy, punctuated by frequent stops and starts. Alex had been silent since they left Austin, and Harriett could barely see her out of the corner of her eye. When Alex finally spoke, the sound of her voice surprised her.

"I see you still enjoy jazz," Alex said.

"I have some other CDs if you want to change it," Harriett said, knowing that Alex had never been particularly fond of jazz.

"This is fine," Alex said, looking out the side window.

"Want to tell me more about the case? We have a long way to go."

"I lied to you at dinner, Harriett," Alex admitted. "Sharon Taggart's case is similar to the Wilkes case in a number of ways. Except that Jared Wilkes was a psychopath, and that's not the case with Sharon."

"How did they catch her?"

"A passerby claims to have seen her and remembered a partial plate number of a car at the scene of the last shooting. It took the police a while, but they narrowed down the description of the car and got lucky."

"But she denies being the shooter."

"Absolutely. But there's no doubt she had the weapon in her possession, and her fingerprints were the only ones on it. Sharon was an accomplished marksman in college. I believe she was on the rifle and pistol team there."

"I'm not clear on how she shot them. Did she just walk up to them?" Harriett asked.

"She didn't actually shoot anyone. She shot at them, but according to the medical examiner, no one was ever hit. All the victims died as a result of injuries after she fired. All of the shootings occurred on busy freeways, and the police believe she shot at the vehicles."

"So the victims killed themselves by their reaction to their vehicles being shot at."

"Yes," Alex said. "There had been a number of incidents over the last couple of years in which motorists reported they had been shot at. Of all those incidents, four died. A couple of others were seriously injured but recovered. In fact, some of the charges against Sharon are actually attempted murder."

"An interesting twist. Drivers killed by their own panic."

"But since the shooter's actions were the proximate cause of the deaths, whoever was responsible can still face a murder charge."

"Second degree at best. She may have planned to fire at the vehicles and not planned for anyone to be killed as a result," Harriett hypothesized. "It shouldn't result in the death penalty. Has the family considered a psychiatric evaluation?"

Alex smiled slightly. "I'm surprised you would even mention that, considering Wilkes."

"Even a first year attorney would have to request an examination. Is Sharon Taggart intelligent enough to fool a shrink?"

"She's extremely bright."

"What about her family? How supportive are they?"

"Very. But I can tell you up front that you probably aren't going to care for Frank Taggart, the husband."

"Why?"

"He's kind of a smart-ass. Parker can't stand him, and I'm sure Sharon's parents only tolerate him because he's married to their daughter."

"What does he do for a living?"

"He's a mechanic for one of the Dallas car dealerships."

Harriett looked at Alex and grinned. "Bet that went over well with the country club crowd."

"I thought Sharon's mother, Clarissa, was going to have a stroke,"

Alex laughed. "No one's ever figured out why Sharon married him. Probably to get away from Clarissa, but you didn't hear that from me. It isn't fair for me to give you my opinions of these people, Harriett. My judgments shouldn't cloud your feelings about them."

"I've always found your impressions about people to be pretty accurate, Alex. But I'll keep an open mind when I speak to the family. Not to change the subject, but how are you planning to get your plane back to Dallas?"

"Paige said she would fly it up later today. She got her pilot's license a couple of years ago."

"She's a very attractive young woman, by the way. She looks like you."

"She reminds me of you sometimes. Pig-headed, straight ahead, no holds barred."

"Is that a compliment or a complaint?"

"The former. She studied advertising in college, you know."

"Really?"

"She's wildly talented, and I tried to convince her to go to New York. We have a few clients who could have helped her get a job with an agency there, but she decided on a different route."

"When she met Senator Collins?"

"She designed campaign materials as a proposal while she was an intern with Stern and Craft. He fell in love with the material she developed, and then he fell in love with her. At least that's what he says happened."

"You don't believe him?"

"I don't know," Alex said, leaning her head against the back of the seat. "I've never tried to influence Paige in any way about whom she saw or what she did, but I think she's too young for Parker. He's twelve years older than she."

"You're twelve years older than I, Alex, and you didn't think I was too young," Harriett said looking at Alex.

"You were already established in your career, Harriett. Paige isn't as mature as you were."

Harriett didn't respond, keeping her eyes on the road ahead.

"Maybe it's because Parker is a politician, but there's something behind all that charm and good looks that I don't completely trust," Alex said. "Guess I'm being a jumpy, over-protective, much older sister."

"Does Paige know Sharon Taggart?"

"Better than I do. They both worked on Parker's last campaign. Sharon's an expert on demographics and wrote most of Parker's speeches for him. He's the one who faces the TV cameras, but she's the brains behind what he's saying."

"Is there anyone who might think they can get to him by going through his sister?"

"That could be an angle, I suppose. You know how politics is."

"There's a good restaurant up ahead. Not too pricey and the food's good," Harriett said. "You up for some lunch?"

"I skipped breakfast, so I guess I could stand something."

Harriett changed lanes and exited the interstate at Salado. Pulling into the parking lot of the Stagecoach Inn, she hopped out of the truck and stretched her legs. Huge pecan trees surrounded the historic two-story building, and the parking lot was two-thirds full.

Alex followed her as she walked through a white picket fence gate and up the steps to the front porch of the restaurant. A waitress seated them at a table overlooking a creek running next to the building. A few children ran around on the bank of the creek, while others held bamboo fishing poles, hoping for something to pass by.

"Do you still fish?" Harriett asked as she watched the scene below them.

"No. You still make your pilgrimages to the lake?"

"I sold the cabin to Wayne Graham a few years ago. It was too far to drive from Austin."

"I'm sorry to hear that. You loved the cabin."

Harriett shrugged. "Wayne takes good care of it, and he left me an open invitation to use it any time I want. If he ever decides to sell, he has to give me first shot at it."

They ordered grilled trout with a side salad. It was dark in the dining room of the Inn, the only lighting the sunlight coming through the windows around the building.

"This is a great place, Harriett."

"I stopped here a few years ago on my way back to Austin and try to come up here when I can. It's so peaceful. They stock trout in the creek down there every spring. I thought about building a place here once, but the traffic is too heavy for a commute."

Alex was looking at Harriett and smiling.

"What?" Harriett asked.

"Nothing. You just sounded like you used to."

Harriett picked up a glass of tea and continued looking at the creek.

"You haven't said anything about my split with Gwen," Alex said.

"It's none of my business, Alex."

"I don't talk about it very often. I suppose that's because it makes me look like a fool. The only time I was ever unfaithful to her was when you and I were together. But it turned out that she had been through a string of lovers over the years."

Harriett couldn't think of anything to say even though she knew that her partner's affairs must have hurt Alex.

"I was furious when I found out. She claimed that I was too busy building my career to be concerned about her needs. She knew about you and me, by the way, but she'd already had two or three lovers before we met."

"I'm sorry, Alex. Really."

The look on Alex's face changed and frown lines creased her forehead.

"What about you? Anyone significant in your life these days?"

Harriett sipped her tea and shook her head. "Between raising Lacey and building the practice, there hasn't been much time to cultivate any serious relationships. I have a comfortable and uncomplicated life." Or at least I did until you walked into my office, she thought.

BY THREE-THIRTY, Harriett was cruising down the LBJ Freeway heading toward the exit to downtown Dallas, and the offices of Winston and Dunne. She pulled into a visitor's parking slot in the parking garage next to the building where the offices were located. She was nervous as she and Alex rode the elevator to the eleventh floor, wondering how much things had changed since her resignation. Alex held the door open for her as she looked around the interior of the offices. Surprisingly little seemed different from her memories.

"I'll let Doug know you're here," Alex said quietly, as she turned down the main hallway.

As they approached Doug Winston's office, Harriett saw a familiar figure sitting at the desk outside Doug's office. Eleanor glanced up as Alex passed her desk and then saw Harriett. In a flash, Eleanor moved from behind her desk to where she was standing and looked at her for a second before embracing her in a hug that had been waiting eleven years.

"You look wonderful, Ms. Markham," Eleanor beamed.

"Thank you, Eleanor. And surely you can call me Harriett considering how long we've known each other."

"Where are you now? Can I get you a cup of coffee?"

"I have a practice in Austin, and yes, I'd love some coffee. It was a long drive."

Alex stuck her head out of Doug's office and motioned to Harriett.

"I'll bring your coffee into the office in a second," Eleanor said, patting Harriett on the back.

Harriett was decidedly underdressed for the offices of Winston and Dunne, but she couldn't have cared less. The ability to dress casually was the best part of her practice in Austin. The moment she entered Doug's office, he swept her into his huge arms and she had difficulty breathing.

"Damn, girl, you look some kind of good," Doug said. "And a helluva lot more comfortable than I am. Have a seat."

"You're looking well, Doug. How is your family?" Harriett asked.

"Writing checks faster than I can put money in the account. But they're all great. David's an associate here now. It's nepotism, but hell, when it's your firm, who's gonna complain?" he chuckled.

"Ownership does have its advantages," Harriett smiled as she glanced around for a chair.

"Alex tells me you've got a good practice going down in Austin now," Doug said as he returned to a beaten up, tired looking leather chair behind his desk.

"We've got enough to keep us busy," Harriett said.

"You have a partner then?"

"Nick Lazslo joined me about five years ago."

"Lazslo. Lazslo. I know that name from somewhere."

"He was teaching law at Virginia before he came to Austin."

"Isn't he a past president of the American Bar Association?"

"Vice-president."

"Right," Doug said, snapping his fingers. "I've read some of his articles in law journals. Sounds like a smart guy."

"He's an excellent attorney."

"How'd he wind up in Austin after UVA?" Doug asked.

"Nick and I attended Yale together. I ran into him at an ABA meeting a few years ago, and he was looking for a change of scenery. Besides, Doug, Austin's not exactly the ass end of the world."

Doug laughed loudly. "Point taken."

A knock at Doug's door announced the arrival of Harriett's coffee, accompanied by cups for Doug and Alex.

"Just the way you always liked it, Harriett," Eleanor said as she handed her a cup.

"Thanks, Eleanor. I forgot to ask about your family"

"Healthy as horses," Eleanor smiled. "I'm a grandmother now, twice."

"Congratulations. Be sure to show me all your grandmother pictures while I'm here," Harriett smiled.

"How is little Lacey?"

"Not little anymore, I'm afraid. I'll talk to you later, and we can trade stories."

After Eleanor left the office, Doug rested his elbows on his desk. "I guess Alex has filled you in on the Taggart case."

"Some. But all I've agreed to do is speak to Mrs. Taggart in a preliminary interview. Nothing more. If this looks like it might be a long, protracted case, I won't be able to leave my clients in Austin to devote months to it."

"I've already told Sharon's parents that. However, we feel relatively certain that you'll be able to win a change of venue on this one. There's been some publicity already, and if you decide to take the case, there's bound to more, considering the nature of the crimes."

"And my prior handling of the Wilkes case. The press is bound to drag that up," Harriett added quietly.

"I'm not as genteel as Alex is when I speak, Harriett. But from what I've seen, I think you might be looking at exactly the same plea as in the

Wilkes case."

"Meaning you think Sharon Taggart is insane?"

"I think it's a distinct possibility."

"You know how tough that defense is, Doug. I'd like to avoid it if possible."

"I'm sure you would, but her family has been talking it around, and the press has gotten a whiff of the rumors already. And despite our warnings, your name has been leaked to the press."

Doug picked up a copy of the Dallas Morning News and handed it across the desk to Harriett.

"It's not the lead story, but it did make the front page," Doug said as Harriett glanced over a short article on page one.

"This is just preliminary guessing," Harriett said. "And at least it's below the fold."

"When will you see Sharon?" Doug asked.

"Later this afternoon would probably be the best time. I want to get in and out unnoticed if possible."

"I'll go with you," Alex said. "I can go in the front and run interference while you enter through the back."

Harriett nodded. "I'd like to freshen up before I meet with Mrs. Taggart. After I speak to her, I'll want to meet with her husband and family members."

"When?" Doug asked.

"The sooner the better. Either tonight or first thing in the morning. I'll want to speak to them separately about thirty minutes apart. I assume I can use your conference room here?"

"I promised you the full resources of Winston and Dunne," Alex said.

Harriett looked at Doug and Alex and cleared her throat.

"I appreciate that," Harriett said. "But if I take this case, you'll have to back away. Winston and Dunne will not be calling the shots. I'll handle this like any other referral. I won't have my client's family running to you if they don't agree with what I'm doing. No matter who's paying the fee, Sharon Taggart would be my only client, and I can't be worried about whose toes I step on."

The bluntness of her statement seemed to surprise Alex, but Doug smiled broadly. "Well, Alex, it looks like our little girl has grown up and left home. You'll have complete and unfettered autonomy in handling the Taggart case, if you decide to take it. You have my personal guarantee, Harriett."

"That's good enough for me, Doug." Harriett said as she stood up, "I think I'll check into my hotel before I visit Mrs. Taggart. When do you want to run your interference, Alex?"

"How about six-thirty? That way you can grab some dinner before you go. You can follow me to central booking. No one will notice your vehicle if I park in front."

Harriett left the office after agreeing to meet Alex in front of the Hyatt at six-fifteen. Doug leaned back in his chair and regarded his partner of thirty years.

"You should've snagged that gal when you had the chance, Alex," Doug said bluntly.

Alex stood looking stoically out Doug's office window and turned to look at her old friend. "I know."

"She still single?"

"Yes."

"Then maybe you should turn on that famous charm of yours."

"It's too late, Doug. Too much time has passed. We're not the same people we were eleven years ago."

"I'd give a lot to see you happy again, Alex. And I know you haven't been since Harriett left."

"I appreciate your concern, Doug, but I'm fine."

"Alice wants you to come over for dinner this weekend."

"I'll let you know."

Chapter
Ten

IT WAS NEARLY dark when Harriett went through the revolving door of the Hyatt and saw Alex parked next to her truck in a parking lot across the street. The only addition to her attire was a suede jacket.

"Is your room all right?" Alex asked when Harriett reached her vehicle.

"Very nice."

"Have you had dinner?"

"No. I took a short nap instead. I'll order up something later."

"Doug set up this interview schedule with the family for you in the morning," Alex said, passing her a five-by-seven-inch slip of paper. "You ready?"

Harriett nodded and climbed into her truck as Alex swung her Mercedes sportster out of its parking space. As she fell in behind Alex's vehicle, she had to smile. One good hit on the accelerator of her truck, and she could squash the sportster like an insect. One of the things she enjoyed most about driving the truck was the feeling of power it gave her, being able to look down on other drivers as she passed them. Two blocks from the George Allen Center in downtown Dallas, Harriett slowed to let the Mercedes get farther ahead of her. As Alex turned in front of the building, Harriett turned down a back driveway and parked near the entrance to central booking. A few seconds later, she was standing in front of the same desk she had stopped at for the Wilkes case. A black officer searched her briefcase and punched a button that admitted her into the interview area.

Interview Room Nine looked pretty much the same as she remembered, a table and two chairs and not much else. The door to the room opened, and she stood to get her first glimpse of her potential client. Although she had seen hundreds of clients in similar circumstances, Sharon Taggart's appearance was somehow different. Her short brown hair was parted down the middle and strands of it fell onto her forehead. Her dark eyes seemed to dart around the room as a female jailer removed her handcuffs and leg restraints. It was almost an instinctive reaction when Sharon rubbed her wrists. The jailer said something to Sharon, and she nodded as she turned to face Harriett for the first time. It was almost as if she had only that moment realized there was another person in the room.

"Mrs. Taggart. My name is Harriett Markham, and I'm an attorney. Your brother has asked me to speak to you," Harriett said.

Sharon looked at her for a moment. "How is Parker?"

"He seemed fine when I saw him. Why don't you have a seat?"

Sharon lifted a chair to move it away from the table, and it seemed to Harriett that she did it to prevent the chair from scraping against the concrete floor and making unnecessary noise in the otherwise quiet room.

"Do you smoke, Mrs. Taggart?"

"Yes, but I shouldn't. It's not good for your health, you know."

"So I hear. But I won't tell anyone if you'd like to smoke."

Sharon shook her head slightly. "That's okay."

"Do you know why you're here, Mrs. Taggart?"

"Uh, they said I killed someone, but I don't know whom. They told me, but I didn't recognize the name."

"Actually they think you killed four people."

There was a question in Sharon's eyes as she frowned.

"Did I know them?"

"I don't know that yet. According to the police report, they found a rifle they believe was used in the commission of the crimes at your home. Was that your rifle?"

"We have a Browning rifle in our house. It's Frank's."

"Have you ever fired it?"

"Yes."

"I understand you're quite a marksman."

"I used to be. Just target shooting. I don't like having the rifle in the house because of Kevin and Laurel, though."

"Are they your children?"

"Yes. They're so curious that I'm afraid they might find the rifle and get hurt."

"The report says the police found it in a garage cabinet."

"I had Frank store it there."

"What about ammunition for it?"

"I'm not sure where that is. Maybe in the attic storage area."

"Could it have been in your car?"

"There might have been some in the trunk, but I don't look in the trunk very often."

"Do you know where you were on Friday, January eighteenth?"

"I'm not sure. I could check my calendar at home."

"You're a teacher, aren't you?"

"Yes, at Highland Park."

"Do you do anything special after school on Fridays?"

"I have to pick up Kevin and Laurel by five. Sometimes we stop by the grocery store for pizza on the way home, or I rent a couple of videos for the kids. The weather was pretty bad in January, so I don't think I did anything out of the ordinary."

"Did you and your husband go out for the evening?"

"We don't go out. Frank and I don't socialize much outside of our family."

"Did you kill Leonard Kaufmann on January eighteenth?"

"No," Sharon answered, her voice flat.

"To be honest with you, Mrs. Taggart, the police seem to have some pretty compelling evidence against you. The warrant to search your home was in order, and you don't seem to be able to explain your whereabouts that night. Will your husband be able to say you were home?"

"I suppose so."

"Is there anything you can tell me in your own defense?"

"How are my children?"

"I haven't met with your family yet, Mrs. Taggart. I only arrived in Dallas this afternoon, but I'll speak to them in the morning."

"They won't let me have pictures of Kevin and Laurel with me. Can you make them let me have them?"

"I'll see what I can do. Can you explain your fingerprints on the weapon?"

"It's Frank's, but I've touched it."

"Your husband's fingerprints weren't on it. Can you explain why?"

Sharon seemed to be concentrating on the table's Formica top intently before she looked up and stared into Harriett's eyes.

"Look, I'm tired of answering questions. Just get the pictures of the kids, okay?" Sharon said with a sudden forcefulness in her voice.

Leaning forward slightly, Harriett said, "I'll get them if the police will allow you to have them."

A twisted smile crossed Sharon's face, "Are they afraid I'll kill myself with a paper cut?"

"I should make my position clear to you, Mrs. Taggart. If I take your case, you have to be absolutely honest with me. You can't hold anything back if you expect me to represent you. I can't..."

"I know," Sharon said leaning her head back and staring at the ceiling. "I know you can't reveal anything I tell you. I'm perfectly aware of my rights and my relationship with my attorney. I'm not a moron, Ms. Markham."

Sharon's eyes slowly lowered until they coolly met Harriett's again.

"It wasn't my intention to be condescending, Mrs. Taggart. But since I don't know you very well yet, I thought I should explain everything as fully as possible."

Sharon shook her head and sighed. "It's all right. If I don't understand something, I'll ask you to clarify if for me. Just check on the pictures, okay?"

"I will."

"And please call me Sharon. That way I'll feel like you're on my side."

"I am on your side, Sharon. You might already know this, but you are the client. I won't take orders from your husband or your parents, or anyone else. If there is a disagreement over my handling of your case, you're the only person who can dismiss me and request a new attorney."

"Well, that's refreshing to hear," Sharon mumbled almost to herself. "Don't you work for Winston and Dunne?" she asked in a stronger voice.

"No. I have a practice in Austin. They've referred your case to me."

"You came all the way up here for my case?"

"Alexis Dunne is an old friend."

"Nice woman, but that partner of hers was a bitch."

"I wouldn't know about that, Sharon. Is there anything else I can get for you besides the pictures?"

"No, I'm fine. Actually, it's very peaceful here."

HARRIETT LEFT THE Allen Center the same way she had entered and drove back to the Hyatt. As she was getting out of her truck, she saw Alex's Mercedes parked nearby. Still carrying her briefcase, she entered the hotel and glanced around the lobby. On her way to the elevator she passed the hotel bar and saw Alex sitting alone at a table against the far wall. Holding the briefcase in front of her, Harriett entered the bar. Alex seemed to be engrossed in reading a folder full of paperwork on the table in front of her.

"Would you like some company, or is this your favorite new hideaway?" Harriett asked.

Alex looked up at Harriett and removed her glasses. "I didn't see you come in. Please, join me," she said as she signaled to a waitress. "How did it go?"

"Hard to tell. She's a little spacey," Harriett answered as she pulled a chair closer to the table.

A young woman came to their table, holding a tray in her hand. "Refill, ma'am?"

"No, I'm fine. But please bring a Chivas on the rocks for Ms. Markham," Alex said. As soon as the woman left the table, Alex turned her attention back to Harriett. "Spacey in what way?"

"She seems fixated on her children right now. I arranged for her to get pictures of them from her wallet before I left. Other than that, she didn't have much to tell me. Didn't know the last victim, admitted she and her husband owned a Browning and that she knew how to use it. Couldn't remember where they kept the ammo. Likes you. Didn't like Gwen."

"Sounds like an eclectic conversation."

"It was," Harriett said as the waitress set her drink down.

"Thank you," Alex said, handing a bill to the waitress. "Keep the change."

"Are you leaning toward taking or rejecting the case?"

"I haven't reached the leaning stage yet. I want to interview her family first."

"Have you eaten dinner?"

"Uh-uh. I'll order something from room service," Harriett said as she picked up her drink.

"Why don't you let me buy you dinner?"

"I'm pretty tired tonight, Alex. Maybe another time. I have to call Lacey before it gets too late."

Alex finished her drink in one swallow and took a deep breath. "I'd like to see you while you're in Dallas, Harriett."

"You've seen me all day," Harriett said, sipping her drink.

"I'd like for us to be friends again."

"We are, Alex."

Leaning back in her chair, Alex smiled whimsically at Harriett. "You're going to make this difficult, and I can't say I blame you. I shouldn't have let you leave Dallas eleven years ago."

"It was the right thing to do. Look, I'm here to review a case, not to rekindle old relationships. I loved you once, Alex, probably more than I should have, but I'm not ready to pick up where we left off. I'm sorry. If I take this case, I can't have it mixed up with a personal agenda."

Alex nodded. "I understand."

Harriett finished her drink and took a deep breath. "I'd better get some rest tonight. Seven will get here pretty early."

As she stood up, Harriett felt a little dizzy and gripped the edge of the table to steady herself. "I'd better get some food pretty quick unless you slipped something in my drink a la Jared Wilkes."

"Not my style," Alex laughed as she rose from her chair. "Come on, I'll walk you to your room."

"I usually hold my liquor better than this."

"When was the last time you ate?"

"When we stopped for lunch."

"That was nine hours ago."

Taking the elevator to the fourth floor, Harriett fished the room key from her purse and opened the door.

"Thanks, Alex," she said as the door opened. "I'll be fine now."

Alex reached inside and switched on a light. Taking Harriett's briefcase, she said, "Go take a shower, and I'll order up something for you. I'll be gone before you're out of the shower."

Not feeling inclined to argue with her, Harriett dropped her purse on the bed and pulled her boots off before making her way toward the bathroom. As she closed the bathroom door, she heard Alex ordering a hot roast beef sandwich from room service, which was one of her favorites.

When she came out of the bathroom draped in a hotel bathrobe, Alex was gone, just as she said she would be. The carpeting felt good under her bare feet as she ran a comb through her wet hair. There had been a time when food would have been the last thing on her mind if she had been alone in a hotel room with Alex. Even now, if she allowed herself to think about being alone with her, she felt a faint but familiar tingling sensation along her thighs, remembering Alex's touch, tender and light. Her thoughts were interrupted by a knock at her door announcing the arrival of her sandwich.

Chapter
Eleven

DRESSED IN A powder blue slack suit over a white silk blouse, Harriett stepped off the eleventh floor elevator and into the familiar world of Winston and Dunne. She turned down a back hallway to avoid the waiting room where Sharon Taggart's family was seated and entered the large conference room. Pressing a button on the conference table, she waited to see who answered.

"Good morning, Ms. Markham," Eleanor's voice came back.

"Good morning, Eleanor," Harriett smiled. "Who's up first?"

"Mr. Taggart. Says he has to get to work."

"Then trot him in, and see if you can round up some coffee, please."

"Right away," Eleanor said.

A moment later, the conference room door opened and Frank Taggart walked toward Harriett. Extending her hand, she introduced herself and offered him a seat. Frank ran a hand through his thinning hair and adjusted his wire-rimmed glasses.

"I'm just going to be asking you a few preliminary questions this morning, Mr. Taggart," Harriett began.

"You're sizing us up to see whether you're gonna take the case or not, aren't you?"

"In a way. I don't know very much about your wife, and the more I know, the more I'll be able to help her later on."

"You're gonna take the case then?"

"I'm inclined to."

"Even if she's guilty?"

"Most of my clients are, Mr. Taggart. But if I don't think I can help her, or if there is a conflict between Sharon and me, then I'm not the right attorney for her."

"Okay. Ask away."

Eleanor came through the back door of the conference room and set a carafe of coffee and several cups on the table.

"Thank you, Eleanor," Harriett smiled.

"There's cream and sugar on the credenza," Eleanor said as she left the room.

"How long have you and Sharon been married, Mr. Taggart?"

"Eight years."

"How did you meet?"

"When I repaired her car. I'm a mechanic."

"How would you characterize your marriage?"

Frank looked at her.

"Is it a good marriage?" Harriett clarified.

"It's had its moments, but it's not exactly like you'd see in some romantic movie where everyone lives happily ever after."

"Has your marriage changed over the last eight years?"

"We got two kids, so yeah, it's changed."

"Sharon's very concerned about her children, Mr. Taggart. You might want to consider letting them see her."

"I'm not taking them down there and letting them see their mother in jail. No way."

"I can arrange for her to see them in another part of the building if you'd like."

"I'll think about it."

"Sharon said the Browning the police confiscated belongs to you. Is that correct?"

"Yeah, it was a Christmas present a couple of years ago."

"From Sharon."

"Yeah."

"Has she ever fired it?"

"I took her out a couple of times. She doesn't like to hunt, so I took her to a firing range."

"Is she a good shot?"

"A regular Annie Oakley."

"Can she hit moving as well as stationary targets?"

"You shoot?"

"Afraid not."

"Well, they got these little round things about the size of a half dollar and painted orange. They swing them back and forth at different speeds and out of synch."

"And she could hit those?"

"Didn't miss a one."

"About how far was she from these moving targets?"

"Oh, forty or fifty yards. Maybe a little more."

"Were you impressed with her shooting ability?"

"I guess so. Didn't think much of it."

"Sharon told me she was at home with you on January eighteenth when the last shooting took place. Can you verify that?"

"Yeah, we were home. We all ate dinner, watched a little TV. Sharon usually gets the kids in the sack around eight or eight-thirty."

"Then what?"

Frank smiled and shrugged, "Then I tried to hustle her into bed. You know, enjoy a little rec time."

"So you and Sharon made love that evening," Harriett said.

"I said I tried, but she said she was too tired. One thing led to another, and we had a spat about it. I finally gave up and went to bed alone."

"When did Sharon come to bed?"

"Couldn't tell you. She was there when I woke up the next morning."

"Does she stay up late by herself often?"

"All the time. She reads, works on the computer. Does just about anything she can to avoid going to bed with me."

"Do you think she's avoiding being physically intimate with you?"

"Sharon's what you'd call frigid. Been that way since Laurel was born. I thought she'd get over it, but so far she hasn't."

"Are you involved with any other women outside of your home, Mr. Taggart?"

"You want to know if I'm cheating on my wife?"

"Yes."

"I've done a little dippin' over the last couple of years. In fact, it was Sharon who recommended it. She told me once when we had a fight that if I wasn't getting what I needed from her, maybe I should look around and find someone else. She just didn't want to know about it if I did."

"So you took her suggestion."

"Yeah. But I never told Sharon about it."

"Do you think she knew anyway?"

"I don't think so, but I doubt she'd care. She's changed, especially recently. Distant. Argumentative. That kind of thing."

"I see," Harriett said, making a notation on her pad.

"I mean once we were horsing around and I grabbed her from behind, just playing around. At first she was laughing. Then I wouldn't let her go when she wanted me to. The woman went berserk. Fought like a tiger and nearly crushed my instep by stomping on it with the heel of her shoe."

"Did you ask her about that?"

"She just said she couldn't stand being grabbed from behind and not being able to get away. Claustrophobia or something, I guess."

"Did she ever behave that way again?"

"Nope. And I never grabbed her and held her like that again, either. Sometimes, I'd try to walk up behind her and get a little grab, you know. She hated it."

"You continued to do it knowing she didn't like it?"

"She's my wife. I've got a right to do some grabbing if I want."

"Do you regard your wife as property?"

"A wife should be willing to have sex with her husband, don't you think?"

"If she wants it, I suppose so."

"You one of them feminist bra burners, Ms. Markham?"

"No," she smiled. "Were there any other times when your wife acted differently or erratically?"

"Can't think of nothing right now."

Harriett stood up and extended her hand to Taggart again. "If you think of anything else you think I should know, please feel free to contact me through the offices here, Mr. Taggart."

As Taggart left, Harriett jotted down a few quick notes before pressing the intercom button and asking for the next relative, Sharon Taggart's mother, Clarissa Parker Collins.

Clarissa Collins was a walking advertisement for good breeding and the social graces. She was impeccably dressed as she entered the conference room, standing tall and erect, her posture straight enough to balance a book on her head.

"Mrs. Collins," Harriett said as she greeted the woman who appeared to be in her mid-sixties, "Harriett Markham. I've been asked by Winston and Dunne to consider taking your daughter's case."

"Of course. But if you don't think you'll take it, I don't know why I should be talking to you."

"Right now, I'm trying to get a clearer picture of Sharon as a person, and even though I haven't officially notified the court that I will be her counsel, anything you tell me will still remain confidential," Harriett explained.

Clarissa Collins brushed off the seat of a chair with a handkerchief and perched herself on the edge of the chair, crossing her thin legs at the ankles.

"I don't know how I can assist you, Ms. Markham. I wasn't with Sharon on the night in question."

"What kind of person would you say Sharon is, Mrs. Collins?"

"She's a nice enough girl, has always been very obedient."

"Never rebellious, even as a teenager?"

"No, never."

"Never got mad or lost control of herself?"

"Once. She was angry with me, as usual."

"Why do you say as usual?"

"I think Sharon resented me for encouraging her to be more social. She didn't enjoy going out that much. It made her an excellent student, but she lacked the social graces one can only acquire through interacting with others."

"She didn't date much then?"

"I can't remember more than once or twice, and they were both younger than she. Hardly what I had expected."

"How did you feel when she got married?"

Clarissa leaned forward slightly and glanced around to make sure no one else was in the room.

"I had mixed feelings. On the one hand, I was relieved when she got married. On the other hand, I wasn't particularly pleased with her choice. Frank doesn't really fit in."

"Why were you relieved?"

"It may sound foolish, Ms. Markham, but when a woman remains single as long as Sharon did and never goes out with men, people begin to talk, you know."

"You thought Sharon was a lesbian?"

"It crossed my mind, but thank God I was wrong. Are you married, Ms. Markham?" Clarissa asked.

"No," Harriett smiled.

Clarissa leaned away from her slightly. "I see."

"Probably not," Harriett muttered under her breath. "Is there anything in particular you dislike about Sharon's husband?"

"He's not very bright, although he thinks he is. Sharon is exceptionally intelligent, has a very high IQ, and I have never understood why she chose to throw it all away on a man like Frank Taggart."

"Perhaps it was a physical attraction."

"I suppose it must have been something."

"You mentioned that Sharon got mad and lost control once as a teenager."

"Yes, we argued, which was unlike Sharon. She never talked back to adults. I made sure of that. But she became extremely angry. When she turned to leave the room, she lashed out with her fist. Actually made a hole in the wall."

"Really?"

"And broke her hand in the process. I told her that violence like that always hurts the person who is angry."

"You think it's better to suppress your anger?"

"Absolutely. Once you calm down and think about what made you angry to begin with, it's never as bad as you thought it was."

"I'm surprised you haven't developed an ulcer, Mrs. Collins. Venting anger is a very natural thing and considered to be quite healthy."

"Unless you take that anger out on members of your own family. I taught both my children that it's wrong to use violence against members of your own family, no matter how much they aggravate you. As a result, I'm confident that neither of them would ever abuse their children nor tolerate it from a spouse."

"What were you arguing about?"

Clarissa wrinkled her nose and shrugged. "I really cannot recall, but I'm sure it was something trivial. One of those teenage things."

"She misses her children very much."

"Sharon is a good mother. There have been times when I thought she might have reacted differently to their behavior, but they are clean and well cared for."

"I appreciate you coming in to talk to me, Mrs. Collins. If you ever need to contact me, please contact Doug or Alex, and they will relay a message to me."

"When will we know your decision?"

"By the end of the day."

As Clarissa left the room, Harriett made more notes and poured herself a cup of coffee. Carrying her cup, she left the conference room via the back door. She needed to move around, and the conference room seemed to be getting smaller and smaller the longer she remained in it. Halfway down the hall, Alex stepped out of her office and handed a memo to her secretary.

"How's it going in there?" she asked when she saw Harriett.

"Okay. I think there's only the father and brother left. Hopefully, that won't take long. I'd like to see Sharon interact with her parents and husband sometime."

"Does that mean you're going to take her case?"

"Yes," Harriett said sipping her coffee.

"Sharon couldn't ask for a better attorney, Harriett. Parker will be here in about an hour."

"That's fine. I'd like to speak to Paige, too, if possible."

"I'm sure she will be here with Parker. She's not actually a family member yet, though."

"You said she had worked with Mrs. Taggart on her brother's election campaign. She might be able to provide a different perspective on her personality."

"I'm sure she'll be more than willing to help if she can."

"I need to get in touch with Wayne."

"Do you have his number? I'll call him for you."

Harriett shook her head. "He doesn't have a phone. I'll drive to the cabin tomorrow morning and talk to him. If you can, call my office and tell Phyllis I'll be back Friday afternoon."

"Be glad to and I'll let you know when Parker arrives."

"Thanks," Harriett said.

Returning to the conference room, Harriett asked Eleanor to send Sharon's father in. Davis Collins was the antithesis of his wife, a plain looking man who could have been any man on the street, belying his financial status.

"What kind of child was Sharon, Mr. Collins?" Harriett began after the preliminary introductions.

"A sweet girl. A daddy's girl, I suppose," Collins smiled.

"Did you spend a lot of time with her when she was growing up?"

"As much as I could, but unfortunately, I was away quite a bit on business back then."

"What kinds of things did you do together?"

"I used to take her fishing and camping. She liked being outdoors even though it made her mother furious when she came home dirty. I think Clarissa has always been a little disappointed that Sharon was too much like me. Our personalities are similar. We're both quiet and enjoy reading. And we both abhor parties and pretentious people."

Collins chuckled pleasantly. "Once Sharon asked me to run away with her during the height of the social season. I could always use business as an excuse to avoid those things, but Sharon sort of got stuck. Clarissa would expend a fortune on the beauty parlor and new clothes for Sharon, but they never took. She'd jump right back into jeans and a T-shirt the second she got the chance and then scrub that crap off her face."

"She didn't enjoy wearing makeup and getting dressed up then?"

"Hated it!" Collins said expansively.

Harriett smiled. She liked this down to earth man.

"Why didn't Sharon just tell her mother that she didn't like those things?"

"She wouldn't have hurt her mother's feelings like that. It wasn't her way. If she had told her, it would have caused a fight, and Sharon would do pretty much anything to avoid a confrontation with Clarissa."

"Your wife told me Sharon once broke her hand by hitting a wall when she was angry."

"Yeah, Clarissa told me about that. It kinda surprised me. Not like Sharon to lose her temper that way."

"Do you know what the argument was about?"

"I was out of town when it happened, and neither of them would discuss it."

"I appreciate your help, Mr. Collins."

"Don't hesitate to call me if there's anything you need from us, Ms. Markham. No matter how this turns out, I won't turn my back on my daughter."

"If you can, Sharon would like to see her children. I can arrange for her to see them away from the jail."

"I'll take them personally tomorrow. Just let me know where to go."

"I'll have someone notify your office as soon as I know."

Chapter
Twelve

"PARKER IS HERE," Alex said as she stepped into the conference room. "How about lunch after you complete these interviews?"

"Check with me later," Harriett said as she looked over the list of questions she had prepared for Sharon's brother. Looking at Alex, she smiled slightly. "And Alex, if you could, ask Eleanor to give me about five minutes before she brings him in."

Collins was dressed in gray slacks and a navy blazer over a lightweight white mock turtleneck pullover. Harriett couldn't shake the idea of how much he looked like a politician. Everything about him seemed rehearsed and preplanned. He grabbed a chair and pulled it closer to her.

"Alex told me you've agreed to take Sharon's case, Harriett. I can't tell you how relieved I am to hear that."

"You're very close to your sister, aren't you?" Harriett asked.

"Despite the five years between us, we've always been close. I used to watch her when my parents went out. It was fun playing games with her. Gave me a chance to act like a kid again."

"What kind of person would you say your sister is?"

"She's very generous. Kind. I don't remember her ever saying anything bad about other people."

"After you left home, did you ever hear your parents complain about her behavior?"

"Well, you know how parents are, Harriett. And Mother has a tendency to overreact when things don't go her way. So if she ever complained, I just blew it off as Mother being Mother again."

"What about your father? He ever voice any problems with Sharon?"

"Never. He used to take her places with him and let her get dirty. Probably just to drive Mother crazy."

"Has Sharon ever told you about problems with her marriage?"

"Nothing serious. Mostly the usual things you'd expect to hear. We don't have enough money. He doesn't do his share of work around the house. Leaves his dirty clothes on the floor. That kind of thing."

"Ever hear Frank complain about Sharon?"

For the first time, Parker Collins seemed uncomfortable.

"He's tried to bad mouth her once or twice, but I stopped him. Sharon deserves someone better than Frank, and if it weren't for Kevin and Laurel, I think she'd split, but Frank's threatened to take the children and disappear if she ever thought about leaving him."

"Do you think he'd do it?"

"Yes. I've offered to move Sharon to Austin to be closer to me several times, but she always said she'd work it out somehow."

"Did Frank have a specific complaint?"

"He's intimated that their sex life hasn't been good enough for him, but I didn't want to get into that can of worms. I suggested family counseling, but I don't think they ever went. When I asked him about it later, he said Sharon refused to go."

"Why would she refuse to see a counselor?"

"My sister is an extremely private person. Always has been. As a child, she could sit for hours in her room thinking. She told me once a few years ago that she had a special place she liked to go to, and when I asked her where that was she just pointed at her head and smiled."

"You mean like a made up place?"

"I suppose."

"I meant to ask your mother, but did Sharon ever have any imaginary friends she played with or talked to when she was little?"

"God, I hadn't thought about that in years. She did have an imaginary playmate once. What was her name? Sharon used to pour tea and serve plastic cookies to her."

"Did she ever introduce you to her friend?"

"No, she said her friend was really shy and didn't like strangers," Parker answered. He closed his eyes and squeezed them tightly. "It was June or Jane, something like that."

"How old was she then?"

"Maybe six or seven."

"Do you know when the friend stopped being a part of her life?"

"Sorry, I don't remember that."

Suddenly, Parker snapped his fingers and said, "Jan! That was her friend's name."

Harriett wrote the name down.

"I understand Sharon helped you with your campaign," she said.

"I couldn't have won without her. She's brilliant at analyzing various voter groups. In fact, she insisted I learn Spanish. At least enough to get me by with Hispanic voters in my senatorial district."

"Was it effective?"

"Very. I think if Sharon had the nerve to leave Dallas, she could make a fortune working in a wider campaign arena."

"Maybe she will if you move on to seek higher offices."

"That's not in the cards right now. There's still a lot to do in Texas."

"Alex tells me you and Paige are getting married next winter."

"Yeah, I guess I've delayed marriage as long as I can. She's a great girl. I think Alex is worried about the difference in our ages, but I hope I can convince her not to worry."

"Do you think there's any possibility that someone might be trying to ruin your political career by framing your sister, Parker?"

"Anything's possible, but none of my opponents have been vindictive enough to do something like this. In fact, one of them tried to hire Sharon to work for his campaign."

"Okay. Well, I know where to find you if I think of anything else. The only other thing I should mention is that I'm going to need a retainer before I can proceed any further."

"I understand. How much will you need up front? I'm prepared to write you a check right now."

"I'll need ten thousand to start. I'll be retaining an investigator to check out some things for me, and he'll need some money to cover his expenses."

Parker pulled a checkbook from his blazer pocket and began writing out a check.

"Not that it matters, but how much do you think this whole thing will run?"

"I don't think a low end estimate of fifty thousand is out of line, but a lot will depend on what we dig up and what defense we decide to use."

"Are you considering an insanity plea?"

"I'm not considering anything right now, but that's one possibility. It has a number of problems, though."

"Like what?" he asked, glancing up from his checkbook.

"Well, for one thing, juries don't like it and don't believe it most of the time. They usually think it's an act to avoid going to jail. Secondly, the burden of proof would fall on us. I'd have to prove Sharon's insane, and the burden goes beyond the reasonableness standard. In Texas, if she knows the difference between right and wrong, she wouldn't be considered legally insane even if she were mentally disturbed. And lastly, if she were proved insane, she could spend the remainder of her life in a mental institution, which wouldn't be much of a step up from life in prison."

"Do you think you can avoid the death penalty?"

"I doubt we'll be facing that. I think murder second degree will be the eventual charge, and it doesn't carry the death penalty. Of course, we can remain hopeful that she'll be acquitted. But right now, quite honestly, that seems to be an extremely remote possibility."

"I wish I knew what happened. What could possibly have driven her to do what she did?"

"We might never know that."

He tore the check out of the checkbook and handed it to her. "Let me know when you need more," he said as he stood and placed the checkbook back into his jacket pocket. He shook Harriett's hand and turned to leave the room. "Should I send Paige in?"

"Please," Harriett smiled, flipping to a clean page in her pad. "It should only take a few minutes."

She was refilling her coffee cup when Paige Dunne tapped on the conference room door and peeked inside.

"Would you like a cup of coffee before we get started, Paige?" Harriett smiled.

"No, thank you," Paige chuckled. "I think I've about reached my quota for the month while I was waiting for Parker."

"He seems quite concerned about his sister's well-being. Are they very close?"

"Extremely," Paige said, rolling her eyes slightly.

"Does that create problems between the two of you?"

"No. I've always gotten along with Sharon and wish I were half as smart as she is. She never forgets anything and can remember the smallest details. During Parker's campaign, she remembered a letter that had arrived at campaign headquarters from some woman who was concerned about some land she owned. It seemed that the taxes had doubled in a year's time, and she didn't understand why. She actually made Parker visit the woman to explain the tax proposals he was going to submit for legislation when he was elected."

"Did you ever notice whether or not Sharon had a temper or acted unaccountably different for any reason?"

"I know she has a temper and the election was a close one. Everyone was pretty tense for a while afterward."

"Did she lose her temper in front of you?"

"Once, but Parker told her she was wrong."

"What was she angry about?"

"We had an engagement party at the Collinses' house over Thanksgiving, and everyone seemed to be having a good time. After about an hour, Sharon and her husband got into an argument and he left. I had never heard her raise her voice before, but her blood pressure was certainly elevated that night."

"Do you know what they argued about?"

Shaking her head, Paige said, "By the time I realized they had been arguing, Frank had already slammed the door and left."

"Have you set your wedding date yet?" Harriett smiled.

"Next winter is as close as we've come so far. It depends on when the legislature adjourns for the holiday and whether there are any late sessions."

"Well, congratulations. I hope you'll be very happy. How is Alex taking it?"

"Like an older sister. She thinks Parker is too old for me."

"She'll get over it as soon as she has nieces and nephews to bounce on her knee," Harriett smiled.

"Somehow that is a picture I just cannot imagine," Paige laughed as she got up.

"I appreciate your time, Paige. I wanted to get a feel for what kind of person Sharon is from someone besides a family member."

"If there's anything I can do to help, I will, Harriett. I know Parker trusts you to do what's best for Sharon, and I'm sure this will all turn out to be a huge mistake."

FOR SEVERAL MINUTES, Harriett read over the notes she had taken during the interviews, but she was tired of being cooped up in the glass and steel office tower. As she was placing her pen and pad back in her briefcase, Alex came into the room.

"Ready for some lunch?" she asked.

"I should go over these notes again," Harriett said.

Alex frowned and walked to the table. Placing her hand on Harriett's briefcase, she flipped it shut.

"Enough is enough. You've been in here taking statements all morning. You need to get your mind as well as your body out of here for a while," she said. Lowering her voice, she looked intensely at Harriett. "You're not going to be able to avoid me, Harriett. I'm suggesting lunch. Nothing else. Now can we please go?"

"Our agreement was that I wouldn't be taking orders from anyone at Winston and Dunne," Harriett said as she stood up.

"On the case you won't be. This isn't about the case."

Impulsively, Alex kissed her, catching her off guard. The softness of her lips hadn't changed and neither had the knot Harriett got in the pit of her stomach when Alex kissed her. She didn't resist the kiss and stopped thinking about complicating her case as her lips parted slightly, inviting Alex's exploration. She had been living a long time with only the memory of Alex's kiss, hoping to find someone else who could make her feel the same way. Alex drew her so close that she could barely breathe, kissing her repeatedly. When she finally pulled away and took Harriett's face in her hands, they were both as breathless as if they had made love.

"Damn," Harriett said, resting her forehead against Alex's.

"I hope this won't complicate your life and distract you from your case," Alex said softly as she stroked Harriett's hair.

"Me, too," Harriett said, looking at her former lover. "But I'm still not ready to rush into anything, Alex."

"All I want to rush into right now is lunch," Alex smiled. "At my age, just the thought of sex makes me hungry."

Harriett laughed as they headed toward the conference room door.

Chapter
Thirteen

THE DRIVE FROM Dallas to Lake Texoma gave Harriett a chance to clear her mind and think. She was torn between wanting to revive her relationship with Alex and knowing logically it was something she should avoid. It would be the simplest thing in the world to sleep with Alex and feel wanted again, but the timing couldn't be worse and she felt like kicking herself. Less than forty-eight hours after coming into her life again, Alex had managed to erase eleven years as though they had been eleven days.

By the time she turned off the highway onto the road that traced the edge of the lake, she was beginning to feel depressed. She wasn't even sure Wayne would be at the cabin. When it finally came into sight, she was glad to see a lone figure sitting on the edge of the fishing pier. The man turned when he heard the vehicle coming his way. The last time Wayne Graham had seen her she hadn't been driving a truck. Stepping out of the cab of the truck, she waved in Wayne's direction, and he seemed unsure whether to wave back or not. Removing her sunglasses, she squinted into the reflection of the sunlight off the water and went toward him. She was nearly to him before he recognized her.

"Got an extra fishing rod?" she asked with a smile.

"In the cabin," he said looking up at her. "What the hell brings you up here, kiddo?"

She squatted down next to her old friend and rested an arm on his shoulder. "I'm here to offer you a job."

"And give all this up? Forget it."

Harriett reached into the pocket of her jacket and pulled out a handful of bills, waving them under his eyes.

"How much?" he asked.

"Three thousand. For starters."

"Must be some case."

"Maybe. That's why I need you, Wayne."

"Well, for that kind of cash, it ain't some dude screwin' his secretary, that's for damn sure."

"Murder times four."

Wayne turned his head and looked at her. "Fuck, Harriett, can't you ever find a client who's content just to knock off one other person?

How'd you get stuck with this one?"

"It was a referral," she said, looking out over the lake.

"From who? Dunne?"

Wayne knew from her silence that he was right.

"You ain't gettin' mixed up with that dame again, are you?"

"No," she lied.

"Right," he said and Harriett knew he didn't believe her. "You check the warrant this time?"

"All the paperwork's in order, and they have the weapon with her prints on it. I might not be able to win this one, Wayne, but I need to find enough to get the sentence lessened."

"Now why would you want to do that for someone who up and killed four people?"

"That's what they pay me to do."

"You over Wilkes yet?"

"No. Are you?"

"Sometimes I make it a whole week without thinking about that son of a bitch. Wish I'd never told you about that warrant," Wayne said.

"Me, too."

"Maybe he is a fruitcake, and he'll never get out of the loony bin."

"He wrote me once," Harriett said softly as she shifted her eyes to the lake. "Right after I moved to Austin."

"How'd he find out where you were?"

"I don't know."

"What'd he say? Thanks?"

Clearing her throat, Harriett looked at Wayne and attempted a smile.

"He said he'd come to visit me someday."

"You reported it, I hope."

"I'm supposed to be contacted if he's ever released."

"It's been nearly twelve years. Think they'll remember?"

"Hope so. Will you take this job?"

"I guess I've caught about every fish in this lake at least once. Might as well. In Austin?"

"Dallas. I need for you to interview the client's co-workers and friends. I'm having a hard time getting a feel for what kind of person she is."

"A woman? Well, that's a new wrinkle. You staying in Dallas?"

"I'm going back to Austin in the morning. It's going to take a while for this to come to trial, and I'll be filing for a change of venue. Right now there's no reason for a judge to grant that. We'll see what the press does once they get more involved in the case. I might need you to do a little Deep Throat work for me."

"Whip up publicity for the case? Ain't that illegal?"

"Not unless you get caught and snitch on me," Harriett smiled.

"I'll start first thing in the a.m."

Pulling a folded sheet of legal paper from her jacket, she handed it to him.

"This is the who, what, when, and where. Don't know the why. I'll book you a room for a week at the Hyatt. Winston and Dunne will bill it out to the client later. If you need more money, they've set up a separate expense account for you. Just contact Doug or Alex, and they'll cut you a check."

"What's the limit?"

"There isn't one."

"I see a whole lot of room service in my future," Wayne chuckled. "Grab a rod."

"I have to get back to Dallas. I want to see my client again before I leave for Austin."

"You'll be sorry. The granddaddy of all bass is waiting out there."

Patting Wayne on the back, she said, "To come this close to shore he'd have to have a death wish."

"Give me about a week, and I'll bring whatever I find to Austin. Haven't had the chance to witness our state government in action for a while."

"We'll have a room ready for you. Thanks, Wayne," she said, kissing his cheek.

He stopped her as she started to walk away, "Hey, I like the truck."

AT FOUR O'CLOCK Thursday afternoon, Harriett entered the back door of the George Allen Center for the last time. The next morning, the family would release a statement to the press announcing that she had been retained to represent Sharon Taggart, as well as their faith that Sharon was innocent of the charges against her. It would be the same old bullshit families always said. After passing inspection, she waited for Sharon to be brought to her. There was a reassuring sameness to the way people were handled in jail.

When Sharon was finally seated across from her, Harriett looked at the shy woman, and somehow the word murderer didn't come to mind.

"Did you get the pictures?" she asked.

"Yes. Thank you."

"I've arranged for your father to bring your children for a visit later this evening."

"I don't want them to see me here."

"You'll meet with them in a conference room on the second floor. No bars, but you won't be able to see your father there. Someone else will bring the children to the room. It's not likely they'd be smuggling a weapon in for you. I can't do anything about the coveralls though."

"That's all right. They'll like the bright orange. You're very kind, Ms. Markham."

"How old are your children, Sharon?"

"Kevin is four and Laurel is almost two. Do you have children?"

"A niece who's eighteen. I became her guardian when she was two, after her parents were killed."

Sharon smiled. "She'll be leaving home soon then."

"I've spoken to your mother, as well as other members of your family."

"That must have been depressing for you," Sharon chuckled.

"They're all concerned about you, Sharon. I've agreed to take your case. They'll announce it tomorrow."

"Thank you."

"I'll be returning to Austin in the morning after I meet with the prosecutor assigned to your case, so we need to go over a few things before I leave. Feel up to a few more questions?"

"Well, I was going to watch the soaps on TV, but I suppose it can wait," Sharon quipped. Then she looked at Harriett. "Sorry. Poor attempt at humor."

"It's important that you keep your spirits up if you can. I've retained a private investigator to interview some of your co-workers and friends for me."

"Why? They won't know anything."

"We might need some character witnesses later. Have you ever had any trouble with any of your co-workers?"

"No."

"Do you like your job?"

"It pays the bills," she shrugged.

"Do they find your work satisfactory?"

"I get good evaluations."

"Has Frank come to see you yet?"

Sharon shook her head.

"Well, I'm sure he will soon."

"It probably doesn't matter, and he's busy with Kevin and Laurel."

"Frank told me that you don't like to be grabbed. That true?"

"Yes."

"Is it just a phobia?"

Sharon's eyes met Harriett's, "Do you enjoy being grabbed?"

"Depends on who it is," Harriett smiled. "Sometimes a man might grab a woman when they're horsing around. It's not uncommon between husbands and wives."

"I don't like feeling...trapped," Sharon said flatly.

"Are you claustrophobic?"

"No. I just don't like for anyone to touch me without my permission. A quirk, I guess."

"Tell me about Jan."

"Who?"

"Parker said you had an imaginary playmate named Jan when you were little."

Sharon laughed. "God! I haven't thought about her in eons. I don't know what I could possibly tell you about someone who doesn't exist. I guess every kid has an invisible playmate at some time. I think I made her up from some story I heard."

"Are you and your brother close?"

"Not so much now that he's in Austin most of the time. He's getting married next winter. I hope I can be there."

"Paige spoke very highly of you."

"She's a sweet girl. Parker's a lucky man."

"Do you think the difference in their ages will be a problem?"

Sharon closed her eyes and rolled her head around on her shoulders.

"An age difference never bothered him before, so I don't suppose it will now," Sharon said cryptically. "There's a lot an older man can teach a younger woman."

"There is something to be said for experience, I guess," Harriett agreed.

"Is Paige a virgin?" Sharon asked, the corners of her mouth turning up slightly.

"Why would you ask that?"

"Just curious. I've read that men like young virginal women, even though they're an endangered species today."

Harriett looked across the table at Sharon. Throwing her head back, Sharon took a deep breath before meeting Harriett's eyes again, arching her left eyebrow.

"Are you a lesbian, Harriett?"

"My personal life isn't pertinent to your case," Harriett said.

Leaning forward on the table, Sharon said, "Ever seen a fabulously beautiful woman and wondered what it would be like to touch her, feel her against you?"

"Have you?"

"When I was younger. But not now." Sharon shrugged as she leaned back in her chair again. "One of those awkward teenage things probably."

Harriett glanced at the clock on the wall behind Sharon.

"Your father will be here with Kevin and Laurel soon," she said.

"I should make myself a little more presentable then," Sharon said.

Chapter
Fourteen

HARRIETT ARRIVED AT the office of Dallas County District Attorney Harry Ward at eight forty-five Friday morning, accompanied by Wayne. Ward's secretary escorted her into his office a few minutes later. She had known Harry Ward when he had been in private practice. During her absence from Dallas, he had run for and been elected District Attorney. Except for a few pounds added to his waistline, he hadn't changed much over the years. He still had a full head of ash brown hair and perpetual frown furrows across his forehead. He stood as she crossed the office to shake his hand, and allowed himself the luxury of a momentary smile.

"Been a long time, Harriett," Ward said, motioning to a chair across from his desk. Setting her briefcase down next to her, she glanced around Ward's office.

"I see this office hasn't changed much," she said with a smile. "It looks pretty much the same as it was under the last DA."

"Continuity. Besides if I moved anything I'd probably never be able to find it again. I expect you're here to feel us out about the Taggart case."

"I've looked over the paperwork your office sent me and..."

"Whoa! I'm not the one handling this case, Harriett. In fact, I have to be in court in about half an hour on another case that's already taken way too much time. I've assigned Taggart to an assistant."

"Then I guess I'll have to meet with him."

"He's just gathering up some things, and then I'll turn the two of you loose on each other in a conference room," Ward said. "To tell you the truth, he wanted this case. Lobbied for it pretty hard so I hope he doesn't screw it up. He's new, so be gentle with him."

"I thought Todd Connor might be the ADA assigned to the Taggart case."

"He was, but another case took a turn we hadn't expected."

The door to Ward's office opened and a young man rushed in, adjusting his tie.

"Harriett Markham, meet Assistant District Attorney Sean Lassiter."

She stood and extended her hand to Lassiter, a tall, thin man with darting ferret-like brown eyes. He shook her hand and released it quickly.

"I have everything set up in a room down the hall," he said more to Ward than Harriett. "Riley will join us in a few minutes."

"Riley?" she asked.

"Yes, Detective James Riley was the lead investigator on this case," Lassiter answered with a smile. "And he seemed unusually pleased when he heard you'd be handling the defense."

Ward looked at his watch and stood. "Well, looks like the bell has rung for round one. I have to get to court. Good luck."

Harriett and Lassiter followed Ward from the office and turned left as he turned right toward the elevators. Wayne fell in behind them. Entering the conference room, she placed her briefcase on the table and removed a pad. Lassiter unbuttoned the jacket to his suit and sat down across from her.

"Mrs. Taggart's representative at the arraignment entered a not guilty plea," he said. "Are you planning to amend that?"

"No. I'm satisfied with the plea. For now."

"Did you find all the paperwork in order?"

"Yes. But I'm curious about how you arrived at the charge."

"The grand jury found it justifiable considering the number of people who died or were seriously injured as a result of your client's actions."

"*Alleged* actions," she corrected, raising her eyes from the notepad to look at him. "From what I've read and seen, the only real piece of evidence you have is the Browning. That hardly seems to justify first degree. You don't have a motive on Mrs. Taggart's part, and the only crime you have the remotest link to is the death of Leonard Kaufmann, which was the result of a traffic accident."

"Ballistics has determined that the same weapon was used in all of the shootings."

"From this Browning?" Harriett asked, looking at the evidence inventory sheet in front of her.

"The shells all came from the same lot as the ones found at the Taggart home. Ballistics confirmed that this Browning left the markings on the shell casings found at each scene."

"I'm afraid no matter which way I look at this case, Mr. Lassiter, unless you're able to prove my client's intent, I don't see anything better than voluntary manslaughter here. There's absolutely nothing here to infer her intent."

"That's ridiculous!" Lassiter huffed.

"The hammer marks on the shells may be consistent with a Browning, but my expert tells me that the hammer marks are inconclusive and could have been made by any Browning in Dallas County or beyond," Harriett lied. "Can I assume you will be introducing the business end of the bullets *allegedly* fired by my client?"

Lassiter didn't answer for a moment. "We were only able to recover one of those."

"And where was it found?"

"Lodged in a telephone pole at the scene of the Kaufmann death."

"Have your forensic people estimated how long it might have been in the pole, or were you planning to make an educated guess?"

"They believe it was introduced to the pole recently."

"I'm not interested in what they believe, Mr. Lassiter, only in what they know for a fact. And a fact that I know is that none of the people who died or were injured were shot. All of their injuries were the result of traffic accidents, many of which happen in Dallas every day."

"And their accidents were caused by your client firing at their vehicles as they drove down the highway, making her actions the proximate cause of their deaths."

"But that, if proven, would only demonstrate reckless disregard, which is still not murder one. My client didn't know any of the victims of the accidents and had absolutely no motive whatsoever to harm any of them."

"The recovered bullet was fired from the Taggart's Browning. And that, Ms. Markham, is not a guess. It's a fact. And by the way, you might want to know that Mrs. Taggart has been identified by the owner of a gun shop in Burleson. He sold her the ammunition for the Browning and remembered her because of the uniqueness of those particular shells."

Harriett hadn't expected this new revelation, but tried not to look surprised.

"I don't see a mention of that on my disclosure sheet. Slip your mind?" she asked.

"It came to our attention after you received those papers. You would have gotten an official notification tomorrow."

"Anything else happen to pop up unexpectedly that you'd like to tell me about?" Harriett asked. "I advise you not to make those omissions a habit."

"We'll continue to strengthen our case against Mrs. Taggart up to the trial date. If that doesn't meet your agenda, I don't see that as my problem," Lassiter shrugged.

"You only have one witness who may or may not have seen the most recent shooting. A Mrs. Emma Sanchez, age sixty-seven."

"She observed your client with a rifle at the Kaufmann scene."

"Has she picked Mrs. Taggart from a line-up?"

"She made a tentative identification of both Mrs. Taggart and her vehicle."

"A dark blue, or possibly black, Ford Taurus." She read from the paperwork in front of her. "Probably aren't more than several thousand of those in and around the Dallas-Fort Worth Metroplex."

"With a partial plate."

"All you have is the first three letters, which make up only one of the DMV codes for Dallas County. How could you possibly have narrowed down thousands of vehicles, most of whose plates begin with those letters, to Mrs. Taggart? That's a leap in deductive reasoning that would have required a crystal ball," Harriett said flatly.

"It's the result of good police work," James Riley said from behind Harriett.

She turned her head to look at Detective Riley. He looked much older, but his eyes told her that he hadn't forgotten Ashley Lawrence.

"What's he doing here?" Riley asked, looking at Wayne.

"Mr. Graham has been hired as an investigator by the defense," Harriett said as she stood up, ready for a confrontation with Riley.

"Well, he ain't gonna find any technical loopholes in this case like he did in the Wilkes case," Riley sneered.

Harriett hadn't expected the Wilkes case to become a part of the discussion so quickly, and the mention of it touched a nerve that was still raw.

"If you'd done your job the right way back then, Wilkes wouldn't have gotten out to kill again," Wayne said as he, too, stood up to face Riley. "You still not willing to take responsibility for your own stupidity, Riley?"

Riley stepped toward Wayne.

"That's enough!" Lassiter said loudly. "Let's pay attention to what we're doing here. You two can settle your private problems later."

Riley took a seat next to Lassiter, but continued to glare at Wayne.

"Mrs. Taggart has no alibi for any of the nights in question," the ADA resumed.

"Innocent people seldom need to recall their whereabouts. Do you know where you were on any of those nights, Mr. Lassiter?" Harriett asked.

"As I'm sure you know, this has been an ongoing investigation by the police department."

"And I know they hadn't been able to come up with anyone as a suspect until they tripped over Sharon Taggart, who had absolutely no reason to commit any of these crimes. Unless you can come up with something more substantial in the way of evidence that links Sharon Taggart to them, I'm going to petition the court for a dismissal of the charges against her."

"The ballistics testimony alone will be sufficient to put her in prison."

"Perhaps, but you won't be able to make a case for anything more than voluntary manslaughter."

"Sharon Taggart wasn't some damn kid out taking potshots at street lights, Ms. Markham," Riley said, leaning forward. "She wanted to cause the deaths of those people. She planned those crimes and carried them out, which is called premeditation and malice aforethought. Her motive is irrelevant. She just had a damn good time doing it."

Harriett slipped her pad back into her briefcase and snapped it shut. "You'll be getting a copy of my petition to the judge this afternoon." She stood and turned to leave, as Wayne opened the door.

"You know, it's hard to believe you'd have the guts to come back to Dallas for this case," Riley sneered.

"Why is that, Detective Riley?" she asked as she turned to face him. "Sharon Taggart needs a defense attorney, and I happen to be a damned good one."

Chapter
Fifteen

EARLY MONDAY MORNING, Wayne strolled out of his hotel's restaurant with the taste of coffee and maple syrup lingering in his mouth and a smile on his lips. He hadn't felt the least bit guilty about ordering the Texas T-bone steak and eggs with a side order of a small stack of pancakes for breakfast, especially since they would be charged to Harriett's client. Before she left for Austin, they had compiled a list of individuals for him to begin interviewing. Chewing on the remains of his toothpick, he unlocked the driver's door of his sagebrush green Chevy Tahoe and slid comfortably behind the wheel. Glancing at the clock on the dash, he estimated that it would take him about twenty-five minutes to make it to Highland Park High School. Plenty of time.

Highland Park High School was located on Emerson Avenue, a few blocks from the Dallas North Tollway. As he swung his vehicle into a visitor's parking area in front of the two-story red brick building, he vaguely remembered his own days in high school. The ten-room county high school he had attended bore little resemblance to the structure in front of him. The spacious grounds were well tended, and everything looked tidy. The school obviously sat in the middle of a solid, upper echelon property tax zone. As he climbed the steps toward the front doors, he secretly made book with himself that everyone he met would be wearing a jacket and tie.

A sign in the front entry welcomed him to the home of the Scots and directed him to the main office. Unlike most of the downtown high schools he had been to over the years, the hallways were relatively quiet except for the sound of morning announcements pouring from the overhead intercom speakers. He pulled open the door to the office and held it for two female teachers as they exited. Teachers sure hadn't looked like that when he was a student, he thought with a smile. If they had, he might have taken more interest in going every day rather than finding something else more entertaining to do, most of which had gotten him in trouble. Still, stealing a glance at the teachers as they moved gracefully down the hallway, his thoughts were interrupted.

"May I help you, sir?" a woman asked slightly louder than necessary.

Turning his head away from the view he had been enjoying, he was disappointed to see a gray-haired woman with pinched lips staring at him. Women who looked like her had made education decidedly distasteful for him.

Placing his meaty hands on the counter, he said, "Yeah. I would like to speak to Mr. Benevidez."

"Do you have an appointment?"

"No I don't." Wayne reached in his pocket and drew out a business card, dropping it unceremoniously on the counter.

"May I ask what this is in reference to, Mr...Graham?" the receptionist asked as she picked up the card and readjusted her glasses to read it.

"Sharon Taggart," he answered bluntly.

"Mrs. Taggart isn't here any longer."

"That's why I'm here. I'm an investigator for Mrs. Taggart's attorney. Is Benevidez in or not?"

"We have cooperated completely with the authorities and already told them everything we knew."

"I'm sure you have, dear, but you haven't told me yet," Wayne smiled benignly.

"If you'll have a seat," she said nodding toward a row of comfortable looking chairs, "I'll see if Mr. Benevidez is available."

"Thanks."

Wayne glanced at the clock hanging on the wall just inside the office doors and sat down. The chairs were not as comfortable as they had looked, and he readjusted his jacket and pulled up his pant legs slightly before reaching for the latest edition of the PTA News. Out of the corner of his eye, he watched the receptionist speak to someone softly on the telephone, all the while casting furtive looks in his direction. Almost ten minutes passed before a distinguished looking Hispanic gentleman in his late forties came into the office and glanced around. The receptionist's eyes led him to Wayne.

The man was well-dressed in charcoal gray slacks with a white dress shirt and navy blue tie, all of which accented his slightly graying black hair and mustache. Extending his hand, the man smiled as he approached Wayne.

"Mr. Graham? Michael Benevidez. How can I assist you?"

Standing as he shook Benevidez's hand, Wayne said, "I appreciate you taking the time to speak to me. I won't take up much of your time."

"Sharon is one of my best teachers, and I will do anything I can to help. Why don't we go to my office?"

A few minutes later, Benevidez sat behind his desk and leaned back, steepling his hands in front of his face, resting his index fingers against his lower lip. Wayne pulled an old notebook and a pen out of his coat pocket and flipped it open.

"Before we begin, Mr. Graham, can you tell me how Sharon is?"

"About as good as anyone would be in her predicament, I guess,"

Wayne shrugged before he began asking questions. "What did Mrs. Taggart teach?"

"Social Studies, but primarily our Advanced Government classes, and I think, one or two sections of World Civilization."

"Overall, was she a pretty good teacher?"

"Superior," Benevidez beamed. "In her second year on the faculty, she was chosen as our Teacher of the Year. The students love her style and were very successful. She got along well with parents and other faculty members and volunteered to assist students with projects for their other classes as well as her own. She was the faculty sponsor for three or four extracurricular activities as well. Some people teach to make a living, but Sharon truly seemed to have a calling for working with teenagers, even the ones no one else wanted."

Wayne laughed, "I can't imagine there would be very many of those in this school."

"You would be surprised, Mr. Graham. Every school, no matter how large or small, or how affluent, has its own little group of troubled students."

"You said she sponsored some activities. Which ones were those?"

"Let's see," Benevidez thought. "I'm sure she was a class sponsor for one of the grade levels. Might have been the junior class because I know she worked on organizing the prom one year. And it seems like she was the sponsor for the Think Tank and Young Lawyers."

"Think Tank? What's that?"

"It's an academic competition between area high schools. Sort of similar to the Jeopardy television game."

"They any good?" Wayne smiled.

"Very good, and we have the trophies to prove it, especially the Young Lawyers. They were second in the State competition a couple of years ago, and Sharon was confident they would make it to the national competition in the next year or two."

"Did you have many opportunities to interact with Mrs. Taggart?"

"Many times. I found her to be cooperative and always with the best interests of the students and the school in mind. There were times we disagreed, naturally, but we were able to reach a satisfactory resolution most of the time."

"What types of disagreements?"

"Nothing huge, and mostly it involved a problem with another teacher whom she didn't think was effectively teaching. But that was something that only started fairly recently."

"Did it lead to other problems?"

"I really don't want to say anything bad about Sharon."

"If you don't, I'm sure someone else will, Mr. Benevidez. It would be better for her attorney to know about any personal conflicts now, so that they aren't a surprise later if they should come up at the trial."

Benevidez thought for a minute before continuing. "About a year or a year and a half ago, Sharon was involved in a verbal altercation with another faculty member, Mrs. Sanderson. I had to separate them and counsel both of them."

"What started the argument?"

"Sharon had a student who was having difficulty in Mrs. Sanderson's class. As I understand it, Sharon went to her room to see if she could help. Apparently Mrs. Sanderson told Sharon that she didn't need any help. She had been teaching for nearly twenty years and didn't need teaching lessons from a younger teacher. Sharon said something else to her and left the room. Just before the bell for the next class, apparently Mrs. Sanderson went to Sharon's room and told her, in front of students, that she would teach her class any damn way she wanted to and that Sharon could go to hell. Sharon called her an incompetent hack, and well, the discussion disintegrated from there. Although they did take the argument into the hall, there was a little shoving involved and another teacher came to get me."

"Did you take any action against either woman?"

"I sent them both home for the remainder of the day to cool off." Chuckling slightly, Benevidez smiled. "Although I did sort of have to agree that Mrs. Sanderson wasn't the best teacher on our faculty, Sharon admitted she hadn't handled it in the best way and formally apologized to Mrs. Sanderson as well as the class. In fact, she used the whole incident as a lesson in how *not* to handle a disagreement."

"Were there any other incidents like that?"

"Never, and I really just chalked it up to the fact that Sharon had only recently given birth to her daughter and was simply under stress."

"If possible, I'd like to have a look at Mrs. Taggart's classroom," Wayne said.

"I think there's a class in there this period, but if you can wait until it's over, the room should be empty for the next period. It was Sharon's conference period."

"Who is teaching her classes now?"

"The district sent a permanent substitute who had credentials in the same subject areas. So far he seems to be working out fine. However, I'm sure the students miss Sharon."

"I'm sure," Wayne said as he pushed himself out of the chair and stretched his back.

"You're more than welcome to wait in the lounge area if you want. There's a coffeemaker, but I can't guarantee how good the coffee is."

FORTY MINUTES LATER, Wayne trudged up a flight of stairs to Sharon's second floor classroom. Closing the door behind him, he looked around at the thirty desks, which were aligned in a semi-circle facing the front dry erase board. The walls were decorated with posters depicting political and historical figures. A map of the world that was painted directly on the wall covered the back wall of the room. Portions of it were filled in, and string lines led from various regions of the world to newspaper and magazine articles concerning world events. Although he had never seen it before in a classroom, there were curtains on all the windows and the whole room had a homey feel to it.

Sharon's desk was situated in the front corner of the room, opposite the door. Two tan file cabinets and a large bookcase sat behind the desk in easy reach of anyone seated there. Pulling out his notebook again, Wayne perused the materials on the bookshelf and made notes to himself. The books appeared to be arranged by subject and were equally divided between American politics and World History. One file cabinet was devoted to curriculum materials while the second was filled with file folders with students' names on each one. Going through the file drawers, he continued making notes as he pulled out a few folders, hoping he would be able to make copies of the material in each.

"Excuse me," a man's voice boomed. "Do you have permission to be in here?"

Turning his head toward the classroom door, Wayne saw a large muscular man filling the entrance, his hands on his hips.

"Sure do. From Mr. Benevidez."

"May I see your visitor's badge?" the forty-ish man asked.

Pulling himself up to his full height, Wayne estimated that they were about the same height and weight, although their weight was distributed a little differently. He reached into his jacket pocket and pulled out the bright yellow plastic clip-on pass.

"Sorry, sir, but we try to keep our eyes open for strangers on campus," the man said as his defensive posture relaxed somewhat.

"No problem," Wayne nodded. "And who might you be?"

"I'm Dylan Fields. My room is across the hall. I just happened to glance in and see you in here."

"Do you know Sharon Taggart?"

"Of course."

"My name is Wayne Graham, and I work for her attorney. If you have a couple of minutes, I'd like to ask you a couple of questions."

"Sure, I guess it'll be okay. How is Sharon? I sure miss having her in here to talk to."

"Why is that?"

"She and I used to have a weekly bull session. You know, bitchin' about the kids and some of our colleagues."

"Were you here when she had her disagreement with Mrs. Sanderson?"

Throwing his head back, Fields laughed. "Hell, yeah! If I hadn't stopped Sharon she would have cold cocked that old biddy."

"Do you know what they argued about?"

"I think it was about some student they had in common. Sharon always picked these loser kids and tried to help them. Sort of like taking in strays, you know."

"Ever know her to lose her temper like that any other time?"

"Nah. It was just one of those things. No one was too sad to see Sanderson retire the next year. She was pretty burned out."

"This school have a Xerox machine?"

"There's one down the hall in the teacher's workroom. I can give you my code to access it."

AFTER LUNCH, WAYNE loaded a box of copies and other materials into his Tahoe and backed out of the school parking lot. He had interviewed two or three teachers, who had all agreed that Sharon was a more than competent teacher and that Mrs. Sanderson had been a bitch. If Harriett needed character witnesses, there were plenty of them available at Highland Park High School. Entering the southbound lanes of the Dallas Tollway, the traffic was light as he made his way back into the downtown area, and the offices of the *Dallas Times-Herald*. Harriett had given him the name of a friend of Sharon's who was a reporter for the daily paper. Other than this one woman, it appeared that Sharon Taggart wasn't eaten up with personal friends. A brief phone call earlier had led to him being granted a brief appointment with Louise Harmon who had agreed to squeeze him in between stories.

When he stepped up to the reception desk of the *Dallas Times-Herald*, he still wasn't certain what he hoped Louise Harmon could tell him. She would probably turn out to be another character witness.

After fifteen minutes of cooling his heels in the lobby, he saw a middle-aged woman walking down a glass enclosed hallway, while apparently engaging in an animated discussion with an older man who kept trying vainly to control his frizzy head of hair by mashing it down with his hand as he talked. A moment later, she approached the desk in the lobby, holding a sheaf of papers. She was a tall woman with a round face framed by short dark hair. Her shirtsleeves were rolled up to her elbows, and her shirt was tucked neatly into her khaki slacks.

"There's a gentleman here to see you, Lou," the receptionist said, pointing in Wayne's direction as he stood and readjusted his waistband.

"Mr. Graham? I'm incredibly busy this morning, so I may have to cut our conversation short if I'm called away."

"I just need a few minutes. Let me buy you a cup of coffee."

"I can give you about fifteen minutes," Lou said as she glanced at her wristwatch and then put her pencil behind her ear. "Deadlines, you know."

Wayne followed her through a security door and down a hallway to a large break room. He poured two Styrofoam cups of coffee and joined her at a table near a window that overlooked the newspaper loading docks.

"Okay, what do you need to know?" Lou asked as she grabbed her cup and tested how hot the contents were. For someone who was supposedly Sharon Taggart's best friend, Wayne hadn't expected Lou Harmon to be so brusque.

"You're Sharon's best friend, aren't you?"

Lou shrugged. "I'm the only one who kept in touch with her after she married Frank I guess, if that's what you mean."

"How did you two meet?"

"What's the difference? I can't see how that would be of any help to Sharon now. It was years ago."

"Humor me," Wayne said flatly. "It's my fifteen minutes. Besides, if you don't answer my questions now, her attorney will have to subpoena you, and I can pretty much guarantee that will take you away from work longer than I will."

Sighing into her cup, Lou finally said, "Sharon worked here one summer as a junior reporter when I was the city editor. I had to review anything she wrote. For a college kid, she was pretty good and took criticism well."

"What kind of stuff did she write?"

"Oh, hell, we stick the summer intern types with the crap no one else wants, so it could have been just about anything. You know, obits, garden parties, movie reviews, those space killer things." Pausing to take a bigger drink, Lou seemed to be thinking about something. When she set her cup down, she smiled. "She really liked the movie reviews when she got assigned to them. Told me once she had been in her university's theater group and had won some acting award. She wanted to major in theater, but Clarissa disapproved of actors and such. The reviews let her fantasize a little."

"Do you know where she went to college?"

"Texas Women's up in Denton," Lou said, glancing at her watch again. "Anything else? Sorry, but we go to press in less than an hour."

"No problem. Did Sharon ever get a chance, maybe at her high school, to get involved in theater again?"

"I never heard her mention it. Closest she ever got was their mock trial team. She called me and asked if I would write a human-interest story on them once. It's like a real trial with a judge and jury. Apparently court etiquette and presentation are more important than actually winning the case. It was interesting, and a few of those kids were actually better than some real lawyers I've seen in action."

"You knew her before her marriage?"

Staring intently at her cup, Lou nodded. "Yeah. She was a different woman back then."

"How was that?"

"She used to know how to have fun. She only married Frank to get away from Clarissa anyway," Lou said as she shifted uncomfortably in her chair.

"How did you get along with Frank Taggart?"

"He's an asshole," Lou answered as Wayne watched the muscles along her jaw tightened.

"He seemed okay when I spoke to him," Wayne shrugged, waiting for Lou's reaction.

Her eyes were flashing as they met Wayne's. "He's a fucking imbecile who mentally abused her. Probably physically, too, for all I know. You didn't know her before...before he destroyed her spirit."

"Tell me how she was."

Lifting her cup to her lips, Lou said, "It doesn't matter any more. She made her choice. I tried to talk her out of it, but she wouldn't listen."

"Were you and Sharon lovers?"

The look in Lou's eyes changed from anger to sadness as she took a deep breath and exhaled. "Like I already said, Mr. Graham, it doesn't matter any more."

"Do you know the rest of her family?"

"I met them a couple of times. Her dad's okay, her mom's too concerned about how others perceive her to be worth much. Sharon and I actually argued about her brother once. She wasn't too happy with an editorial I wrote about him and let me know it," Lou chuckled. "For a while it was like the old Sharon had been resurrected."

"I'm guessin' you didn't give him a ringing endorsement," Wayne smiled.

"He's a hack who gets by on his looks and charm. Hell, my dog knows more about the problems of this senatorial district than he does. But the voters don't really care as long as the candidate looks good while he's lying out his ass."

"When was the last time you saw Sharon?"

"About a year ago, I think. She called me out of the blue, crying. Said she needed help."

"What was her problem?"

"After Laurel was born, Sharon seemed more unhappy than usual. When I got to her house, she wanted me to take her to the Dallas Mental Health Center." Clearing her throat Lou said, "She said the kids were driving her crazy, and she was afraid she might hurt one of them."

"Did you take her?"

"Of course. We signed in and waited around for a couple of hours before anyone would talk to her."

"Did they help her?"

"Hell, no. Someone came out and told her they didn't deal with postpartum problems, and she should see her regular physician for an anti-depressant. But as far as I know she never did. Like I said, that was the last time I saw her. I figured she worked it out." Looking at her wristwatch, Lou stood up and tucked the back of her shirt further into the waistband of her slacks. "Look, Mr. Graham, I really do have a deadline in less than an hour."

Wayne drained his cup and tossed it in the trash as they walked out of the break room. "I appreciate your help, Lou."

Stopping momentarily Lou looked at Wayne. "How is Sharon?"

"Holdin' up okay so far, I guess."

"If you see her, tell her...tell her I hope everything works out for her. She deserves a break."

Unlocking his car door, Wayne took a deep breath and squinted up into the growing heat of the Texas afternoon before settling into his car and returning to his hotel room.

Chapter
Sixteen

DESPITE THE SUNNY cloudless blue sky overhead, a biting wind smacked into his face, making him pull the collar of the lightweight jacket up to cover his neck. He felt like shit and hadn't slept worth a damn the night before. It had been a long time, and the air smelled different as it blew through the chain link in front of him. He smiled benignly and waited while the final paperwork changed hands, needing only one last signature.

The old man had kicked off a couple of years earlier. He hoped he had suffered when he keeled over a few minutes after the board meeting. His attorney told him that money had been transferred into a trust. He fingered the bank card in his pocket and smiled. The old man had always been generous to a fault, believing he could buy his son's love. And he had been right. He loved his father's money, and he had been making plans for years to put it to good use.

He closed his eyes and saw her face in his mind, wondering how much she had changed since the last time he had stared into her eyes. He had seen the hint of fear in them and that was all he ever needed. Just that fleeting hint of fear in her eyes had kept him going for nearly twelve years. He had promised her he would drop by for a visit, and now dear old Dad had given him the means to do that.

He was jerked away from his thoughts by the sound of metal scraping and watched as the security gate slid open. Just outside the gate, a black and yellow cab sat idling. He would spend his first night of freedom fucking and drinking. Then it would be time to get on with the plans he had been making and storing in his mind for too long. She was waiting for him. He wanted her to suffer, but not all at once or too quickly.

Glancing up at the two-story red-bricked guard tower, he smiled as he stepped through the gate.

Chapter
Seventeen

AT HARRIETT'S REQUEST, Wayne, working through Winston and Dunne, made arrangements for Sharon to meet with members of her family and videotaped the meetings over a two-day period. Early the following Monday morning, he gathered up the videos and his notes, checked out of the Hyatt and headed for Austin, arriving before noon.

Harriett came out of her office and hugged Wayne warmly.

"Nice place, kiddo," Wayne noticed. "Beats that antiseptic cell you called an office at Winston and Dunne."

"Got anything interesting for me?" Harriett asked as she looked down at the box he was carrying.

Before Wayne could answer, a man came briskly down the hall toward them. "Do we have a sewing needle around here, Harriett?" the man asked. "I just popped a damn button on my shirt."

"Phyllis probably has one. Nick, this is Wayne Graham. Wayne, Nick Lazslo, my law partner."

Nick smiled, extending his hand to Wayne. "I've heard a lot about you, Mr. Graham."

Taking Nick's hand, Wayne noticed the man's friendly open face with deep blue eyes behind his wire rimmed glasses. "Well, you can't believe everything Harriett says."

"You mean you're not really Superman, Dick Tracy, and father confessor combined?"

Wayne laughed. "But then again sometimes she does tell the truth."

"Wayne has been looking into the Taggart case for me," Harriett said.

"Great!" Nick said. "I hope you found something Harriett can use. This is going to be a rough one, I'm afraid."

Nick's concern seemed genuine, and Wayne liked his openness.

"Why don't you sit in while Wayne shows me what he has?" Harriett asked.

"Let me find a needle and thread first. I'll be there in a minute."

Wayne followed Harriett into her office and set the box on her desk.

"Nice guy," he observed.

"He's an excellent attorney, too. I was lucky when he agreed to join me. What do we have here?"

"Interview summaries and videos of your client at work and with her family."

"Does Sharon know you videotaped her?"

"No, but I don't think she'll sue you over it. Especially if you get her off."

"I wouldn't put much money on that," Harriett said as she read the labels on the videos.

Reaching into the box, Wayne dropped two stacks of papers on the desk. "These are copies of some materials I found in her filing cabinet, and a list of books on her bookshelf. Pretty interesting reading, if you're a lawyer."

When Nick entered Harriett's office, she was reading the interview statements. "Have you seen the videos, Wayne?" she asked.

"Yep."

"Got an opinion?"

"You ain't paying me for my opinion, kiddo."

Looking at him, she smiled. "I trust your opinion. What do you think?"

"The cops didn't make any mistakes on this one. The evidence is pretty convincing. I think she shot at those cars and caused the accidents that killed the people in them. It's kind of interesting that none of the cars had passengers, almost like she picked ones with only a driver. Three others survived though, so I guess you could say she didn't mean for anyone to get killed."

Nick stood behind Harriett and picked up the evidence inventory sheet.

"Pretty impressive evidence," he said. "Gun, ammo, fingerprints, powder residue, an eyewitness, and no alibi. Too bad you're not the prosecutor."

"The only thing missing is a motive," Wayne said.

"They don't need a motive for a conviction. Is she nuts?" Nick asked.

"Not from what I've observed. Just confused," Harriett shrugged.

"Claiming a memory loss?"

"No. Claiming categorically that she didn't do it even in the face of all this evidence," Harriett frowned.

"When did the shootings start?"

"About a year and a half ago," Harriett said.

"I think you're going to find that a lot happened about a year and a half or two years ago," Wayne said. "Everyone I've talked to has made some reference to that time period. That she changed around then in some way, but they weren't very specific about what the change was."

"What did the people you spoke to say about that time?" Harriett asked.

"Her principal said Sharon had a falling out with another teacher about a year or so ago. Other teachers said she became suddenly withdrawn around the same time. Two years ago she had her second kid, and a friend said it affected Sharon somehow. She became distant and began cutting herself off from everyone. Was depressed enough to seek help at a mental health clinic. It's sort of a common thread running through the interviews. Plus, I think you might find my interview with Louise Harmon interesting. She didn't come right out and say so, but I'd bet my pension that she and Sharon were lovers."

"Her mother said she once suspected that Sharon was a lesbian."

"Could be bi," Wayne shrugged.

"Let's see a movie," Harriett said. "Sorry I can't offer you any popcorn."

Wayne picked up a video and slid it into a TV-VCR combination on Harriett's bookcase.

"Who's this?" Harriett asked.

"The husband," Wayne said as the video flickered and began. "It's the most useful tape."

Nick closed the blinds behind Harriett's desk before taking a seat.

Frank Taggart was waiting in a spouse's visiting room as Sharon was brought in.

"Nice looking woman," Nick observed.

Sharon took a seat across from her husband and asked, "How are the kids?"

"How do you expect them to be with their mother in jail?"

Sharon smiled slightly. "Dad brought them to see me a couple of days ago."

"If I'd known what he was going to do, they wouldn't have gotten out of the house."

"I met them in another room, not here."

"What did you tell them?"

"That I'd be home soon and not to worry. We just talked about what they were doing in day care mostly, and they brought some pictures they drew for me."

"The shit's gonna hit the fan soon, Sharon. When the trial starts, it'll be in the papers. People will ask the kids questions."

"You have to keep them away from all that, Frank. It's a mistake."

"You know, you've done some dumb shit stuff before, but even I can't believe you're stupid enough to do something like this. How do you think it makes me look?"

Sharon didn't speak and looked away from her husband. For a moment, the video camera caught her face, causing Harriett to sit up and watch the video intently.

"Since you're not the one sitting in jail, I'd say you're looking pretty damn good, Frank. Is that why you're here? So I can feel sorry for you? We have to face this together."

"We haven't done anything together in years."

"When I get out of here, maybe we should see a counselor."

"You wouldn't go the last time."

"I don't mean a sex therapist. A family counselor."

"We wouldn't have problems if you didn't protect that pussy of yours like it was one of the crown jewels. If it wasn't for that, we wouldn't have any problems."

"Can we have a conversation just once without you bringing up sex?"

"Look, Sharon, I'm sorry you're in here, but I don't think a therapist or a counselor is going to help us. I'll stick with you through the trial, but I've already spoken to an attorney about a divorce."

"When did you do that?"

"A month ago. Before this mess."

Sharon leaned forward on the table, "Before or after you raped me?"

Frank laughed derisively, "Shit, girl! I never raped you."

"I'm sorry, Frank. You're right. Was it before or after you 'fucked me for my own good?'" The forcefulness behind her statement surprised Harriett, and she glanced at Wayne and Nick to see their reactions.

"It didn't hurt you none," Frank Taggart said.

"Well, what woman wouldn't enjoy having your dick shoved up her ass?"

"You didn't say nothing about it, and I know you came. If I could've gotten to what I wanted to begin with, I wouldn't have been forced into that," Frank shrugged. Leaning closer to Sharon, he lowered his voice. "Besides, now that we've done it that way, I kinda liked it. When you get out of here maybe I'll give it another shot."

"You won't get the chance. Do it to whoever the hell you're seeing behind my back."

"Already did, and she loved it."

Sharon stood up abruptly. "Get the hell out of here! And don't do me any favors by coming back."

"When I go, the kids go with me. If you get out and want to keep seeing Kevin and Laurel, you'll give it up any time I want it. Otherwise, I hope you can remember what their faces look like."

Sharon swung her fist to strike Frank, but he grabbed her arm and twisted it, forcing her to turn her back to him. As Harriett, Wayne and Nick watched, Frank Taggart held Sharon from behind, fondling her as she struggled to get away from him.

"Relax, baby," Frank said. "This is supposed to be a conjugal visit."

"Please don't, Frank," Sharon said. Although the quality of the video shot through the two-way mirror was not the best, Harriett could see tears running down Sharon Taggart's cheeks.

"Uh-uh. To tell you the truth, it turns me on when you put up a fight. Feel that," he said as he pulled her closer against him.

"Let me go, you bastard!" Sharon seethed as she attempted to thrash around in Frank's arms.

Ignoring her, Frank led her toward a cell cot next to the wall and forced her down onto it. Releasing her, Frank ordered Sharon to remove her orange coveralls. For an interminable minute Sharon became quiet and stared at Frank as he stood over her. Then a smile crossed her lips as she pulled down the zipper on the front of the coveralls, sitting up to let them fall away from her shoulders.

"I've seen enough," Harriett said.

"No," Wayne said. "Wait. The best part is coming up."

"Other than being a very poor choice of words, Wayne, I don't have any desire to watch a rape. This is in the county jail, for Christ's sake. Where the hell are the guards?"

"Just wait, okay?"

Harriett forced herself to look at the television scene again. Sharon had gotten up and unfastened her bra, exposing well-developed breasts to her husband.

"Is this what you want, Frank?" Sharon asked softly as she touched herself seductively.

"You know it is," he answered.

Sharon moved toward him, still smiling, moving her eyes up and down his body. "You wanna fuck me, baby?"

Frank seemed dumbfounded as she pressed her body against his.

"I want you to fuck me."

"Why do you always play this stupid game, Sharon?"

She kissed his neck and ran her tongue around his ear. "Because I like it, and I know how much it turns you on."

Sharon raised herself on her toes and drew Frank's mouth to hers until they melted together.

"Watch this," Wayne said over his shoulder.

Sharon's hand found the zipper on Frank's pants and pulled it down. Frank Taggart was lost in whatever he was feeling and was oblivious to his wife's hand as it wandered along his crotch. Finally she slipped her hand into his pants. As he felt her hand, Frank looked at Sharon and smiled. The smile left his face abruptly, replaced by pain.

"What the hell are you doing, Sharon? That hurts."

"I'm just showing you how much I love you, baby. It won't hurt you any. You might even like it," she purred.

"Stop it, goddammit!" Frank yelled.

"Uh-uh," Sharon said. "Just relax, Frank."

This time it was Taggart trying to get away from his wife.

"Don't move, Frank. You'll hurt yourself if you struggle. If I slip, I might accidentally rip a hole in one of these balls you're so proud of."

Frank stopped moving, but there was still pain on his face. Sharon pulled him closer to her.

"Look at me, Frank," Sharon ordered. When he failed to do so, a slight movement of her hand inside his pants resulted in his immediate obedience.

"Do I have your complete attention, Frankie boy?"

Frank nodded and looked at Sharon.

"You're never going to hurt her again. And if you even think about taking off with her kids, I'll hunt you down and kill you like the motherfuckin' animal you are. Understand?"

Frank nodded again.

"I missed those other people because I wanted to miss them, but you know what a good shot I am. I won't miss you. If she'd let me, I'd rip your balls out right now and get it over with."

Giving his crotch one final squeeze that doubled him over, Sharon released Frank and pushed him away from her. Calmly, she slipped her bra and coveralls back on.

"You'll recover, Frank. This time. I'll have someone watching you and the kids, so don't think about doing anything stupid."

Sharon went to the door of the room and knocked, stepping back to wait for a guard to open the door.

Wayne stopped the tape. "Did you catch that last part?" he asked.

"Yeah, rewind it a little," Harriett said.

The three of them watched the last segment two more times before turning the tape off.

"What do you make of that?" Harriett asked Wayne and Nick.

"I'd like to know who 'her' is," Nick said.

"What are you thinkin'?" Wayne asked.

"I'm thinking that I don't know whom I just saw on that tape," Harriett answered. "I've met with Sharon Taggart. Except for being fixated on her children, she was nothing like the woman I just saw."

"What about the husband?" Nick asked. "You met him, too, didn't you?"

"His behavior doesn't surprise me. He mentioned their sex life wasn't as good as he wanted it to be."

"You think he raped her?"

"Sounds like he might have. I'd sure like to know exactly when that happened."

"Well, I don't think good ole Frank is gonna tell you," Wayne said.

"All he told me was that they had a fight, and he went to bed and fell asleep on January eighteenth. According to him, Sharon was home when he went to bed and when he woke up the next morning. I wonder if that was the night he raped her."

"You gonna ask Sharon?"

"Unless you can find a peeping Tom who might have seen what happened."

"You think your client's crazy?" Nick asked.

"I don't know if she's crazy, but I know she's guilty. The only chance she'll have is an insanity plea and a change of venue. Either way, we need the change of venue. How much press is the case getting in Dallas?"

"Not too bad."

"I need for it to pick up before I make my motion, Wayne."

"Okay. Give me a call at the Hyatt tomorrow about what you're planning on doing about the change of plea," Wayne said as he sat up and rubbed his face.

"And keep an eye on Riley and what he's doing. I don't want anymore of that 'it's just come to our attention' crap. If Lassiter and Riley are holding out on us, I want to know about it."

"When are you going to be back in Dallas?"

"Book me a room at the Hyatt for Wednesday through Friday, will you?"

Harriett was in the kitchen opening a Diet Coke when Nick joined her. She smiled when she saw him. Despite Nick's professorial look, she liked having him around. He always had a clear head about the law and was absolutely incorruptible.

"How's your case load, Nick?" she asked.

"I can see the light at the end of the tunnel, thank God," he said as he retrieved a soft drink from the refrigerator.

"I might need your help. I'm requesting a change of venue for the Taggart case."

"To Travis County?"

"Uh-huh."

"Publicity problems, I suppose."

"If Wayne does his job right, there will be soon."

"Want to put something together this evening?"

"If you don't have other plans."

"Well, I was planning to water my plants tonight, but I guess they can survive one more day," Nick smiled. "Listen, have you thought any more about speaking to my class at the law school?"

"I'm not that good a lecturer, Nick."

"You're the best criminal attorney I know. With your experience you have a lot of valuable things to tell them. They all think they're Matlock."

"If we get a change of venue, I guess I'll owe you."

"I'll see how that comes out before I set a date for you. Let's get busy. When do you want to file the motion?"

"In a few days. Probably Thursday. I'm going back to Dallas Wednesday afternoon."

"Tell you what. I'm winding up my last pending case tomorrow. Maybe I'll go with you. Haven't ever been to Big D."

"I'll have Wayne book you a room."

Chapter
Eighteen

"I DON'T KNOW why I let you talk me into this, Helen," Harriett said.

"Because you need to get out and socialize at least once a year," Helen said with a smile.

"I'm not sure cruising the club scene qualifies as socializing," Harriett responded. "I'm leaving town tomorrow, and I haven't even packed yet."

"What the hell, Harriett," Helen shrugged. "We won't be out that late. Besides, I'm your shrink, and I'm telling you that you need to relax a little before you get any deeper into this new case you've taken on."

"I can't stay out too late, or I'll be a menace on the highway tomorrow." Harriett knew that Helen enjoyed going out to the clubs while Erik was perfectly content sitting at home with a good book. She hated that she might have to cut the evening short.

"This is the best gay country-western club in the city," Helen said as they approached The Corral on Austin's famous, or infamous, Sixth Street. "And I know how much you love to dance."

"Not that I get many chances to do that any more," Harriett replied. Her single status had never worried Harriett as much as it had Helen. She had chosen to let her life revolve around raising Lacey and establishing her legal practice to the virtual exclusion of her own personal life.

"Didn't get to dance with Alex while you were in Dallas, I'd guess," Helen said knowingly.

"Alex is the past," Harriett said quietly.

"Yeah, right," Helen said as she pulled open the front door to The Corral.

The loud beats of a song by Brooks and Dunn crashed into the two women as they stood for a moment to let their eyes adjust to the dim lighting inside the club.

"IDs, ladies," a cowboy with a large dark bushy moustache said loudly.

Both women pulled driver's licenses from the pockets of their jeans and held them out for the man to examine.

"Good to see you again, Dr. Mortensen," he smiled, with amazingly white teeth showing beneath his moustache.

"Looks like a pretty good crowd for a Tuesday night, Tommy," Helen smiled back.

"Not bad, but give it an hour, and all the dykes comin' from the ladies basketball game will show up. Then things will really be jumpin'. Enjoy yourselves ladies," he said before stopping the next group coming through the doors.

An hour passed quickly as Harriett and Helen danced two or three dances with each other as well as other women. Finally, they sat at a table to catch their breath and enjoy a much needed drink. Harriett wasn't much of a drinker, but dancing and a cold beer seemed to go together like a good meal and fine wine.

"See any interesting possibilities?" Helen asked, between sips of her beer.

"Not likely anyone would find a meaningful relationship in a bar," Harriett laughed.

Placing her hand over Harriett's, Helen said, "Sometimes a passing fancy is better than nothing."

Harriett frowned at her friend's implication. "Is that what you think I need, Helen? A quick lay?"

"I didn't say that. But now that you mention it, it couldn't hurt. "

"Some psychologist you are," Harriett smiled.

"Sex relieves tension, and you're wound pretty tight right now. How long has it been since you were with someone, Harriett?"

"Longer than I care to think about, but tonight I plan to relieve my tension by dancing."

She watched couples moving around the crowded floor and enjoyed watching the women together. They ran the gamut of proficiency from barely able to move to exhibitionists. She was amazed at some of the women who were together. As her eyes scanned the crowd, she noticed one couple in particular. They seemed comfortable together and moved gracefully around the floor, adeptly avoiding the other couples who seemed intent on intercepting them. The taller woman was dressed in well fitting light blue jeans and a loose fitting, long sleeved white Oxford shirt. She was at least five nine or ten, with broad shoulders and an athletic build. She was obviously not afraid to stand erect and didn't try to hide her height. The lights from the spinning light ball overhead caught her short amber hair and made it sparkle. She wore steel-rimmed glasses and had an easy smile. The women moved so fluidly together that it seemed to Harriett that they must have been dancing together for a long time. Her partner, a graceful, slender blonde with long hair, was four or five inches shorter, but they both carried themselves with an elegant flair that naturally drew attention to them.

"They're very good, aren't they?" Helen interjected.

"They're amazing," Harriett nodded.

"So which one do you prefer? The femme or the butch?"

Looking at Helen and smiling slowly, Harriett answered, "You know I have a weakness for tall, athletic butches."

"That would have been my guess," Helen laughed.

When the music ended the two women on the floor hugged briefly and parted company. Harriett watched as the shorter woman left the floor and walked to a group of women seated near the back of the room. The taller woman made her way to the bar and placed an order. Carrying a single bottle of water, she joined another group at a table, talking and taking large gulps of her water.

"Well, maybe they aren't a couple after all," Harriett said. "Hard to tell sometimes."

"Let's dance," Helen said as a slower song began. "Finally something more my speed."

HE WATCHED FROM the shadows at the far end of the front bar, nursing the same drink he's had since he followed them inside. It was a decent enough bar and a beer was a beer. No one had approached him and that was fine with him. It wasn't really his scene, but he wanted a chance to observe Harriett. She had been attractive eleven years ago, and it pissed him off that she hadn't changed much over the years. Her life had gone on as if nothing had happened. When his keepers had begun trusting him a little, he had followed any news he could find about Harriett Markham. She had managed to keep a pretty low profile but wasn't invisible. The last article he found about her included a photograph. She had attended a political fund-raiser accompanied by her niece. In fact, he had barely noticed Harriett at all. But the niece was definitely someone he would like to get closer to. Much closer. He could almost feel her long legs wrapped around him as he pictured the blonde's body moving rhythmically and sensuously beneath his. He closed his eyes so his mind could process nothing but the feeling of indescribable pleasure his body was experiencing. Just the thought of the possibilities made him painfully hard.

HARRIETT AND HELEN wove through the crowd onto the floor and joined other women who had obviously waited for slower tunes, so they could dance closer to their chosen partner. As they made their way easily around in the perpetual circle, Harriett noticed the tall woman watching the dancers on the floor. For a second or two, she seemed to be watching them, and their eyes met briefly, a slow smile making its way across the woman's lips.

When the music wound down, Harriett and Helen left the floor and headed back to their table. As soon as they were seated, Harriett took another drink as she waited for the next song to begin. The music started slowly, but she recognized it. Shania Twain's "You've Got a Way" had been one of her favorite songs since it first came out.

"I love this song," she smiled.

"Then would you like to dance?" a voice behind her asked.

She turned and looked up at the woman she had seen dancing earlier. She looked at Helen, who laughed. "You go, girl!"

The woman held her hand out to Harriett, and it was warm to the touch when she took it. Leading Harriett to the dance floor, the woman seemed to be dancing before they blended with the other couples. As soon as they were on the floor, she spun Harriett into her arms and moved confidently onto the steps. She was a skillful lead and, holding Harriett close, guided her wherever she wanted her to go. Harriett hadn't danced with anyone who could lead so well in many years and felt comfortable being held closely by the woman, finding the light scent of her cologne intoxicating. As the final refrain of the song faded away, the woman smiled and held Harriett's arm up to spin her around one last time before walking her back to her table.

"Thank you," Harriett smiled. "I enjoyed that very much."

"My pleasure," the woman smiled back. Nodding to Helen, the woman moved away.

"Y'all looked great together out there," Helen beamed.

"She's a wonderful dancer," Harriett said.

"What's her name?"

Harriett looked at her blankly and made a face. "I don't know. We just danced."

"Boy, you have been out of circulation too damn long," Helen laughed.

"She didn't ask my name, either," Harriett shrugged. "Maybe she just likes to dance."

"So go ask her to dance again. Won't hurt my feelings one little bit. Unless, of course, you don't have the guts," Helen dared.

"Maybe I will," Harriett grinned, accepting the challenge. "Can you request a song here?"

"If you tip the DJ about five bucks," Helen said as she picked up her long neck bottle.

Twenty minutes later, Harriett approached the tall woman who was leaning against the edge of the bar. "Excuse me, I've requested a song. Would you care for another dance?"

The woman smiled at Harriett and shrugged, "Sure."

"I'm sorry, but I didn't catch your name," Harriett said.

"Jess. And yours?"

"Harriett. Shall we?" Harriett asked extending her hand as "Shut Up and Kiss Me" began.

"Good choice," Jess laughed.

Harriett smiled. "Do you shuffle?"

"I think I can manage," Jess said.

Harriett and Jess made the song theirs. As Helen watched them together, she smiled to herself. Even if Harriett never met the woman again, she was having a temporary affair right there on the dance floor. They both seemed to be enjoying themselves as Harriett moved gracefully through the quick spins and turns of the dance. Helen had always known that Harriett was a sensual woman who had managed to suppress her personal life for the sake of her niece and professional appearances. This was the real Harriett, laughing and open, unafraid to be herself. All she needed was someone to share her life. Helen wasn't sure that someone was Alexis Dunne.

When the song ended, Harriett led the woman back to their table.

"Helen, this is Jess. Jess, this is my friend, Helen. She's straight," Harriett said.

"I'm sorry," Jess laughed as she shook Helen's hand.

"Sometimes so am I," Helen chuckled.

Jess held Harriett's chair as she was seated and was half seated herself when a beeper chirped. Jess reached for a pager clipped to her belt and pressed the button.

"Well, ladies, my apologies, but duty calls. I enjoyed dancing with you, Harriett. And Helen, it was a pleasure to meet you," Jess said briefly. "Maybe I'll see you here again sometime."

Harriett watched as Jess walked away, the black lighting making her white shirt glow.

"Bummer," Helen sighed.

Chapter
Nineteen

SHE WAS OBVIOUSLY drunk. And just as obviously underage. But she did look older than her seventeen years. He had learned a long time ago that it wasn't the looks that gave away their age. It was their actions, the uncertainty in their eyes, and most importantly, their desire to experience things girls of their age probably had never experienced before...except in the sexual fantasy world of their own minds or on the pages of a syrupy crotch throbbing romance.

It was easy for him to pass himself off as a member of the university set. He didn't think he looked his age, and he had worked hard to keep himself in excellent physical condition. Sometimes he sat in a dark back corner of a bar and watched, waiting for just the right girl, leaving alone. After all, he did have standards and knew exactly what he was searching for. It had to be perfect every time. Otherwise, why bother.

Tonight was going to be one of those perfect nights. He knew it while he was dressing, and he knew it now as he approached the young woman. She was apparently with friends. None of them males. Just a giggly gaggle of girls, none of whom were sober enough to remember one man in a crowd of men. He approached the bar, standing next to the blonde, blue-eyed all-American girl wearing a UT sweatshirt and impossibly tight fitting pants. No underwear, he thought. Nice ass. He smiled at her as he ordered a drink. She smiled back at the interest in his eyes. Her giggling friends watched as the flirting began at the bar, moved to the dance floor, and finally disappeared out the door. A couple of mixed drinks on top of the beer she had already had made it so easy that he almost changed his mind. But Harriett had done this to him. Watching her with the woman at the bar earlier had made him unbelievably horny, driving him to seek out someone to play the lead in his fantasy.

Once they were inside the van, she hadn't left him much choice. She was eager and he was aroused. So what the hell? He would give her a night to remember, even though she would never be able to tell her friends about it.

Parking in an out of the way area of the campus, he pulled her into the back of the van, roughly pulling the sweatshirt over her head, exposing her supple breasts with their erect pink nipples. Her sexual inexperience was obvious, and he almost laughed at her attempts to be sexually sophisticated. The funny thing was it might have worked on someone younger and less experienced than he. When he finally tired of her inadequate efforts, he rolled her onto her back, staring at her, smiling beneath him. His hands slid up her body to her neck. Slowly squeezing his hands tighter, he waited for the look. The look that said she was ready for the ultimate sexual experience. After a few moments, he felt her hands on top of his, trying to loosen his grip. Her mouth opened, but no sound escaped. He felt her hands weaken and looked deeply into her wide eyes. There it was...the terror. Shifting his weight slightly between her legs, he continued staring into her eyes as he drove his erection quickly and deeply into her. Loosening his hands, he ground into her as she gasped for air, her semi-limp body being crushed beneath his. He held her arms down and let his body take over. Her body jerked violently and unexpectedly as he sank his teeth into her breasts, biting and sucking at them while his penis continued to slam into her again and again.

He felt her struggling under him and looked into her eyes again and smiled. He knew he could continue for hours. She was recovering some of her strength, but was still disabled by alcohol. He stopped and withdrew from her, remaining on top. He still had an erection. She was begging him to let her go, but it was too late. He knew how this had to end. He knew there was only one way he would ever be satisfied. He needed that look...one more time.

He ran his hands down her arms to her breasts. The tender skin was already beginning to bruise. He kissed each one softly, his hands moving to her throat. She realized what he was going to do and fought against him. Sitting up, he slapped her viciously, bloodying her lip. With his hands encircling her neck he pressed against the sides of her neck. Within seconds her eyelids began to flutter. Using his thighs to spread her legs farther apart, he forced himself into her again. Stupid bitch is dry, he thought. With each stroke he managed to penetrate deeper and deeper and his hands tightened more with each thrust. His hands left her throat, and she wasn't moving as he continued to ravage her rag doll body. He had to relieve the unbearable pressure that had built up inside him, but it wasn't working.

Withdrawing from her once again, he rolled her onto her stomach. He knew she wouldn't be fighting back this time. Spreading her ass cheeks, he pushed into her anus, tearing skin that didn't feel anything any more. He didn't need to be careful. He needed to get off, and this bitch was going to do it. As he drove into her, he closed his eyes and pictured the one he really wanted. The one he would soon have. The silken blonde hair. The long willowy legs encircling him as he fucked her over and over in his mind. The thought of it gave him the sexual release he needed, and he was sweating and breathing heavily, gasping for air just as the girl with him now had done. It was an exquisite pleasure.

Chapter
Twenty

BY THE TIME Harriett and Nick arrived at the Hyatt in Dallas, Wayne had obviously been a very busy man. As she walked past a newspaper vending machine in front of the Hyatt, the Taggart case was front-page news. There were pictures of Harriett and Sean Lassiter on the front page of both major Dallas papers. An inside story recounted the Wilkes case and had interviews with everyone associated with that case who would agree to be interviewed. Wayne had almost done his job too well. A reporter approached Harriett as she was getting the key to her room, demanding a statement. She and Nick escaped into an elevator to get to the safety of their rooms. Harriett arranged to meet Wayne and Nick in her room.

"I want to thank you for that greeting I received when I arrived," she said as soon as Wayne walked into her room.

"It's just the beginning, kiddo. You said you wanted a change of venue."

"You didn't have to tell them where I was staying."

"I didn't. They all know how to let their fingers do the walking."

"Maybe I should contact my agent," Nick said wryly.

"First time in Dallas, Nick?" Wayne asked.

"Yep."

"Maybe you and me can sneak out of here later. I know a couple of places you might enjoy."

"I want publicity, Wayne. I don't want my partner arrested with one of your hooker friends. Who leaked the information in the papers anyway?"

"Better you don't know, but Riley isn't happy about it, and Lassiter is crappin' in his Brooks Brothers suit. You know how fast gossip spreads, especially if it's a lie," he grinned.

"I hope it's enough. I have to talk to Sharon," Harriett said as she opened her briefcase. "And you two need to read over this stuff."

She handed Nick and Wayne a stack of Xeroxed papers.

"What the hell is this?" Wayne asked.

"Information about dissociative identity disorder, formally known as multiple personality syndrome. Helen Mortenson put it together for me before we left Austin."

"Harriett's arranged a meeting with the judge tomorrow to change the plea to not guilty due to mental disease or defect," Nick said.

"I can't believe you'd resort to NGRI, Harriett," Wayne said.

Taking a deep breath, Harriett said, "Before I can do anything, I have to convince Sharon to take this plea. If she won't, then I'm back to square one because Lassiter isn't going to turn loose of murder one. He's like a damn dog with a bone."

"When are you planning to talk to Taggart?" Wayne asked.

"Very shortly. And this time, I'm going in the front doors. If I convince her, I'll announce it to any reporters who are there."

"You ready to handle questions about Wilkes?"

"Guess I won't have a choice. Tomorrow I want you to contact these men," she said, handing a paper to Wayne. "One of them is here in Dallas, but the others are out of state. Offer them their fee and room and board to conduct psychiatric evaluations of Sharon. If they're available, make the arrangements as soon as possible."

"What if she won't agree?" Nick asked.

"She has to," Harriett frowned.

NINETY MINUTES LATER she pushed her way through a group of reporters and entered the front doors of the Allen Center. She was standing when Sharon was brought into the interview room. Waiting for the officers to remove her client's handcuffs, Harriett grew impatient, but remained standing as Sharon pushed her hair back and sat down.

"You lied to me Sharon," she stated flatly.

"I haven't lied about anything, Harriett."

"Why didn't you tell me you bought the ammunition for the Browning?"

"I haven't. No since we first bought the rifle."

"That's bullshit, Sharon!" Harriett said, raising her voice. "They found the store that sold it to you. Want to try again?"

"I didn't buy any ammunition," Sharon insisted.

"If you keep lying to me I can't help you."

Sharon looked down at her hands and appeared to be deep in thought. Harriett waited but her patience was already at its limit.

Slapping her hand down on the table, Harriett demanded, "Look at me, goddamn it!"

When Sharon did look up at Harriett her face was relaxed.

"Guess I should've gone a little farther from home, huh?" Sharon stated matter-of-factly.

"So you did buy the ammo?"

"Well, of course, I did. Wasn't likely she would ever get up the guts to do it."

"Who?"

"Sharon."

Harriett watched as the woman's lips curled into an easy smile. Slowly, the woman looked around the room.

"Depressing place."

"Excuse me?" Harriett said.

Slowly the woman's head turned back to Harriett.

"I'm Jan. But you'd already figured everything out but that, hadn't you?"

"Not exactly."

"Oops."

Harriett kept her eyes on the woman who now claimed to be Jan as she sat down. Jan laughed out loud at the look on Harriett's face. Just as suddenly, her face became solemn.

"How much trouble is she in?" Jan asked.

"Neck deep. The prosecution is pressing for murder one. There's a possible death sentence attached to it."

"Damn! I really fucked up this time."

"You want to tell me about it?"

"Maybe I shouldn't."

"Don't you want to help Sharon?"

"Shit. I been doing that my whole life. I need a break."

"Jan. Wasn't that the name of Sharon's imaginary playmate?"

"Ta-da!" Jan said expansively.

"Do you communicate with Sharon?"

"No. I just get stuck with all the shit she doesn't want to deal with."

"Like what?"

"Sex, anger, stuff like that."

"Is Sharon angry?"

"Hell, if your life was as pathetic as hers, you'd be pissed off, too. Stuck with that bastard pig Frank."

"Does Frank know about you?"

Jan laughed and pulled a leg up under her. "I've been with him a few times, but he doesn't have a clue. I made him think he was some kind of stud duck, which, believe me, he ain't."

"When you say you've been with him, what do you mean?"

"What do you think I mean? I fucked him. I wouldn't dignify what he does as making love. Things have to be really tense before I sleep with him."

"I know what he did when he visited here last week."

"What?"

"I know he grabbed you and tried to force you to have sex with him."

"Then I guess you know he didn't quite pull it off. You think I'd let that animal rape me the way he did her? I'm not afraid of that asshole."

"But Sharon is."

"She's afraid of everything."

"You're responsible for the shootings, aren't you?"

"I didn't shoot anyone, Harriett," Jan smiled. "Those people killed themselves."

"You're culpable, which means..."

"I know what it means. I'm not stupid," Jan snapped.

"Sorry. I forgot that Sharon taught law as part of her class."

"Sharon didn't teach shit. She couldn't hack it any more."

"You're teaching her classes?"

"For about two years. It's kinda fun. I was teacher of the year, you know."

"I've seen a video of you in action. Very impressive."

Jan performed a mock bow from her seat and smiled.

"Where is Sharon while you're teaching?"

"Resting, I guess."

"But it is Sharon who goes home every evening?"

"Of course. After a long hard day at the office, you think I want to go home to that asshole Frank Taggart? Pul-eeze," Jan said, rolling her eyes.

Harriett took a deep breath and exhaled slowly.

"I'm going to request a psychiatric evaluation."

"For what? I ain't nuts. Besides, I thought you said the other day that this was a bogus charge."

"Not if you did it."

"But Sharon didn't do anything. We don't need any shrinks in here fuckin' everything up and askin' how Sharon got along with dear old Mommy and Daddy or how traumatic her potty trainin' was."

"If you're a personality separate from Sharon, we could amend the plea to NGRI. A psychiatrist would be able to testify that Sharon has a mental defect."

"And then what, spend the rest of my life in a mental institution?" Jan asked, getting up from her seat. "No, thank you. I only came out today because you pushed Sharon too far. But I'm not talkin' to any shrinks and neither is she. At least if we go to jail, we'll be away from everyone who's ever hurt us."

"She needs help."

"To get rid of me you mean. But you know what, I kind of like it here."

"I'll bet you do. Do anything you want and let Sharon take the blame."

"Look, I've been takin' shit for her for over twenty fuckin' years, and all I've got to show for it are bad memories. You know what it's like to have nothin' but bad memories? I'm thinkin' about stayin' out."

"What about Sharon?"

"What about her? She'd never be able to protect herself anyway. I can just let her go to sleep. Let her go somewhere where she won't have to worry about pain and anger anymore."

"If you're the one who suffers the pain and anger, won't you be one-sided without her? After all, she created you."

"Because she couldn't handle life in the big bad world. She'll never be able to. So what's the point of her even stayin' around?"

"Time's getting short," Harriett said. "I haven't been able to convince the prosecutor to lessen the charge. Sharon could face the death penalty based on the physical evidence they have, and I have no doubt the State will demand it."

"What are you sayin'?"

"I'm saying that I'm not left with much except an insanity plea on her behalf, but I can't do that without Sharon's permission."

"Do you think she's crazy?"

"I think she has some problems that would qualify as a legitimate affirmative defense. She'll have to give the okay, and then you'll both have to trust me."

"What happens if they don't believe she's crazy?"

"She could be just as bad off. This is a last resort defense. She'll have to be evaluated by psychiatrists from both sides."

"I already told you I wasn't gonna talk to any shrinks," Jan said.

"We don't have a choice, Jan," Harriett said calmly. "If I can't go forward with this defense, Sharon will be executed and you'll both die."

"You're askin' me to commit suicide anyway by going away."

"I'm asking you to let me save Sharon. Then maybe you and she can come to grips with one another. You're strong, Jan. She needs that part of herself. And I think you need her."

"She's a pathetic weakling."

"She's a caring, gentle person. If she's executed will you come out to take the punishment? Or will you leave her alone and bewildered?"

"I'll do what I have to to protect myself."

"Then do it now. When people understand what happened to her, they'll get help for you, too."

"You know what happened to her?"

"No, but from what I've read, it must have been a childhood trauma of some kind. Is that right?"

Jan smiled at Harriett. "I guess that depends on your point of view."

"Will you let her agree to a change in the plea?"

"Why not? I like to shock people anyway."

Pulling a paper from her briefcase, Harriett laid it on the table and handed a pen to Jan.

"Sharon has to sign this."

Taking the pen, Jan said, "She doesn't do anything I don't want her to do."

Signing the paper, Jan handed the pen back to Harriett. "Now what?"

"I'm requesting a change of venue as well," Harriett said as she glanced at the signature before slipping the document back into her briefcase. "I hope to get the case moved to Travis County."

"Where the hell is that?"

"Austin. It's more liberal, and a jury might be more open-minded to the plea than a Dallas jury."

"Whatever. When does the shrink arrive?"

"The first one will probably be here tomorrow sometime."

"The first one! How many fuckin' people do I have to talk to?"

"I'm arranging for three, and I don't know what the prosecution will bring in."

"Shit, why worry about pleadin' insanity. By the time they get through, we won't have a brain left worth keeping."

"I don't want to mislead you," Harriett said. "This won't be a walk in the park. Juries don't like this plea, and the burden of proof is on us."

"You mean you have to prove she's crazy."

"Yes. And that whichever one of you pulled the trigger didn't know the difference between right and wrong."

"That's some swell job you got, Harriett."

Chapter
Twenty-One

IT WAS NINE-THIRTY that evening by the time Harriett returned to the Hyatt. As soon as she entered her room, she collapsed on the bed. Sitting up a few minutes later, she called Wayne and Nick, arranging to meet them in the bar for a drink.

When they had all been served, Harriett took a long drink.

"What do you think?" she asked looking at the two men.

"She agreed?" Nick asked.

"Someone signed her name to the document. Lassiter won't fight the insanity thing. He doesn't have to prove a damn thing, so his job will be easy."

"Too bad the rules changed, or he'd be busier than a shithouse rat," Wayne said.

"Did you look over the papers I gave you?"

"Yeah," Nick said. "But you're still stuck with the right-wrong standard."

"Well, she admits she did it, but she doesn't think she did anything wrong. Malicious mischief at best. The victims overreacted."

"She had to have known people might get a little overwrought if they were being shot at," Nick said.

"But did they know that?" Harriett asked. "How would the average driver cruising down the highway know they've been shot at?"

"A bullet zippin' through the windshield would probably be their first clue," Wayne snorted.

"Why not a blowout? Or a rock hitting the windshield? Have we got the accident reports?"

"Yeah."

"Did the reports mention a bullet hole in any of the windows?"

"The cars were pretty messed up, Harriett. Ever seen what's left after a head-on collision with a light pole or another car at fifty or sixty miles per?"

"So how would the prosecution know the cars were even shot at? If bullets went through the windshields they had to have lodged somewhere inside the vehicles. Lassiter has to be withholding something to act as sure as he is. Wayne..." Harriett began.

"Yeah, yeah, I'll look into it. I know someone at ballistics."

Harriett smiled at the older man and patted his hand.

"You know someone everywhere, thank God," she said. "I want to see where these accidents took place. And at the same time of day."

"She told you she shot at the cars, Harriett," Nick said.

"But Lassiter doesn't know that, Nick," she nodded.

"Well, you can't have it both ways," Nick said over his glass. "You can either disprove their evidence or go for insanity. But you can't do both."

"I'm betting they have more than the one bullet they told me about. If Lassiter is holding them back and I can prove it, I want him off the case. I'm going to hold the insanity motion for a while."

"You can check out the scenes of the crime tonight if you want to," Wayne said. "They all happened after dark."

WAYNE DROVE HARRIETT'S truck as he took her and Nick to the sites where the accidents had taken place. Each faced a bridge or embankment. As Harriett made her way around the areas overlooking the highways, she had an unobstructed view of the oncoming traffic. At the scene of the Kaufmann accident, the last shooting, a steep grassy embankment ran between the main highway and an access road.

"Where did the witness say she saw Sharon?" Harriett asked as she looked around.

"Claims she saw her coming from up there," Wayne said as he pointed up the grassy area.

Harriett climbed up the embankment and lay down on the grass. Wayne and Nick joined her a moment later.

"Good view," Wayne said.

"Where did Mrs. Sanchez see the car?"

"On the access road," Wayne said, motioning over his shoulder.

"I want pictures of this whole area at night." Looking back at the traffic, Harriett asked, "How fast do you estimate those cars are going?"

"Over the speed limit. Maybe sixty-five or seventy."

"Could you hit an oncoming vehicle at this range, Wayne?"

"Probably. The car ought to run into the bullet."

"Lassiter said they took a slug from a telephone pole here at the Kaufmann scene. Where did the vehicle end up?"

"It hit the median and flipped over a couple of times. Finally came to rest down there in that culvert."

Harriett raised her body to see the spot Wayne had indicated.

"I only see one telephone pole between here and there. The rest are aluminum light poles. I wasn't very good in geometry, but from this angle I don't see how a slug could make it into that pole."

"It might have ricocheted off the pavement and then hit the pole," Nick offered.

"I bet you believe the magic bullet theory from the Kennedy

assassination, too," Wayne chuckled.

Looking at her investigator, Harriett said, "I'm beginning to think that either this wasn't where Sharon was lying in wait, or that bullet didn't come from any telephone pole. Have you seen it yet?"

"I saw what they claimed was the slug," Wayne said. "Right caliber, but the ballistics report was iffy about whether or not it came from the Taggart Browning."

"Was it damaged, like it had struck a pole?" Harriett quizzed.

"I seen worse. A telephone pole ain't that dense," Wayne shrugged.

"Why would they show us a bogus bullet?" Nick asked. "That would be stupid."

"Riley," Harriett answered as she got up and started down the embankment toward her truck.

"Riley hates Harriett because of what happened in the Wilkes case," Wayne finally answered as he sat up. "Hell, for all I know, he's squirreled evidence away that Lassiter don't even know about yet. Harriett nearly ruined Riley's career back then. She used information from me to get the case thrown out of court. Not long after that Wilkes killed again. She's had a hard time living with that one."

"The Wilkes case was just one of those things."

"Yeah, well, the prick got off on an NGRI. That's why she's been hesitant about usin' it for this case."

"Sometimes it's the right thing."

"And sometimes it ain't."

"It's been over eleven years, Wayne. Besides, they couldn't possibly have known Harriett was going to take the Taggart case."

"Riley might have known soon enough to bury the evidence under a mountain of red tape. Remember, they didn't have to make the disclosure until they knew officially who the defense attorney would be."

"She got this case from Winston and Dunne, didn't she?"

"She got it from Dunne. She and Harriett were....close, once upon a time. I've known Harriett a long time, but I wouldn't swear she's gotten over her," Wayne said as he paused on the embankment. "You met the legendary Alexis Dunne yet?"

"No."

Slapping Nick on the back, Wayne said, "Well, maybe this will be your lucky week, counselor."

Harriett was quiet during the drive back to the Hyatt, sitting between Wayne and Nick. Wayne returned to the bar for a nightcap while Harriett and Nick took the elevator to their floor.

"Wayne cares about you very much, Harriett," Nick said.

Harriett smiled slightly, "He's been watching out for me since my father died."

"What time do you have to appear before the judge in the morning?" Nick asked as the elevator door opened and they stepped out.

"Eleven. He's working us in between a couple of other motions."

"Do you want to run over your presentation?"

Looking at her watch, Harriett said, "Yeah. Maybe once."

IT TOOK HER less than thirty minutes to sum up her arguments for moving the trial to Travis County. She had a collection of newspaper stories, and interviews of the victims' families. As a backup, she had prepared a file on the publicity surrounding the Wilkes case. At the bottom of the Wilkes file were four sheets of paper. She looked at them and frowned.

"What's that?" Nick asked as he removed his glasses and rubbed his eyes.

"Death threats."

"What?"

"Wayne gave them to me earlier today," she said.

Nick took the papers from her and read over them.

"Are these legit or something Wayne planted?"

"They're the real deal. But they're also my trump card. Wayne got them from the newspapers after the re-hash stories about the Wilkes case began appearing."

"You should have reported these to the police, Harriett."

"The Dallas Police have better things to worry about than crank calls, Nick."

"They threaten your life, for Christ's sake."

"Pretty convincing argument for moving the trial, don't you think?" Harriett smiled.

"The sooner the better. You shouldn't be alone."

"I assume Wayne told you about Wilkes," Harriett said.

"Just the basics."

"Then you can understand why people might get worked up over the case and my involvement in it. I have to do a good enough job tomorrow, so I can get out of here."

"What if the judge won't grant the change?"

"Then I guess I'll have to hire a bodyguard or start packing a gun."

For the first time since joining Harriett's legal practice, Nick was nervous despite her calm demeanor. She had lived with an attorney's worst nightmare and was looking at the possibility of repeating it. It was one thing to talk about the lofty ideals of the law and another to live them, jeopardizing your own life in the process.

THE FOLLOWING MORNING, Harriett presented her motion for a change of venue forcefully. The arguments against the motion by Sean Lassiter were equally forceful. The fatal blow to the prosecution's arguments was the death threats made against Harriett. Nick escorted her from the courtroom with the judge promising he would make a decision the following day.

She paused in the corridor outside the courtroom to get a drink from a water fountain while Nick went ahead to the elevators. When she turned, Riley was standing behind her.

"Cute stunt," he said.

"If my motion is rejected, I'll expect personal security from the police department for the duration of the trial," Harriett said calmly.

"This one ain't gettin' away to kill again."

"That isn't up to either of us. Fortunately, juries make those decisions. So you do your job and I'll do mine."

She tried to step around him, but Riley blocked her path again.

"Are you planning to dance this do-se-do all day, Riley? I have to meet with my client."

"Maybe if you ask me real nice, I'd move."

"Go to hell," Harriett said as she pushed him away.

Riley grabbed her arm and stopped her, "Assaulting a police officer, counselor. That's pretty stupid."

"So is assaulting an officer of the court," Nick said.

"This isn't any of your business, buddy, so take a hike," Riley growled.

"If you don't release Ms. Markham immediately...," Nick began.

"You'll do what? Sue me?" the detective smirked. "I'm all shook up."

In a move Harriett hadn't anticipated, Nick knocked Riley's hand away from her and stepped between them. Nick was about the same height, but Riley outweighed him by at least fifty pounds. The disadvantage didn't stop Nick from getting nose to nose with the burly detective.

"If I catch you harassing Ms. Markham again, you'll be more than just shook up. The newspapers recorded the threats against Ms. Markham, and I'm tempted to have your voice analyzed to see if it matches any of those threats. If I find out it does, I'll drag your ass into court and fuck you over so bad, you'll wish you were walking a beat again," Nick said in a low steady voice. "Is my position crystal clear to you, Mr. Riley?"

The detective tried to stare Nick down, but it didn't work. Riley blinked first, and Nick moved to let him pass before escorting Harriett to the elevator.

"Thanks," Harriett said as the elevator door closed.

Nick smiled at her. "Jesus, that ape could have ripped my head off."

"That was a pretty gutsy move, Nick."

"Remember to carve that on my tombstone. Here lies Nicholas Lazslo, Gutsy But Stupid."

"That wasn't a bad idea about the voice check though."

"Yeah, except the newspapers didn't record shit. I wonder if there's a bar near here."

Chapter
Twenty-Two

MID-MORNING FRIDAY the judge granted Harriett's motion for a change of venue citing the threats made against her as his primary reason. She arranged to meet with Dr. Richard Talbot at eleven for a preliminary report on Sharon Taggart's mental evaluation.

"You understand, Ms. Markham, that I would need to spend much more time with Mrs. Taggart to give an in-depth report," Talbot said.

"Of course, doctor, but right now I need your preliminary findings. I haven't filed a motion to change her plea yet."

"I wouldn't have any difficulty testifying that Mrs. Taggart absolutely needs psychiatric help. The dissociative disorder is almost certainly there, but it is extremely difficult to say whether she has more than one personality or merely a single disturbed personality."

"Did you speak to Jan?"

"I spoke to Sharon when she claimed to be Jan."

"But you didn't believe her?"

"The change was so slight it was hard to tell. I finally had to hypnotize her."

"Did that reveal anything?"

"The theory is that early childhood trauma, such as sexual abuse, can develop into the creation of an alter personality. The child uses this personality to escape whatever pain he or she is encountering, essentially suppressing the memory of it quite effectively."

"Was Sharon sexually abused as a child?"

"I have no doubt whatsoever that Sharon was an abused child, but even under hypnosis, she was reluctant to talk about it. That leads me to believe that she was very young when it occurred. I did get her to recount an early memory of holding a man's penis in her hand, and she was quite specific about that."

"Did she say it was her father who abused her?"

"No, she didn't. It might not have been. It could have been someone close to her family and not a family member."

"Well, where do we go from here, doctor?"

"I'll see her again in the morning."

"If she says anything my investigator can track down and verify, let me know."

"I trust you're going to have her examined by someone other than me."

"Yes. I have two other experts lined up, but not until she's transferred to Austin the first of next week."

"I won't allow any videotaping of my meetings with her, but if you'd like to observe our session in the morning, I won't object to that."

After Talbot left her room, she and Nick spread out the information they had about dissociative disorder on the bed. Sitting on the bed, they began looking through the paperwork again.

"When are you going to make the NGRI?"

"As soon as they move Sharon to Austin. Might as well make Lassiter do the running back and forth between Austin and Dallas. Make a list, Nick."

"Of what?"

"First, the points I'll need to drag out of the witnesses. I have to have at least one, and hopefully more, psychiatrists say she has a mental defect. I already know the prosecution's expert will say she doesn't, so I need some guidelines about what to ask. Second, I need a list of cases that are even remotely similar to this one."

"Guess I get that part," Nick said as he wrote on a pad.

Before Harriett could continue, they were interrupted by a knock on the door.

"Must be Wayne," Harriett said. "Come in!"

The door opened, and Alexis stepped into the room. When Harriett saw her, she looked surprised.

"I hope I'm not interrupting a strategy session," Alex said, glancing at Nick.

"No," Harriett said as she stood up. "We were just sketching out a few preliminaries."

"I heard you got the change of venue. Congratulations."

"Thank you."

Alex smiled at Nick and walked toward him.

"I don't believe we've met," she said. "Alexis Dunne."

Nick got up to accept the hand Alex extended toward him. "Nick Lazslo." Nick understood immediately why Harriett had been attracted to the woman.

"I'm sorry," Harriett said. "Nick is my law partner and will be helping me on the Taggart case."

"I'm sure she'll need all the help she can get," Alex said. She turned to Harriett. "Are you still considering a change in her plea?"

"Yes. She agreed to be evaluated by independent experts. One of them saw her today."

Glancing back at Nick, Alex said, "Could I speak to you for a moment....alone?"

"Um, listen, Harriett, I can look over some of this in my room, and we can discuss it on the way back to Austin tomorrow," Nick said as he picked up his coat.

"Thanks, Nick. I'm sorry about this," she said, following him to the door.

"Not a problem."

Harriett closed the door and walked back toward Alex.

"What can I do for you, Alex?"

"I thought I might take you to lunch if you haven't already eaten."

When she glanced at the clock next to the bed it was already after one.

"That sounds harmless enough," Harriett smiled.

AFTER LUNCH AT the Carriage House, a dimly lit restaurant where patrons paid for the privacy the lack of wattage offered, Alex drove Harriett to the condominium she purchased after the separation from her partner. It was comfortably and simply furnished, yet formal enough to make a visitor aware of dirt on their shoes. Slipping her shoes off, Harriett smiled contentedly as her feet sank into the luxurious carpeting.

"It's lovely, Alex. And somehow it seems to suit you better than your old house."

"I really don't spend that much time here, but I can give you the two dollar tour."

"Do you still cook?" Harriett asked as they left the kitchen.

"I've collected quite a few new recipes since the last time I cooked for you."

"I still don't cook much."

"Is that how you've managed to stay so slim? By not eating?" Alex smiled.

"It isn't intentional because, God knows, I love food, but it seems silly to get carried away cooking for just Lacey and myself."

Harriett smiled inside as she looked at Alex. Around clients, Alex always seemed to have a smile on her face and exuded charm. But in private, her smiles were less frequent and her more serious nature had often turned into a deep passion when they were together.

Harriett walked to a set of French doors that opened out onto a small covered deck. The Dallas skyline covered the horizon.

"Nice view," she said.

"You should see it at night," Alex said walking up behind her. "It's beautiful then."

"Do you ever wonder what people are doing in those buildings late at night when the lights are on?"

"Probably staring out at us, wondering what we're doing."

Harriett laughed. "Now there's a scary thought. Like watching someone with binoculars and finding them looking back at you."

"You haven't changed at all, Harriett."

"Everyone changes," she said softly. "Everything changes."

"Not everything. You're still beautiful," Alex said, sliding her hands down Harriett's arms.

"Did you bring me here to seduce me, Alex?" Harriett asked as she continued gazing at the skyline, feeling her skin react to Alex's light touch.

"Is that what you think?"

She turned toward Alex. Looking at her still took her breath away. "Maybe."

Alex kissed her forehead. "You said you weren't ready to rush into anything."

"I'm not."

"You can't know how much I've hated not being with you," Alex said. Leaning closer she kissed Harriett softly. "How much I've hated not being able to touch you."

Moments later they were slowly undressing one another, leaving a trail of clothing into the bedroom as they renewed a relationship placed on hold for too many years. There was something familiar about their physical intimacy that was unhurried and prolonged, each taking the time to appreciate the other's body. It was well after dark when Alex drove Harriett back to the Hyatt.

As she got off the elevator on her floor, she saw Wayne leaning against the wall outside her room.

"Is something wrong, Wayne?" she asked as she unlocked her door.

"Yeah," Wayne answered. "We got a problem."

"Well, come on in and tell me about it."

Harriett tossed her purse on the bed and slipped her shoes off.

"So what's this big problem?" she asked as she ran her fingers through her hair.

"The problem is that you're lettin' yourself get tangled up with Alex Dunne again."

"What?"

"I said..."

"I heard what you said, Wayne," Harriett frowned. "And I resent the hell out of what you're insinuating. I'm not some kid who needs to be watched."

"Come on, Harriett. Remember who you're talkin' to. I've been down this road before. She talked you into her bed today, didn't she?"

"You're not being paid to pry into my private life, which, I might add, is none of your damned business," Harriett snapped.

"I don't give a shit if you like it or not. I ain't got a family of my own, so I adopted you and Lacey. I won't stand around and watch while you throw everything away tryin' to recapture something it's taken you years to get over." Wayne stepped closer to Harriett. "You can't let what you're feelin' between your legs do your thinkin' for you, honey."

"Go to hell, Wayne. Just do what you're being paid to do," Harriett said as she stalked into the bathroom and slammed the door.

Chapter
Twenty-Three

BY NINE THE next morning, Harriett and Nick sat behind a two-way mirror and watched as Dr. Talbot placed Sharon Taggart under hypnosis for the second time.

"You know anything she reveals under hypnosis won't be admissible," Nick whispered.

"You don't have to whisper, Nick. She can't hear us. I need any lead we can get about her abuse as a child."

"If it points to her family you'll be biting the hand that feeds you."

"I know."

On the other side of the mirror, Sharon slipped into a deep sleep, her eyes closed as her head lolled slightly to one side.

"Can you hear me, Sharon?" Talbot asked gently.

"Yes," Sharon answered, barely audible.

"I'm going to count backwards from ten. I want you to go back five years in time as the numbers decrease. Do you understand?"

Sharon nodded.

"Nine," Talbot said softly. "Now you're twenty-five years old. Eight and you're twenty."

Talbot continued counting slowly and speaking softly until he finally reached five.

"How old are you, Sharon?" he asked.

"I'm five."

"That's very good. What are you doing?"

"Playing."

"Are you alone?"

Sharon shook her head. "Parker is with me."

"What are you and Parker doing?"

"Playing a game."

"Is it a fun game?"

"I don't like it. Parker likes it."

"Does the game have a name?"

"No."

"Can you explain it to me?"

"No," Sharon frowned.

"What is Parker doing, Sharon?"

Sharon's eyes flew open and seemed to look through Talbot.

"Don't want to, Parker," she whined. "Don't like it."

Hearing a conversation in her head, Sharon shook her head and closed her eyes again. She began shaking her head rapidly. "No, no, no," she repeated. She was perspiring and becoming agitated

"Sharon," Talbot said. "When I count to six, I want you to move five years ahead. Do you understand?"

Sharon nodded, her demeanor becoming calmer as Talbot uttered the number.

"Do you feel better now, Sharon?" he asked.

"Yes."

"Tell me about Parker."

"He's my brother. I love him. Mother said I should love my brother."

"Do you love Parker?"

"Yes."

"Can you trust Parker?"

"Parker watches me."

"Do you and Parker still play together?"

"Sometimes. Parker is getting too old for games though."

"What do you and Parker do together?"

"Nothing bad," Sharon said after a hesitation.

"I know," Talbot reassured her.

"I don't like his friends."

"Why?"

"They hurt me sometimes."

"But Parker doesn't hurt you?"

"No," Sharon smiled. "Parker loves me."

"How do his friends hurt you, Sharon?"

Sharon readjusted her position in her chair and frowned. "Parker told them not to. It was an accident."

"Was Parker there when you were hurt?"

"I won't play the game if Parker's not there."

"Can you describe the game?"

Sharon opened her mouth and breathed through it, squeezing her eyes more tightly shut.

"It's a secret game. I'm not supposed to tell."

"But you want to tell someone, don't you? It's hard to keep a secret all to yourself."

"Parker said I shouldn't tell."

"I want you to rest, Sharon. In a moment, I'll count back to ten. When I reach ten you will be the age you are now. You won't remember anything we've talked about today and you will feel rested and peaceful. Do you understand?"

"Yes."

Talbot returned Sharon to the present and awakened her from the hypnosis. They chatted for a few minutes before Talbot excused himself and left the room. A moment later he joined Harriett and Nick.

"Why did you tell her to forget everything?" Harriett asked.

"Because when you draw Jan out again, I don't want her to be repeating what Sharon said."

"But I thought Jan knew everything that happened to Sharon," Nick said.

"If the theories are correct and if she exists at all, Jan would have been suppressed by the hypnosis and unaware of what Sharon was doing during that time," Talbot explained.

"What did you mean when you said when I draw Jan out?" Harriett asked.

"Jan trusts you. I don't think there's any doubt that Sharon was sexually abused as a small child. The likely offender is her brother and perhaps later his friends. She's too attached to her brother to tell us what he did, but if Sharon indeed created Jan to deal with the abuse, Jan will have no attachment whatsoever to the brother. In fact, she might even want to hurt him. Sharon has a deeply rooted belief that a person should never hurt another member in his or her own family; the old blood is thicker than water idea. That may be why she said that Parker never hurt her. In essence, it didn't happen to her. It happened to Jan, who isn't really a family member."

"Thanks for clarifying that, Doc," Nick said.

"It's a complex disorder, Mr. Lazslo," Talbot smiled.

"Sort of makes you long for your basic, run of the mill whacko," Nick said.

"Will Sharon let Jan tell me what happened to her as a child?"

"She'll resist it, but from what I've observed on the videos, Jan exists as a genuine separate personality and is becoming stronger. In addition she's extremely angry and violent."

"If Jan has been around for what, twenty-five years, why is she just now acting out her anger?"

"Personally, Ms. Markham, I believe the husband might have pushed her over the edge. That's not anything based on fact, but it's obvious that Sharon's husband has probably also been sexually abusive."

"They've been married eight years, Doctor. Why would Jan wait this long if she was involved in an abusive relationship with her husband?"

"Maybe he hasn't always been abusive. If it's a recent development on his part, Sharon might have lived with it until the level of abuse rose to a level that could no longer be tolerated. If the deaths of those people started about a year and a half ago, I'd look for changes in their marital status that have occurred within at least the last two years."

"Everyone we've talked to has mentioned a change in Sharon's behavior within the last two years, beginning about the time her daughter was born."

"Did she begin cutting herself off from friends and isolating herself?"

"Gradually, yes. A former friend said Sharon sought help at a mental health facility but was turned away."

"It's possible she may have gone through a serious bout of untreated postpartum depression after the birth of her second child. But since she wasn't diagnosed by anyone, there's no way to tell. Maybe Jan can fill in the details for you, if Sharon lets her. You will have to be careful though, Ms. Markham, not to attack Sharon verbally. Jan won't allow you to hurt her. She is Sharon's protector."

"I told you to take those karate lessons," Nick smiled.

"She might not hurt you physically, but if she knows everything Sharon knows, she might go after you some other way."

"What should I tell her if she asked where you are?" Harriett asked Talbot.

"Tell her I'll be back in a few minutes. That I had a long distance phone call."

Harriett took a deep breath and left the viewing room to speak to Sharon.

"Ms. Markham," Sharon said as Harriett entered her room. "Dr. Talbot is here. He just left."

"I saw him. He had to take a phone call and said it would be all right if I spoke to you until he got back."

"They told me they were moving me Monday."

"Yes. A court in Austin will hear your case."

"Does that mean I won't be able to see Kevin and Laurel?"

"Not for a while. But your case has a better chance away from Dallas County."

Sharon frowned.

"Maybe Frank can bring them to Austin on weekends to see you," Harriett offered.

"I can ask him, but he might be too busy."

"I'm sure he's worried about you."

Sharon looked hard at Harriett, her eyes narrowing slightly.

"He's only worried that he won't get enough pussy from that whore he's fuckin'."

"It's good to see you again, Jan," Harriett said.

"Wish I could say the same."

"I'm only trying to help Sharon out of the mess you've gotten her into."

"That why you brought that Talbot guy in?"

"Yes. But Sharon won't tell him much."

"She don't know much," Jan smirked. "Listen, you got a cigarette?"

Harriett reached into the pocket of her jacket and tossed a pack of cigarettes to Jan. Lighting a cigarette for her, Harriett watched the woman fill her lungs with smoke and exhale slowly.

"You know," Harriett said, "I'm surprised you let Sharon control what you do so much."

"She doesn't control what I do. I just respect her wishes...most of the time."

"Can you tell me about Parker?"

Jan blinked hard several times and looked at Harriett.

"Depends on what you want to know."

"Did Parker ever hurt Sharon?"

"No."

"Did he hurt you?"

Jan smiled slightly. "That's pretty slick, Harriett. Must be why good old Mom and Dad are so willing to paying your substantial fee."

"Actually, Parker is paying my fee."

"No, shit!" Jan laughed. "That cocky bastard."

"Well, he knows Sharon wouldn't do anything to hurt him. Isn't that what her mother taught her?"

"Sharon learned that lesson better than he did."

"Did he hurt you?"

"He didn't mean to. It was an accident."

"Will you tell me about it?"

"Nope," Jan said inhaling more smoke.

"So I guess Sharon is still in control then. Maybe you're not as strong as you think?"

Jan stood and glared at Harriett.

"She should be careful," Talbot said. "She might have stepped over the line with that question."

"You told her not to attack Sharon," Nick said.

"It's not a good idea to attack Jan, either. She's the violent one, remember?"

Jan's face softened slightly. "Are you deliberately trying to provoke me, Harriett?"

"I'm trying to get to the truth, and you're not helping."

"I told you I did it, for God's sake. What else do you want?"

"I want to know why you did it. I demand to know why. Otherwise, they can wheel a gurney in here right now and stick the needle into Sharon's arm."

"They ain't gonna do that. She didn't do anything."

"I thought you were supposed to protect Sharon. If you don't cooperate with me, you're going to be responsible for killing her. Maybe you're mad at her because she palmed off all her pain on you. Are you trying to kill Sharon?"

Jan ignored the question, lighting a second cigarette with the butt of the first one.

"Proof of your existence is the only thing that might save Sharon. Otherwise, the DA will slam dunk her ass at trial."

"Who cares," Jan said in a bored voice.

"I care, the people at Winston and Dunne care, her brother cares."

"Parker doesn't give a shit," Jan retorted sharply. "He's just trying to cover his own ass. They're all trying to cover their asses and that includes those friendly fuckers over at Winston and Dunne. Especially that bitch Alex."

Harriett was surprised by the seething anger in Jan's voice. "Do you think they're all out to get you?"

"Fuck no!" Jan laughed. "They're just doin' what they do and bein' who they are." Staring intently at Harriett, Jan asked, "You know Alexis Dunne pretty good, don't you?"

"I was an associate with her firm a long time ago."

"Yeah?" Jan grinned as she leaned closer to Harriett. "I heard it was a lot closer relationship than that, counselor."

"Shit," Talbot breathed.

"What?" Nick asked.

"She knows something that she thinks will give her an advantage over Harriett."

"I'm not here to discuss my former employer, Jan," Harriett said.

"Don't you want to discuss Alex?"

"I'd rather discuss your relationship with Parker."

"It was close. Real close," Jan smiled. "Like your relationship with Alex. Did Alex ever hurt you when she fucked you?"

Harriett was unsure where to take her discussion with Jan.

"How did Parker hurt you?" she continued.

"I already told you that it was an accident," Jan said with a dismissive wave of her hand. "Alex is an attractive woman. A little older than I like, but still very sensual, in her own way."

"What was Parker doing when he accidentally hurt you, Jan?" Harriett asked, still trying to direct the conversation away from Alexis Dunne and their past relationship.

Jan smiled at Harriett, allowing smoke to slowly escape through her mouth and nostrils.

"He just got a little carried away," Jan finally said.

"How old were you?"

"Five or six."

"What did he do that hurt you, Jan?" Harriett asked, grateful the subject had swung back to Parker.

"Well, I'll tell you, Harriett. He stuck his dick a little too far down my throat, and I couldn't breathe, so I bit him. That what you're looking for?"

"I'm sorry, Jan. I know it must be a painful memory for you."

"Not as painful as it was for Parker," Jan laughed. "Neither of us ever made that mistake again."

"Then it wasn't an isolated incident."

"Hell, no. And I got so good at giving blow jobs that he started inviting his friends over to join us."

Anger was beginning to strain Jan's voice even though she seemed relaxed and kept a faint smile on her lips. Crushing out her cigarette, she leaned back in her chair and held Harriett's eyes with hers.

"This is the way it went, okay. All his buddies would line up and pull their pathetic little dicks out. Then Sharon would go from one to the next on her knees, making them all salute. She usually managed to go away after the first one."

"Where was Parker?"

"Watching to make sure she didn't get hurt again even though it really wasn't Sharon. He's a very caring brother, and he never knew the difference."

"Jesus," Harriett muttered under her breath.

"Besides she could do him anytime."

Harriett turned away from Jan and looked at the mirror while taking a deep breath.

"Of course, later there weren't as many blow jobs," Jan said.

"I'm sorry," Harriett said, turning back toward Jan.

"I said, later there weren't as many blow jobs."

"When did they stop?"

"Oh, they didn't stop. But when Parker and his buddies started fuckin' Sharon, there wasn't as much time for other things."

"How old was she when that started?"

"Eleven. No, twelve. Parker said she wasn't ready until then."

"How did the sex start?"

"Same as the blow jobs. Parker taught her what to do and I did it."

"She had sex with Parker first?"

"You gotta learn somewhere," Jan said casually. "Hurt like a son of a bitch. But after the first few times, it wasn't so bad."

"Did you enjoy it?"

"Well, that's a little personal, don't you think?" Jan said with a smirk. "Do you enjoy it?"

"I wasn't having sex when I was twelve."

"When *did* you start having sex, Harriett?"

"When I was an adult and could consent to it."

"I'll bet there were still a couple of times when you really didn't want to though, but did it just to satisfy your lover. Times when you knew you shouldn't but did anyway."

"No, there wasn't."

"You knew you shouldn't with Alex, but you did. I guess you must have wanted it real bad since you knew she was already taken."

"Why do you keep bringing Alexis Dunne into this, Jan? Just to rattle me?"

"Maybe," Jan shrugged. "It's not much fun being the only one on the hot seat."

"If I'm honest with you, will you be honest with me?"

"You mean trade secrets?" Jan smiled.

"Yes."

"Cool. You first."

Taking a deep breath, Harriett glanced at the mirror and said, "You're right. I did sleep with Alex while she had a partner, and I knew it was wrong, but I did it anyway. That good enough?"

"And did you crave it? Couldn't get enough of it?" Jan asked in a low sultry voice.

Harriett could feel the heat rising up her neck as she saw Jan's pleasure in her discomfort. "Yes," she finally stated.

"Well, of course you did! Otherwise you wouldn't have kept going back to her for more. Honesty is the best policy, don't you think?"

"It can be very therapeutic, yes."

"Guess it's my turn," Jan smiled broadly, sitting up in her chair and leaning her elbows on the table.

"I fucked her, too," Jan announced.

"Who?"

"Alex. I fucked her, too," Jan answered with a smile. "Or I should say she fucked me."

"What!"

"You're right, Harriett," Jan said exhaling loudly. "The truth is therapeutic, even if it hurts like hell. God damn! I feel better already, don't you?"

Harriett stood up and went to the door of the interview room.

"Don't you want to know how good she felt, Harriett? Or maybe how good she made me feel, over and over again," Jan purred. "An incredible lover, but then, you already know that. And that delicate little tattoo on her thigh was delicious."

Jan began laughing as the door opened and Harriett left the room. She had to get out of the building to breathe again. She heard Nick's voice behind her but didn't stop until she was standing outside the attorney's entrance. She wasn't sure whether to believe what she had just heard. She had allowed a client to get to her and felt like she was being sucked down by quicksand.

"Harriett," Nick said softly from behind her.

Harriett held a hand up to stop him from talking without turning around.

"I just need...a moment," she managed to say as she took in oxygen through her mouth.

Turning slightly, Harriett put her hands out and leaned against the wall.

"Thinking about stepping away from this one?" Nick asked.

"Yeah," she said as she pushed away from the wall. "But what reason would I offer the judge? I'm sorry your Honor, I request a release as defense counsel because I just found out my client was fucking my ex-lover." Crossing her arms in front of her and stepping into the sunlight, she squinted as she looked up. "A conflict of interest my ass. What a joke."

Looking back at Nick, she smiled. "I walked into that like a beginner. Incredible."

"We knew she was very smart, Harriett."

"She's sadistic. She enjoyed watching me squirm."

"She's probably lying just to get a rise out of you. You were pushing her pretty hard."

"Then she could be lying about Parker, which shoots the shit out of my case. But," Harriett said, shaking her head, "I don't think she's lying about either one. I need Wayne to find out whom Parker's friends were in high school and check them out. I can't just take her word for it. Maybe he can track down someone who'll be willing to admit they sodomized and had intercourse with a child."

"And the thing with Alex?"

With the still vivid memory of Alex touching her, inside her, less than twenty-four hours earlier, Harriett said, "I'll deal with that one." Turning away, she walked back toward the entrance of the county jail.

Chapter
Twenty-Four

HARRIETT WAS QUIET most of the way back to Austin that afternoon. Nick wished there was something he could say to make her feel better, but didn't have a clue where to start. He spent over an hour reading and re-reading the information on dissociative identity disorder Harriett had collected. Finally, Nick pulled his glasses off and closed the folder, stuffing it back into his briefcase.

"The criteria for DID seem clear-cut enough," Nick said.

She looked at him, and said, "It's the sudden appearance of the second personality that bothers me. If Sharon developed this alter personality as a child, where the hell was Jan all these years?"

"Maybe she wasn't stressed enough between fifteen and twenty-eight to bring her out. Besides, there are statements by the mother, a friend, and one co-worker that might imply Jan has come out sporadically before."

"You mean when she was angry?"

"Yeah."

"Even if that's true, there's no way those people would have known they were dealing with a different personality. I'll have to stick pretty much to what we know happened in the last couple of years."

"Looks that way. Have you thought of a way to get around the only important thing you have to show in the trial?"

"You mean the right and wrong standard?" Harriett asked as she signaled to change lanes.

"Unfortunately in Texas, it doesn't matter if she's crazier than a June bug," Nick said. "If she knew what she did was wrong, but did it anyway, then she's just plain old guilty. Period. End of defense."

"First, I have to establish that Sharon has a second personality. Jan knows the difference between right and wrong, no matter how warped her knowledge is. But the important part is that Jan doesn't believe she did anything wrong. Since Jan performed the actions and Sharon had no awareness of them, it's irrelevant whether Sharon knows the difference between right and wrong because she wasn't the perpetrator. How does that sound?" she asked.

"Jesus, sounds like you'll need a road map designed by Rand-McNally to get a jury to follow what's going on. A list of the cast of characters might be a good idea, too," Nick answered with a chuckle.

"Kind of makes you wish you'd chosen another profession, huh?"

"Sometimes. My law students would think this was something created for a TV movie. Does Lacey have a game tonight?" Nick asked glancing at his wristwatch.

"They have a bye tonight, but play next Tuesday," Harriett smiled. "A couple more wins and her team will be in the play-offs. Why don't you come to the house with me? We can scratch up something for dinner."

"Works for me, but you'll have to drop me at the office later to pick up my car."

When Harriett pulled the truck into her driveway, she saw a blue car parked at the curb and frowned.

"Company?" Nick asked as he closed the truck door.

"Devon. Lacey's boyfriend. She said they had to work on an experiment for biology class," Harriett answered as they walked to the front door of the two-story, red brick townhouse.

The house seemed quiet as they entered until they heard giggling coming from the living room. As they reached the entrance to the living room, they saw Lacey and Devon on the couch. Devon was holding Lacey in his arms, kissing her passionately. Nick coughed loudly when he saw them. Devon got up quickly, adjusting his clothing.

"Ms. Markham," he said. "We didn't hear you come in."

"That much is obvious," Harriett said coolly as she crossed her arms and looked at Lacey. "Is this the biology experiment you said you'd be working on, Lacey?"

Lacey got up slowly. "We have to wait a couple of hours before we can check the last sample."

Nick smiled. "Does it involve studying the chemical changes in saliva resulting from sexual arousal?"

"Nick!" Harriett said sharply as Lacey and Devon laughed. "That's not helping."

"Sorry," he shrugged.

Turning back to Devon, Harriett said, "Don't you have someplace to be, Devon?"

"Yes, ma'am. I need to run home and change."

Lacey took Devon's hand. "I'll be right back," she said as they walked to the front door and left the townhouse.

"What's so damn funny, Nick?" Harriett fumed as Nick laughed softly.

"They weren't doing anything, Harriett, and I think you scared the shit out of that kid."

"Lacey knows better than this."

"It could have been worse. You could have found them upstairs."

"If we'd been later I might have."

"Stop it, Harriett. Lacey wouldn't let the situation get that out of hand and you know it. She's too smart for that."

"When it comes to sex, brains don't always outweigh desires."

"Does that observation come from personal experience?"

Harriett looked at him, remembering that only two days earlier she had let her desire overrule her brain, and frowned. "As a matter of fact, it does. Are there any other personal questions you'd like to ask me?"

Lacey strolled back into the living room. "I'm sorry Aunt Harriett, but we really weren't doing anything. And by the way, you had a phone call earlier. I wrote the number down and stuck it on the fridge."

"Thank you, sweetheart," Harriett smiled.

"Devon's picking me up around eight. Okay?" Lacey asked.

"Leaving your poor old maiden aunt home all alone again, huh?" Harriett kidded.

Harriett took the number from the refrigerator door and walked to the kitchen phone. She leaned against the wall and punched in the number. "Grab yourself a beer, Nick. I wish Lacey would write down the caller's name, so I wouldn't have to waste time with magazine salesmen."

Three rings later a voice answered. "Sex Offenders. Raines."

"This is Harriett Markham. I was told I had a phone call from this number."

"Oh, hi, Harriett. I don't know if you remember me. This is Jess Raines. I met you at The Corral a week or so ago."

"Of course, I remember," Harriett smiled as the woman's face floated through her mind. "How can I help you?"

"Actually, I was wondering if you might be free for dinner this evening," Jess said.

"I just got back in town. It's been a very stressful week for me. Did you say Sex Offenders when you answered the phone?"

"Yeah. Sorry about that. I probably should have left my home phone. But I was hoping to hear from you before I left work."

"You work at Sex Offenders?" Harriett inquired. Nick was looking at her and she shrugged.

"I'm an investigator with the Attorney General's Office. Listen, I understand if you're too tired to go out. Maybe another time," Jess said.

"You know what, Jess? I'd love to go out for dinner this evening. I'm really not up to cooking and my niece is going out anyway."

"Great! Give me your address, and I'll pick you up. What time is good for you?"

Harriett glanced at the kitchen clock. "Is eight okay?"

"Perfect. And you don't have to get all dressed up. We'll make it a casual evening."

"All right." Harriett smiled. "By the way, how did you get this number? It's unlisted."

"Well," Jess laughed, "I am an investigator. That's why I get the big bucks. See you about eight."

Harriett hung up the phone and went to the refrigerator. Pouring a glass of iced tea, she looked at Nick. "I have a date," she smiled.

Chapter
Twenty-Five

JESS HAD SPENT nearly an hour deciding what to wear for her date with Harriett Markham. She was nervous, and if she still smoked and drank, she would have already had several of each. She hadn't been on a date in nearly two decades. Except for the fact that Harriett was an attractive woman, a lawyer and knew how to dance, Jess realized she didn't know another damn thing about her. She had seemed nice enough at the club, and it was only a dinner date. It was better than sitting around the house reliving the memories of everything she had lost, feeling Renee's phantom touch next to her in bed every night. Looking at her reflection in the mirror as she ran a brush through her hair, she knew Renee wouldn't have wanted her to live this way.

At precisely eight o'clock, Jess, who had finally settled for pressed jeans, boots and a charcoal tweed jacket over a white t-shirt, took a deep breath and pushed the doorbell of Harriett's townhouse. When the door was opened a few moments later by a tall, slender, blonde teenager wearing a ratty sweatshirt and well-worn jeans, Jess wondered if this had been a good idea after all.

"Can I help you?" the girl asked.

"Hi. I'm Jess Raines. I'm here to pick up Harriett," she answered with a smile.

"Come on in. My aunt will ready in a minute."

"Thanks," Jess said as she stepped inside.

Lacey extended her hand, "Lacey Markham."

"It's a pleasure, Lacey."

As Jess was shaking hands with Lacey, Harriett came down the stairs. Jess thought she looked even better than she had at the club, if that was possible. She was glad Harriett's idea of casual matched her own and thought she might faint when Harriett smiled at her. Coming up next to her, Harriett hugged her briefly. Noticing the same subtle scent she had noticed the evening they met, Harriett inhaled it deeply.

"You look very nice, Jess."

"So do you." Jess blushed.

"What time will you be home, Lacey?" Harriett asked as she turned her head back toward her niece.

"We're just going to a movie and catching something to eat

afterward, so not too late. Maybe midnight," Lacey shrugged.

"That's fine, sweetheart. You two be careful."

"We will. And what time will you be home, Aunt Harriett?" Lacey grinned, glancing at Jess.

Harriett also looked at Jess and smiled. "I'm not sure."

"Well, have fun," Lacey said as she hugged Harriett. "I'll see you in the morning."

As Jess backed her sapphire blue Durango out of Harriett's driveway, she said, "Your niece is very attractive."

"Thanks. She's graduating from St. John's Prep this year, and I worry about her sometimes."

"That's understandable." Jess looked across the seat at Harriett. "I hope you're hungry."

"I could eat a cow right now," Harriett laughed. "At least you know there's nothing wrong with my appetite."

"Perfect," Jess grinned. "I hope a thick steak, baked potato, and salad will do the trick."

Nearly half an hour later, Jess pulled into the drive of a large split-level ranch style house on an oversized, tree filled lot and turned off the ignition. Seeing the look on Harriett's face, she said, "I grill the best steak in town. And we won't have to leave a tip."

Jess helped Harriett out of the Durango and escorted her to the front door. Before she unlocked the door, she looked at her date and said, "If you're uncomfortable, we can go somewhere else, Harriett. I'd understand, but, honestly, dinner and some good conversation are the only items on my agenda."

Harriett smiled at her. "Sounds good to me."

When they entered the house, Harriett saw a table for two already set. Jess lit candles on the table and flipped on the stereo. Soft, melodic sounds of Kenny G crept into the room.

"Make yourself at home," Jess said as she slipped her jacket off and flipped on the kitchen light. "How do you like your steak?"

"Medium rare," Harriett said as she looked around. "This is a beautiful house, Jess."

"Thanks. It's a little big for just me, but I can't bring myself to part with it. There are some drinks in the fridge. Help yourself while I get a fire going," Jess called over her shoulder.

Harriett took a wine cooler from the refrigerator and continued to look around the front rooms of the house. The hardwood floors shined, and there were glowing embers in the oversized fireplace. An eclectic collection of paintings and prints adorned the walls while bare beams crossed the ceiling of the main room. To Harriett, it had the feel of a large cabin in the middle of the city. She glanced at pictures on the mantle and took one down to examine it more closely. Jess was smiling broadly in the picture and had her arms around a smiling woman with long corn silk hair.

"That's me and Renee," Jess said softly, walking up behind her. "In better times."

"Where is she now?" Harriett asked.

"She was killed in a traffic accident about four years ago."

Harriett replaced the picture carefully on the mantle and turned toward Jess. "I'm sorry, Jess. You must miss her very much. How long were you together?"

"Twelve years, and I still miss her every day. But life goes on and she wouldn't want me to stop living. We had a great life," Jess smiled. "It'll take a little while for the charcoal to burn down. Why don't we take our drinks out to the patio?"

Jess took a bottle of water from the refrigerator and led Harriett outside into a large enclosed patio. Setting her water on the table, Jess walked over to a large brick grill that took up one corner of the patio. Harriett joined her and rested a hand lightly on Jess's shoulder. It was a familiar gesture that reminded Jess of the evenings she and Renee had spent preparing dinner before it was all taken away.

"This is a beautiful grill," Harriett said.

Swallowing the lump that had formed in her throat, Jess glanced at her. "I built it a few years ago. If the weather is cold it can double as an outdoor fireplace," she said as she poked at the charcoal, rearranging a few of the briquettes.

"It's very quiet here," Harriett observed.

"It's great, isn't it? Never hear any sirens or traffic out here. Just peace and quiet. It sort of reminds me of home."

"Then I suppose that means you're not from Austin."

"I'm originally from Stamford, north of Abilene, but the employment opportunities were much better here."

Jess smiled when she saw the look on Harriett's face. "What?"

"I grew up in Anson."

Setting her poker down, Jess frowned. "Well then, I guess you know that means I'll have to take you home. We both know that Stamford and Anson are mortal enemies."

"Only on the football field or basketball court and only when you're sixteen or seventeen," Harriett laughed.

Slipping an arm around Harriett's waist and giving her a gentle squeeze, Jess smiled, "Thank God or I'd have to eat two steaks by myself."

Twenty minutes later, Jess carried two large Porterhouse steaks outside and placed them over the hot coals. "These shouldn't take too long," she said.

Harriett half reclined on a chaise lounge and watched Jess intently. The wine cooler had relaxed her, and the faint smell of mesquite smoke and sizzling beef made her mouth water. She felt comfortable around Jess and wanted to get to know her better. She had left Dallas that morning without seeing or talking to Alex. Had her evening in Alex's bed meant anything more than that they had missed one another? Her thoughts were interrupted by Jess's voice.

"There are two salads in the refrigerator and potatoes in the oven. Would you mind getting those out while I finish these up?" Jess asked.

"Anything else I can get ready?" Harriett asked as she stood up.

"You should find whatever you want for the potatoes in the fridge, and since I didn't know what kind of dressing you liked, I got one of just about everything," Jess chuckled.

By the time Harriett had everything else ready and on the table, Jess opened the French doors from the patio and carried the steaks inside and set them on two plates on the kitchen island.

"Well, these look perfect to me," she proclaimed as she cut into the steaks and smiled at Harriett.

After dinner, filled with interesting, but light conversation, Jess and Harriett sat on the couch in the living room, drinking coffee. "I might not have to eat again for a week," Harriett said. "That was a fabulous meal, Jess. Thank you."

"It was my pleasure. I love to cook, and steak happens to be my specialty."

"Well, you can prepare them for me anytime," Harriett sighed contentedly.

"I'll remember that," Jess smiled over her coffee cup.

Looking at Jess, Harriett said, "Tell my about Renee. She was very beautiful."

Jess swallowed and set her cup down, glancing at the picture on the mantle. "Yes, she was. Don't know exactly what to tell you about her. She was a teacher at a local high school, and she loved her job and her students."

"And I'm sure they loved her, too."

"Half the kids at her school came to her funeral. It was amazing," Jess smiled slightly. "I should be so lucky when I die."

"How did you meet? If you don't mind me asking."

"I pulled her over for speeding and issued her a ticket," Jess chuckled. "Best ticket I ever wrote."

"You said she was killed in an accident," Harriett said softly.

"Actually it wasn't an accident. I just call it that. It was murder."

In answer to the look on Harriett's face Jess leaned back on the couch and continued. "Drunk driver. Son of a bitch was stopped by the police three or four hours later and still had a blood alcohol level of two point four. He was so blitzed that he didn't even know he had run her off the road and killed her. Got a minimal sentence for vehicular manslaughter even though he already had two or three DUIs on his record. That really pissed me off."

"I'm so sorry, Jess," Harriett said. "I can't imagine how much it must hurt."

"Renee and I bought this house together," Jess said with a slight smile. "When she found it, she was so excited. It was a dump. I was surprised the city hadn't declared it unsafe for human habitation, but I wound up signing my name on the bottom line anyway. It took us four or five years to get it close to what we wanted. When she di...was killed, the insurance paid it off. That's why it's hard for me to part with it. It sounds stupid, but somehow it still lets me feel connected to her."

Running her hand down Jess's arm, Harriett caught her eye as Jess turned toward her. "It's not stupid, Jess. You loved Renee very much, and the home you made together is beautiful. May I see the rest of it?"

"Sure," Jess shrugged. Standing, she took Harriett's hand and began the tour.

Each room in the expansive home had been decorated to reflect the personality of its inhabitants. The downstairs included the living room, a large combination den and game room complete with pool table and jukebox, a guest room, bathroom, kitchen, and laundry room. Jess stopped midway down the first floor hallway and flipped a switch inside the last downstairs room.

"This is where I spend most of my time," she said glancing into the room. "It's not completely picked up, but not too bad for me. My office."

The walls of the room were covered with trophies, plaques, and pictures. As Harriett made her way around the room, she read the inscriptions on the trophies and smiled at the pictures. Obviously, Jess had been a basketball player in her high school and college years, and if the trophies and plaques were any indication, Harriett assumed that she had been a very good player.

"A jock, huh?" she laughed over her shoulder.

"Only in my younger and wilder days," Jess chuckled. "But I had a good time."

Harriett followed Jess back into the living room. "What's upstairs?"

"The master suite," she answered. "Basically just an oversized bedroom, sitting room, and master bath."

"I've never seen a bedroom that took up an entire floor before," Harriett said.

Pressing a switch at the bottom of the stairs, theater style lighting illuminated each step as Harriett followed Jess up the stairs and into the largest bedroom she had ever seen. Plush burgundy carpeting covered the floor, which held a minimal amount of furniture. The far wall of the room was floor to ceiling windows with French doors opening onto a second story deck. Moonlight filtered through a skylight over the king size bed.

"Oh, my God!" Harriett breathed. "There's so much space."

"The problem with most people is that when they find themselves with extra living space, they feel an irresistible urge to fill it up with something. I've always preferred simple over extravagant." Jess turned a dial near the entrance to the room and brought the lighting up for a better view of the expansive room. "Just the way I was raised, I guess."

"This is incredible, Jess. Really."

"Thanks," Jess smiled. "The bath has a garden tub with a Jacuzzi that is very relaxing after a tough day."

Harriett wandered around the room and master bath and couldn't get over how impressive it was. Standing next to the bed, she ran her hand over the wood on the headboard.

"This is lovely. What kind of wood is this?" she asked as she ran her hand over the smooth surface.

"Birdseye maple," Jess said, shoving her hands into her pockets. "I saw some a couple of years ago and fell in love with its uniqueness. Found a retired furniture maker and had him construct this bed out of it for me." Seeing the look on Harriett's face, Jess answered her unasked question. "This isn't the bed Renee and I shared. I couldn't stand having it here. Too many memories," she said, her voice cracking slightly. "I'm sorry."

Harriett reached out and squeezed her arm gently. "I didn't mean to bring back bad memories, Jess," she said softly.

"It's okay. Talking about the bad times allows us to cope with problems and makes it easier to talk about good memories. If I don't talk about it, I'll never be able to get on with my life."

"Now you sound like my psychologist," Harriett said.

"Well, to tell you the truth, Harriett, Helen Mortenson was my psychologist for a while after Renee died. That's how I got your unlisted number," Jess grinned.

"That witch!" Harriett laughed. "Isn't that a breach of confidentiality or something?"

"How about another cup of coffee and some dessert?" Jess offered.

"And maybe more good conversation," Harriett said as she took Jess's hand and moved toward the stairs.

AN HOUR LATER Jess had been bombarded with questions about her past and her work until she finally threw up her hands. "Are you this relentless when you question witnesses in court?"

"Sorry, occupational hazard," Harriett smiled.

"Now that you know everything about me except maybe my shoe size, tell me about Harriett Markham. And I should tell you that I'm a trained interrogator, too."

Leaning back against the sofa, Harriett sighed, "Pretty boring story."

Jess rested her arm along the back of the sofa and looked at Harriett. "You know pretty much all there is to know about Renee. Anyone significant in your past?"

"That's a little complicated," Harriett answered, clearing her throat.

"How so?"

"There was someone a long time ago. She was a senior partner in the law firm I worked for in Dallas. It was intense, and I know now, a mistake."

"Did you love her?"

Harriett looked into Jess's eyes. "Very much."

"And..." Jess coaxed.

"I was involved in an extremely difficult case, which resulted in my leaving the firm and moving to Austin."

"And she just let you go?"

"She already had a partner, which I guess made me the 'other woman.' So it was for the best."

"But you don't regret it," Jess stated.

Harriett smiled slightly. "No, I don't regret it."

"Do you still love her?"

"I'll always love her, but I'm no longer in love with her. She was an important part of my life once." Harriett couldn't bring herself to divulge the temporary rekindling of her affair with Alex. Maybe someday, but not that night.

Jess glanced at the mantle clock and sat up. "Damn, it's after one. Your niece is probably wondering where you are."

"I'm fine, and Lacey doesn't wait up for me when I go out for the evening."

"You said it had been a stressful week," Jess said as she got up and carried their coffee cups to the kitchen. "I just thought you might be getting tired."

Harriett followed Jess into the kitchen and helped her rinse and load their dinner dishes into the dishwasher. For a few minutes there was an awkward silence between them. Being with Harriett had made Jess realize how much she hated being alone and how much she missed Renee.

"I really enjoyed dinner tonight, Jess," Harriett said. "The food was delicious, and the conversation was wonderful."

"I'm glad. It's been a while since I've had anyone over for dinner," Jess said quietly. In fact, it's been more than a while since I've been with anyone I'd want to get to know better, she thought as she glanced at Harriett. "We'll have to do it again sometime."

"I'd like that," Harriett smiled warmly. She had been pleasantly surprised at how comfortable being with Jess was. There was a quiet shyness about her that she found intriguing.

"Would you like to go to the club tomorrow night? Maybe have dinner someplace before we trip the light fantastic?" Jess offered.

"So I can spend my evening fighting off other women who want to dance with you?" Harriett teased. "Your services seemed to be in great demand the last time you were at the club."

Stepping closer to her, Jess smiled, "I promise to turn down my legions of admirers and save every dance for you."

"Well, who could possibly turn down an offer like that?" Harriett laughed.

Chapter
Twenty-Six

"I COULD LOSE my job if they catch you in here, Wayne."

"Look, Kelsey. I know the prosecution or Riley or both have more than they're telling us. And I know you're the techie who ran the tests on the fuckin' rifle. Were the bullets a match or not?" Wayne pressed. Howard Kelsey was the best ballistics technician in north Texas, but he was also your basic Harvey Milquetoast. He couldn't be bribed, but he sure as hell could be intimidated.

"All six that I examined were from the same lot the police found at the defendant's home. The firing pin marking on the shells were consistent with that model Browning and the lands and grooves matched as well. The bullets were all lubricated, which means..."

"Yeah, yeah, I know what it means. They travel faster out of the barrel. So what?"

"Well, why would anyone need a bullet that travels faster if it's gonna run into a target moving toward it at sixty or so miles per. Just seems like an unusual choice. If they hadn't been such specialized bullets, there's no way they could have been traced to your client. Pretty stupid, if you ask me."

Wayne scratched his beard stubble. "Or it was pretty smart. So you have the six bullets, right?"

"I did, but Riley has them now. Signed them out as soon as I gave him my results." Kelsey shrugged. "He said something about being afraid we would lose them before the trial."

"Did he sign a chain of custody voucher?"

"Yeah."

"Well, I need a copy of it, Howie. Taggart's attorney has a right to see it."

"I can't give you that! They'll know where you got it!"

Grabbing the man by the front of his lab coat, Wayne said, "Look, you little pissant, I'm not gonna waste my time arguing with you, and I don't have time to run the paperwork through channels. By the time I do that, those fuckin' bullets could be any damn place." Reaching into his coat pocket, Wayne shoved a sheet of paper in front of Kelsey. "This is what they said they had. One! One fucked up point and a few shells. You know damn well Riley's gonna claim you lost the others, you moron!"

"That son of a bitch!"

Shoving Kelsey away, Wayne ordered, "So give me a copy of the other ballistics reports."

Kelsey scurried away from Wayne and pulled a large binder from a shelf over his desk. Flipping through several pages, he eventually removed two pages and took them to the lab copier.

"Those bullets were fired over about a year's time. How did you tie them together?" Wayne asked.

"It was Riley's idea. I guess the circumstances were similar enough that he asked me to compare the bullets and casings from the other cases to the last one...Kaufmann."

"Then I'll need the log form for each shell." Wayne lit a cigarette.

"Hey! You can't smoke in here, man."

"So give me a ticket. I need a copy of the log for the rifle, too. When did it come in?"

"About a week or so after the bullet from the Kaufmann case, I think."

WITH THE COPIES of the ballistic reports in hand, Wayne settled in his Tahoe and pulled out his cell phone.

"Well, you were right," Wayne announced as soon as Harriett answered her phone. "They're squirreling away the real bullets for a rainy day, and I got the paperwork to prove it."

"Where did they find them?" she asked.

"Lodged in the passenger seats of the vehicles. So the shots had to have gone through the windshields, and the drivers would have known they were being shot at."

"What about the windshields? Where are they?"

"Can't use them. Too mangled up in the collisions."

Harriett removed her glasses and pinched the bridge of her nose. "Are they hiding anything else we should know about?"

"Not that I could ferret out. But from configurin' where the bullet they showed us had to have been fired from to hit the telephone pole, I'm guessin' that it might have been a plant. Maybe from a Browning, but not from any shots your client might have fired."

"That was probably Riley's genius at work again," Harriett sighed.

"So we know they have the rifle, unused ammo, shell casings, and the spent bullets from the scenes. What else?"

"They got some of her clothes with powder residue, and her fingerprints are on just about everything in the county."

"Then I'll be forced to amend the plea soon."

"What are your experts sayin' so far? Is she nuts or not?"

"I hope so, but the final reports won't be ready until the end of the week. I want you to do a little deep digging for me, Wayne."

"How deep?"

"According to Dr. Talbot we could be looking into a multiple personality defense for the NGRI. The generally accepted cause is early childhood trauma, probably sexual abuse."

"What about all that shit I found at the school? You know Lassiter's people have probably seen all them books about the insanity defense."

"Reading a few books doesn't prove you aren't insane."

"Well, I'd have to think she was fakin' it if I was the prosecutor."

"I'll have to worry about that if and when Lassiter brings it up. In the meantime, I want you to find out who Parker Collins's friends were in high school and locate as many of them as possible. Then I might need you to talk to them and bring them back for the trial if necessary."

"I can do that, but I'll need a refill on the retainer."

"I had two thousand transferred into your account this morning," Harriett said.

"Okay, kiddo. When will your client arrive?"

"Monday afternoon. They'll call from the county jail after she's been processed."

"How soon do you think it'll be before the trial begins?" Wayne asked.

"Two, maybe three weeks," Harriett said. "Depends on how long it takes them to get their experts on board."

"Rumor in Dallas is that Donald Stevenson is their guy, you know," Wayne said.

"Fabulous," Harriett muttered.

Chapter
Twenty-Seven

"YOU'RE IN A good mood this evening," Harriett observed as Jess guided her Durango through Austin traffic Saturday evening.

Jess smiled as she looked across the car at Harriett. She was feeling better than she had in the last four years. She certainly couldn't deny her physical attraction to the woman beside her. "I am in a good mood. So far I've had a great meal and stimulating conversation, and am about to spend the rest of the evening dancing with a beautiful woman at my favorite club. Who wouldn't be in a good mood with all that going for her?"

"Thank you, Jess." Harriett hoped the dim lighting in the car prevented Jess from seeing her blush.

A little before ten, Jess swung the Durango into a private parking garage across the street from the Corral and rolled the window down to pull a ticket from the entry gate. After parking the car in a vacant slot on the third level of the garage, Jess walked around to the passenger side and helped Harriett out of the vehicle. As Harriett took Jess's hand, she intertwined their fingers. Jess couldn't believe how stunning Harriett looked. Tan jeans showed off a figure that anyone would be proud of, and her light brown hair hung loosely down to her shoulders. Jess was in the mood to dance, and it had been a while since she had danced with anyone she gave a damn about.

"Let's go show them how it's done," Jess smiled as she closed and locked the SUV.

The Saturday night crowd hadn't found its way to the Corral yet, and Jess couldn't help but notice that there was plenty of space on the dance floor.

"Would you like a drink?" Jess asked.

"Maybe later," Harriett said.

Jess saw their reflection in a floor-to-ceiling mirror that ran the length of the bar and even she had to admit that they made an attractive couple. She was only slightly taller than Harriett and everything about them seemed to fit together. She slipped her arm around Harriett's waist and drew her closer. "You look beautiful tonight."

"So do you," Harriett said, shifting her weight slightly to lean against Jess's shoulder.

As soon as a new song began, Jess led her onto the dance floor, and taking her into her arms, began a slow two-step. She fit so well against Jess's body that it was as if they were one person as they glided smoothly together. Jess reached up, and using her fingertips, brushed Harriett's hair back from her face, seeing the tenderness in her eyes as Harriett looked at her, softly stroking the back of Jess's neck.

It was nearly midnight when Jess asked, "Ready to go?"

"I think I'll request something to finish our evening," Harriett smiled.

"What did you request?" Jess asked when she returned a few minutes later.

"It's a surprise, but I used to love dancing to it."

"Ah," Jess grinned, "I love a mystery."

"She promised to play it next."

"How much did you have to pay her?" Jess laughed.

The music stopped and a moment later, a deep driving drumbeat began swelling through the speakers as Harriett stood and took Jess's hand.

"Do you remember this one?" she grinned. "Now we'll see how good you really are."

Jess laughed as she followed Harriett onto the floor, already feeling the beat of "Hungry Eyes."

She pulled Harriett into her arms and moved immediately into the dance. Other patrons of the bar seemed stunned not to be hearing the usual country-western tunes that had been playing all evening. As their bodies touched and teased one another, Jess placed her hands on Harriett's hips and pulled her into the sultry, suggestive dance. Eventually, a number of other couples joined them, but neither woman seemed to notice. As the music began to fade away, Harriett kissed Jess lightly and said, "Now I'm ready to go."

HARRIETT OPENED THE front door to her townhouse, reaching in to flip on an inside light.

"Coffee?" she asked.

"Sounds perfect," Jess answered, following her into the kitchen and leaning against the counter as she scooped grounds into the coffeemaker.

"I haven't had as much fun as I had tonight in a long time, Jess. Thank you," Harriett said, taking two mugs from the cabinet next to the sink.

"I'm glad. I had a great time, too."

An uncomfortable moment passed between them as they waited for their coffee. Neither of them wanted the evening to end, but both seemed uncertain what to do about it.

Clearing her throat, Jess said, "I should be getting home after this."

Bringing her eyes up to Jess's, Harriett asked, "Are you trying to get away from me, Jess?"

"No, of course not. I just....," Jess started.

"Do you remember that song we danced to the night we met?" Harriett interrupted.

"Which one?"

"Shut Up and Kiss Me," she said huskily, stopping inches from Jess.

Jess smiled as she leaned forward and kissed her softly, shyly. Harriett wrapped her arms around Jess's shoulders and pressed against her, enjoying the closeness and warmth of Jess's body as her lips parted slightly, inviting her to deepen their kiss.

"Stay with me tonight, Jess," she whispered as strong arms caressed her.

"I...I want to," Jess breathed, "but I can't. I'm sorry."

Breaking their embrace, Harriett looked at her, an unasked question in her eyes.

"I...um...I haven't been with anyone since I lost Renee. It isn't you, Harriett. God knows you're beautiful and desirable, but I want to know more about you than just your body. I don't want us to rush into anything."

Kissing her softly, Harriett smiled. It hadn't been long since she had said the same thing to Alex only to give in to her desires. She hadn't heard from Alex since that evening. It had been a mistake that she didn't want to repeat. "It's been a long time for me, too. I understand, Jess. Thank you."

Harriett filled their mugs with coffee, offering Jess cream and sugar.

"Would you still consider going out with me again?" Jess asked as she stirred creamer into her mug, suddenly afraid to hear the answer.

"Absolutely," Harriett smiled. "How would you feel about letting me fix a late breakfast for you tomorrow morning?

AT NINE FORTY-FIVE Sunday morning, Harriett opened the front door of her townhouse to greet Jess.

"Good morning," she said cheerfully. "Hungry?"

"Starving," Jess said as she followed her into the kitchen.

"Pull up a stool. This will be ready in a minute" Setting a cup on the counter, Harriett poured a cup of coffee for her. Before she could return to preparing breakfast, Jess stopped her and pulled Harriett's lips to hers. "Thank you for last night," she said.

"It was wonderful," Harriett smiled, meeting her lips a second time. "There's milk in the fridge and sugar in the canister. The paper is on the dining room table."

Jess was amazed at how natural everything felt when she was with

Harriett. She was sipping her coffee and glancing through the paper when Harriett set an omelet in front of her. "Hope this is okay," she said.

"It looks delicious," Jess smiled, diving into her food as she continued to read.

Harriett picked out a section of the paper and began reading while she ate as well. "Hey, guess what?" she said with a chuckle. "The city council's decided that MoPac needs to be extended."

Jess laughed. "It needed that almost as soon as they completed it."

After a few minutes, Jess stopped eating and picked the paper up. "Damn," she said under her breath.

"What?"

"Another girl was killed last night." Looking at Harriett she asked, "Didn't you say your niece attends St. John's Prep?"

Chapter
Twenty-Eight

"YES, WHY?"

"The victim is...or was a student there, too."

"Let me see that," Harriett said, setting her fork down. She quickly scanned the small article. "Jesus, I know this girl."

Glancing over her shoulder toward the stairs leading to her niece's room, Harriett said, "She's still asleep. I should tell her before she finds out some other way. I'm sorry, Jess."

"Go take care of her. Can I use your phone for a minute?"

"Sure. It's in the kitchen."

While Jess was gone, Harriett went upstairs and looked into Lacey's bedroom. Only a swatch of blonde hair could be seen from under the covers. Sitting on the edge of the bed, she gently rubbed Lacey's back. Stretching and groaning loudly, Lacey opened her eyes and smiled at her aunt. "Just getting home?" she teased.

"No, but I got home late and didn't want to wake you," Harriett said.

Sitting up and plumping up her pillow, Lacey leaned back and said mischievously, "I want details, all the gory details."

"Maybe later, Lace. I'm afraid I have some bad news, sweetheart," she frowned as she reached out and pushed a strand of hair from Lacey's face. "Corey Chandler was killed last night. It was in this morning's paper."

For a moment, Lacey didn't react, too stunned to speak. "How....," she finally managed.

"I don't know any more than I've told you right now. The paper didn't have any details," Harriett said softly. Taking Lacey into her arms and hugging her tightly, she whispered, "I'm so sorry, honey."

When Harriett released her, a tear was making its way down the teenager's cheek. "I should call Devon. We saw her last night."

"Come downstairs and I'll fix you something to eat," Harriett offered.

"That's okay, Aunt Harriett. I'm not very hungry."

She left Lacey as she was dialing Devon's number. She found Jess sitting at the kitchen table, writing notes on a legal pad Harriett kept near the phone.

"Is she all right?" Jess asked as Harriett rested her hands on her shoulders and looked at the legal pad.

"I think so. What's this?"

"I just got a few more details from a friend of mine at APD. This is the second case like this in as many weeks. Last week it was a UT freshman named Marion Alexander."

"Are you involved in the investigation?" Harriett asked as she sat down next to Jess.

"Only in a peripheral way. I ran the last case through the offender files, but didn't get any hits on the MO. Must be a new freak in town."

"Did the first girl die the same way?"

"Raped and strangled after being picked up in a club. Apparently no one saw anything suspicious either time."

"What about the autopsy reports? Were either of them drugged?"

"Marion Alexander was clean and the tox report on Corey Chandler won't be ready for a few days. Why all the questions, Harriett?"

"Corey was a classmate of Lacey's," Harriett shrugged. "I'm just concerned." A niggling feeling crept into Harriett's mind, but she shook it off when Lacey came into the kitchen wearing a bathrobe pulled tightly around her. Sitting at the table, she pulled her feet up under her and hand-brushed hair over her head revealing red-rimmed eyes.

"Are you all right?" Harriett asked as she placed her hand on Lacey's knee.

Lacey nodded. "Devon is coming over in about an hour. We're going to the Chandlers' for a few minutes."

Looking at Jess, Harriett said, "Lacey and her boyfriend saw Corey last night."

"When did you see her, Lacey?" Jess asked quietly.

"After the movie, about eleven, I think."

"Was she with anyone?"

"She was with a couple of other girls from school. She told us she had her sister's ID, and they were going to a club for a few laughs," Lacey said as tears began to form in her eyes again.

"Did she mention which club?" Jess inquired.

Lacey shook her head and blinked, letting a tear escape and roll down her cheek. "I should have asked, but kids at school do that kind of thing all the time. I should have tried to talk her out of it."

"It wasn't your fault," Jess said strongly. "There's no way you could have known what would happen. Were you very close to Corey?"

"We had some classes together and used to hang around together a lot. Then we both started dating and sort of drifted apart. She told me a few days ago that she had met someone she really liked."

"Another student?" Jess asked.

"No, she said he was older. She thought he was a grad student at UT."

"Do you know a girl named Marion Alexander?"

"I don't think so. The name doesn't ring a bell," Lacey answered.

Later that morning Harriett followed Jess to her Durango and waited for her to get settled behind the wheel. "I'm sorry about Lacey's friend, Harriett," she said. "Will she be okay?"

"It might take a while, but I'm sure she'll be fine," Harriett smiled.

"I'll call you tomorrow," Jess said as she turned the key in the ignition.

"Better let me call you. I have a client from Dallas whose trial has been moved here. She's supposed to arrive tomorrow. After that I'm afraid my work schedule is going to be pretty erratic."

Pulling a pen from her visor, Jess wrote her home phone and pager number on the back of a business card. "You can always reach me at my cell number," she smiled as she handed Harriett the card.

Leaning into the vehicle, Harriett hugged her tightly and kissed her. "I *will* call soon," she whispered emphatically.

"DO WE KNOW where the prosecution team is staying in Austin?" Harriett asked Nick as they went over their case notes and the faxes Wayne had sent of the ballistic reports.

"The Red Lion."

"I'll contact them later about my new motions. Ought to make their day."

"Do we know when our other experts are flying in?"

"Olson is in the air even as we speak, but Renick can't get away until Wednesday. A car is picking Olson up and bringing him here late today," Nick said. "How soon do you think it'll be before the trial begins?"

"A few weeks," Harriett said. "Wayne told me the prosecution expert will be Donald Stevenson. I need to know everything about him, anything I can use to attack his testimony."

"What's wrong with him?" Nick asked.

"Another player from the Wilkes case," she explained. "Stevenson always testifies for the prosecution in cases like this. Wrote the book on disproving multiple personality as a defense. After the Wilkes case, he founded some organization back east devoted to debunking claims of insanity and has been very successful since then. He and Renick aren't on the best of terms, so we'll have to make sure they don't accidentally run into each other."

"Are you going to see Sharon when she arrives?" Nick asked.

"Since she's my client, I don't have much of a choice."

"I'll go with you," Nick offered.

"I can handle it," she said.

"But..."

"I said I can handle it, Nick. Just make sure your calendar will be clear when we get ready to pick the jury," Harriett said.

WHEN SHE RECEIVED the phone call notifying her of Sharon Taggart's arrival, she wasn't looking forward to seeing her client. Before leaving her office, she placed a call to Judge Howard Landers's office requesting a time to present her motions. Then she called Sean Lassiter and gave him the time for the motion hearing the next morning at the Travis County Courthouse.

A little after three Harriett was waiting for Sharon to join her. The time for niceties had passed.

"It's crunch time, Sharon," she said as soon as the woman sat down. "You can't be bullshitting me from now on. Understand?"

"Yes."

"Tomorrow morning, I'm amending your plea to not guilty by reason of mental defect. The prosecution will be playing hardball from then on. This is the only chance you have to avoid prison and rebuild your life."

"But I didn't do anything, Ms. Markham," Sharon said softly.

"Yes, you did, Sharon. The evidence is strong enough to prove it. Tomorrow and Wednesday my last two experts are going to evaluate you. After that, at least one expert for the State will evaluate you. We'll probably be in court in two or three weeks."

"Wait," Sharon frowned. "I don't understand. This is too confusing."

Harriett looked at Sharon. "I know you don't understand, Sharon. You'll have to trust me more than you've ever trusted anyone before. Can you do that?"

"Yes," Sharon said after a pause.

"Good. The last time I saw you we were talking about Parker. Do you remember that?"

"Yes."

"Do you remember any of Parker's friends?"

"No."

"None of them?"

"I don't remember their names now. It's been so long."

"Have you ever seen any of them around Dallas?"

"No."

Getting nowhere with her client, Harriett took a chance and decided to change tactics.

"Frank will be here for the trial. I talked to him this morning."

"Really?"

"He said he couldn't wait to see you again. He asked if I could arrange a conjugal visit here. It shouldn't be a problem," Harriett said as she doodled on her legal pad and waited. When she finally looked up at Sharon, she tossed a pack of cigarettes on the table in front of her client and asked, "Do you need a cigarette?"

"What I don't need is a fuckin' conjugal visit with Frank fuckin' Taggart!"

"You handled him the last time, Jan. It's important that your family appears to be supportive."

"They're not my family, they're hers. You still pissed because I told you about me and Alex?"

"Why should I be? That's ancient history."

"I thought we agreed to tell each other the truth, Harriett."

"I am telling the truth. Alex and I no longer have a relationship. Would you like to tell me about Parker's friends?"

"I already told you I fucked them."

"Were you alone with them?"

"Parker was always there, watching. I think it turned him on, you know."

"Did Sharon ever resist what was happening?"

"She tried, but hell, she was too little to put up much of a fight."

"Did Parker keep her from resisting?"

"He'd put his hand over her mouth and tell his buddies to hurry up. Usually in the middle of this fun and games Sharon would go away and leave me stuck with it."

"This is tough, Jan. I wish I didn't have to know so much."

"What the hell," Jan shrugged. "One thing for sure, no one's ever going to hurt me or her again. How specific do you want?"

"I have to establish the sexual abuse to make the case."

Jan took a deep breath before beginning. "Parker would get her ready for company. Isn't that a quaint way of putting it? Anyway, at first, I didn't come out until she couldn't stand it any longer. Later, I would appear when she knew company was coming."

"Didn't you fight back?"

"Once, but it made Parker really mad."

"What did he do?"

"Nearly smothered me to death with his hand. I might have passed out. I can't remember much about that time. When Parker's friends got to the house, they would come to Sharon's room two at a time with Parker and do their thing one after the other while Parker talked to her, so she wouldn't think about it. She...I was just this... this thing on the bed."

"How old was Sharon when this stopped?"

"About thirteen or fourteen, I think. The last time was pretty bad."

"Different from the other times?"

"Yeah. She had to be taken to a hospital."

Harriett cleared her throat, "What happened?"

Jan's hand was shaking as she placed a cigarette between her lips, lit it, and inhaled deeply.

"Things just got out of hand. Parker told them it would be the last time. He was leaving for college the next week. When his friends found that out, they called all their friends who might want one last piece of ass. I don't remember what time they started."

"Where were her parents?"

"Some social function."

"Do you know what time they left?"

"There was a dinner and then a dance. Maybe five-thirty or six. The first boys showed up as soon as they were out of the driveway."

"In pairs?"

"Yeah."

"Do you know how many boys were there that night?"

Tears filled Jan's eyes and spilled down her cheeks as she drew deeply on her cigarette.

"How many on a football team?"

"Twenty-two, offense and defense."

"Sounds about right."

"Jesus Christ," Harriett breathed.

"It wasn't too bad until the end. Then Parker left to take a piss or something."

"He left you alone with the boys?"

"Yeah. Said he'd be right back and made them put rubbers on before he left. One was on top of me the second Parker left the room, but he stopped before he was finished. When he got up I thought it was over, you know," she said blinking rapidly at Harriett.

"But he locked the door and said something to the other boy and they started laughing. The second one pulled his rubber off, and they both got on the bed. I started to scream for Parker, but he slapped my face and told me not to make a sound. I was really scared."

Jan stopped and wiped her face, closing her eyes, which forced more tears down her face.

"Do you need to take a break?" Harriett asked gently.

When Jan opened her eyes, there was a defiant look in them. "No."

Taking a ragged breath, she continued, "They rolled me on my side with one behind me and one in front. The one behind me pulled my leg up. I didn't know what was happening until I felt the pain. I couldn't scream because the other one put his hand over my mouth. He said, 'Just let it lay in there a minute until she relaxes.' Then he told me to open my mouth and said if I hurt him, he'd kill me. The pain was so bad that I couldn't think. I felt his penis against my lips and opened my mouth; then his head was between my legs. I heard him laugh and say 'go ahead but keep your balls out of my way'."

Slamming her fist on the table, Jan looked at her attorney. "There wasn't a fuckin' thing I could do. They were animals. I couldn't move my arms or legs and had to breathe through my nose when I could. His dick blocked my breathing and made me gag. I thought I was going to die like that when I heard Parker banging at the door, but they wouldn't stop."

"What did Parker do?"

Jan smiled weakly. "He said he'd take care of it," she said quietly.

"How did he take care of it?"

"He took Sharon to the doctor for his daddy's company who admitted her to a private hospital he ran," Jan said with a laugh. "Turned out to be a nursing home. One kid with a ripped up asshole and fifty skeletons on respirators."

"What did her parents say when they found out?"

"Parker called his mother at the club and told her something. Next thing I know, I'm in a nursing home."

"Her parents had to have suspected something."

Jan looked at Harriett for a moment and shrugged.

"Did you ever hear any of the boys' names?"

"The only one I remember was a guy they called Jerry. Hung like a donkey. Ripped me up pretty good that last night. I can't remember the names of any of the others now. Been too long."

"After Parker went to college, all this stopped then?"

"Except for Parker. She still did him until she went to college. Really looked forward to his coming home for the holidays, you know. Want to hear something hilarious?"

"I could use a laugh right now."

"Parker wanted Sharon to visit him while he was in college. He was the president of his fraternity. Makes you wonder what he was planning for initiation, doesn't it?"

"Um, Sharon's not still sleeping with Parker, is she?"

Jan's face changed and Harriett recognized the look immediately. "That's Paige's problem now. Hope she likes group sex."

Harriett wrote on her pad and turned it toward Jan.

"Do these dates mean anything to you?"

Jan took the pad and sniffed as she looked at it. "Should they?"

"I don't know. That's why I asked."

"Well, the first one is Laurel's birthday."

"What about the others?"

Jan studied the list and tapped the pad with her finger.

"I don't know the exact dates, but one of these was about the time Sharon put her dog to sleep. She already had the mutt when she met Frank, but he hated it. And when Laurel was about six months old, she got hurt pretty bad. Might have been the third date."

"How was Laurel hurt?"

"Sharon left the kid alone while she was cleaning up the kitchen. The kid decided to try walking and fell. Hit her head on a table or something, knocked out a tooth, and bled like a stuck pig. Sharon was nearly hysterical, but got the baby to the doctor right away."

"Was there any permanent damage?"

Jan laughed, "Hell, they crammed that tooth back in the socket, and the damn thing stayed there until it fell out on its own a year or so later."

"She was lucky."

"Not after Frank found out. Sharon felt bad because she wasn't careful enough. She was eaten up with guilt, and then that shithead Frank wouldn't even let her hold Laurel or feed her. Accused Sharon of trying to kill the kid. Said she was too stupid to live. Ugly scene."

"What was Sharon's reaction to what Frank did?"

"She went away for a while."

"What did you do, Jan?"

Without looking up, Jan said, "You know what I did, Harriett. Is that what these dates are?"

"Yes."

Jan lit another cigarette and resumed looking at the list. "Now this last date I know. It's recent. That's the night Frank raped me after they had a fight. I don't remember anything special for this other one though."

"You know, Sharon seemed to have you pretty much under control until Laurel was born."

"Things weren't too bad until then. She really got down on herself after the kid was born, and that's about the same time Frank decided to turn into a shithead. Have you told her about me yet?"

"No, but I'll have to soon, so she'll understand what's happening."

Chapter
Twenty-Nine

SEAN LASSITER AND his assistant were already seated at the prosecutor's table when Harriett and Nick entered the courtroom. Harriett didn't acknowledge his presence as she took her seat and opened her briefcase to remove copies of her motion. A few minutes later, the door behind the judge's bench opened and Judge Howard Landers took the two steps up to his chair as Harriett and Nick rose, followed by Lassiter and his assistant.

"Be seated," Landers said, adjusting his glasses. "I understand you have a motion to present to the court, Ms. Markham."

"Yes, your Honor," Harriett said as she stood. "If it pleases the court, I'm filing a motion to amend my client's plea from Not Guilty to Not Guilty by Reason of Mental Disease or Defect."

Moving to the prosecutor's table, she tossed a copy of her motion in front of the prosecutor. He began looking over the paperwork as Harriett presented a copy to Landers.

"You understand, Ms. Markham, that by choosing an affirmative defense you are taking the burden of proof from the prosecution and placing it on your own shoulders?" Landers asked, flipping through the motion.

"I understand my burden as well as the possible consequences of my actions. My client has been apprised of the ramifications of the change in her plea, and you will find an affidavit signed by her to that effect attached to the motion."

"Mr. Lassiter," Landers said. "Do you have an objection to the change in plea?"

Rising, Lassiter said, "I've only now received a copy of the motion, your Honor. May I be granted a few minutes to look over it?"

"Take five," Landers said as he leaned back in his chair and waited.

Landers looked at his watch and said, "Response, Mr. Lassiter."

"The State has no objection to the change in the plea, your Honor."

"I should think not," Landers said. "Motion to change the defendant's plea to not guilty by reason of mental defect is granted. I will order an independent psychiatric evaluation of the defendant," Landers said flipping through a calendar in front of him. "Hoping everything goes smoothly, I'm going to schedule jury selection in *State v. Taggart* for April twenty-ninth and a trial date for May sixth. Last day for motions will be three days prior to the beginning of the trial. Satisfactory?"

"Satisfactory with the defense, your Honor," Harriett said.

"Satisfactory with the prosecution, your Honor," Lassiter said.

As Landers left the bench, Nick said, "You got the best judge for this case."

"Yeah, and now I'm going to need the best jury, too."

WAYNE CALLED HARRIETT'S office early that afternoon. "Well, there's good news and bad news. Want it in any special order?" he asked.

"At this point it probably doesn't matter," she said, leaning back in her chair.

"Okay, I got the names you wanted, but Parker Collins was a popular guy. Practically hung out with every jock in North America."

"You can narrow it down to the football team and eliminate any girls."

"Okay, but they're spread out to hell and back."

"Keep up with your frequent flyer miles, and you can take a vacation when this is over."

"What am I looking for, Harriett?"

"You're looking for a guy who's willing to admit that he had sex with a ten-year- old girl and continued to do so for about two years. Or a guy who will admit to sodomizing a six-year-old and then progressed to more serious sex with her. The only name I could get from Sharon was Jerry somebody."

"Jesus, Harriett! Who's gonna admit to some shit like that? Guy'd have to be a pervert."

"Then find me a pervert with a conscience, Wayne. Two would be even better."

"Two pervs. I'll put that on my wish list. Makes my bad news sound good."

"What's your bad news?"

"Stevenson will arrive there tomorrow."

"Oh, well, it's not a perfect world. I've got Nick looking into it. I have a couple of other things for you to check," Harriett said.

"Hell, I haven't finished this list yet, kiddo."

"I don't think this will take long. First, go back to Sharon's friend and ask her what mental health clinic Sharon went to. If she signed in, I need a copy of it. Second, find out the name of the doctor for Collins Industries fifteen or sixteen years ago and whether he was associated with, or owned, a nursing home. If he's still alive, talk to him to see if he admitted Sharon there as a patient during the summer of 1984 or 1985. If he won't cooperate, let me know, and I'll have his records subpoenaed. Third,...."

"Wait a sec. I ain't a fuckin' stenographer," Wayne growled. "Okay, go ahead."

"Third, find out whom the Taggart's veterinarian is and get the date Sharon had her dog put down. It would have been within the last two years. Fourth, find out who treated Laurel Taggart for an injury she received when she was about six months old. I want the actual date of the injury. Get all that?"

"Yeah. Which of these is the most urgent?"

"The perverts. I don't care or want to know how you get them to talk, Wayne. Promise them anonymity. The statute of limitations on that expired years ago, and my client isn't interested in pressing charges. I have to have them. I need everything as soon as possible. Judge Landers has set jury selection for April twenty-ninth. I want a report every day from now until the trial, Wayne. Fax me any paperwork you get and call with anything else."

"Will do and you try to take it easy, kiddo. Got me?"

"Gotcha," Harriett smiled.

HARRIETT HAD JUST leaned back and begun reading over the papers in front of her when she was interrupted by the intercom. "You have a call on line two, Ms. Markham."

Lifting the receiver while still trying to read, Harriett said, "This is Harriett Markham."

"Having a good day, counselor?" a welcoming voice asked.

"I am now." She smiled as she combed her hair back with her fingers. "How are you, Jess?"

"I'm good. How is Lacey today?"

"Better, but Corey's death really shook her up. They're planning a memorial at school in a couple of days."

"And your case, how's that going?"

"We're still looking for a few witnesses, but hopefully we'll be ready by the time the trial begins."

"You will be. Well, I'll let you get back to work. I...uh...I just wanted to hear your voice," Jess admitted softly.

"Ah, was that you breathing on the phone last night?" Harriett smiled.

"Don't give me any more ideas than I already have," Jess laughed.

Chapter
Thirty

HE SCANNED THE living room slowly. There was no need to hurry. He had watched them both leave for the day less than an hour before. Maybe he would even stay for lunch.

Moving into an office off the living room, he sat in Harriett's chair, closed his eyes, and leaned back. The air outside the gate had smelled better than the air inside, and the only thing separating one from the other had been a chain link fence. He hadn't taken anything with him other than a small suitcase. You don't accumulate much in eleven years when you can't go anywhere. Eleven fucking wasted years! He hadn't planned on being stuck that long, but it had given him plenty of time to plan everything down to the smallest detail, and just thinking about it aroused him. He wondered what she would say when she saw him again. It had been a long time. Casually, he opened the desk drawers and sifted through paperwork.

Half an hour later he went upstairs. Harriett's bedroom looked homey and smelled the way he remembered her smelling. Not looking for anything in particular, he wandered into the adjoining bathroom to search the medicine cabinet. It was remarkably free of prescription medication, containing only a few over the counter cold medicines.

He took his jacket off and tossed it on the bed before he went to the dresser and pulled a drawer out. Sitting down on the bed, he placed the drawer in front of him and examined its contents. The clothing in the drawer felt cool as he touched it, and he closed his eyes to imagine how it would feel if Harriett was wearing it. Holding up a slip, he let it slide over his arm slowly and smiled to himself.

He neatly refolded and stacked the lingerie on the bed as he took each piece out and examined it. As he replaced the last drawer, he opened a jewelry box on top of the dresser and looked at an assortment of necklaces and earrings, leaving them as he found them.

The second bedroom was much more interesting, but then a teenager's room was always a voyage of discovery. Pictures and old corsages hung from a corkboard near the four-poster bed. He didn't know this smell. He picked up a pillow from the bed and pressed it to his face. No, he didn't know this smell, but he would soon enough, and not from a pillow. It was fresh and clean. He was going to like that.

He had seen the girl the day before. Just another anonymous stranger watching from the bleachers. She had been wearing sweats as she stretched the muscles along the backs of her legs while she talked to her team members. Someone must have said something funny because she tossed her hair away from her face and laughed. She was tall and that was good for track.....among other things. A whistle blew and Lacey began stripping out of the sweat suit. The girls ran warm-up laps, and he moved his binoculars to observe the movement of their breasts as they rose and fell in rhythm to the running. It was going to be so easy. He would have liked more of a challenge, but he would have to make the best out of it. In the end, it wouldn't matter anyway. Jesus! She had long legs. The thought of them encircling his body had given him a hard-on. She would be worth the eleven years he had been waiting.

The contents of the teen's drawers revealed someone who hadn't yet achieved the maturity and sexuality of a woman. Some of the lingerie showed that the owner of the clothing was approaching the dividing line between girl and woman. Women knew more and played more games. That was why young girls were so appealing. They were open, submissive, and eager to experience the meaning of womanhood, trying to prove they were worldly-wise even though they didn't have a clue. And he would be willing to teach this one. Soon.

On the dresser was an assortment of pictures. Grandparents. Friends. The girl smiled perpetually in several of the pictures with her family and friends. A small heart shaped frame showed the girl with a boy about her age leaning against a tree. The boy had his arms around her waist, and they looked happy. He could almost feel his arms around her and knew it wouldn't be long before she would enjoy how it felt to be touched by a man instead of a boy. He slipped the frame into his jacket pocket and left the room.

A few days earlier he had watched as Harriett descended the steps of the Austin detention center. He had been tempted to approach her, but the time hadn't been right...yet. Patience. What was that old saying? All good things come to he who waits. It had been this long. A few more days wouldn't matter one way or the other. He couldn't wait to see the look on her face. It had always been the look on their faces. The fear, then the terror. Which would terrorize Harriett more? Her own safety or the safety of her niece? He had been within a few feet of Harriett, and she never knew he was there. He liked his invisibility. She was older but still in good shape. He smiled to himself as he contemplated the decision of which one to visit first. It didn't really matter since they would both be dead afterward anyway.

Chapter
Thirty-One

LATE TUESDAY AFTERNOON Harriett was at her desk, going over a brief she had been neglecting when Phyllis buzzed her over the intercom.

"Yes, Phyllis," Harriett answered.

"Ms. Dunne is here to see you, Ms. Markham," Phyllis announced.

"Send her in."

Alex smiled when she entered Harriett's office.

"What are you doing here, Alex?" Harriett asked.

"We hadn't heard from you in a while, and I thought I'd come down to see how the case was going," Alex said as she approached the desk.

"It's out of Winston and Dunne's hands at this point. Would you like some coffee?"

"No, thanks. I thought I might persuade you to have dinner with me."

"I can't, Alex."

Alex walked behind Harriett's desk and kissed her on the cheek.

"Having problems with the case?"

"You know how the insanity defense is. It's a crap shoot at best."

"You can't spend all of your time working on the case, or it'll drive you crazy," Alex said with a smile.

Harriett looked at Alex and then lowered her head.

"I was going to call you tomorrow, Alex," she said, ignoring the hand that was traveling across her tense shoulders.

"Then I've saved you the cost of a phone call."

Coughing slightly, Harriett said, "I need some information. For the case."

"You know I'll help if I can."

"I need to know the exact date you slept with Sharon Taggart," she said without looking at Alex.

"What?" Alex laughed. "Where did you get that?"

"Sharon said....well, I won't tell you exactly what she said, but she said you and she had been lovers."

"She's lying, Harriett. I know her, but there was never anything between Sharon Taggart and me."

"I don't care whether it was serious or casual sex, Alex," Harriett said forcefully. "But I need to know the damn date."

"You must believe her then."

"Sharon was quite detailed about it, including a reference to your labrys tattoo. If memory serves me right, there aren't many ways just anyone could see that. I might have to call you as a witness."

"There isn't anything I could offer in the way of testimony that would help your case," Alex said, stepping away.

"State of mind would be very helpful. I have to know whether or not you slept with the woman, Alex. And I don't really give a damn about your motives."

"Just preparing the best defense for your client?" Alex asked with a hint of sarcasm in her voice.

"That's right."

"It was just one of those things." Alex shrugged as she moved away from Harriett and sat down. "I never intended for it to happen."

Harriett smiled, "Talk about deja vu."

"It wasn't the same thing, damn it."

"Was it your idea?"

"Of course not. She approached me."

"How was she?"

"You don't need to know that," Alex snapped.

"Was her behavior unusual?"

"She was extremely aggressive."

"Was that the only time?"

"No. The last time we were together I told her it was a mistake. It shouldn't have happened. It couldn't happen again. Ever."

"How did she react to that?"

"She didn't. She just smiled and got dressed and left without saying another word."

Harriett sat down at her desk and flipped her calendar back.

"And when did you break off your liaison with her?"

"After Thanksgiving last year. The affair started two or three months after Gwen and I called it quits, and as much as I hate to admit it, I was flattered by the attentions of an attractive young woman. I think the last time we were together was the Friday or Saturday after Thanksgiving, but I honestly don't remember."

Harriett looked at the calendar and then picked up her legal pad, glancing through her notes.

"Saturday, December first," she said. "Number three died that night."

"What the hell are you saying?" Alex demanded. "That the woman killed someone because I had sex with her?"

"No. Because you rejected her. It was the only date I couldn't tie to some event."

"It didn't mean anything, Harriett," Alex said quietly.

"Will you testify about what you just told me, or will I have to subpoena you?" Harriett asked.

"You won't need to do that," Alex said with a frown.

"I probably shouldn't be telling you this, Alex, but some very unsavory testimony is going to come out during this trial. A lot of people are going to be hurt."

There was a hint of irony in Alex's voice as she said, "I knew you were a great attorney, Harriett. But I'm beginning to wish I'd never referred this case to you."

"So am I. I've already found out more than I ever wanted to know."

IT WAS NEARLY dark when Harriett pulled her glasses off and rubbed her eyes. Standing up, she stretched the kinks out of her back. I could really use a good massage, she thought as she picked up a stack of folders and slipped them into her briefcase. The Taggart case was consuming almost all of her time, and Nick had to pick up most of her overflow. Nothing had ever disrupted her from her usual routine so much, and she wished she had never taken the case. Her thoughts were disrupted by the sound of loud voices moving down the hallway toward her office. She was halfway around her desk when her office door burst open and she saw Parker Collins walking toward her, followed by an obviously distraught Phyllis.

"Can I help you, Senator?" she asked as calmly as possible, wondering if Nick was still in his office.

"What the fuck do you think you're doing?" Collins said loudly.

"If I knew what you were talking about I could answer your question, but..." she began.

"I received a phone call from an old friend who said he had been interviewed by your investigator."

"That's probably correct. Mr. Graham is doing some background research for Sharon's case."

Phyllis was hovering near the office door uncertain what she should do, although bringing coffee seemed out of the question considering the circumstances. Looking around Collins, Harriett cast a reassuring smile at her secretary.

"You can return to your desk, Phyllis. Thank you," she said. "I need to speak with Senator Collins privately. Please tell Mr. Lazslo that I need to see him before he leaves, though."

From the look on Phyllis's face Harriett knew that Nick was already gone, but hoped the idea that someone else might be there would prevent Collins from doing anything rash. Judging from the fire in Collins's eyes, she hoped she was right.

"Please have a seat, Senator," she offered.

Collins glared at her and sat down, crossing his legs as they waited for Phyllis to leave and close the office door behind her. As soon as the door clicked shut, he was on his feet again with both hands pressed flat on Harriett's desk.

"Background my ass," he seethed. "I don't know what the hell my sister has told you, but it does not involve my friends."

"Actually, Senator," Harriett said as she sat behind her desk again, "it does. Surely, you understand that I have to verify everything my client tells me no matter where it leads. She's made some fairly serious accusations, some of which, if true, might exonerate her, which is what you hired me to do."

"I didn't hire you to drag my name through the mud or slander the reputations of my friends."

"What exactly did your friend say when he called you?"

"He said your investigator told him he was investigating allegations of child abuse involving Sharon," Collins seethed through clenched teeth.

"Well, Mr. Graham is nothing if not blunt and to the point," Harriett said. "Sharon alleges that you and your friends used her for sex for several years. Rather I should say, Sharon's imaginary playmate alleges that."

"That's bullshit! I never had sex with my own sister. A person would have to be crazy to insinuate something like that!" Collins ranted.

"Exactly my point," Harriett smiled. "If Mr. Graham cannot find anyone to substantiate her claim then it will further bolster our plea of insanity."

Collins's face brightened somewhat as it began to return to its normal color. "I see. And surely you can see how upsetting these charges would be to my friends."

"Yes, I can see that. However, if what we suspect is true, and you, in fact, did molest your own sister and allowed your friends to do the same, I can also successfully use that to prove our plea. Either way, it's a win-win situation for Sharon. I should tell you, however, that I believe my client. She has been extremely graphic about what you did to her, and no one's imagination is that good."

Leaning back over the desk, Collins brought his face as close to Harriett's as possible. "You will *not* use this defense on my sister's behalf. Do you understand me, Ms Markham?"

Standing quickly, she faced the man who disgusted her. "I *will* use this defense, and I *will* drag out every perverted thing you ever did to Sharon. You're the reason she did what she did. Innocent people died because of it. She might go to prison, but everyone will know what you and the others did. Now get out of my office before I call the police and have you removed."

A wisp of a smile crossed Collins's lips as he straightened his tie and readjusted his jacket. "You will regret it if you continue, Ms. Markham," he said calmly. "I will see to it personally. I can and will destroy you, so watch your back." Collins's eyes narrowed slightly as he turned to leave. Opening the office door, he smiled again. "And please give my regards to your lovely niece. Lacey, isn't it?"

Harriett's hands were shaking as she sat back down and leaned her head against the back of her chair. She had never mentioned Lacey to anyone associated with the Taggart case except Sharon and then only in passing and certainly not by name. She wasn't sure what she should do. Collins had threatened her personally, but the threat to Lacey was a veiled one at best. With no other witnesses to their conversation it would only be her word against his if she involved the police.

"My God! Are you all right, Ms. Markham?" Phyllis asked as she re-entered Harriett's office. "I've never seen anything like that."

"I'm fine, Phyllis. Thank you. I think we should call it a day, don't you?"

Chapter
Thirty-Two

HARRIETT WAS SOUND asleep when she was awakened by someone shaking her shoulder.

"Get up, Aunt Harriett," Lacey prodded.

Harriett peeked over the top of the bedcovers and could barely make out Lacey's face in the semi-darkness of her bedroom.

"What's wrong?" she croaked.

"Nothing. You promised you'd go jogging with me this morning. Remember?"

"Was I drunk when I promised that?" she asked as she sat up in bed. "What time is it?"

"Almost six. So get up and get dressed," Lacey answered as she went through the bedroom door.

She fell back onto her pillow and sighed. Next time she would ask more questions, especially those related to time.

When Harriett came down the stairs, Lacey was jogging in place in the entryway. She smiled when she saw Harriett's face.

"Don't worry, Aunt Harriett. We can start off at a slower pace until you wake up."

"Thanks."

Lacey opened the front door. Locking the door behind her, Harriett went down the steps.

"It's cold," she said.

"You'll warm up once we get going. Come on."

Following her athletic niece, Harriett remembered how much she hated exercise in any form. She had never participated in sports in school and joined choir to avoid physical education classes.

Lacey jogged slowly, allowing her aunt to keep up with her. Periodically, the girl would stop and run a series of wind sprints. Half an hour later, they were halfway down a jogging path in a wooded area about a mile from the townhouse. Lacey stopped and looked at Harriett.

"Let's take a break," Lacey said.

"Excellent idea," Harriett huffed, resting her hands on her knees. "Is this your idea of a good time?"

"It's good for your heart and lungs."

"Only if your lungs don't explode, and your heart doesn't stop beating. Can we sit down for a few minutes?"

"Uh-uh. You don't want your muscles to get cold. It's better to keep moving, at least a little."

Harriett made a half-hearted attempt at keeping her muscles warm, but really wanted a cup of hot coffee and a doughnut.

"You like Devon, don't you, Aunt Harriett?" Lacey asked.

"He seems to be a nice enough boy. Why?"

"Just wondering," Lacey shrugged.

Harriett stopped trying to move and looked at her slender, attractive niece.

"Are you having a problem with Devon?" she asked.

Lacey smiled slightly, "It's not really a problem, but we've been going out a long time."

"And Devon would like a little more out of your relationship?"

"Something like that."

"Haven't we already had the infamous birds and bees talk?"

"You've always been very open with me about stuff like that, but it's one thing to talk about it abstractly and another to deal with it in reality."

"I don't care if every muscle in my body freezes up, I have to sit down for this discussion, Lacey."

They found a park bench nearby and Harriett had never been so grateful to sit in her life. Taking a deep breath, she asked, "Is Devon pressuring you to sleep with him?"

Lacey laughed lightly. "I don't think sleep is what he has in mnd."

Smiling despite herself, Harriett said, "I keep forgetting that kids today don't speak in euphemisms anymore."

"How old were you when you made love the first time?" Lacey asked

"That's a little personal, sweetheart," Harriett answered, dodging the question. She had tried to be as open with Lacey as possible, but had never brought her personal life into their discussions. "Do you mean had sex or made love? They aren't the same thing, you know."

"Have you ever had sex with a guy?"

"Once."

"What happened?"

Clearing her throat slightly, Harriett said, "I discovered that being with a man wasn't what I wanted."

"Was that when you decided that you liked being with a woman more?"

"I didn't really decide that, honey. I think I always knew. It just took me a while to accept it. I finally met someone I cared about and haven't questioned my lifestyle since."

"Did you feel guilty about it?"

Harriett smiled. "For a while I imagined that everyone who looked at me knew about it. And of course, I worried that Mom and Dad would find out. But now I realize that relationship was mostly experimentation on my part. I think, now, that we just used each other."

"Was it different when you met Alex?"

"Yes," Harriett smiled.

"You never talk about her anymore."

Harriett took a deep breath and looked at the early morning rays of sunlight filtering through the trees.

"That was a long time ago, Lacey. It wasn't meant to be. I'm surprised you still remember Alex. You were pretty young."

"Did you love her, Aunt Harriett?"

"Of course, I did, sweetheart. Very much. But people change and life goes on."

"Was that why we moved to Austin? Because of Alex?"

"No, but Alex and I both knew it was the right thing to do."

"I wish you'd find someone. I don't like the idea of you being lonely."

"I'm forty-five, Lacey. The pool of nice, eligible women in my age range is somewhat limited."

Smiling mischievously, Lacey said, "What about Ms. Raines? You like her well enough to see her more than once. Not to mention she's a total babe."

"I like Jess very much," Harriett smiled, "but it's a little early in our relationship to say more than that."

"Well, you've gone out with other women, but you've never brought any of them home before. I know you've always wanted to protect me, Aunt Harriett, but I'm really not as naive as you think I am."

"I've never wanted my lifestyle to cause you a problem, sweetheart."

"What you do with your personal life isn't any of my business. You've always done what's most important to me. You've cared for me and loved me more than most of my friends' parents. And I love you very much, Aunt Harriett."

"I love you, too, Lacey," Harriett said as she hugged her niece.

"All I want is for you to be happy," Lacey smiled. "And according to my health teacher you're at your sexual peak."

"Jesus, Lacey! Is that what my tuition money is paying them to teach you?" Harriett laughed.

Lacey stood up and stretched her legs on the bench before jogging in place again.

"Ready to head for the house?" she said.

Harriett got up and stretched a little.

"I can't tell you what to do about Devon, sweetheart. Everyone has to do what he or she thinks is right. Just think about it and then be careful."

By the time Harriett and Lacey resumed jogging along the path that led out of the park, other early morning joggers were on the path.

"I didn't think there would be anyone as dumb as we are out here," Harriett said.

"There are always a lot of people here. That's why I come here. It's not safe to be around here alone."

Actually, Harriett's body was beginning to get accustomed to the moderate pace they were jogging, but she knew it wasn't an activity she would enjoy on a regular basis. A number of joggers passed them going the opposite direction. Some of them seemed to recognize Lacey and waved or nodded to her. Occasionally an overly energetic runner would run past them wishing to cover the ground more quickly. The exit from the park was within her sight when a runner moved past her. She barely noticed him until he was already past her. The hood of his sweatshirt hid his face.

Lacey had moved well ahead of Harriett and the runner fell in between them and stayed there as they neared the road which encircled the park. Although it was away from town, cars looking for a less congested route through Austin had begun traveling the road. Harriett herself had cut through the park a number of times in her truck. The runner between Harriett and Lacey increased his pace enough to get closer to Lacey. With the road only a few yards away, the runner glanced over his shoulder at Harriett and smiled. It was a man wearing sunglasses. Other than that, she couldn't tell much about him except that he seemed to be an average height and weight. He slowed as Lacey slowed, remaining slightly behind her. Harriett began to get an uneasy feeling about the man and increased her own pace to get closer to Lacey.

Lacey came out of the trees less than ten yards from the roadway and prepared to stop. Before she could stop completely, the man behind her reached out and pushed her toward the road. Lacey was startled by the push and planted her feet to stop her forward momentum. Her running shoes slid on the gravel that lined the road, and she looked up to see a car coming toward her. The man reached out and grabbed her, pulling her away from the road.

"Lac-e-y!" Harriett screamed.

The man looked back toward Harriett and smiled again. Turning his head, he glanced quickly up and down the road. He said something to Lacey and then darted across the road and disappeared as Harriett reached her niece.

"What the hell was that?" Harriett asked, trying to catch her breath. "Are you all right?"

Lacey nodded and looked at her. "He shoved me."

"What did he say to you?"

"That he was sorry. Then he told me I should learn to watch my step and so should Harriett. How did he know your name, Aunt Harriett?"

The memory of Parker Collins leaning over her desk flew through

Harriett's mind creating an involuntary shiver along her spine. "I don't know, but let's get out of here, and I don't want you jogging anymore for a while. And no arguments. You might be eighteen, but I'm still your guardian."

Chapter
Thirty-Three

AN UNSEASONABLY COLD wind escorted Wayne through the front entrance of Larabee Premier Motors in Scottsdale, Arizona. His flight to Phoenix had been less than pleasant, as the plane had encountered turbulent weather somewhere over New Mexico. On more than one occasion, sudden air pockets had left his stomach several hundred feet higher than his body, and he had been thankful when they had finally landed. At least he could stop at a bar in the airport and not worry about hitting his mouth.

Now fortified by his bourbon on the rocks, Wayne ambled toward a reception island located near the rear of the showroom floor. He stopped on his way to the desk to admire a white Mercedes Sportster with a red leather interior. Tearing himself away from the pricey vehicle, he grinned at the well-dressed woman seated behind the reception desk.

"How may I help you today, sir?" she smiled pleasantly.

"Is Mr. Larabee in?" Wayne asked.

"I'm sure he is." Pressing a button on the intercom, the woman spoke to whoever picked up on the other end. Replacing the receiver on its holder, she smiled up at Wayne. "Mr. Larabee is in the service area. If you would like to take a seat, he'll be with you in just a few minutes."

"Thanks," Wayne smiled. "I'll just look around and hope my numbers come in on the lottery."

Tapping a folder against his thigh, Wayne meandered through the showroom admiring the vehicles on display. He's heard that Mercedes were good cars, but they would never be in his price range. Only people like Alexis Dunne could afford such a ride and feel comfortable driving one.

"Excuse me," a low voice said.

Wayne turned to look into the round face of a clean-cut man with obviously styled hair. It was cut to project the image he needed to convince customers that he was hip, but could still be trusted. He wore black dress pants and a matching vest over a dazzling white dress shirt, complete with cufflinks.

Extending his hand, the man introduced himself. "I'm Thad Larabee. Loretta said you were looking for me. What can I show you today?"

"You own this dealership?"

"Yes. At least part of it. The other part belongs to the bank." Larabee laughed easily.

"My name is Wayne Graham, Mr. Larabee. I'm an investigator for an attorney in Austin, Texas. I need to ask you a few questions about a case she is working on."

"I'm not aware of any litigation involving either me or my company." The hint of a frown passed over Larabee's face.

Looking around the showroom, Wayne leaned toward Larabee slightly. "The case is a personal one and kind of sensitive. I think you'd be more comfortable if we continued this conversation in your office," Wayne said pointedly.

"Of course," Larabee nodded. Pausing at the receptionist's desk and instructing her to hold all of his calls, Larabee led Wayne down a long paneled hallway and into a glass enclosed office. Wayne dropped his folder on Larabee's desk as he pulled an upholstered chair closer and waited for Larabee to assume his position behind the desk. As he sat, Wayne noticed a family picture sitting on the front corner of Larabee's desk. Larabee was dressed casually and smiling, as was the woman Wayne assumed was his wife. They were propped up on their elbows in front of a stone fireplace, two young children, a boy and a girl, beamed into the camera as they nestled against their parents.

"This your family?" Wayne smiled.

"Yes," Larabee answered as he took the picture from Wayne, smiling affectionately at it before replacing it on his desk. "Now what is this visit about, Mr. Graham?"

"How old are your kids?"

"Jacob is ten and Heather is six, but I'm sure you didn't come here to inquire about my family."

Opening the folder now on his lap Wayne said, "No, I didn't. Do you know a woman named Sharon Taggart?"

Larabee seemed to think for a few minutes, mentally searching for a recollection of the name, before shaking his head. "No, I don't. Sorry."

"You went to high school in Dallas, didn't you?"

"Well, actually it was in Highland Park, just north of the downtown area."

"While you were in high school, did you know a Parker Collins?"

"Yeah." Larabee seemed to brighten at the memory. "He and I were on the school football team together for a couple of years."

"Have you been in contact with him recently?"

"I left the Dallas area right after I graduated and haven't been back. My parents moved to Arizona, and I followed them to attend college. I haven't really seen anyone from back then in fifteen or twenty years."

"Were you ever at the Collinses' house, you know, for parties or anything like that?"

Larabee shifted in his chair and began to look slightly

uncomfortable. "I might have been a couple of times. It was a long time ago."

"Yes, it was. Mr. Collins is a State Senator from the Dallas area now."

"I figured Parker would end up doing something like that. He was a very popular guy when I knew him."

"Yeah, I heard that everyone, especially the boys, enjoyed being invited to his home when his parents were away."

Spreading his hands in a sign of resignation, Larabee said, "You know how teenage boys are. If we had the chance to sneak a few alcoholic drinks we did."

"That's true," Wayne chuckled. "Not to mention getting a little pussy every now and then, too, right?"

Larabee eyed Wayne closely and leaned forward in his chair. "What is this really about, Mr. Graham? If you have a question in mind, why don't you just spit it out, and stop beating that poor bush to death?"

"Can I assume that you did know Sharon Taggart then?"

"I knew Sharon *Collins*, Parker's sister. Apparently she's gotten married since then."

"Mrs. Taggart has been arrested for homicide. She claims she was sexually molested by her brother and his friends when she was a small child. Do you know anything about that, Mr. Larabee?"

Larabee pulled open the bottom drawer of his desk and lifted out a bottle of Crown Royale and two glasses. As he spun the top from the bottle he glanced up at Wayne, "Would you care to join me?"

As Wayne took a swallow of his drink, enjoying the feel of it coating his throat, Larabee leaned back holding his own glass. "I wondered if that would ever surface."

"Want to tell me about it?"

For the next hour, Thad Larabee recounted what he knew about what had gone on inside the Collinses' home almost twenty years earlier. To Wayne, the man seemed relieved to finally tell the story. Despite that, Wayne couldn't feel sorry for Larabee. What he told Wayne involved more than mere youthful indiscretion, and even though Larabee wouldn't face prosecution for what he did, the incident had obviously troubled him. As he told his story, he glanced repeatedly at the picture of his own daughter.

Wayne left Larabee Premier Motors with the names of other male classmates. As he drove back to the Phoenix Airport, he called Harriett on his cell phone to let her know she had at least one pervert who corroborated her client's story. If he was lucky, he could be in Tampa, Florida late that evening in search of pervert number two.

Chapter
Thirty-Four

"I DON'T BELIEVE I let you talk me into this," Harriett said as Nick held the door into the lecture hall open for her.

"It's because you're a sucker for a sob story," Nick said with a smile. "And you owe me big time for agreeing to help with the jury selection."

"I know, but I have a million things to do. Opening arguments are in four days."

"No one knows that better than I do, Harriett. That's why I arranged for you to do this before the case goes to court. You need a break from the case right now."

"Do they know I can't answer any questions about it?"

"Yes. These aren't first year law students."

As Harriett followed Nick down an aisle toward the podium at the front of the room, she glanced around. The room resembled every law classroom she had ever been in, with elevated seats that gave it the feel of a small auditorium. The front of the room was arranged in the same manner as a miniature courtroom. Students presenting a case could be easily observed by other students in the audience. She had almost forgotten about giving the presentation that day and was dressed in slacks and a tweed jacket over a gray turtleneck sweater. When Nick called to see if she was ready, it had taken her a few minutes to remember where she had put her notes. She opened her briefcase and scanned the few pages she had hastily thrown together, hoping it would be enough to fill the hour and a half Nick had allotted her. As she slipped her glasses on, Nick bent down next to her.

"I'll make a brief introduction, and then they're all yours," he said.

"Are you staying or throwing me to the wolves?" she asked with a smile.

"I'll be around. Try to leave about thirty minutes for a question and answer session at the end."

"No problem."

The low buzzing of voices stopped when Nick stepped up to the microphone.

"Ladies and gentlemen," he said. "Today, I have invited a respected member of the bar whose specialty is criminal law, and who, incidentally, happens to be my law partner, to speak to you. Harriett Markham has been practicing criminal law for twenty years and has an impressive record of victories on behalf of her clients. After Ms. Markham completes her remarks to you, she has agreed to address any questions you may have. Ms. Markham," Nick said, looking back at Harriett.

Harriett walked to the podium and placed her notes on it. She had never been comfortable using notes for anything other than preparation, believing that juries instinctively didn't trust an attorney who didn't know his or her case well enough to present without the crutch notes provided. Stepping to one side of the podium, she looked at the students and smiled slightly.

"I wish Mr. Lazslo hadn't put in the part about practicing law for twenty years. It makes me feel over the hill," she said to scattered laughter.

"How many of you are considering specializing in criminal law?" she asked. Surveying the room, she saw half the students raise their hands.

"And of those who plan to practice in that area, how many would rather put the bad guys away?"

Most of the same hands went up.

"I hope you realize how difficult it is to do that. As prosecutors, you must prove your cases to a jury beyond a reasonable doubt. I, on the other hand, get to spend my time discrediting your witnesses and excluding your evidence. I only have to deal with one or two clients at a time," she said, sliding her hands into the pockets of her slacks. "You, however, may be juggling dozens of cases in various stages of preparation at any given time. If I'm good at my job, my clients will be paying me substantially more than you'll be earning. Anyone want to change their minds about putting the bad guys away?"

There was a low buzz of conversation among the students as they considered what she had said.

"Conversely, if you lose a case you are defending your client may hate you and threaten you or sue you because he or she thinks you didn't represent him or her very well. Every defense attorney hopes to be able to defend in a case in which lives are at stake and to be able to carry that case to a successful conclusion on behalf of his or her client. I'm sure you already know that ninety-five percent of all criminal defendants are guilty. However, they must be defended as zealously as the innocent five percent. Any attorney unwilling to put forth his or her best effort only for the innocent should consider another profession."

Nearly an hour later, Harriett reached the end of her prepared remarks.

"To be a successful attorney does not mean making thousands of dollars on every case, although no one objects to making money. However, the happiest and most content attorneys are those who truly love the law and take seriously their oath to assist their clients to the fullest capacity within the confines of those laws and the canons of legal ethics. I would be glad to answer any questions you might have at this point, and I will attempt to answer them, even if they are beyond the scope of my remarks," Harriett concluded.

Picking up a glass of water from the podium, she took a drink as she waited for the first question. As she set the glass down, she pointed to a young woman in the fourth row.

"Do you believe that women in legal practice are competitive with their male counterparts, or are there the same limitations women have in other professions?"

"I have found that anyone, male or female, who puts forth his or her best effort practicing the law can be successful. At one time, I was a senior associate with a large, well-known firm and didn't experience any difficulties because of my gender. Unfortunately, there are women in every profession who might use the gender issue as an excuse for their failure to move up. Just work incredibly hard when you start, never believe that you are God's gift to the legal profession, never stop learning, and everything will fall into place."

A young man in the front raised his hand and stood, "Of the ninety-five percent you know are guilty, have you ever felt you personally let any of them down?"

"I believe I have represented every client as well as I could have. Have I ever let any of them down personally? I don't believe so. There have been clients I wasn't crazy about representing, of course. But at that point you have to overlook the person and remain faithful to the law and the spirit of the law."

"Are there any criminal defendants you would not take as a client?"

"I like to think not."

"Are you less zealous about representing clients who have been court appointed than the ones who pay your full fee?"

"This is certainly a money hungry little group you have here, Mr. Lazslo," Harriett said over her shoulder. "I am fortunate enough at this point in my career for money not to be the determining factor in client selection. Hypothetically, those clients who come to you through court appointments are among the neediest clients. And incidentally, a rather large percentage of those clients fall within the five percent I mentioned earlier."

"How do you handle getting a client off when you know he's guilty?" a young woman asked.

"That's a difficult question to answer. However, if an attorney has performed his or her duties with a clear conscience, then he or she will have to learn to take it in stride. It certainly happens. Get over it and move on."

A man in his mid thirties stood up near the middle of the

auditorium. "Have you gotten over the Wilkes case yet?" he asked.

For a moment, Harriett didn't believe her ears. She couldn't believe that any of the students would have known about the Wilkes case. Quickly, she glanced back at Nick, who got up and joined her at the podium.

"Is he one of your students?" she asked softly as Nick reached her.

"No. I'll take care of it," Nick said, leaving her side.

Turning back toward the man, Harriett cleared her throat.

"Ladies and gentlemen, the case this gentlemen is referring to was resolved before it came to trial," Harriett explained. "Occasionally, you may have cases that, for one reason or another, are settled prior to the adversarial process."

Students in the auditorium watched as Nick approached the man and spoke to him briefly. The man smiled as he spoke to Nick and finally shrugged. As he left the room, he turned his head toward Harriett and grinned as he slipped on a pair of sunglasses that looked suspiciously like the ones the mysterious jogger had been wearing.

"That concludes today's presentation," Nick said as he rejoined Harriett at the podium. "Briefs for your assigned cases are due at our next meeting. Be prepared to argue both sides."

Nick stood with Harriett as the students began filing out.

"I'd be willing to bet serious money that son of a bitch Collins was behind that," Harriett said.

"He said he was paid by someone to show up here today, but didn't know who. Think he's responsible for the jogging incident, too?"

"I don't know. I'll ask Wayne to find someone to keep an eye on Collins. He might just be trying to rattle me."

"Is he succeeding?"

Harriett looked at Nick. "Yes."

"I THINK YOU should make this section on your burden stronger," Nick suggested as he read Harriett's draft of her opening remarks to the jury that afternoon. "Emphasize that you know the burden of proof is yours and that you welcome it."

"Okay, how about this...," Harriett said as the intercom buzzed.

"Yes, Phyllis," she answered as she jotted notes in the margins of her statement.

"Ms. Raines from the Attorney General's Office is here to see you," Phyllis said.

"I called a friend about Collins," Harriett said, pressing the intercom button. "Send her in please, Phyllis."

Harriett moved around her desk and greeted Jess at the door to her office. Turning toward Nick, she said, "This is my law partner, Nick Lazslo. Jess is an investigator for the Attorney General."

Jess approached Nick as he rose and extended her hand. As they shook hands, Harriett noticed a pistol in a shoulder holster under Jess's jacket.

"Please have a seat," Harriett said.

Unsure what Harriett's co-workers knew about her personal life, Jess said, "I understand you have a problem that may or may not involve my department at the AG's office."

"Harriett is representing a client who is accused of murder," Nick explained.

"Actually multiple murders," Harriett added.

"And that would be Sharon Collins Taggart?" Jess asked, looking at papers in her portfolio.

"Yes," Harriett answered.

"You had the case transferred here from Dallas County, and your client is pleading insanity. Correct?"

"Yes," Harriett nodded. "Recently, my client's brother threatened me and my family. Since then two incidents have occurred, one of which directly involved my niece and caused me some concern for her safety."

"The brother originally hired Harriett to defend her client and now isn't very happy about the way her investigation is going," Nick added.

"Sounds a little like you're biting the hand that feeds you," Jess frowned.

"I'll do whatever is in the best interest of my client," Harriett snapped defensively.

"I'm not making a judgment," Jess smiled. "Just want to make sure I get all the facts straight. Did you know the individual you had contact with?"

"No. He claims he was hired anonymously to carry out the stunt at the law school, and although I believe he was the same man involved in an attack on my niece, I can't prove it. I need to know what my options are, other than filing a restraining order. My client's brother is a member of the state legislature, and I can't allow this threat to distract me from the case."

"I certainly understand your concern," Jess said as she ran her fingers through her short amber hair. She knew that Harriett wouldn't breach her client's confidentiality. "But there really isn't anything the Attorney General's office or the police department, for that matter, can do until a criminal offense actually occurs."

"Which means what?" Harriett asked as she leaned forward on her desk. "There's not a damn thing I can do to protect either myself or my niece?"

Jess answered, "I didn't say that. Give me a day or two to look into it. It's really outside the jurisdiction of my section, but I'll check around to see what, if anything, can be done. In the meantime, feel free to call me any time. I'm used to phone calls in the middle of the night," she said, smiling at Harriett.

"And that's it?" Nick asked.

"Pretty much," Jess shrugged as she stood up. "I'll do what I can, but I can't promise anything."

"We'd appreciate anything you could do," Nick said, shaking Jess's hand again.

Turning to Harriett, she said, "Would it be possible for us to speak alone for a moment?"

As Jess looked at her, Harriett saw a penetrating intensity in her hazel-green eyes that she hadn't seen before. Jess waited for the door to the office to close before she spoke again. "Why didn't you call me about this before now?"

Leaning against her desk, Harriett nodded. "I can't compromise my client's confidentiality because of an unsubstantiated threat against me."

"I know you can't tell me anything about the case, but I wish you had told me about the threat sooner, Harriett," Jess said pointedly. "I could have found someone to watch you both."

"Well, I've told you now," Harriett retorted as tears began forming in her eyes.

Stepping closer, Jess reached out and drew Harriett to her.

"I can't let anything happen to Lacey, Jess. I wouldn't be able to stand it," Harriett said weakly, tightening her grip around Jess.

Chapter
Thirty-Five

"LADIES AND GENTLEMEN, Sharon Taggart is charged with causing the deaths of four human beings and serious bodily injury to three others," Sean Lassiter began his opening statement. "They had no relationship to her whatsoever. They were simply random anonymous targets who happened to wander into her path. There is no dispute about what Sharon Taggart did. She took a high-powered rifle, lay in wait, and fired it at oncoming vehicles on a busy Dallas freeway not once, not twice, but on seven separate occasions during a two-year period. In easily understood terms, the law states that an action is murder in the first degree if there is either the intent to cause serious bodily injury or the act that caused the death of an individual was clearly dangerous to human life. No one can argue that the defendant's actions meet both these criteria. Sharon Taggart is responsible for the deaths of four innocent people.

"I know what you're thinking, ladies and gentlemen. Anyone who would do such a thing must be crazy. They must surely be insane. And we would all like to believe that because it is incomprehensible to us that any normal person would do what Sharon Taggart, in fact, did. However, in order for Sharon Taggart to prove she is innocent because she is insane, she cannot rely on the medical definition of insanity. Medically, she may very well be insane. That, however, does not make her legally insane, and therefore, not responsible for her actions. To be insane in the eyes of the law, Ms. Markham must prove by the weight of the evidence presented that her client did not know the difference between right and wrong at the time she committed the crimes. It's really a very simple test. Either she knows she committed a wrongful, therefore, illegal act or she doesn't.

"Because the burden of proof in this case falls on the shoulders of the defense, I don't have to do a thing. I can sit over there in that chair and listen to the testimony the same way you will and still draw my salary. However, I represent the interests of the people of the State of Texas, and I must challenge the evidence the defense will present. I plan to do that vigorously so that Sharon Taggart will not be able to look at any of you through the scope of a high-powered rifle and snuff out your life or anyone else's as though it wouldn't matter to anyone.

"The State will call witnesses to challenge the claim of mental disease or defect, as will the defense. However, I believe the State's witnesses will convince you that Mrs. Taggart is, in fact, not insane. She is simply guilty. She has confessed that she committed the offenses she is charged with, and the State will show that she had the ability to form the requisite intent to commit those crimes. By claiming that she was insane at the time, she is hoping that you will say her actions were okay. That the lives of her victims didn't matter."

Smiling at the jurors, Lassiter shook his head slightly. "You know, the interesting thing about a plea of not guilty by reason of mental defect is that if you, the jury, reject that plea, if Ms. Markham fails to satisfy her burden, it means that Sharon Taggart is guilty of the crimes she stands accused of and will be punished accordingly. If, however, you believe Ms. Markham's rendition of the facts, Sharon Taggart will still be punished by being incarcerated in a mental facility for an indeterminate length of time. Either way, Sharon Taggart will be punished. Which institution Sharon Taggart will be sent to depends on your decision. Thank you."

Taking a deep breath, and smiling briefly at Sharon, Harriett rose from her chair and approached the jury box, pulling her glasses off as she walked toward them.

"Ladies and gentlemen, my name is Harriett Markham, and I represent the defendant in this case, Sharon Collins Taggart," Harriett began, indicating who Sharon was. Following Harriett's instructions, Sharon looked at the jury with little emotion on her face.

"The decision before you during these proceedings will be to determine whether Sharon Collins Taggart is not guilty of the crimes she's charged with committing due to a mental disease or defect. In essence, your job will be to decide whether Sharon meets the requirements put forth by the State of Texas for insanity or not. The decision will be yours alone. My job is to prove to you, beyond a reasonable doubt, that my client is not responsible for her crimes because she has a mental defect or disease that rendered her incapable of knowing the difference between right and wrong, and therefore, incapable of understanding the nature or consequences of her actions. In order for my client to prevail, you must believe there is more evidence supporting her claim of insanity than there is to disprove it.

"Mr. Lassiter, who represents the interests of the State of Texas, has been relieved of his burden, and his job is to question the evidence I present for your consideration. The defense will prove that Sharon Taggart suffers from a mental defect severe enough to prevent her from forming the requisite intent for the crimes she is accused of committing, thereby make her not legally responsible for her actions. I will present expert witnesses who will testify to Mrs. Taggart's mental condition. The State will also call expert witnesses to the stand who will deny that my client, in fact, has any such mental defect. Unfortunately, when we deal with experts in any field, there will be differing opinions. In part, this is because we are only dealing with opinions about an intangible when we deal with matters of the mind. We can't touch, feel, smell, or taste mental illness. And yet we have all seen people who have behaved in a manner that seemed insane to us. A person who deliberately walks into the path of an on-coming vehicle might seem to be performing an insane action until we examine the reason he took that action. Perhaps he was depressed. Perhaps he was drunk. Perhaps he was blind or got something in his eye. Perhaps he thought he could get across the road before the truck reached him because of a depth perception problem. Once he is dead, medical tests would tell us, without question, whether he was drunk or blind. But how would we know if he was depressed, had a cinder in his eye, or had a depth perception problem? We wouldn't know and would have to rely on the opinions of experts as to what led him into the path of the vehicle. If we dug into the person's past, we might indeed discover a problem we couldn't have known from merely looking at him. Only then would we understand what led to his death."

Glancing toward Sharon for effect, Harriett saw Paige Dunne slip quietly into the courtroom and make her way to an open seat halfway down the gallery area. She wished the young woman hadn't decided to watch the proceedings and lowered her head to gather herself before continuing. "Sharon Taggart appears to be what most of us would consider normal. She appears to lead an average normal life. She has parents, a brother, a husband, and two children. She holds a responsible job that brings her into daily contact with hundreds of young people who have been entrusted to her. She grew up in what appears to be a stable, affluent home. But appearances can be deceiving. The realities of Sharon Taggart's life cannot be seen by looking at her because they are locked away in her mind. Through a series of witnesses, I will reveal the realities of her life to you and feel compelled to warn you in advance that the testimony you will hear will not be pleasant. It will be graphic and disturbing, but it will provide you with the evidence you will need to determine, with a clear conscience, that Sharon Taggart, a victim of incest at the hands of her brother and abuse at the hands of her husband, is not guilty by reason of mental defect and as a result was incapable of forming intent or determining the rightness or wrongness of her actions."

Harriett paused for a moment, maintaining eye contact with the jurors while she waited for the ripple of whispers among the observers in the courtroom to fade away before resuming her remarks.

"What the witnesses will reveal will certainly be challenged by Mr. Lassiter. That is his job. But no matter how well Mr. Lassiter does his job, there can be only one verdict in this case. The prosecutor will take his job seriously. I will take my job seriously. Once this case is turned over to you, Sharon Taggart has the right to expect you to perform your job seriously as well. Thank you."

Stealing a glance at Paige Dunne as she returned to the defense table, Harriett felt profoundly sorry for the young woman and the part the case had forced her to play in hurting her. Judge Landers called for a fifteen-minute recess to allow the jury to prepare for a full day of testimony. As soon as Landers left the bench, Harriett conferred briefly with Nick to get his opinion on the reactions of the jurors to the opening statements.

"I thought they looked fairly open to hearing the testimony. Lassiter gave a good opening, so I'm glad yours was what they heard last," Nick said.

"I'm seeing Landers in chambers before we leave today. The courtroom will need to be cleared of spectators before Parker's high school friends take the stand Monday."

"Personally, I can't believe Wayne found one, let alone two men willing to testify about molesting Sharon."

"I didn't ask him how he got them to agree, and frankly, I don't want to know," Harriett said.

"Lassiter will object to clearing the courtroom," Nick said.

Harriett shrugged, "Let him."

Turning to leave the courtroom, Harriett saw Sean Lassiter still sitting at the prosecution table looking over a sheaf of papers. On her way past the bar, she stopped momentarily at his table.

"Can I help you?" he asked without looking up from his paperwork.

"That was an excellent opening statement," she said, walking away before he could respond.

On her way out of the courtroom, Harriett saw Alex and Paige standing in the hallway with Senator Collins. Paige jerked away from Collins when he tried to wrap his arm around her, and he and Alex appeared to be involved in a heated discussion. As Harriett took a drink from a nearby water fountain, Alex walked up next to her.

"Are Sharon's incest allegations true?" she asked quietly.

"You know I can't tell you anything about the case, Alex," Harriett answered, wiping sprinkles of water from her mouth. "But I am asking Judge Landers to clear the courtroom for some of the testimony."

"Paige is extremely upset."

"I'm sorry she had to hear my remarks, Alex. It wasn't my intention to hurt her. You might want to keep her away from the trial as much as possible. A great deal of the testimony would certainly upset her even more than she already is."

"Are you talking about my testimony?"

"As well as that of the other witnesses," Harriett nodded.

"I'm not worried about your questions, Harriett."

"I'll fend Lassiter off as much as I can, Alex. I'm sorry. I wish things could have turned out differently."

"Me, too. Great memories, though," Alex smiled.

"The best," Harriett said, touching Alex's arm gently before walking away from her for the last time.

Jess leaned against a wall watching as Harriett and Alex talked. There seemed to be a familiarity in the way they looked at one other, and their body language spoke volumes. They made an attractive couple, and it was obvious to her that the two women had once possibly been lovers for an extended period of time.

"Harriett," Jess said as Harriett walked toward her, obviously distracted by her own thoughts.

"Oh, Jess," Harriett said, "I'm sorry. I didn't see you."

"Complex case you're dealing with," Jess observed. "I caught a part of it before the recess."

"Very complex," Harriett smiled.

"Has anything else unusual happened to either you or Lacey?"

"I've had a couple of hang-up phone calls, but that could have been anything."

"It's not exactly kosher, but I have someone keeping an eye on Senator Collins."

Harriett reached out and placed her hand on Jess's shoulder. "I appreciate that very much. I'm really more concerned about Lacey than I am about myself."

"I understand," Jess nodded.

"Why don't you come over tonight?" Harriett asked with a smile. "Lacey and her boyfriend will be there and maybe Nick. We're considering Chinese."

"Sound great," Jess smiled.

"It's a date." Harriett lightly squeezed Jess's arm before she turned to leave.

WELL, ISN'T THAT sweet, he thought as he watched the two women. Harriett has found a new lover. Glancing back toward Alex, he smiled. Perfect. Walking away from one lover and into the arms of a new one at virtually the same moment. He couldn't believe his good fortune. He could have reached out and touched Harriett when she moved past him. It would have been so easy. Too easy. Would she have recognized me? he wondered. He didn't think she would have, but was certain she would have recognized his voice. He had called her house a few times hoping Lacey would answer, but had only heard Harriett's low and sultry voice telling him to leave a message. All he had left was the sound of his own breathing before he hung up. He wondered if he would find Lacey's voice as inviting as her aunt's. Bending over for a drink of water, he watched Harriett disappear into the courtroom. He didn't know how much longer he could wait. Not much longer, he thought as he walked down the hall away from the courtroom. Not much longer.

Chapter
Thirty-Six

JESS PULLED TO the curb in front of Harriett's townhouse. It would be dark within thirty minutes. Checking her hair in the rearview mirror, she stepped from the Durango. As she started up the steps, the front door opened and she was nearly run over by Lacey. Grabbing her to keep from falling, Jess asked, "Whoa, what's the rush?"

Lacey laughed. "I'm sorry, Ms. Raines. We're on our way to pick up dinner."

"Please, just Jess," she smiled. "I don't want to feel any older than I already am."

"Jess, this is my boyfriend, Devon Shore. Devon, this is Aunt Harriett's date, Jess Raines."

As she shook Devon's hand, she decided that he and Lacey made a nice looking young couple. Devon had an open face and a genuine smile.

"Go on in," Lacey said as she took Devon's hand. "We won't be gone long."

She watched as the two teenagers climbed into Harriett's truck and backed out of the drive. When she turned back to the front door, Harriett was smiling at her. Jess walked up the steps and greeted her with a light kiss. "Cute couple," she said.

"Them or us?" Harriett asked.

Laughing, Jess answered, "They're cute. We're fabulous."

Harriett wrapped her arm around her waist and escorted her into the living room. "Jess, you remember Nick?" Harriett asked as Jess nodded. "And we have a surprise guest as well." Jess saw a bear of a man who appeared to be in his late fifties or early sixties hoist his body from the sofa. "This is Wayne Graham, my investigator."

She took a step toward Wayne and shook his hand firmly. "A pleasure, Mr. Graham."

"Not many people say that to me. You a cop?" he asked.

"I'm not on the streets anymore," Jess nodded.

"Jess is a special investigator with the Attorney General's office," Harriett added.

AS THE ADULTS got acquainted, Lacey drove the big blue pickup through Austin streets toward Harriett's favorite Chinese restaurant.

"How long did they say it would be before the order was ready," Devon asked.

"About an hour, but it could be sooner," Lacey smiled at him across the truck.

"Or maybe longer," Devon smiled back. "Makes me glad your aunt's favorite Chinese place is on the other side of town."

Lacey switched lanes and guided the truck into traffic on the interstate highway. Devon knew immediately where she was going. Three cars behind them a dark car entered the highway. That big truck was so easy to follow, he thought. Might as well have a fuckin' neon sign on it. There wasn't any reason to stay behind them since they didn't have a clue he was following them. Speeding up, he passed a couple of cars and fell in directly behind the truck, driving much too closely.

"What's that idiot doing?" Lacey asked. "If I stop, he'll run into me."

Devon glanced back, but couldn't see who was driving the vehicle behind them. "Take the next exit, and let the jerk have the road," he frowned.

Lacey turned off while the car stayed on the highway and sped past them. A few turns later Lacey brought the truck to a stop on a grassy area overlooking Town Lake and turned off the ignition. Without a word, she moved closer to Devon and kissed him. Pulling her closer, he kissed her deeply, allowing his hands to wander.

With its headlights off, the black car eased to a stop. Through the trees he could see the silhouette of the truck. Ah, young love, he thought. Groping and gasping their way through a quickie in the cramped cab of a pickup truck. Slowly he made his way through the trees toward the truck. The windows were already beginning to fog.

Devon shifted himself on the seat and lowered Lacey onto the seat, his hands pushing her sweater up over her breasts. "You're beautiful, Lacey," he whispered as his mouth took in one of her breasts. Her breathing became heavier as her hands pulled his mouth harder against her breast.

Crawling to the truck, he could hear laughter and panting sounds from inside. As he slowly raised himself nearer the driver's window, the window was almost completely fogged over except near the bottom. Through the rapidly closing slit he watched as Lacey's half-naked body moved beneath the boy's mouth. Yes, she would be very hot, he thought, as he felt his own body react to what he saw. Lacey's hand flew up to the window, momentarily startling him into ducking down again. The sounds of increasing teenage passion had aroused him quickly to the point of painfulness. Unzipping his pants, he reached inside and coordinated his hand movement with the sounds from inside the truck.

When he could bear it no longer, he came and was barely able to suppress his own groans of satisfaction.

"Devon," Lacey said breathlessly, "Please stop. Please."

He heard shifting inside the vehicle and thought, Don't stop now, kid. Nail that little cunt. Glancing up at the window, he saw blonde hair against the glass.

"I'm sorry, Devon," she said softly.

"It's okay, Lace. Besides, if we wait much longer to pick up dinner, your aunt will get suspicious."

Lacey glanced at the dashboard clock and sat completely up, "Shit! We better get going."

The man moved quickly away from the truck and back to his vehicle. Lighting a cigarette, he waited until the truck passed before starting his engine. Fifteen minutes later, Lacey and Devon left the Beijing Dragon Restaurant and backed out of the parking lot. As they entered the interstate heading back to Harriett's townhouse, he fell in behind them again. Sporadically he moved closer and then fell back, finally turning his headlights on bright and remaining at a distance he knew would shine the lights into Lacey's rearview mirror.

"What is this?" Lacey said. "Night of the moron! I can't see a thing." Devon reached up and flipped the switch on the rearview mirror to deflect the headlights behind them, but the headlights in the side mirrors were just as intense. Lacey signaled to turn off the highway, and the car followed her. Making several more turns, she was unable to shake the vehicle behind her. Finally, she slowed and pulled over to the curb. The car stopped behind her, but the driver didn't get out.

Pulling away from the curb, Lacey reached down and picked up Harriett's mobile phone, punching in numbers as she watched the car continuing to follow her. Harriett picked up the phone at home and heard Lacey's shaking voice say, "Aunt Harriett, someone is following us, and I can't lose them. I'm afraid to come home."

"Hang on," Harriett said.

A moment later, after a fast explanation, Jess was on the line. "Where are you, Lacey?"

"Uh...I'm not sure. Devon, what's the next street?"

Jess could barely hear Devon in the background. "We're on Woodland and just passing Briar Hill," Lacey relayed.

"Okay," Jess said calmly as she quickly wrote street names on a pad near the phone. "Don't stop, Lacey. Harriett will be giving you directions to follow. I'll intercept you and the mystery car in a few minutes, okay?"

Jess handed the phone back to Harriett and walked quickly to the front door. As she jumped off the front steps and ran to the Durango, the door behind her opened. As she got into her vehicle and turned the key, Wayne wedged himself into the passenger seat, fastening the seat belt as they sped away.

"You're armed, I'm guessin'," Wayne growled.

Reaching under the driver's seat, Jess pulled a Glock from a hidden holster and laid it on the seat next to her. "And you?

Wayne pulled a .357 from under his coat. "Never leave home without it."

Ten blocks from Harriett's townhouse, Jess whipped the Durango to the curb, turned off the headlights, and rolled the driver's window down. "They should be here anytime now," Jess said, almost to herself.

In less than a minute, the headlights of two vehicles came over a rise in the road. The first vehicle was Harriett's truck. The second a low slung dark vehicle that remained less than a car length behind the truck. Flipping on her headlights, Jess screamed away from the curb. Reaching under her seat, she stuck a police light on top of the Durango. The red light swept across the dark vehicle which abruptly swung around the truck and accelerated. As Jess followed the car, Wayne leaned out his window and yelled to Lacey, "Go home!"

Jess's Durango had plenty of horsepower, and she managed to keep the other vehicle in sight, but wasn't really gaining on it. "Can you make out the plate?" she asked Wayne.

"Looks like the bastard covered it with mud or somethin'," Wayne shook his head. "Can't see a fuckin' thing. This the best this heap can do?" he demanded.

Jess goosed the accelerator and moved closer, concentrating on the taillights of the car ahead of her. "This road ends three or four blocks ahead," Jess said. Suddenly, brake lights from the car lit up, and it slid to a stop as the driver's door flew open. As she stopped the Durango and jumped out, she saw a dark figure run into a wooded area to her left. "Radio's in the console," she yelled at Wayne as she grabbed her gun and a flashlight and sprinted off. "Call in this location."

Jess estimated that she couldn't be very far behind the other driver as she moved into the brush, her Glock held out in front of her. Her anger that anyone would get so close to Lacey or Harriett fueled her, but she knew she couldn't allow herself to get careless now. As she moved deeper into the darkness of the wooded area, she stopped periodically and looked for branches moving after being disturbed or to listen for the sound of someone moving in the decayed vegetation on the ground. A snapping sound to her left caused her to drop to one knee and swing the pistol and light around, only to be greeted by the glowing eyes of a stray cat before it retreated further into the foliage.

"Shit," she muttered as she stood once more, crouching as she moved from tree to tree.

HE RECOGNIZED THE woman searching for him from earlier that day at the courthouse. He was close enough to overpower her and kill her. His hand clenched and unclenched the handle of his knife as he contemplated his options. It would hurt Harriett if she lost her new lover, and he didn't want to do that. He wanted to be the one to hurt her. She would understand the message he had left for her. As he heard the sirens of other vehicles approaching the area he retreated, using the noise they were making to cover his movements.

TWENTY MINUTES LATER, patrol cars lined the street, spotlights probing into the darkness. A police helicopter circled overhead. Most of the houses appeared to be abandoned as officers searched each one. As Wayne leaned against the Durango, drawing heavily on a cigarette, Jess slowly made her way back toward him. She was frowning.

"I'm gatherin' you lost him," Wayne stated the obvious.

"Yeah. Goddamn it!" she seethed as she threw her flashlight into her car.

"Well, I'm hungry from all this excitement," he said as he pushed himself away from the car and crushed out his cigarette.

When they drove up to Harriett's house, there was a patrol car in the driveway. Inside, officers were taking statements from Lacey and Devon. Harriett came up to them. "Who was it?" she asked.

"I never saw his face," Jess explained.

Harriett frowned and Jess was furious that she hadn't been able to apprehend the man. "I don't think you should stay here, Harriett," she said. "Whoever it was probably knows where you live."

"I'm not going to run away and hide, Jess. It would just give him more power over me."

Taking Harriett's arm, Jess led her into the kitchen. "Why don't you and Lacey stay at my place for a while. At least give us a chance to locate the guy."

"We'll be fine here."

"If you won't come to my house, then I'll be forced to stay here," Jess said. "Your choice."

Placing her hands on Jess's shoulders, Harriett finally said, "Let's have dinner, and then I'll decide. Okay?"

"Where's the food?" Harriett asked as she and Jess returned to the living room.

Lacey jumped up, "Oh, I left it in the truck when we got home. I'll get it, but it's probably cold by now. I'm sorry."

"That's why God invented microwaves, sweetheart," Harriett smiled.

"I'll get it," Wayne said as he trudged out the front door. A couple of minutes later, he carried in two large plastic grocery bags full of food and handed them to Harriett. Turning to Jess, he said quietly, "Join me outside for a minute."

Jess followed him to Harriett's truck. "Walk around her truck...slowly. Tell me if you see anything unusual," the investigator said as he lit another cigarette.

Jess looked at him blankly, but did as he told her. She walked around the truck twice. Once at normal height and a second time bent at the waist. As she came around the rear of the truck the second time, she stopped. Looking at Wayne, she asked, "Got a flashlight?"

When Wayne shook his head, she walked to the Durango and retrieved her flashlight. Squatting next to the truck, she ran the beam down the body of the truck. "Fuck me," she breathed.

"Whaddaya think it is?" Wayne asked coolly.

Glancing up at him, Jess said, "You know damn well what it is. Some guy whacked off and finger painted with his own semen."

"Yep, that's what I thought. Just wanted another opinion," he said gruffly. "Better get the lab out here to impound this truck. Whoever it is sure ain't tryin' to be very subtle."

Jess flipped open her phone and punched in a number. "Unfortunately, it's not illegal to jerk off, even if it is on someone's private vehicle."

"Whatcha gonna tell Harriett?"

Looking back at the truck and the word "*soon*" scrawled on it, she looked at Wayne. "I'm going to tell her that her life has been threatened, and she should take it very seriously."

"Well, there goes dinner," he exhaled.

AFTER WATCHING HER truck being loaded on a tow truck and hauled away, Harriett and Lacey packed bags, and Jess loaded them into the back of her Durango. Wayne agreed to stay at Harriett's just in case anyone uninvited showed up. Arriving at her home, Jess showed Lacey to a downstairs bedroom and made sure she had everything she needed to be comfortable.

Joining Harriett in the master bedroom, Jess took off her jacket and locked her Glock away in the nightstand. Harriett began unpacking as Jess cleared a place for her clothes in her closet and chest of drawers.

"How long do you think we'll have to be here?" Harriett asked.

"Probably long enough for the lab to process the car that followed Lacey and your truck," Jess shrugged.

"I'll need to rent a car."

"I'll arrange for one tomorrow after I drop you off at your office. Anything special?"

"How about something non-descript that looks like every other damn car on the road?"

"That's probably a good idea," Jess frowned slightly. "Listen, Harriett, if you want, I can sleep downstairs."

"If anyone should sleep downstairs it would be me. I'm the one displacing you."

"I don't look at it that way. But I don't want Lacey to get the wrong idea."

"And exactly what idea would that be, Jess?" Harriett asked shortly. "That you and I are sleeping together? We both know *that's* not true."

Jess was taken aback by the rebuke in Harriett's voice, but chose to ignore it.

"I'm sorry, Jess," Harriett said softly. "I'm so sorry. Tonight has just been...stressful."

"I won't let anyone hurt you or Lacey."

Crossing the room, Harriett put her arms around Jess and hugged her tightly. "Let's get some rest," she whispered. "We're both a little jittery right now, and my client's trial starts in earnest tomorrow."

"I'll be back in a minute. I need to check the doors and set the alarm," Jess nodded.

Harriett finished putting her clothes and bathroom items away. She had just begun undressing, pulling her shirt over her head, when she had the feeling she was being watched. As she turned, she saw Jess leaning against the door facing of the bedroom. She could feel her eyes caressing her body, clothed only in her bra and half zipped jeans. Jess's eyes wandered slowly up Harriett's body until their eyes met.

"You are so beautiful," she said softly as Harriett moved slowly toward her, stopping less than a foot from her. "You take my breath away."

Harriett continued looking into Jess's eyes as she reached up and touched the side of her face without speaking. Her hand came to rest on the back of Jess's neck, and she pulled her closer. In a rush of desire she had been struggling with since they first met, Jess took Harriett in her arms and kissed her deeply. Her kiss was filled with a longing and need she hadn't felt since she had lost Renee, and Harriett responded to it eagerly. As Jess's lips moved along her neck and shoulders, Harriett closed her eyes and reveled in the feel of Jess's hands on her skin. Almost as quickly as she had begun, Jess stopped and held Harriett in her arms.

"I should sleep downstairs," she said.

Harriett couldn't believe what she was hearing. "What's wrong, Jess?"

"Nothing."

"Then why do you seem so...reluctant to be with me?"

"I'm not. This just isn't the right time. Your plate is full with the trial and now with whoever is stalking you. You don't need me to complicate things even more."

Harriett held Jess's eyes with her own as she began unbuttoning her shirt. Running her hands under it she heard the quick intake of breath as her hands spread and flattened against Jess's abdomen and ribs. "I want to be with you, Jess, but you keep pushing me away."

"I want you so much that it scares the hell out of me, Harriett. I never thought I would meet anyone who could make me feel like this after Renee."

"I can't be Renee for you, Jess."

"You don't need to be. Renee is...dead."

"And you're still alive. When are you going to forgive yourself being alive and wanting to enjoy life again?"

Jess's eyes penetrated Harriett's as if she were trying to see what was in her mind. Her hands softly touched Harriett until they found their way into her jeans and caressed her buttocks. Kissing her with a series of small teasing kisses, Jess let her mouth wander as Harriett ran her hands through Jess's hair and pulled her mouth back to her own. She couldn't remember ever wanting anyone so much before, not even Alex.

HARRIETT WAS AWAKENED in the gray pre-dawn by Jess's lips on her neck, and the feel of her hand moving lightly over her hip. She rolled toward her and drew her into a slow, lingering kiss. It had been so long, and her body reminded her how good it could feel to be loved and desired.

"Don't you ever get tired?" Jess asked between kisses.

"I'll never get tired of you. I love the way you make me feel when you touch me."

"Ah! Then I don't have to ask if you'll still respect me in the morning."

"It is morning," Harriett chuckled.

"Time flies when...," Jess started with a grin.

"Shut up and kiss me," Harriett growled seductively.

Jess laughed and kissed her again.

"I'm sorry, Harriett," she said as she stroked along Harriett's back, dreading that they would soon have to leave the bed and dress for work.

"For what?"

"I'm sorry I didn't make love with you before now. I don't know what was wrong with me. Scared, I guess."

"Well, there is *definitely* nothing wrong with you. And you were more than worth the wait."

Jess pulled Harriett on top of her and swept her tousled hair away from her face.

"I'll never let anyone hurt you, Harriett. I promise." She had promised to always protect Renee and failed. She had promised to protect her younger brother and also failed. But this time Jess was determined not to fail again.

"I know, my love. Unfortunately, I need to grab a quick shower and get ready for court." As Jess watched her naked body slide toward the edge of the bed, Harriett looked over her shoulder and smiled. "I don't suppose I could convince you to wash my back for me?"

Chapter
Thirty-Seven

HARRIETT SAT PATIENTLY through the first two days of the prosecution's presentation to the jury. So far, everything Lassiter had offered was undeniable. The rifle belonged to the Taggarts, and Sharon's fingerprints were on the barrel and stock. However, as Harriett pointed out, it wasn't unusual that her prints were on the weapon since it was in her home, and she had used it. The firearms expert from the state forensics lab testified that the rifle had been recently cleaned, and there was no way to determine when it was last fired by Sharon or anyone else, for that matter.

While she was actually enjoying picking at Lassiter's witnesses' testimony, she knew the strongest State evidence against her client hadn't been presented yet. Smiling to herself, she was looking forward to her cross-examination of Detective James Riley. She listened attentively to the testimony of Emma Sanchez, purportedly an eyewitness to the Kaufmann shooting. Mrs. Sanchez was an older woman, in her late sixties, but had no trouble pointing directly at Sharon and identifying her as the woman she had seen leaving the embankment near the freeway carrying a rifle. In her cross-examination, Harriett used a map of the area of the crime and asked Mrs. Sanchez to point out where she had been when she witnessed the events of that February evening. Then she had an enlarged photograph of the location, taken at the same approximate time of night as the crime, displayed for the jury. The picture showed an individual on the embankment, and from the location already pointed out by Mrs. Sanchez, it would have been virtually impossible to identify the woman in the picture. In fact, it could have been a man with long hair. Despite Harriett's best efforts, Mrs. Sanchez adamantly refused to alter her testimony or to question her identification of the defendant. Deciding that nothing more was to be gained by badgering the woman, Harriett ended her questioning, but left the enlarged photo on an easel facing the jury.

AS JAMES RILEY readjusted his body in the witness chair and took a drink of water from the glass next to him, he watched Harriett flipping through her legal pad. He hated her, but he was determined not to allow his feelings to distract him from answering her questions. He suspected she might try to provoke him into an outburst that would cause the jury to regard him as a less than credible witness. In his experience, that was always the case when police officers testified. The key would be to remain calm.

"Detective Riley," Harriett said rather quietly, forcing Riley to lean forward slightly in order to hear her. "You were assigned to the task force formed to investigate the freeway killings after the third shooting, weren't you?"

"That's correct."

"Did you ask for the assignment?"

"No, I was pulled from another case to work on the task force."

"And your particular area of investigation for the task force was initially the third case. Is that correct?"

"Yes."

"How many of the shell casings were recovered from the shootings?"

"There were six. One at the site of each shooting, except one. No casing was found at one of the scenes, and it was assumed the perpetrator policed the area before leaving."

"In your experience, isn't it rather atypical for a woman to have committed crimes such as the ones my client has been charged with?"

"It's a little unusual," Riley agreed.

"Isn't it true that most crimes committed by women are generally spur of the moment crimes of passion or self-defense?"

"Objection," Lassiter said. "The witness is not an expert in the psychology of criminals."

"He's a trained detective with nearly twenty years experience in dealing with a wide variety of crimes and criminals," Harriett argued. Glancing at Riley, it struck her that she was actually calling him an experienced and competent police officer.

"Overruled. The witness may answer the question," Landers intoned.

Looking back at her old nemesis, Harriett said, "Detective?"

"Yes, ma'am, the task force initially believed that the freeway shootings were committed by a man."

"Detective Riley," she continued. "You testified that the shell casings that were introduced into evidence today were purchased by my client. Is that correct?"

"Yes, it is. She was positively identified by the clerk who sold them."

"When items, such as ammunition or shell casings, are submitted to the state laboratory, the police officer who delivers them signs a chain of custody voucher, don't they?"

"That's the procedure," Riley smiled.

"And after it's tested, the evidence is then held in the evidence locker at the lab until it's needed for trial or to match to other similar evidence. True?"

"Yes."

"Approach the witness, your Honor?" Harriett asked.

Landers motioned her forward, and she picked up a copy of the chain of custody voucher as she walked toward the witness stand. Leaning her elbows on the railing, she handed the paper to Riley. "Is this the chain of custody voucher for the shell casings in the Taggart case, detective?"

"It would appear to be," Riley said as he looked down at the sheet.

"Could you please read the name of the last person who had possession of the shell cartridges that were tested by the state lab before this trial began?"

"James Riley," the detective said clearly.

"Why didn't this evidence remain in the evidence locker with other pieces of evidence?"

"I was instructed to take it to a second evidence locker by Mr. Lassiter," Riley answered, nodding his head toward the prosecution table.

"How long was this evidence in the prosecution's possession?"

"A couple of months. Until we made an arrest in the case."

"Isn't it true, detective, that Mr. Lassiter presented the defense with fraudulent evidence during the initial disclosure?"

"Objection, your Honor. Is defense counsel accusing the prosecutor's office of something?" Lassiter asked.

Turning to face her opponent, Harriett smiled slightly. "Perish the thought, Mr. Lassiter." A wave of snickers and giggles swept through the gallery as Judge Landers tapped his gavel to restore quiet to his courtroom.

"Overruled," he said. "Continue."

Returning her attention to Riley, Harriett continued, "The bullet the defense originally received, Detective Riley. Was that from one of the scenes?"

"Yes, the Kaufmann scene. It was located in a telephone pole nearby."

"Was it later determined that that particular bullet was not related to the crime?"

"Yes."

"Thank you, detective. I have no further question for this witness, your Honor," Harriett said.

"Redirect, Mr. Lassiter?" Landers asked.

"No, your Honor," Lassiter responded.

At the end of the third day of testimony, Sean Lassiter rested the State's case. Harriett knew he was simply waiting for her to begin presenting evidence to support Sharon Taggart's claim of mental defect. It seemed to Harriett that he had actually presented a rather mediocre case based on the evidence he had at hand. She had managed to raise some points of doubt with each witness, even though it still might not have done enough damage to win.

"IS MS. MARKHAM in?" Jess smiled as she stood at Phyllis's desk.

"They got in from court about half an hour ago, Ms. Raines," Phyllis smiled back. "They're in the kitchen."

"Rough day?" Jess asked as she walked into the small kitchen area of Harriett's offices. Harriett had already changed from the suit she wore to court, her bare feet propped up on a kitchen chair. Nick had shed his jacket and tie and was concentrating on a diet soda.

"The rough days haven't gotten here yet," Harriett answered as she stood and joined Jess, kissing her lightly. "Just the preliminary wrangling. Drink?"

"I'll get it," Jess said crossing toward the refrigerator. "How did things go in court today?"

"Not bad. We didn't hear anything we didn't expect," Harriett said as Jess pulled out a chair and straddled it, resting her arms on its back. Harriett ran her hand down Jess's back and smiled. "And how was your day?"

"Not bad. The lab lifted a couple of partial prints from the car that followed Lacey last night, but the vehicle was stolen. They're running them through the system."

"What about my truck?" Harriett inquired.

"They found a few smudged fingerprints on both the driver's side window and door panel. It will take a while for the DNA test results to come in on the semen on the back quarter panel," Jess said matter-of-factly. "Hopefully, we'll get something from the prints."

Harriett shivered slightly. "That's disgusting. When could anyone have possibly done that? Surely I would have noticed something like that."

Jess took a long drink of her soda and cleared her throat. "I stopped by Lacey's school earlier this morning and talked to her and Devon about it. It seemed harmless enough at the time, but apparently they enjoyed some private time together before they picked up dinner last night. Neither of them saw anything, but I'm sure someone might have followed them."

Harriett sat up quickly. "What are you saying, Jess? That some pervert watched them?"

"I don't know anything for a fact, Harriett. It's all purely speculation until we catch him. But, yes, I think someone approached the truck, observed whatever they were doing and became aroused."

"They could have both been killed," Harriett seethed. "And for what? Teenage petting!"

"They couldn't have known this could happen, Harriett," Nick said. "They're too young to think about things like that."

"That doesn't excuse anything, Nick," Harriett said angrily. "This is inexcusable."

Harriett stalked off to her office and slammed the door.

"She's scared," Nick observed.

"She should be," Jess said.

AFTER DINNER, HARRIETT spoke to Lacey alone in Jess's spare bedroom. She rejoined Jess as she was rinsing dishes and putting them in the dishwasher.

"It's hard to stay mad at her very long," Harriett sighed. "She had already told me that Devon was getting more serious lately. But I don't think I'll have to worry about that anymore for a while. At least not until they catch whoever was responsible."

"If we're lucky we can match the DNA. The fingerprints are a long shot, and if the system can't match the fragment we found, we might not be able to catch him. So far, whoever did it hasn't done anything too serious. Perverted maybe, but mostly minor offenses. It could have been a park prowler."

"I know. Can I borrow your office for a little while? I need to look over my notes for court tomorrow."

"Of course, you can. I'll clear a space so you can work."

By ten o'clock, Harriett turned off the office light and wandered into the front of the house. Hearing voices and laughter, she made her way into the family room as Jess was racking up balls on the pool table. "Who's winning?" she smiled.

"It's a tie so far," Lacey replied. "Do you want to play?"

"No, I think I'll let you two play for the championship."

"You can be the cheerleader," Lacey laughed. "Like when you were in high school."

"You were a cheerleader?" Jess asked.

"And a damn good one," Harriett answered as a slight blush crept up her face.

"I'll bet you were real cute," Jess chuckled.

"Hmm," Harriett said as she sat in a swivel rocker, pulling her feet up under her. She felt relaxed as she watched Jess and Lacey concentrate on their game. Both were competitive women, and she knew that Jess wouldn't throw the game to make Lacey feel good. Harriett had never let Lacey win, either. She might never win, but the challenge to improve was more important than winning. She was glad that Jess and Lacey seemed to get along well. She knew she was falling in love, and for the first time saw what a family life of her own might be like. It was something she had never had, or could have had, with Alex. On a lucky shot, Lacey managed to take the final game from Jess who demanded a rematch the following evening. Kissing Harriett good night, Lacey left them alone in favor of a shower and sleep.

"She's a great kid," Jess smiled as she put the pool cues in the rack and switched off the light over the table.

"I've been very fortunate," Harriett nodded. "Sometimes, I think she's more grown up than I am."

Jess took a bottle of brandy from behind the bar in the family room and poured two small snifters. "This will help you relax," she said, handing one to Harriett.

Harriett sipped the brandy slowly. It felt good going down. Taking a deep breath, she said, "Thank you, Jess. For everything."

"You don't have to keep thanking me, Harriett," Jess smiled. "I'm glad to do whatever I can to help. Besides, my job does sort of dictate that I do something."

Harriett rose from the rocker and carried her snifter back to the bar. "Just doing your job, huh?" she said.

Jess tilted her head and leaned toward Harriett. "This isn't in my job description," she said quietly as her lips met Harriett's. Setting her snifter on the bar, she wrapped her arm around Harriett's waist and pulled her closer, kissing her deeply, her tongue tasting the brandy that lingered in Harriett's mouth. She ran her hands up Harriett's back and buried them in her hair, kissing her repeatedly and passionately. As Jess caressed her body and nibbled along her neck, Harriett took a deep breath.

"If you don't take me to bed soon, Jess, I'll be too exhausted to represent my client in the morning."

"Either way, you'll be tired." Jess grinned as she flipped the light switch off.

"But it will be a satisfied tired," she said, tracing Jess's lips lightly with her tongue, eliciting a groan of anticipation.

Chapter
Thirty-Eight

"ARE YOU READY to call your first witness, Ms. Markham?" Judge Landers asked the following morning as soon as the jury was reseated and settled.

"Yes, your Honor," Harriett replied as she stood at the defense table. "The defense calls Dr. Raymond Talbot to the stand."

As soon as Dr. Talbot was sworn in and seated, Harriett addressed him.

"Dr. Talbot, where did you receive your psychiatric training?"

"I received my medical training at Columbia University. After I elected psychiatry as a specialization, I did my residency at Johns Hopkins Medical Center in Baltimore, Maryland."

"Did your training acquaint you with a variety of mental problems?"

"Yes. After my residency, I became a staff psychiatrist at Presbyterian Hospital in Dallas."

"How long have you been at Presbyterian Hospital, Doctor?"

"A little over twenty years."

"Approximately how many times have you testified in court concerning the mental status of defendants?"

"Maybe fifteen or twenty times counting testimony for both the State and the defense."

"Then the State has also asked you to perform independent psychiatric evaluations?"

"Several times."

"Do you receive a fee for your services?"

"I receive a standard consultation fee."

"Is the fee the same when you testify for both the defense and the State?"

"Yes."

"Your Honor, I request that Dr. Talbot be recognized as an expert witness in the field of psychiatry for purposes of this trial."

"No objection," Lassiter said.

"The court recognizes Dr. Talbot as an expert in psychiatry. Continue Ms. Markham," Judge Landers instructed.

"Dr. Talbot, are you acquainted with the defendant, Sharon

Collins Taggart?"

"Yes, I am."

"Under what circumstances did you meet Mrs. Taggart?"

"1 was contacted by your office to conduct a preliminary psychiatric evaluation of her mental status."

"When did you conduct your initial evaluation?"

"While Mrs. Taggart was being detained in the Dallas County Jail approximately two and a half months ago, in February."

"Can you, in layman's terms if possible, tell the court the result of your evaluation?"

Readjusting himself in the witness chair, Talbot shifted his weight to allow him to look easily at the jury.

"Sharon Taggart is a thirty-year-old female who presented a variety of symptoms."

"What symptoms did Mrs. Taggart present, Doctor?"

"She appeared to suffer from a relatively mild form of depression, characterized by self-deprecation and low self-esteem. In addition, she had periodic memory losses that coincided with significant events in her life. She was reserved when I first met with her, almost shy. Using common psychiatric questions, I attempted to trace the root cause of her symptoms."

"Were you able to do that?"

"Mrs. Taggart's symptomatology became extremely complex during my meetings with her. At our second meeting, I began to suspect that she might be suffering from dissociative identity disorder."

"Would you briefly explain what you mean by dissociative identity disorder, Dr. Talbot?"

"At one time, it was better known as multiple personality syndrome," Talbot said to the jury. "The name of the illness was changed to dissociative identity disorder in 1994 by the American Psychiatric Association."

"Were you ever able to prove or disprove your suspicions about Mrs. Taggart?"

"Through hypnosis, I was able to determine that Sharon has a second alter personality who calls herself Jan."

"Were you able to communicate with this second personality?"

"Only with great difficulty, but that is the nature of the disorder. Jan, the alter personality, is Mrs. Taggart's protector. Part of the protection she provides actually involves preventing Sharon from doing anything that might make other people believe she is what some would call crazy."

"Is Sharon Taggart crazy, doctor?"

"Objection," Lassiter said. "Ms. Markham is leading the witness."

"Rephrase, Ms. Markham," Landers said.

"What can you tell this court about Sharon Taggart's mental state, doctor?"

"Sharon Taggart is an extremely bright woman of above average intelligence. She functions normally at a responsible job, is married, and has two children. She absolutely is not a raving lunatic," Talbot said. "Nevertheless, she does suffer from a dissociative identity disorder. The word 'crazy' wouldn't apply concerning Mrs. Taggart or anyone else, however, since it has no standing in either medical or legal terms."

"What would the prognosis for her future be if she were to receive competent psychiatric help?"

"DID is one of the most treatable mental disorders if the treatment is long-term, and the patient follows through with the entire treatment program."

"What would cause a person to develop this particular disorder?"

"It's generally accepted that the onset of the disorder occurs due to some type of early childhood trauma. When children can't deal with whatever pain or grief or terror they are confronting, they retreat into their own mind and create another personality as a coping device."

"How early in childhood would the trauma probably occur?"

"Certainly during an early developmental period. Usually before the age of nine."

"Are we talking about something like an automobile accident, or the death of a loved one?"

"Those things could lead to the creation of a separate personality. However, far and away, the most common cause is some form of repetitive child abuse from which the child cannot physically escape. Their reaction is to escape mentally. Some of the patients I have treated refer to it as 'going away.'"

"What does that mean?"

"It means that the host personality takes a rest and allows the second, or alter personality, to experience whatever pain was intended for the host."

"Seems like this second personality would become a little hostile toward the host for going away."

"Sometimes. But if the alter personality's primary function is to protect the host, as in Sharon's case, there wouldn't be much anger directed at the host. The alter is simply doing its job."

"If the alter personality were to become angry, whom would he or she direct the anger at?"

"Anyone who threatens the host in all likelihood."

"Is Sharon Taggart's second personality a protector?"

"Yes, and she's become quite bitter, especially recently."

"What, if anything, in Mrs. Taggart's past could have led to the development of a second personality?"

"From my interviews with her, it is my opinion that Sharon Taggart was severely abused as a child during her formative years."

"What form of abuse was she subjected to, Dr. Talbot?"

"In all the years I have been practicing psychiatry, I can't remember another patient who was subjected to the varieties of abuse that Sharon Taggart was, Ms. Markham. Sharon was sexually abused by a member of her own family as well as by an array of strangers. In addition, she was verbally, and I suspect, emotionally abused by her mother."

"Is it your testimony that Sharon Taggart was the victim of incest?'

"Yes. At the hands of her brother."

Murmurs swept through the court spectators, as Harriett read looks of shock and disgust on the faces of the jurors.

"But Sharon Taggart loves her brother, doesn't she?" Harriett continued.

"Sharon herself doesn't have a recollection of what happened to her. On the other hand, Jan, the alter personality, is quite graphic in describing what happened."

"Can you explain why Sharon isn't angry at her brother?"

"Sharon was taught by her mother from a very young age that it was wrong to hurt another member of her family. It's a deeply ingrained part of her personality. Deeply ingrained enough that even the alter personality balks at hurting a member of Sharon's family and turns her anger and aggression against others outside the family as a substitute."

"Too bad Sharon's mother didn't make as big an impression on her son," Harriett said as she looked toward the jury box.

"Objection," Lassiter said. "Editorializing."

"Withdrawn. Doctor, what would happen that could cause Sharon's alter personality to react violently?"

"Extreme stress that Sharon couldn't handle would almost certainly do it. In particular, anything that reminded her vividly of prior abusive situations."

"In your opinion, Doctor, is Sharon Taggart insane?"

"Insanity is a medical term, Ms. Markham. Medically speaking, yes, Sharon Taggart has a serious, but curable, mental defect."

"Are you aware of the legal definition of insanity, Dr. Talbot?"

"Yes. In this state, the only determination is whether a person knows the difference between right and wrong and is able to comprehend the consequences of their actions."

"Does Sharon Taggart know the difference between right and wrong?"

"I believe she does."

"And does Jan, her alter personality, know the difference between right and wrong?"

"Yes."

"Does that mean that Sharon is guilty?"

"It's more complex than that. As a person with dissociative identity disorder, Sharon is not in contact with her alter personality and has no cognitive control over what she does. In essence, Sharon Taggart was not present when a crime was committed. For her part, Jan adamantly believes that she hasn't done anything wrong."

"Jan doesn't believe shooting people is wrong?"

"She didn't shoot anyone. She shot in the general direction, and if the drivers overreacted to that, she feels absolutely no responsibility for the consequences of their actions. In the final analysis, Sharon Taggart bears no responsibility whatsoever because she mentally wasn't there."

"Thank you, Dr. Talbot. No further questions at this time, your Honor. However, I reserve the right to recall this witness for clarification purposes at a later date."

"Mr. Lassiter, do you have questions for this witness?"

"Yes, thank you, your Honor," Lassiter answered as he looked at the legal pad in front of him.

"Dr. Talbot, when you examined Mrs. Taggart, you used hypnosis in order to reach your diagnosis, is that correct?" Lassiter began.

"Yes. It's the most effective method for determining the presence of the disorder."

"Isn't it true that many psychiatrists believe hypnosis is an unreliable method?"

"I wouldn't say many, but, yes, some do believe it's unreliable."

"When you hypnotized Sharon Taggart for the purposes of diagnosis, did you ask to speak to her other personality?"

"Yes."

"In actuality, weren't you suggesting to Mrs. Taggart that she had more than one personality?"

"No, I didn't suggest the disorder to her."

"But you did when you asked for a new personality."

"I didn't ask her to create a new personality, Mr. Lassiter. I asked to speak to one who was already there."

"Did Sharon Taggart tell you under hypnosis that her brother molested her?"

"No."

"A moment ago you said..."

"I said she had been molested, but not that Sharon told me. Jan revealed that part of Sharon's history. Sharon wasn't aware that it had happened."

"Isn't it possible, Doctor, that by asking to speak to Jan, you were providing Sharon with a way to divulge information that she otherwise wouldn't have told you?"

"Absolutely."

"So you encouraged her to invent Jan, didn't you?"

"No. If I suggested under hypnosis that Sharon have hallucinations, that doesn't mean she would suddenly start having them. In fact, if she did, I would be extremely suspicious that she was faking it. I cannot give Sharon Taggart more than one personality through hypnosis anymore than I can give her tuberculosis through hypnosis. It's either there or it isn't."

Lassiter had made a mistake by allowing Dr. Talbot to get into a lengthy discussion of hypnosis, and Harriett couldn't restrain a slight smile.

"No further questions at this time, your Honor," Lassiter said as he leaned back in his chair.

"Redirect, Ms. Markham?"

"Dr. Talbot, is Sharon Taggart aware of the existence of her alter personality?"

"She is now but was not aware of her existence when I first examined her."

"Does she speak to Jan?"

"No."

"What is the relationship between Sharon and Jan?"

"As I said, Sharon was unaware of Jan's existence. However, Jan has quite an extensive knowledge of what Sharon has done. She's an observer, but does not communicate with Sharon."

"If Jan decided to do something, would Sharon be able to stop her?"

"Since she didn't know Jan existed, I doubt she would have been able to stop her. And even if she suspected Jan's existence, she still might not have been able to control what Jan was doing, especially recently. The Jan personality has been growing progressively stronger over the past two years or so."

"No further questions," Harriett said.

Throughout the remainder of the first day of testimony Harriett presented two other evaluations by psychiatrists, both of whom had reached independent conclusions that Sharon Taggart was suffering from dissociative identity disorder brought about by childhood sexual and emotional abuse.

As court adjourned for the day, Harriett sent a request to Judge Landers to meet with him privately in chambers. Landers granted the request and notified the prosecution of the meeting. As soon as Sharon had been taken from the courtroom, she and Nick joined Lassiter and his assistant, in Landers's office. Landers hung his robe on a hanger and ruffled his hair with both hands as he sat down behind his desk.

"What can I do for you, Harriett?" Landers asked with a smile. Harriett had argued a number of cases before Howard Landers since moving to Austin. He was a friendly man who enjoyed a relaxed atmosphere in his courtroom. Despite that, he tolerated no shenanigans from attorneys. In her estimation, Landers was one of the fairest judges in the state.

"The defense has completed its expert testimony, Judge Landers. Tomorrow, I will be calling two witnesses whose testimony is potentially embarrassing and certainly graphic in nature and content. For the sake of the witnesses, as well as my client, I am requesting that the courtroom be cleared during their testimony," Harriett said, handing Landers a list of scheduled witnesses.

Landers looked over the list and handed it to Lassiter.

"What's the basis for your request?" Landers said, leaning back and placing his hands behind his head.

"These witnesses have only agreed to appear if they are given some sort of anonymity. Short of placing paper bags over their heads, clearing the courtroom seemed to be the only logical remedy," Harriett explained.

Landers smiled. "What do you think, Mr. Lassiter? Do you object to having the courtroom cleared?"

"The public has the expectation of open courts, your Honor," Lassiter said.

"Yeah, yeah. I know all that idealistic law school bullshit," Landers said as he looked at Nick. "Sorry, Nick."

"The families of the victims have a right to hear the testimony against Mrs. Taggart," Lassiter continued.

"What they will hear, Mr. Lassiter, won't make them feel any better," Harriett said.

"The State opposes the clearing of the courtroom, your Honor," the prosecutor finally said.

"Why am I not surprised?" Landers chuckled. "Do you believe your witnesses will perjure themselves if they are faced with a full courtroom, Harriett?"

"Possibly. They face public humiliation by testifying. If the courtroom is not cleared, I will be forced to treat them as hostile witnesses. Frankly, I prefer not to attack my own witnesses."

"Who are these people...Larabee and Meier?" Landers asked.

"High school acquaintances of the defendant's brother who are willing to testify to the extent and nature of the sexual abuse suffered by my client, and their complicity in that abuse."

"Why would they agree to testify to such a thing? Just being solid citizens?" Landers frowned, not expecting an answer. "Where are you going with this, Harriett?"

"My case is built around the fact that Mrs. Taggart has a personality disorder created by childhood abuse, which included sexual abuse of an incestuous nature. These witnesses will help establish that to the satisfaction of the jury."

"You're not requesting the same anonymity for other witnesses, I see," Landers said.

"Considering what I already know, Judge Landers, I have absolutely no desire to protect any of the other witnesses from public ridicule," Harriett said coolly.

"That sounds a little vindictive, Harriett, and that's not like you."

"I'm sorry, your Honor, but this is an unusual case."

Landers looked at Lassiter and shrugged. "I'm going to grant the request to have the courtroom cleared for the testimony of these two witnesses. It's only important that the jury hear them, Mr. Lassiter."

"Thank you, your Honor," Harriett said.

As the attorneys left Landers's chambers, Nick said, "What about the others? You'll have to ask permission to treat them as hostile."

"I know, but I didn't want to push my luck right now. When they balk at testifying about their actions, Howard will grant that request. He hates recalcitrant witnesses."

Chapter
Thirty-Nine

RISING FROM HER seat, Harriett said, "Your Honor, the defense calls Thaddeus Larabee to the stand."

At Harriett's request, and over the objection of Sean Lassiter, Judge Landers had cleared the courtroom of spectators. The only persons remaining in the courtroom were Harriett and her client, the prosecution team, and the jury. Harriett remained standing as she waited for the bailiff to bring Thad Larabee to the witness stand. As she saw Larabee enter the courtroom, Harriett rested a hand on Sharon's shoulder and whispered to her.

Larabee wore a gray two-piece business suit for his court appearance. As he passed Harriett, he glanced momentarily at Sharon. Waiting for the bailiff to administer the witness oath, Harriett looked over the questions she had prepared for Larabee and Meier. Although they were her witnesses and their testimony would provide strong evidence that Sharon had been abused as a child, Harriett knew she would have a difficult time not showing her own feelings concerning what she already knew about the men.

As soon as Larabee had given the court stenographer his full name and his Scottsdale, Arizona address, Harriett was ready to proceed. Larabee looked nervous as he waited.

"Mr. Larabee, do you know the defendant Sharon Collins Taggart?"

"Her brother and I were friends. We met in junior high and then attended high school together."

"Would you characterize your friendship as a close one?"

"There were four or five of us who always hung around together."

"How old was Mrs. Taggart when you first met her?"

"I don't know exactly. She was pretty young. Maybe six."

"And how old were you at that time?"

"About twelve or thirteen."

"Would it be fair to say that you spent time at the Collinses' home?"

"Objection," Lassiter said. "Leading."

"I'll rephrase," Harriett said before Judge Landers could render a ruling. "When, if ever, were you at the Collinses' home, Mr. Larabee?"

"Lots of times. We used to spend the night over there at first. Then later when we were in high school, Parker would throw parties at his house when his folks were out of town."

"And where was Sharon during your visits?"

"At home. Parker babysat her."

"Who attended these parties?"

"Just some of the guys we knew."

"Any girls?"

"Not usually."

"What did you do at the parties at the Collinses' house?"

"Watched TV, listened to music. Sometimes we would sneak in a few beers."

"Was Sharon involved in these parties?"

Larabee loosened his tie slightly in anticipation of where he knew the questions were leading.

"Sharon," Larabee began, glancing toward Sharon, "she stayed in her room, mostly."

"Why?"

"Parker told her to wait there."

"What was she waiting for, Mr. Larabee?"

Larabee's eyes looked down at his hands as he cleared his throat.

"She was waiting for us."

"Why would you go to her room?"

"We would just go up there to fool around."

"I'd like for you to be very specific, Mr. Larabee. What do you mean exactly by fooling around?"

"We molested her, okay?" Larabee said forcefully, looking at Harriett. "At first, it was just touching and looking when we were young, but it sort of got out of hand after that."

"How old were you when these molestations began?"

"About thirteen."

"And Sharon was about six?" Harriett reiterated as she looked at the jury.

"Yeah, about that," Larabee said quietly.

"Was there penetration of Mrs. Taggart's genital area?"

"Objection, leading," Lassiter said as he stood.

"The witness is perfectly free to answer either yes or no, your Honor. The question did not direct the witness in either direction," Harriett responded.

"Overruled. The witness may answer," Judge Landers said.

"Was there penetration of Sharon Taggart's genital area, Mr. Larabee?"

"Yes. Manually."

"Were these molestations performed by more than one boy?" Harriett asked as she watched the faces of the jurors. They were riveted to Larabee's testimony.

"Like I already said, there were four or five of us. We went to

Sharon's bedroom together."

"What generally occurred after you arrived in her bedroom?"

"Parker always went in first. Then the rest of us would go in. Parker would have undressed Sharon and have her on the bed. The first time we just looked, but Parker told us it would be okay if we touched her after that, and he would have her touch us."

"Did Sharon have a reaction to this touching?"

"Not at first. I think Parker told her it was a game or something like that."

"Objection, your Honor. Mr. Larabee's response is speculative."

"Sustained. Ms. Markham?"

"Was there ever a time when the nature of these visits changed?"

"When we were around fifteen. None of us had any experience with sex, and we were just curious, you know."

"Go on, Mr. Larabee."

"We would go to Parker's house and have oral sex."

"Were these acts performed on Mrs. Taggart or vice versa?"

"By her, but she was still pretty young. About eight or nine."

"Do you know how Mr. Collins persuaded his sister to perform oral sex on his friends?"

"He told her it was what big girls did," Larabee replied with a frown.

"Did he tell her this in front of you?"

"Yes."

"Can you describe for the court how this activity was carried out?"

"We would line up, and Sharon would get on her knees in front of us and move from one of us to the other."

"Sort of like a group blow job, Mr. Larabee?"

Lassiter jumped to his feet before Larabee could answer, "I object, your Honor."

"Withdrawn," Harriett said. "Were you alone with Mrs. Taggart when these incidents occurred?"

"No. We were all there watching. A few times Sharon would get fussy and not want to continue, but Parker always convinced her to do all of us."

"When, if ever, did these visits move beyond mere sodomy?"

"I don't remember exactly, but by the time we graduated from high school we were all pretty frequent visitors at the Collinses' house."

"When you were seventeen or eighteen and Sharon was about twelve or thirteen?"

"Yes."

"At that time were you and your friends sexually active with Sharon Taggart?"

"Yes."

"Were you alone with her in the room then?"

Shaking his head, Larabee said, "Parker didn't want anyone alone with her because she might get hurt. We had to go at least in pairs. We would both have intercourse with her while we were there."

"What was her reaction by this time?"

"She was less cooperative as she grew older."

"How did Mr. Collins handle her reticence?"

"I don't know about with any of the others, but once while I was there, he grabbed her and threw her on the bed and held her down. He had to hold his hand over her mouth. That was the last time I ever went to the house. When I saw him holding her down like that, I couldn't do it. Sharon was crying and begging him to make us go away, but he just told her to calm down and do it. The quicker she let us, the sooner he would let her go."

"How long did Mr. Collins use his sister to provide these free sexual favors for his friends?"

"I don't know. I never went back after that day. But they weren't free."

"Excuse me?" Harriett said. The very idea that the exchange of money might have been involved had never crossed her mind, and Jan hadn't mentioned it.

"I said they weren't free. Well, at first the touching stuff was. But after we all got used to it and kept coming back wanting more, we had to pay him."

"How much did you pay him?"

"At first it was ten for the oral sex and later twenty-five for the intercourse."

"Do you know what that kind of arrangement is more commonly called, Mr. Larabee?"

"Parker was pimping his sister to his friends. Is that what you mean?"

"Yes, thank you. Do you have any other direct knowledge about sexual activities involving Sharon Taggart?"

"I ran into Parker over the Christmas holidays about a year and a half after we graduated, and he invited me over to his place for a party."

"What do you believe he meant by that?"

"The same as usual. Sex with Sharon."

"How old would she have been at that point in time?"

"About fourteen."

"Did you ever have an occasion to see Sharon Taggart after the last time you were at her house?"

"I ran into her at a mall once."

"Did she speak to you at that time?"

"Yes. We talked about school and a few things like that."

"Did she appear to harbor any animosity toward you?"

"No. I asked her if Parker's friends were still coming by the house, and she said they were. But it seemed like we were talking about two different things."

"I have no further questions for this witness, your Honor," Harriett said.

"Mr. Lassiter. Cross?" Judge Landers asked.

"Thank you, your Honor. Mr. Larabee, you stated that you only personally witnessed Mrs. Taggart resisting these sexual liaisons once, isn't that correct?"

"Yes."

"She never resisted your advances, did she?"

"Well, no, but..."

"That's sufficient, Mr. Larabee," Lassiter interrupted. "Isn't it possible that Mr. Collins was giving this money you say you paid him to his sister?"

"That wasn't my impression."

"But it is possible, isn't it?"

"I guess so."

"In fact, it's possible that collecting this money was her idea, isn't it?"

"Objection," Harriett said. "The prosecution is asking the witness to speculate, and a child the age of my client at the time of these sexual liaisons could not possibly have had the requisite intent necessary to set up such a monetary venture."

"Sustained."

"Did she want to have sex with you?"

"I don't know."

"Did she ever kiss you voluntarily?"

"Yes."

"Did she ever resist what you were doing to her?"

"No."

"Did she touch your genitals?"

"Yes."

"And she was spontaneous in her reaction to you, isn't that correct?"

"I don't know what you mean by spontaneous?"

"Did she know what she was doing?"

"She seemed to."

"And weren't her physical reactions to sex the same as any young woman's?"

"I don't know."

"You had sexual intercourse with other young women in high school, didn't you?"

"Yes."

"And were the physical reactions of Sharon Taggart dissimilar from those of those young women?"

"No."

"So Sharon Taggart was sexually well versed by the age of thirteen?"

"I suppose."

"She knew what to do to turn you on, didn't she, Mr. Larabee?"

"Yes."

"She used her hands?"

"Yes."

"Her mouth?"

"Yes."

"She encouraged you to go further, didn't she?"

Larabee glanced at Harriett before answering. "Yes."

"And you liked it, didn't you?"

"Yes."

"And *she* liked it, didn't she?" Lassiter hammered.

"I don't know."

"Did the defendant tell you she liked it?"

"Yes."

"And she asked you to do it again, didn't she?"

"No," Larabee answered. "She never did."

"You weren't alone with her in the room, is that what you testified to on direct?"

"Yes."

"So as a rule you watched another young man have intercourse with Mrs. Taggart after you had satisfied yourself, is that correct?"

"Yes."

"And her physical reactions to the second young man were the same as they had been to you. True?"

"I didn't watch very closely."

"But she kissed him, touched him, and encouraged him to continue as you watched. Isn't that true?"

"Yes."

"And she didn't resist the other young man?"

"No."

"In fact, she seemed to rather enjoy herself every time, didn't she?"

"Objection," Harriett said. "The witness isn't a mind reader, your Honor. He can't possibly know whether Sharon Taggart was having a good time or not."

"Sustained."

"No further questions, your Honor," Lassiter said after glancing at his legal pad.

FOLLOWING A TWENTY-minute recess, Harriett rose. "Your Honor, the defense wishes to call Jacob Meier to the stand."

Jacob Meier entered the courtroom and walked purposefully to the witness chair, raised his right hand and swore to tell the truth, the whole truth, and nothing but the truth. He unbuttoned his jacket and took a deep breath before looking toward Harriett.

"Mr. Meier, will you please tell the court how you came to know the defendant, Sharon Collins Taggart?" Harriett began.

Coughing slightly, Meier leaned toward the microphone and spoke. "I met Mrs. Taggart through her brother, Parker Collins."

"How old were you when you first met her?"

"I believe I was around thirteen."

"And what was the nature of your relationship with the defendant?"

Meier's eyes darted toward the jury box. He closed his eyes for a moment before answering. "Parker would invite a few of us over to his house when his folks were gone for what he called 'a pussy party'."

Harriett hoped the surprise she felt at her witness's statement didn't show on her face. Although she had done a pre-trial interview with Meier, she hadn't expected the particular wording she was hearing. She glanced at the jury quickly before continuing, and it was obvious that Meier had the jurors' complete attention.

"Would you please explain what that phrase meant to you, Mr. Meier?"

"It meant that we were all going to have sexual intercourse with Parker's sister," Meier said in a clear, unwavering voice.

"Was sexual intercourse always involved?"

"It didn't start out that way. At first it was oral sex performed by Sharon. The actual sexual intercourse didn't begin until later. To the best of my memory, I was about fifteen or sixteen when that started."

"And that would have made my client perhaps ten or eleven?"

"About that, yes."

"Was there ever a time when the nature of these 'parties' changed?"

"An activity like that isn't something that can exactly be kept a secret for long, Ms. Markham. By the last time any of us were at Parker's house, there must have been at least fifteen or twenty guys involved."

"All in the same evening?"

"Yes. I'll never forget that night as long as I live."

"What made it different from the other times you had been at the Collinses' home?"

"Everything just seemed to get out of control that night. Parker lost control of what was happening, and he left his sister alone with a couple of us."

"Can you describe for the court what happened that evening, Mr. Meier?" Harriett asked quietly as she leaned forward on the defense table.

"We had all been drinking and smoking pot most of the evening. Throughout the evening, five or six pairs of guys had followed Parker to his sister's room. Finally someone tapped me on the shoulder. When I looked up, it was Parker. He told me that if I wanted to get any, I'd better go on up because Sharon was getting a little hard to handle. The guy who went up with me was this big lineman, Jerry Phelps. It was his first time at Parker's, and he was really excited. Like he'd never seen a naked girl before." Meier paused and took a drink of water from a glass next to the witness stand.

Clearing his throat, he shook his head slightly and continued his testimony. The courtroom was as silent as a tomb. "Jerry and I stripped off our jeans and jockey shorts, and Parker handed rubbers to both of us and told us to put them on. We did, but then there was shouting downstairs. Parker told us to wait and left the room. Before I knew what was happening, Jerry closed the bedroom door and locked it. He looked at me and grinned and said, 'I ain't taking no sloppy seconds or thirds.' So we....," Meier's voice cracked and he stopped to take several deep breaths.

"Are you all right, Mr. Meier?" Judge Landers asked. "Do you need a short recess?"

Meier looked at Harriett and Sharon before looking up at Landers.

"No, your Honor. It's just that this is extremely difficult for me to admit to."

"Please continue, Mr. Meier," Landers instructed.

"Jerry and I both removed our rubbers and got on the bed. I held Sharon down and put my hand over her mouth while Jerry got behind her and....and penetrated her anally. He was a really big guy, and when he pushed into her, her eyes went wild with pain. I told him to slow down, and let it rest inside her until she relaxed. She closed her eyes real tight for a minute, and when she opened them again, she looked at me and seemed almost calm. I took my hand away and forced her to do me orally, but it became obvious to me, even as drunk as I was, that she was having a hard time breathing. So I stopped and told Jerry to pull out. That we were done. But Jerry wouldn't stop. He just kept pounding away at her like a jackhammer. When he finally did get off her, there was blood on the bed, so he must have hurt her pretty bad. Jerry was so hopped up that he couldn't get rid of his erection and wanted to wait a few minutes and do her again. But by then she was too messed up, and Parker was banging at the bedroom door. She just curled up into this little ball like she didn't notice that we were still there. She looked so small," Meier's voice faded away.

"What happened after Mr. Collins got into the room?" Harriett asked.

"He took one look at his sister and told us the party was over. I told him I thought she needed to go to the hospital, but he said he would take care of it."

"What did he mean by that, Mr. Meier?"

"I really don't know, Ms. Markham. I got dressed and left. I never went back."

"Can you tell the court what happened to Jerry Phelps, Mr. Meier?"

"Jerry died a few years ago," Meier said. "I heard he shot himself but don't know that for a fact."

"I know this has been difficult for you, Mr. Meier. Why did you agree to present this testimony today?"

"Because I still have nightmares about that night, Ms. Markham. I have a little girl of my own, and the idea that she might fall victim to predators like we were scares the shit out of me. I'm not proud of what I did and can never make up for it, but if my testimony helps Sharon, then I know I've done the only thing I can do," Meier answered, as a tear left his eyes and moved down his right cheek.

"Thank you, Mr. Meier. The defense has no further questions of this witness, your Honor," Harriett said as she stood and concluded her direct examination.

"Cross, Mr. Lassiter?" Landers asked.

Lassiter tapped his pencil against his legal pad and stood. "The prosecution has no questions of this witness, your Honor."

Chapter
Forty

THE AFTERNOON OF the third day of defense witnesses, Harriett covered the basic information about Sharon's childhood through a series of questions before getting to the heart of her questioning of Clarissa Collins.

"When did you suspect that Sharon was sexually active, Mrs. Collins?"

"Before she was a teenager."

"Dr. Wilder, a company physician with Collins Industries, has testified that you brought Sharon to him when she was twelve because you believed she was active at that time. Is that correct?"

"I took her to Dr. Wilder, yes."

"Did you suspect your daughter was having sex before she was twelve?"

"I may have. I don't remember exactly when I became suspicious."

"What did Sharon do that made you suspicious?"

"She began to talk about sexual matters, and I couldn't imagine that she would have read about the things she was talking about. She must have experienced them."

"Did Sharon have a boyfriend when she was eleven or twelve?"

"No. Sharon was a rather unattractive girl at that age. Awkward."

"How did Sharon feel about her brother?"

"They have always been very close, even though Parker is six years older than Sharon. She adored him because he was her protector. He took her places with him and made sure his friends were nice to her."

"When did Parker start watching Sharon while you went out, Mrs. Collins?"

"When he was about eleven or twelve. He was very responsible when he was young."

"When did you first become aware that your son was molesting Sharon?"

"That never happened," Clarissa answered defiantly. "Parker wouldn't molest his sister. He loved her."

"Didn't Sharon tell you that he was sodomizing her when she was five or six?"

"Well, she said something about Parker touching her once, but I told her she was mistaken. Parker gave Sharon her bath many times when I was busy. She misinterpreted what he was doing, that's all. It was nothing. When I explained it to her, she never mentioned it again."

"How did you explain the fact that he inserted his fingers into her vagina, Mrs. Collins? Just doing a thorough cleansing?"

"Objection," Lassiter said. "Counsel isn't allowing her witness time to answer one question before asking another."

"Sustained."

"Did you tell Sharon that her brother wasn't doing anything wrong by putting his hands on her genital area?"

"Yes. And I spoke to Parker about it."

"What was his explanation?"

"That it had been innocent. He was bathing her and his hand slipped."

Harriett chuckled slightly and looked at Clarissa, "His hand just slipped right in there, did it? I haven't heard a line that weak since I was a teenager, Mrs. Collins."

"Objection," Lassiter said. "Counsel is testifying."

Harriett looked over her shoulder at him and saw the hint of a smile on Lassiter's lips. "Withdrawn, your Honor."

"The jury will disregard Ms. Markham's commentary," Landers said looking at the members of the jury. "And it will be stricken from the record."

"Was it common for Parker to have his friends come over to your house when he was there alone with Sharon?"

"Mr. Collins and I didn't have any objection to his friends visiting as long as they didn't make a mess."

"Was there ever an occasion when Sharon complained about his friends?"

"She told me that they would sometimes come into her room, and she didn't like that."

"What was your response to her complaints, Mrs. Collins?"

"I reminded Sharon that good manners meant being hospitable to guests in our home."

"How hospitable do you think Sharon should have been?"

"Ms. Markham, I taught both my children to have excellent manners. Sharon knew how to behave when we had guests."

"She knew she should lay on her back on the bed and spread her legs for them. Is that what you mean?" Harriett asked sarcastically.

Clarissa's face turned red. She looked at Judge Landers. "Do I have to sit here and listen to obscenities like that? What she's implying is...is disgusting."

"I couldn't agree with you more, ma'am," Landers said. "But we've already heard some fairly disgusting things during the course of testimony. Continue, Ms. Markham."

"I know you don't believe your son was molesting his sister. Do you believe his friends were molesting her?"

"Objection, your Honor," Lassiter said. "Unless Mrs. Collins was present at any of these alleged molestations, she cannot testify to something she didn't witness."

Landers looked at Harriett and shrugged, "Sustained."

Harriett glanced at the jurors. For some reason, the testimony of Clarissa Collins had taken on comic proportions. The woman was in total denial concerning the actions of her son, and Harriett almost felt sorry for her. Almost.

"Mrs. Collins, what if I told you that this court has already heard testimony from two of your son's high school friends who admitted that they had sodomized and had sexual intercourse with Sharon from the time she was six until she was nearly thirteen?"

"I would say that they were lying. All of Parker's friends came from the finest families."

"What if I told you they both swore, under pain of perjury, that they had paid Parker to use Sharon to provide these services?"

Clarissa Collins couldn't answer for a moment, and Harriett was afraid the woman was going to break down on the stand.

"Parker would never hurt Sharon. He loved her," Clarissa reiterated.

"But he allowed his friends to hurt her and to pay for the privilege of doing so. Isn't that how Sharon wound up in the nursing home operated by Dr. Wilder in 1984?"

"Sharon was raped by a boy she was seeing."

"In your deposition, and again in your testimony today, you stated that Sharon never had dates when she was in school and certainly was not dating at the age of twelve. In fact, you have intimated that you believed your daughter was a homosexual before she married. Isn't that true, Mrs. Collins?"

"I don't recall saying..."

Harriett stood up. "Would you like to see a copy of your deposition, which you signed, to refresh your memory, Mrs. Collins?"

"No. I did tell you those things."

"Were you lying then?"

"No."

"So Sharon didn't have any boyfriends she would sneak out of the house to rendezvous with?"

"No."

"Then how can you explain the injuries which led to her being treated by Dr. Wilder?"

"Parker called me at the country club. He said one of his friends had raped Sharon in her room while he and some other boys were shooting pool downstairs. He didn't know what to do."

"Why didn't you tell your husband and rush home or to the hospital to be with your daughter?"

"It was already done and over with when Parker called. I was afraid my husband would kill the boy responsible if I told him."

"Were you ever aware of the extent of her physical injuries from that incident, Mrs. Collins?" Harriett asked.

"I knew she was hurt, Ms. Markham. But she was fine when I brought her home."

"Approach the witness, your Honor?" Harriett asked.

Landers nodded and Harriett walked to the exhibit table and picked up a piece of paper.

"Mrs. Collins, would you please read the underlined portion of Sharon's medical record from that night to the jury?" Harriett asked, handing Clarissa the paper.

Clearing her throat, Clarissa read, "Twelve year old female. Contusion to left side of the face. Bruising, minor tearing and swelling noted at the back of the throat. Numerous bruises and bite marks along the inside thigh area. Genital area red and swollen. Patient complains of abdominal pain. Significant tearing in the rectal area."

"Did you seek psychiatric help for Sharon after this rape?"

"No. She recovered from it. We never discussed it again."

"I have no further questions for this witness," Harriett said as she returned to the defense table and sat down, shaking her head at the fact that Clarissa Collins had deluded herself for so many years.

Sean Lassiter declined to cross-examine Clarissa Collins. As she stepped down from the witness stand, she paused momentarily next to Harriett and looked at her daughter. Sharon looked straight ahead, refusing to look at her mother.

Chapter
Forty-One

"MR. TAGGART," HARRIETT said, beginning the fourth day of testimony, "how did you meet your wife, Sharon Collins?"

"I fixed her car. We started dating not long after that."

"How would you characterize your relationship?"

Frank shrugged and looked at the judge, "Pretty much the same as any other couple when they start dating, I guess."

"Approximately how long did you and Sharon date before you were married?"

"About eight or nine months."

"What was her family's reaction to your marriage?"

"They acted happy enough, but I knew they weren't crazy about me."

"Did that bother you?"

"Couldn't have cared less. I wasn't going to be living with them."

"How long were you married before your children were born?"

"About four years before our son was born. My daughter came along a couple of years later."

"Children can sometimes place a burden on a family financially and emotionally," Harriett said. "Were there any noticeable changes in your relationship with your wife after your children were born?"

"No. Sharon was a good enough mother."

"Was there ever a time when you thought she wasn't a good mother?"

"No."

"Not even after your daughter was injured in January of 1999?"

"I thought Sharon should have been more careful, that's all. I warned her that Laurel was getting ready to start walking, and she should watch her more closely."

"What happened that caused your daughter's injury?"

"Sharon left her alone to do something, and I guess Laurel decided that was a good time to start walking. She fell and hit her head on a table."

"How severely was she injured?"

"She had a bruise on her cheek and knocked a tooth out."

"Was she treated for her injuries?"

"Yeah. Sharon took her in to the doctor right away. She didn't even lose the tooth."

"What was your reaction to Laurel's injuries?"

"I was upset, naturally."

"Did you blame Sharon for Laurel being hurt?"

"It was her fault. I told her she couldn't leave the baby alone."

"Would you say that Sharon was upset as well?"

"I guess she was. She kept telling me how sorry she was. She knew she should have listened to me."

"Did you refuse to let Sharon feed Laurel that night or even to hold her?"

"You bet. She deserved to be punished. But I might have overreacted a little."

"What was her reaction to this 'punishment'?"

"She got mad and said she was going out for a little while."

Picking up a copy of a hospital report, Harriett said, "Your Honor, I request that this copy of the hospital record regarding the injuries to Laurel Taggart be marked defense exhibit eight."

Harriett presented copies to Landers and Lassiter and then handed a marked copy to Frank Taggart.

"Would you read the date on the hospital record, Mr. Taggart?"

"January 10, 2000."

"Are you aware that January 10th, 2000 was the night Jerome Roth was fatally injured in an automobile accident after someone fired a shot at his vehicle?"

"No."

"Other than this one incident, you believe Sharon is a good mother, don't you?"

"Yes."

"Was she a good wife as well?"

Frank looked at the defense table for a moment. Sharon leaned forward and rested her elbows on the defense table and smiled slightly.

"Yeah. She did the best she could. She always had dinner ready when I got home. The kids were clean and healthy."

"Was Sharon working?"

"She didn't work until after Laurel was born in 1999."

"What changes, if any, occurred in your personal relationship with Sharon after your children were born, Mr. Taggart?"

"Like I already said, she was a good mother."

"I'm not interested in how she treated her children. How did she treat you?

"Did the frequency of your lovemaking decline, Mr. Taggart?"

"Yeah, a little, I guess. I didn't notice."

"Really?" Harriett asked with mock surprise. "How frequently would you say you and your wife had sex prior to the birth of your son Kevin?"

Frank smiled sheepishly and glanced at Sharon. "Often enough."

"Once a week? Twice a week? Nightly?"

"I didn't mark the nights on my calendar, Ms. Markham."

"Was there ever a time when you complained to your co-workers that your sex life with your wife was non-existent?"

"No, I..."

"How about if I called Charles Renniger to testify, Mr. Taggart?"

Frank glared at Harriett.

"Didn't you complain to Mr. Renniger that you weren't quote, 'gettin' any' from your wife?"

"Objection! Ms. Markham is badgering her own witness, your Honor."

"Ms. Markham?" Landers asked.

"Your Honor, the relationship of this witness to his wife, or the lack of it, goes to my client's state of mind. Permission to treat this witness as hostile," Harriett said.

"Granted," Landers said. Looking at the jury, Landers said, "Ladies and gentlemen, by allowing Ms. Markham to treat Mr. Taggart as a hostile witness, she is allowed to ask him leading questions which may not be objected to by the prosecution. Continue, Ms. Markham."

"Thank you, your Honor. Isn't it true that you told Mr. Renniger that you and your wife weren't having sex at all, Mr. Taggart?"

"Yeah, I told him that," Frank sulked.

"And was that true?"

"After Laurel was born, Sharon practically locked me out of the bedroom."

"Did the same thing happen after your son was born?"

"Not as bad. Less, but not a total freeze out."

"Did Sharon's demeanor, the way she acted in general, change after Laurel was born?"

"She was quieter. A little down, but as soon as she got her job she was happier."

"And you believed your sex life would improve at that time, didn't you?"

"I hoped so."

"But it didn't."

"No."

"I imagine that was very frustrating for you."

"You could say that."

"Tell me, did you discuss this problem with your wife?"

"I tried to. I said maybe we needed to see a counselor or something."

"And she refused?"

"Just kept putting it off."

"Isn't it true, Mr. Taggart, that you brought home pornographic videos and made your wife watch them with you in an attempt to increase her interest in sex?"

"Yeah, so what? Didn't work."

"Is it true that you were in the habit of grabbing your wife from behind?"

"It wasn't a habit. But I grabbed her a few times. She's my wife."

"Isn't it true that you knew Sharon didn't like being grabbed from behind? In fact, hadn't she asked you not to do it?"

"It was just playing around. That's what men and women do, Ms. Markham. But then someone like you probably wouldn't know anything about that," Taggart smirked, looking at the jury. "You only know what happens between two women."

"Your Honor," Harriett said calmly, "please instruct the witness not to editorialize. I ask that his last remark be stricken."

"Objection," Lassiter said. "Counsel can't object to her own witness's statements, no matter how hostile, when she opened this line of questioning herself."

"Overruled," Landers said. "I will not allow my courtroom to become an open forum for the purpose of airing personal grievances. The witness's remarks concerning Mrs. Taggart's attorney will be stricken. The jury is instructed to disregard them. Continue, Ms. Markham."

"You ignored your wife's request that you not grab her, isn't that true?"

"She got over it."

"Isn't it true, that when you grabbed her and refused to release her, that she became hysterical?"

"She tried to get away, yeah."

"Did you release her when she struggled to get away?"

"I was just playing."

"Trying to get a little, Mr. Taggart?"

"Yeah."

"Isn't it true that on one of these occasions when she couldn't get away, that she hurt you?"

"Yeah."

"You slapped her after that, didn't you?"

"You ever had someone stomp on your instep? Hurt like a son of..." Frank began as he looked at the jury. "It hurt. I slapped her, but it was like a knee jerk reaction to being hurt."

"What did she do after you slapped her?"

"She apologized," Frank said.

"Did you have sex immediately after that?"

"Yeah. She insisted."

"And I suspect you didn't fight it very much."

"It was a game. She always pretended not to want sex and wound up liking it once I got her in bed."

"Do you remember January eighteenth of this year?"

"What about it?"

"Was there anything special about that date?"

"No."

"Isn't it true you and Sharon had a fight that evening?"

"We could have. I don't remember."

"You had a few drinks with your friends after work that evening, didn't you?'

"I might have."

"According to Mr. Renniger and another man," Harriett said as she looked at her notes, "a Kenneth Payne, you had several drinks with them before you went home."

"Then I guess I did. So what?"

"Does drinking make you amorous, Mr. Taggart?"

"I don't know."

"Does it make you more aggressive?"

"No."

"Isn't true that on January eighteenth you arrived at your home after several drinks and demanded sex from your wife?"

"No."

"And isn't it true that Sharon declined your advances?"

"That wouldn't have been anything new."

"Isn't it true that at approximately ten o'clock on January eighteenth you physically attacked your wife, Mr. Taggart?"

"No."

"You grabbed her and took her into your bedroom, didn't you?"

"We went in the bedroom."

"Where you then ripped her clothes from her body and forced her down on the bed."

"That never happened!"

"Then didn't you hold her face down on the bed while you sodomized her?"

"That's a fuckin' lie!" Frank said loudly.

"And didn't Sharon beg you to stop?" Harriett pressed.

"No, she..."

"She what, Mr. Taggart? She wanted it? She liked it rough?"

Frank looked at Sharon and smiled, "She came."

"Did she struggle initially?"

"She usually did." Frank cast a quick glance at Sharon as he answered.

"That turned you on, didn't it?"

"Because I knew she would stop trying to get away in a few minutes."

"And did she?"

"Yeah," Frank said, continuing to look at Sharon. Harriett glanced at her client and frowned slightly. She knew Sharon Taggart was no longer sitting at the table.

"What happened when she stopped struggling?"

"I let her go. Do you want me to tell you what she did then?"

"We're all breathless with anticipation to know how this romantic evening ended, Mr. Taggart."

Leaning forward in the witness chair, Frank looked at Sharon with a crooked smile. "She told me to put my hands under her hips and raise them, so I could get at her better. Then I didn't have to do a damn thing but stay there on my knees while she moved her hips with me inside her. Real slow at first. Then faster and faster until she knew I couldn't hold it back any more and we both came. Is that what you wanted to hear, Ms. Markham? It wasn't rape. Sharon consented."

Harriett was disgusted and looked to see if any of the jurors, particularly the women, seemed to be equally uncomfortable. Sharon had leaned her head back and was looking at the ceiling of the courtroom with a smile on her face.

"Had you and your wife ever had anal intercourse before?"

"No."

"Did she ask you to stop?"

"She didn't mean it."

"You raped her, Mr. Taggart, didn't you?"

"That's only your interpretation."

"What did Sharon do afterward?"

"Nothing."

"She just laid there?"

"She pulled a cover over herself and went to sleep."

"She didn't speak to you?"

"No."

"And what did you do?"

"I went to sleep."

"Rape can be pretty exhausting, can't it?" Harriett asked sarcastically. Out of the corner of her eye, she saw Sean Lassiter start to rise from his chair. "Withdrawn. Was Sharon in bed when you woke up the next morning, Mr. Taggart?"

"Yes," Frank answered.

Turning toward the jury, Harriett said, "At some time after eleven in the evening on January eighteenth, two thousand and six, a bullet went through the windshield of Leonard Kaufmann's vehicle causing him to lose control of it. He died instantly as a result of his vehicle colliding with a utility pole."

Turning back toward Frank, Harriett said, "Did you know that, Mr. Taggart, or were you too busy sleeping off a night of good sex? No more questions for this witness, your Honor," Harriett said as she returned to her chair at the defense table. Waiting for Lassiter to cross-examine Taggart, Harriett looked at Nick and shrugged. Sharon leaned toward Harriett and touched her arm.

"You ever done it that way, Harriett?" Sharon whispered.

"No, Jan. I haven't."

Chapter
Forty-Two

AFTER A TWO-hour recess for lunch, Harriett called to the stand the witness she had been dreading since the trial began.

"Defense calls Alexis Dunne to the stand," Harriett announced.

Harriett avoided looking at the prosecution table as she waited for Alex to enter the courtroom and be sworn in. As she looked down at her notes, Nick reached behind Sharon and tapped Harriett on the shoulder.

Leaning back, he said, "Do you want me to take this one?"

"Thanks. I can handle it."

"You sure?"

"Yeah," she smiled. "It's okay."

By the time Harriett looked at Alex, she was seated and taking a deep breath. They both already knew what was coming, and Harriett planned to get through her questions as quickly as possible.

"Ms. Dunne, do you know the defendant, Sharon Collins Taggart?"

"Yes. My law firm handles legal matters for Taggart Industries in Dallas, and her brother is engaged to my sister."

"Have you ever had an occasion to spend time alone with Mrs. Taggart?"

"I met Mrs. Taggart during her brother's campaign for the state legislature two years ago. I enjoyed her company several times after that."

"As a result, did you and my client become intimate?"

Alex's jaw tightened and for a fleeting moment, Harriett wished it hadn't been necessary to ask the question. "We became involved in a sexual relationship that lasted approximately a year," Alex answered as she looked at Sharon.

"When was the last time you saw Mrs. Taggart?"

"She called my office and asked if she could see me regarding a legal matter just after Thanksgiving of last year."

"Did she indicate what the legal matter was?"

"She said she was considering a divorce and wanted to know her legal options concerning the division of their property and custody of their two children."

"Did your secretary schedule an appointment for Mrs. Taggart?"

"Mrs. Taggart asked to speak directly to me. I explained that my appointment calendar was booked until the following week, but finally agreed to meet with her at my office the evening of December first. About six-thirty."

"What happened when Mrs. Taggart arrived at your office, Ms. Dunne?"

"We discussed the Taggart's property holdings and other assets, which were fairly negligible. I told her I didn't think she would have any problem being awarded custody of her children. Certainly, her parents had the financial resources to tie Mr. Taggart up in court for months, and I didn't believe he would be able financially to challenge her custody claim."

"Did anything else transpire during your meeting?"

"Sharon and I had a sexual liaison in my office afterward," Alex stated.

Clearing her voice slightly, Harriett asked, "What, if anything, happened after you and Mrs. Taggart were intimate?" She couldn't bring herself to look at Alex as she asked the question and pretended to look over her notes on the table. Turning her head slightly, she saw Sharon look up at her and smile. Returning her attention to Alex, Harriett said, "Ms. Dunne?"

"Afterward, as callous as it must have seemed, I told Sharon that the relationship between us was a mistake. It should never have happened. I knew better, but allowed myself to be seduced anyway."

"What was her reaction when you told her it had been a mistake?"

"At first she laughed. Then when she realized I was serious, she became distant. She left about ten minutes later."

"Do you remember what time Sharon left your office?"

"Not exactly, but I believe it must have been around nine or nine-thirty."

Turning to face the jury, Harriett said, "And at eleven-thirty that same night, Elizabeth Pennington died in an automobile accident on the freeway. No further questions, your Honor."

"Cross, Mr. Lassiter?" Landers asked.

"I have no questions for this witness, your Honor," he said.

HARRIETT WAS LOOKING forward to a long weekend. Before the first witness of the fifth day could be called, Landers had announced that trial would not resume until the following Tuesday due to a personal family matter, which would take him out of town. She had already elicited and heard enough sickening testimony in just four days to last her a lifetime and would enjoy the three-day break with Jess. Since the trial had begun, no other unusual events had occurred either to her or Lacey.

Rising from her seat, Harriett said, "Your Honor, the defense calls Parker Collins."

Collins entered the courtroom and walked directly to the witness chair to be sworn in. Harriett was amazed at how calm he appeared despite the fact that everyone in the courtroom was already aware of what he had been accused of, including his fiancée, Paige Dunne.

"Permission to treat the witness as hostile, your Honor," Harriett requested.

"Granted," Landers ruled.

"Senator Collins," Harriett began as he took his seat, "we've already heard four days of testimony concerning abuse suffered by your sister when she was a child."

"I did not molest my sister, Ms. Markham," Collins said, shaking his head. "She's made up stories like that since she was little to get my parents' attention."

"Are you telling this court that your sister was not abused?"

"She's always told my mother lies about me. I can't put up with them any more, not even to save Sharon from prison."

Squinting slightly, Harriett asked, "Are you aware, sir, that we have sworn affidavits from two of your high school friends saying that they sodomized and sexually molested Sharon from the time she was six until she was at least thirteen? And that both claim they paid you money for the privilege of doing that?"

Collins's face slowly drained of color as he searched for a response.

"That's a lie," he finally said. "Sharon was raped by one of my friends when she was twelve or thirteen, but I didn't find out about that until after it was over."

"Is that when you took her to Dr. Wilder?"

"Yes. I'm sure Sharon had to have been traumatized by the rape, and now she's dumping all of that over onto me. I should have been watching her more closely, but I thought I could trust my friends."

"Sharon thought she could trust you, sir. Guess you were both wrong. Which one of your friends do you claim raped Sharon?" Harriett asked.

"I don't remember now. It's been a long time ago."

"How about Jerry Phelps?" Harriett asked as she picked up a legal pad from her desk.

"Or maybe Raul Santiago? Or David Curtis? Or Steven Lanier? Are any of these names ringing a bell for you, Senator?"

"They knew Sharon had been raped."

"Which one raped her!" Harriett demanded.

"Phelps did."

"Isn't it convenient that Jerry Phelps is dead now and can't dispute your story?" Then she smiled slightly, "But then there are Thad Larabee and Jacob Meier. They have a slightly different story, although Meier did mention Phelps."

"Then Jake can tell you Phelps raped Sharon."

"Actually he did tell the court that happened. And he knows

because he was in the room when the rape occurred."

"I didn't know that," Collins frowned.

"Then you must have a profound memory loss because Meier swears you were there also."

"That's not true," Collins said.

Standing up quickly and placing her hands on the defense table, Harriett said, "Didn't you leave Sharon alone with two of your friends, and thereby allowed Jerry Phelps to brutally rape her?"

Collins shot out of his chair. "That's a fucking lie!"

"Sit down, Mr. Collins!" Landers ordered.

Harriett waited for Collins to compose himself.

"Sharon herself corroborates Mr. Meier's story."

"Sharon's crazy," Collins blurted out.

"Isn't it true that you charged your friends a fee to have sexual intercourse with your own sister? And that you, and you alone, ensured that she cooperated by holding her down on the bed and threatening her if she screamed?"

"No...that's a lie," Collins stated. "Sharon never objected, and I was never paid any money by my friends."

"In other words, you only watched while your friends violated your sister over and over and over, for free, for nearly seven years just because you were being a good host. Is that your testimony, Senator?"

Collins slumped back in the chair. Harriett looked at the faces of the jury members and walked back to the defense table.

"No further questions of this witness, your Honor."

"The prosecution has no questions for this witness, your Honor," Lassiter said quietly.

Standing at the defense table, Harriett said, "Your Honor, I move Parker Collins be arrested and charged with perjury, based on his testimony in this courtroom today."

Nodding slightly, Landers said, "Bailiff, take Senator Collins into custody on the charge of perjury."

"Thank you, your Honor. The defense rests."

Chapter
Forty-Three

HARRIETT WAS TIRED as she pulled herself up from her desk and stretched. The Taggart case was taking its toll on her, and she knew it. The remainder of the afternoon and into the evening she had worked on her preliminary closing remarks. Lately, she had begun to believe she needed to take some time away from her practice and devote more time to herself and her new relationship with Jess. Carrying her coffee cup into the kitchen of the office, she washed it and placed it in the drainer. A few minutes later, she finished picking up a few things in the kitchen and returned to her office for her briefcase. She wanted to immerse herself in Jess's Jacuzzi, soak away her problems and make love with Jess...several times. She glanced at her wristwatch and smiled. Jess was sure to be in the middle of preparing dinner.

She was only a step or two into her office when she was grabbed roughly from behind and a hand clamped over her mouth. Quickly, whoever grabbed her spun her around and pushed her hard against a wall, momentarily stunning her. The hand covered her mouth again, but this time she felt a stinging sensation under her chin and froze.

"If you try to scream, the sound will never make it out of your mouth. I guarantee it," a man whispered.

Terrified, Harriett tried to remain calm, but it was a losing battle. Her head was pounding from hitting the wall. She blinked her eyes open and felt a shiver run up her spine as they focused on the man in front of her and widened in stunned surprise.

"Happy to see me again, Harriett?" Jared Wilkes asked with a grin. "Do you know how many times I've dreamed of this moment?"

Harriett felt the tip of his knife pierce the skin under her chin slightly and closed her eyes. "Twelve fucking years," Wilkes said slowly, dragging his words out. "Look at me!" he demanded.

She felt her breath quicken even though she tried to control it. When she opened her eyes again she hoped Wilkes couldn't read the fear in them.

"I've been watching you for a long time. At the bar, in court, passing you on the street. Nice home, too. Sexy lingerie," he said as he brought his mouth closer to her ear. "Has your new girlfriend seen you in it yet? I could have killed her that night she chased me, you know.

And Lacey, I can't wait until I meet her," he leered.

At the mention of her niece's name, Harriett brought her hands up in an attempt to push Wilkes away. He laughed as he shoved them away. "I'm going to take my hand away from your mouth now, so we can talk," he said quietly. "But I'm going to keep the knife right here," he continued, jabbing it slightly into the skin under her chin, making her wince.

Wilkes slowly removed his hand and she began to breathe through her mouth to take in more oxygen.

"What do you want, Jared?" she asked, her voice wavering slightly as she felt the tip of the knife on her skin with every word, making her tilt her head further back in order to speak without pain.

"You know, this is a really nice little office you have here," Wilkes said, ignoring her question. "I've been in here a couple of times looking around. Bet you didn't know that."

"No, I didn't."

Wilkes pulled her away from the wall and wrapped an arm around her throat, moving the knife to her back. "Let's go," he said as he pressed against her back.

With Wilkes guiding her from behind, Harriett made her way down the hallway and upstairs to the rooms that had been her home before Nick joined her practice. They had been converted into storage for old files long before and were seldom used. Wilkes stopped her in front of an upstairs room and opened the door. As soon as they were inside, he closed and locked the door before flipping on a small light. She couldn't believe what she saw. A mattress lay on the floor and Wilkes had covered the window with a black drape. Her body tensed, and she knew he could sense it as well.

"Do you like it?" he asked.

"What do you want, Jared? You can leave right now, and I won't report this. If you do anything else, you'll only be making things worse for yourself."

Wilkes shoved her away from him, and she turned to face him. The corners of his mouth curled into a wicked smile. "Undress," he ordered.

When she failed to make a move, he twirled the handle of the knife in his hand and moved toward her. Instinctively, she began backing away from him, but there was no place to go in the small room. He teased her with the knife until she found herself against a wall. Swiftly, his free hand grabbed her throat, and he held her against the wall. She could barely breathe as he began unbuttoning her blouse. With a flick of the knife in his hand, she felt her bra come apart and saw his eyes as they surveyed her upper body. She closed her eyes as he ran the tip of the knife around her breasts. Releasing her throat, he grabbed her arms and slung her onto the mattress.

With more strength than she thought she had, she swung her fist and caught Wilkes on the left side of his head. A moment later she was stunned as his hand struck her face. Before she could react, he was on top of her, pulling her skirt up with one hand and holding her by the throat with the other. Cold metal raked against the inside of her thigh as her underwear fell away. Pushing himself up slightly, he looked down at her.

"Is this your worst nightmare, Harriett?" he asked. "I've been watching Lacey, you know. I hope her boyfriend hasn't done her yet. When I'm through here, I think I'll pay her a little visit and find out. I could've already had her but decided to save the best for last. After all these years, I bet you're still wondering what all those girls went through."

She tried to move from under him, but her efforts only made him smile. He leaned down closer to her face and whispered, "Let me show you."

JESS WAS TURNING down the flame under a pot of potatoes that had finally come to a boil when Lacey came into the kitchen. "Smells great," she said. "When will Aunt Harriett be home? I'm starving."

"I thought she'd be here by now," Jess frowned. "I talked to her a couple of hours ago, and she was finishing up then. Call her office and tell her there won't be any food left if she doesn't get here soon."

As she was running water over a head of lettuce for a salad, Lacey walked back into the kitchen. "She doesn't pick up at her office. All I got was her service. Maybe she's on her way home."

Jess had to smile. She liked the idea of her house being referred to as Lacey and Harriett's home. The cell phone in her pocket vibrated, and she looked at Lacey as she fished it out. "Probably her now." Flipping the phone open, she didn't recognize the number on the display. "Jess Raines," she said.

A moment later, she shook her head at Lacey. "It's my office. Call Harriett's cell. Maybe she's stuck in traffic," she said calmly. As soon as Lacey left the room, Jess returned to her own phone. "Repeat that," she said.

WILKES KISSED HARRIETT'S cheek as he encircled her neck with his hands, slowly squeezing and cutting off her oxygen. Within a few seconds, she could feel her body going limp and knew she would lose consciousness. As her eyelids fluttered, he opened his hands, and she gasped for air. Weak from the strangulation, gasping for air, she was powerless as Wilkes ran his hands between her legs and pushed them apart. Her brain was sending signals to her body, but it wasn't responding correctly to the messages as he penetrated her roughly. As her body began responding to the oxygen she was taking in and the pain she felt, his hands found her throat again. The more frenzied his attack became, the tighter he gripped her throat.

JESS BROUGHT THE Durango to an abrupt stop behind two patrol cars and left the driver's door open as she quickly exited the vehicle and ran toward the officers who were standing two houses down from Harriett's office. Catching her breath, she said, "Anything?"

"The building is dark inside, but there's a tan Chevy in the back drive," one of the patrolmen answered.

"Then she's inside," Jess said. Pointing at two of the officers, she ordered, "You two, take the back. When I give the signal go in. We'll go in the front." Drawing her Glock, Jess and the patrolmen moved rapidly toward the office. Looking in the front windows, she tested the front door. Stepping in front of it, she nodded to one of the officers. "Tell them to break the back glass and go in," she said as she struck the front glass with her elbow.

HARRIETT'S THROAT WAS dry and ached as her eyes opened. As she tried to move, she felt a stabbing pain in her groin. A hand ran across her breasts and down her abdomen, causing her abdominal muscles to tighten involuntarily. Wilkes's face appeared over her once again and a chill ran through her. "Please...," she started as tears filled her eyes.

Seeing the fear in Harriett's eyes, he smiled. "I could keep this up all night, but I have a date with Lacey later and don't want to keep her waiting too long," he said, his hands taking her by the throat again, slowly beginning to close. Harriett knew she was going to die as lights exploded inside her head, followed by a roaring in her ears as she lapsed into unconsciousness.

A quick search of the offices revealed nothing out of order until Jess glanced up the stairs leading to the upstairs storage area. A small shaft of light came from under the door at the top of the landing and Jess took the stairs two at a time with a patrol officer right behind her. She turned the doorknob and when she found it locked she lowered her shoulder and rammed into it. She barely had time for her brain to register the scene in front of her before she squeezed off two quick shots. "Call an ambulance!" she screamed to the officer behind her.

Chapter
Forty-Four

HARRIETT LAY STOICALLY on an examination table, a warm blanket covering her as she shivered. She couldn't remember ever feeling so cold. The bruises on her face and neck had begun to darken into an ugly purple. She barely remembered being undressed, Wilkes's blood being washed from her face and upper body as she trembled.

"Are you all right?" Jess asked softly.

Nodding slightly, but not looking at her, Harriett brought a shaking hand up and pushed strands of hair behind her ear. She didn't want Jess to see her like this.

"Lacey.....," she managed to say.

"She's safe," Jess assured her.

When Harriett finally looked at her, Jess saw tears had begun forming in her eyes. Her heart went out to Harriett, and she took her in her arms, holding onto her tightly, allowing her to cry as long as she needed to. A light tap on the door announced the arrival of a doctor wearing green hospital scrubs, followed by a nurse.

"Ms. Markham," the doctor said softly. "I'm Dr. Jacobi. I know this is an extremely difficult time, but we need to perform an examination."

"I know," Harriett nodded.

"Are you a relative?" Jacobi asked Jess as he pulled latex gloves on.

"A friend."

"Then you'll have to wait outside."

"I want her to stay," Harriett said in a firm voice as she wiped her face.

"I'm afraid that violates hospital policy, Ms. Markham," Jacobi said.

"I don't give a damn what it violates," Harriett said forcefully, even though the strain of speaking made her throat ache. "I'm an attorney, and I promise not to sue you because you let her stay."

"I'll need to perform a pelvic exam and take several swabs as evidence."

"I know the procedure," Harriett said flatly. "Just do it and get it over with."

Jess took Harriett's hand and held it tightly, turning her back to what was happening as a nurse prepared Harriett and set out medical implements. She couldn't imagine the humiliation Harriett was going through and tried to block out what the doctor was saying during his examination. Periodically, she flinched and squeezed Jess's hand tighter. Despite the fact that the exam room seemed cold enough to hang meat in, beads of perspiration appeared on her forehead. Picking up a towel hanging near the exam table, Jess wiped Harriett's face. She opened her eyes and kept them on Jess during the remainder of the exam. This is my fault, Jess thought. I should have been keeping a closer watch on her. It seemed that the doctor was taking an eternity to complete his examination and, although she tried not to think about what the doctor was doing, Jess picked up scraps of the doctor's explanation to Harriett and his instructions to the nurse. At last the doctor turned off the exam light and moved to the side of the exam table.

"You have some tearing, which is to be expected, as well as considerable bruising, Ms. Markham. It might take several days for them to heal, and you'll probably have some discomfort until it does. Do you have children?"

"No."

"Well, the treatment is about the same as with new mothers. Sitz baths and then apply heat to the area to reduce the pain and speed healing."

"What about...diseases?" Harriett asked as she squeezed Jess's hand again.

"We'll send slides to the lab to determine the presence of any STDs. I evacuated the vaginal area, but I'll give you an injection to prevent pregnancy. Do you have any other questions you'd like to ask?" Jacobi asked, patting her on the shoulder. "I recommend you make an appointment with your own gynecologist for a follow-up. Someone will be here shortly to photograph the bruises for the police."

"Can I go home after that?" Harriett asked.

"I want to admit you for observation, at least for tonight. I'm sure there won't be any complications, but occasionally we see some hemorrhaging. I'll write an order for a sedative tonight and a prescription you can take home. If you'd like I can request a psych consult. Sometimes rape victims have a delayed reaction even after they've healed physically."

"No," Harriett said. "I have a friend who's a psychologist. I'll contact her."

Jacobi patted Harriett on the shoulder before leaving the room. Jess excused herself and followed him out.

"Can you get her a private room, doctor?" she asked.

"I'm sure we can. We should have her in a room in less than an hour."

"I'd like to stay with her."

Jacobi smiled and said quietly, "I won't tell anyone if you won't."

FORTY MINUTES LATER, Jess accompanied Harriett to her room. As soon as the nurse had taken her temperature, pulse and blood pressure, she left to get the prescribed sedative.

"Jess," she said softly. "I want to take a bath."

Nodding silently, Jess helped her out of bed and could tell by the way she moved that she was hurting and wished there was something more she could do. She knew from experience that Harriett would remain in the shower, running the hot water over her body, for a long time, attempting to wash away the memory of what had happened. It was nearly half an hour before she emerged from the bathroom, holding a hospital gown tightly around her body and crawled back into the hospital bed.

As she settled back against a pillow, she looked at Jess. "When did he get out?"

"Last month," Jess answered, stroking Harriett's damp hair.

"I don't remember how I got here," Harriett said, her voice wavering slightly. "I only remember his hands around my throat...him...inside me...I..."

Jess gathered Harriett in her arms and held her. "Don't talk about it right now, honey," Jess whispered. "Just rest. You're safe now."

"Call Wayne and ask him to stay with Lacey," Harriett said, struggling to keep her mind clear. "I'll need a continuance. Get Nick to contact Judge Landers."

"Don't think about the case tonight," Jess said.

Harriett drifted off to sleep a few minutes later, and Jess slipped out of the room.

PACING LIKE A caged animal outside the emergency room, Jess wished she hadn't given up smoking. A car pulled quickly into the parking lot and stopped abruptly. Nick and Lacey jumped out of the vehicle and ran toward her.

"Where is she?" Nick asked breathlessly.

"In her room. They gave her a sedative, and she's sleeping," Jess answered.

"What the hell happened?" Nick demanded as Wayne joined them.

"I'm sorry. It's my fault," Jess said quietly, shaking her head. "I should have been watching her more closely."

"I want to see her right now!" Lacey said forcefully and Jess could see the fear and anger in the girl's eyes.

"She's in Room 442, but she's asleep."

Lacey pushed past her and entered the emergency room doors with Nick close behind her.

Taking in a deep breath and exhaling slowly, Jess asked Wayne, "Does Lacey know what happened?"

"We only told her Harriett had been assaulted," Wayne answered as he pulled a pack of cigarettes from his coat pocket and offered her one. Every fiber of her body wanted to take it, but she shook her head.

"So what went down tonight?" Wayne said as he exhaled a cloud of smoke.

"When it started to get dark and Harriett hadn't come home yet, I figured she was still at her office." Jessie leaned back against the building and rubbed her face with both hands. "The tail I had on Collins didn't report anything. Then I got a call from my office. They finally matched one of the partials from the stolen car to Wilkes's prints and matched DNA from the semen on Harriett's truck with that from the two girls who were murdered here not long before that."

"Go on," Wayne said as he flipped his cigarette away.

Clearing her throat, she continued, "I called for back up and drove to Harriett's office. Her rental was still in the driveway, but there weren't any lights on inside. We went into the house as quietly as possible and saw a light from under an upstairs door, but by the time we broke in....."

"You saved her life, Jess," Wayne said, resting a big hand on her shoulder, "That's all that matters."

Jess smiled weakly at him, "Hope she'll feel the same way. What hospital did they take Wilkes to?"

"None. Croaked in the ambulance. DOA," Wayne answered with a smile. "Good shootin'."

"No great loss to humanity," Jess said, pushing her body away from the wall. "There'll be a shitload of paperwork to fill out since he died and a shooting review board. I need to turn in my weapon. I'm...I'm so sorry, Wayne."

"No way you could have known," he said gently.

Chapter
Forty-Five

JESS AND LACEY helped Harriett out of the Durango the next afternoon as Wayne and Nick pulled in behind them. Lacey put her arm around her aunt's shoulders while Jess walked ahead to unlock the front door.

As they reached the front steps, Wayne put his arm around Harriett and hugged her briefly before escorting her inside.

"Can I get you anything, honey?" Wayne asked as they entered Jess's living room.

Managing a small smile, she said, "I could use a double bourbon, straight up."

"I'll get it," Lacey volunteered.

Harriett looked around before moving to the overstuffed sofa near the fireplace. Sitting gingerly, she drew her legs up under her and leaned her head back. Lacey returned with her drink as Jess came down the stairs from the bedroom.

"You should get some rest," Jess said as she stood behind Harriett and placed her hand on he shoulder, feeling her body flinch slightly at being touched.

Harriett shook her head and frowned. "I'm all right."

"No, you're not," Wayne said.

Harriett shot him a look and snapped, "It happened, okay. I'll get over it."

"Not alone you won't, and you know it," he said.

Setting her drink down, Harriett got up quickly from the couch to confront him, biting her lower lip to control her pain.

"I don't want you here!" she said loudly, her voice quivering slightly. "I don't want anyone with me! Or are you too fucking stupid to understand that?"

"Take it easy, Harriett," Jess said, glancing at Lacey. "You're mad as hell and have a good reason to be, but Wayne's right. The sooner you can talk about it, the better off you'll be."

"And who came up with that brilliant piece of bullshit," she said as she wiped her nose with the sleeve of her sweatshirt.

"Actually, Helen told me that when I called her from the hospital," Jess replied calmly.

"Fabulous! Is she going to drop by, too?" she snapped.

"If you need her to. None of us can begin to imagine what you've gone through. If you can't talk to us, then call her."

"You're damn right you can't imagine it, Jess. Shit! I couldn't imagine it either. But when it happened, there wasn't a goddamn thing I could do about it."

"You're alive, Harriett. That's what's important," Jess said, placing her hand on Harriett's arm.

Harriett slapped Jess's hand away and struck her chest with her fist. "And where the fuck were you?" she said loudly. "You were supposed to protect me! You promised you wouldn't let anyone hurt me!"

Stunned by the outburst, Jess started to reach out to pull her into her arms, but the anger in Harriett's eyes stopped her.

"I know. I'm sorry," Jess said softly. She knew she had let Harriett down. Just the way she had let Renee and Clayton down. The only difference was that Harriett had survived.

"Sorry? Sorry doesn't quite cut it, Jess! I trusted you," Harriett snapped as she pushed past Jess and went up the stairs.

"She'll be okay," Jess said calmly.

"I'll call Landers for a week's continuance," Nick said.

"She just needs some rest," Wayne grumbled. "And so do I. I'll be at Harriett's if you need anything, Jess."

Jess walked out with Wayne and Nick. When she returned to the house, she saw Lacey leaning against the front door.

"You okay?" Jess asked.

"I don't know what I'm supposed to do," Lacey said quietly.

"Just be there for her. You're all she has, so you'll have to be strong for her."

Lacey stuck her hands in the pockets of her jeans and walked slowly back into the house. "She shouldn't have said what she did to you, Jess."

"She's upset and has a reason to be, but she's a strong woman surrounded by people who love her. It might take a while, but she'll be okay, Lacey."

"I hope so."

HARRIETT SLEPT UNTIL early evening. She felt sore all over and walked into the bathroom to wash her face, carefully avoiding looking at herself in the mirror. She found Jess and Lacey standing at a kitchen counter peeling potatoes when she finally went downstairs.

"Feeling better?" Jess asked when she saw Harriett enter the kitchen.

"Much," Harriett said nervously, glancing between Jess and Lacey. "I'm sorry about earlier, Jess," she said quietly. "I didn't mean..."

"You don't have to apologize, Harriett. Especially not to me. You have every right to be mad."

"I'm not mad at you."

"I know that," Jess smiled as she pushed her glasses up with the back of her hand. "Right now you need to eat a good meal."

Harriett smiled back at her. "Can I help?"

"Sure. Why don't you whip up a salad? I think Lacey and I have everything else under control."

"What are you concocting?" Harriett asked as she looked in the refrigerator.

"I have no idea," Lacey laughed. "This is sort of free form cooking using whatever we could find."

"Sounds delicious," Harriett said sarcastically.

Harriett carried lettuce, tomatoes, cucumbers, and green onions to the counter and pulled a knife from a drawer. Jess glanced at her and saw her staring at the knife.

"Nick called Judge Landers at home earlier," Jess said, breaking Harriett's trance. "He's granting a week's continuance. Said he'd contact Lassiter's people about it."

"I'm sure that will piss Lassiter off. He probably thinks I conjured this up as a delaying tactic," Harriett said

"He's an asshole, in case you hadn't noticed."

Harriett laughed lightly. "It's crossed my mind."

"Landers said he'd be open to a longer continuance if you needed it."

"I have to face people sooner or later, Jess, so they can all stare at me and get it over with."

"It wasn't your fault, Aunt Harriett," Lacey said. "It was that asshole Wilkes's fault."

"When I took his case twelve years ago, I set all this in motion."

"That's ridiculous," Lacey protested. "Personally, I think you have a legitimate lawsuit against the State. They were supposed to warn you that he was out and they didn't."

"How's that salad coming?" Jess asked. "We're almost ready here."

"If I ask a question, will you two give me a truthful answer?" Harriett asked.

"Depends on the question," Jess said as she set plates on the kitchen table.

"How bad do I look? I haven't had the guts to look in a mirror yet."

"I've seen you look better," Jess smiled. "Purple isn't really your color."

"Makeup can do miracles these days," Lacey shrugged.

Harriett laughed as she put salad into three bowls and set them on the center kitchen island. Turning around, she moved behind Jess and placed her hands on her shoulders and leaned forward against her.

"Well, it smells delicious, whatever the hell it is," she said.

AT ELEVEN-THIRTY that night, Jess was sitting cross-legged on the sofa going over paperwork. They had talked for a long time over dinner, and she was glad that Harriett had been able to laugh even though she knew that Wilkes was never out of her mind. She had insisted that Lacey keep her date with Devon and the house was quiet.

Pulling her glasses off, she leaned back on a stack of pillows to rub her eyes when she heard Harriett's voice coming from the bedroom. Bolting up, she took the stairs two at a time and slowly pushed the door open. Harriett was thrashing around in the bed and talking in her sleep. Sitting on the edge of the bed, Jess called her name quietly and shook her gently, her nightshirt damp to the touch. Harriett jerked up in bed, breathing heavily as Jess turned on the lamp on the nightstand. As soon as she recognized her, Harriett covered her face with her hands.

"Bad dream?" Jess asked softly as she pushed damp hair away from Harriett's face

"He was right here. I saw him as clearly as I see you now," Harriett said exhaling loudly.

"Maybe you should take a sedative."

Harriett shook her head. "Not unless I want to spend the rest of my life on them."

"Your clothes are soaking wet and so are the sheets. Why don't you change while I take care of these?"

Harriett carried dry clothes into the bathroom, and Jess pulled the sheets off the bed and had replaced them by the time Harriett returned.

"There you go," she said. "Good as new."

Harriett climbed back in bed and laid back as Jess took the old sheets into the bathroom and placed them in a hamper. Returning, she stood over Harriett, smiling down at her.

"Can I get you anything?"

"I'm fine, but I wouldn't mind a little conversation."

"Sure," Jess said, as she sat on the bed next to Harriett.

"Have you dealt with many...rape victims, Jess?" Harriett asked.

"More than I wanted to," Jess said softly. "Just remember that none of this was your fault, Harriett."

"You're a good woman, Jess."

"Yeah, I'm a real jewel," she smiled.

"Do me another favor?"

"Anything."

As Harriett looked at Jess, her eyes glistened and she blinked hard.

"Please hold me, Jess. I don't want the thought of his hands on me to be the last thing in my mind before I go to sleep tonight."

Jess pulled the bed quilt up and slid under it, switching off the lamp on the nightstand. Wrapping her arm over the woman she knew she had fallen in love with, she wished she could erase everything that had happened in the last two days as she gently stroked Harriett's body until she heard the soft rhythmic sounds of sleep.

"HELLO, HELEN," JESS said as she stepped aside to let Helen Mortenson in the house.

Helen hugged Jess briefly and looked at her closely. "Are you all right?"

"Yeah. Of course. Why wouldn't I be? Nothing happened to me," Jess frowned.

"Something most certainly did happen to you, Jess. Someone you care about has been hurt. You wouldn't be human if you weren't affected," Helen said. "Do you need to talk about it?"

"No, Harriett needs you more than I do."

"Call my office and make an appointment then." Making sure Jess was looking at her, Helen added, "Soon."

"Harriett's in the den," Jess nodded. "I was just fixing some lunch for us. Can I get you something?"

"Whatever y'all are having," Helen smiled.

Helen was startled at Harriett's appearance, but smiled broadly as she greeted her with a long, warm hug. "How are you feeling, dear?"

"Sore mostly." Harriett shrugged as she sat down gingerly and leaned against the wing arm of the couch.

"That will go away in a few days, and the bruises will fade as well. How are you feeling up here?" she asked, tapping the side of her head.

"Confused," Harriett admitted. "A little afraid. Pissed off. Glad he's dead."

"He was an extremely sick man. I'm surprised he was released."

"Jess...Jess called the State hospital. The doctor there said he had been a model patient."

Helen laughed. "Yeah, well, one of the definitions of 'model' is an imitation of the real thing. I'm sure Wilkes did whatever he thought they expected from a sane person."

Harriett stared at her for a moment. "Interesting idea."

"Depends on how good an actor he was, and how overworked the staff was. But we're not here to discuss Wilkes. How are you sleeping?"

"Pretty good. I've had a few nightmares, but Jess wakes me up before they get too bad."

"Are you taking a sedative?"

"Just the first night. I don't want to become dependent on them. I need to deal with what happened and move on."

"It did happen," Helen said, taking a deep breath. "You were raped, Harriett. There wasn't anything you, or anyone else, could have done to prevent it. Jared Wilkes wasn't going to be stopped."

"He told me he had been watching me. He was in my home, my office. He was at the bar the night you and I were there. He watched Lacey..." Harriett said as her voice caught.

"What were you feeling when he attacked you?"

"Scared. I couldn't believe it. I wanted to kill him," Harriett answered. Tears trickled from her eyes as she looked at Helen. "He...he hurt me, Helen, and he still is. He made sure that he always will. He took away how I see myself. The way other people see me. I'm glad he's dead!"

"I haven't heard you say what he did yet. You need to say the words out loud, Harriett," Helen pressed gently.

Harriett buried her face in her hands and wept. "I can't, Helen."

"Of course you can. They're only words. They can't hurt you."

"He raped me!" Harriett finally sobbed. "Oh, God! He raped me! He took everything away."

Helen moved to wrap her arms around Harriett. "Shhh. He didn't take away your life. You're still the same woman you were before. You didn't cause this, but you have to accept it and learn to deal with it."

"Jess...she hasn't...she won't touch me...not the same way...not since that night," Harriett cried into Helen's shoulder.

"She doesn't want to hurt you," Helen soothed. "She knows you need time to heal."

"But she is hurting me," Harriett said, lifting her tear-stained face. "She sees me as a victim. I'm damaged goods."

"No, she doesn't. She's hurting, too, because she wasn't there to protect you and blames herself."

"Oh, God, Helen, I said terrible things to her."

"Jess loves you, Harriett. She knows you didn't mean what you said." Pausing for a moment, Helen caught Harriett's eyes. "You didn't mean it, did you?"

"Of course not. I apologized, but I don't think she believed me."

A light knock at the den door interrupted them. Helen walked to the door and opened it.

"Lunch is ready," Jess said, holding two plates.

"It looks fabulous," Helen beamed as Jess set up two tables and placed the plates on them.

"Not joining us?" Helen asked.

"My office called and I have to go in." Glancing at Harriett, she said, "The review board needs to see me." Leaning forward she kissed Harriett lightly. "I'll pick up something for dinner, okay?"

Helen watched the interaction between the two women closely. They both seemed unsure of themselves, and it was creating a gulf she wasn't sure they could cross.

WHEN LACEY OPENED the door of Jess's house that evening, Jess handed her a couple of bags while she juggled the rest.

"What's this?" Lacey laughed.

"Dinner, of course. You know your aunt doesn't cook, and I haven't noticed you reading any recipes lately either," Jess teased as she kicked the door shut.

"Aunt Harriett!" Lacey called. "Jess is home with dinner!"

"I decided we should finally have that Chinese dinner we missed," Jessie said as she went into the living room. Clearing everything from the coffee table, she set the bags down and threw pillows on the floor.

"Should I get plates?" Lacey asked.

Jess looked at Harriett and smiled. Turning to Lacey, she said, "You don't eat Chinese takeout on a plate, sweetheart. You pass the containers around and eat out of them. But," she said dramatically, "you have to be on the floor and absolutely no forks allowed. That's cheating."

"I don't know how to use chopsticks," Lacey laughed. "I'll starve to death."

"Come on, both of you. I don't want to give more than one lesson. It's easy. In fact, you can almost shovel the food in with chopsticks. So pull up a pillow."

There were rounds of laughter as Harriett and Lacey tried to get the hang of using chopsticks, with Lacey cheating occasionally by using her fingers. An hour later, most of the cartons were empty and everyone was full. Lacey excused herself to finish her homework, leaving Jess and Harriett sitting on the living room floor, leaning against the couch.

Taking Harriett's hand and kissing it, Jess said, "I'm sorry if I've seemed a little distant lately, Harriett. I had a lot on my mind, but the good news is that the shooting review board cleared me today."

Harriett reached up and touched Jess's face. "I knew they would."

"Well, I know a pretty good attorney who might have helped me if it hadn't worked out," Jess smiled, pushing herself up. Gathering up the remains of dinner she carried them into the kitchen. As she rinsed out their glasses, Harriett joined her and leaned against the counter. "Thanks for being here when I needed you, Jess. And for saving my life."

As Harriett looked at her, Jess touched her cheek softly and leaned forward to kiss her lightly. As her eyes searched Harriett's face, she could feel the familiar warmth of Harriett's body close to hers, wrapping her closely in her arms. As her hands moved across Harriett's back, their lips met and Jess lost herself in their deepening kiss, the first they had shared since the night that had changed everything between them. There was no hesitancy on Harriett's part as she responded again and again to the demands of Jess's mouth. They clung to one another, neither wanting to break the contact between them. Jess's hand slid down Harriett's side and found its way along her thigh. Feeling her body tense, Jess was snapped from the passion that had engulfed her. Taking Harriett's face in her hands, she brought their kiss to an end.

"I'm sorry," Harriett whispered, her voice catching.

"It's too soon, Harriett," Jess said.

"I...I'm going back to my place in the morning. I need some time alone to think," Harriett said, not meeting Jess's eyes.

"About us?" Jess frowned.

"And other things."

Chapter
Forty-Six

"YOUR HONOR, THE people call Dr. Donald Stevenson to the stand," Lassiter announced as he rose from his chair at the prosecution table the following Monday morning.

Harriett turned in her chair and watched as the bailiff escorted a tall dapper looking man in his late sixties to the witness stand. She had read the transcripts of a number of trials in which Stevenson had been called as an expert witness for the prosecution. After his interview with Sharon, his conclusion that she suffered from no mental defect had come as no surprise. Nick hadn't been successful in finding a chink in Stevenson's armor, leaving her left with the hope that he would say something she could attack in her cross-examination.

"This guy's a fuckin' asshole," Sharon whispered as she leaned closer to Harriett. It only took a quick glance for Harriett to realize that Jan had been the voice in her ear.

"But a credible asshole," Harriett whispered back with a smile.

Lassiter led Stevenson through a serious of questions that easily established him as an expert in psychiatry. She listened intently to his testimony, throwing in a few objections mostly intended to interrupt Lassiter's flow of questioning. Occasionally, she had to pinch herself to stay awake and noticed that the psychiatrist's sonorous monotone was lulling the jurors to sleep as well. Lassiter was halfway through his direct questioning of the witness when Nick slid into the chair on Sharon's left and pushed a folder across the table toward Harriett. She looked at him and received a broad smile in return.

Trying to keep half of her attention on what Stevenson was saying, she quickly flipped through the pages inside the folder and leaned forward to grin at Nick, mouthing a thank you. Leaning back in her chair again, she waited for Lassiter to conclude his questions. Stevenson testified, to no one's amazement, that Sharon showed no evidence of mental illness and that nothing in her background supported her claim of multiple personalities. He gave her credit for being an accomplished actress, even mentioning that she had won an award in college as the lead actress in the play *The Three Faces of Eve*. It was his belief that she was using that experience to perpetrate a fraud in her own defense. By the time Lassiter completed his questioning and passed Stevenson to

Harriett for cross-examination, she was prepared to dispose of him as quickly as possible.

"You have very impressive credentials, Dr. Stevenson," Harriett observed.

"Thank you, Ms. Markham," Stevenson replied with a smile.

"When you took your examinations for licensure were there any requirements pertaining to your personal history?"

"I'm not sure what you mean."

"Well, in order for me to be licensed as an attorney in this, or any other state, I have to show that I had never been convicted of a felony offense. Do either the American Medical Association or the American Psychiatric Association have similar stipulations before they grant a medical license?"

"Of course."

"Has Donald Stevenson always been your legal name, sir?"

"Objection, relevance, your Honor," Lassiter said.

Rising from her seat, Harriett responded, "You Honor, the defense would like to enter the police record of Donald Stefanofski into evidence for the purposes of impeaching this witness as an expert."

"Side bar, your Honor," Lassiter said.

Motioning both attorneys to the bench, Landers covered the microphone in front of him and leaned forward. "What is all this, Harriett?"

"I have evidence that the witness changed his name and that prior to that he was indicted and convicted of a felony offense which would negate the prosecution's claim that he is an expert. He should never have been granted a license to practice and without said license he has been practicing psychiatry illegally."

"That's crap and you know it! Your Honor, the prosecution would never offer up testimony from such a witness," Lassiter protested.

"Maybe you should have done your homework better," Harriett snapped. "If I found it you should have as well."

"Dr. Stevenson has testified in dozens of trials."

"Maybe those should be revisited as well."

"Enough," Landers said as he looked over the paperwork Harriett had given him. Looking at Harriett, an eyebrow slightly raised, he said, "He was nineteen years old when this happened, Harriett."

"It still doesn't absolve him of the lie. He served eighteen months and changed his name immediately after his release in a deliberate attempt to hide his involvement in a crime," Harriett said.

"What crime?!" Lassiter demanded.

"The paperwork says sexual assault, counselor," Landers said, handing the papers to Lassiter.

"This is teenage sex, for Christ's sake," Lassiter said. "It happened nearly fifty years ago. It in no way abrogates the validity of his testimony."

"It does if he has been practicing without a valid license," Harriett said. "And if the license is invalid then his testimony should bear no more weight than my gardener's."

Looking back at Lassiter, Landers shrugged. "She's right, Mr. Lassiter." Turning his eyes back toward Harriett, he frowned, "Step back, counselors."

Lassiter and Harriett returned to their respective seats as Landers addressed the court. "You may step down, Dr. Stevenson." Waiting as the confused witness left the witness stand and was escorted from the courtroom, Landers smiled at the jurors.

"Ladies and gentlemen of the jury. Dr. Stevenson has been disqualified as an expert witness. Anything he testified to as an expert will be stricken from the record and you are instructed to disregard it. Mr. Lassiter, do you have another expert you would like to call as a witness?"

Rising, Lassiter said, "No, your Honor. The people were relying on the testimony of Dr. Stevenson."

"Objection to the use of the title of doctor regarding the previous witness," Harriett said as a formality. "It unduly lends credence to his testimony regardless of your Honor's admonition to the jury."

"So noted," Landers nodded.

Harriett knew using the information Nick had found was a cheap trick, but it was the best she had to counter Stevenson's testimony. In all likelihood, he wouldn't lose his license considering the length of time since his felony conviction, and she knew Landers didn't like having stunts pulled in his courtroom. She would have to face those consequences when and if they arose.

HARRIETT HADN'T HEARD from Jess since she and Lacey had moved back to the townhouse. She had slept off and on, alone in her own bed for the first time in nearly two weeks. It felt strange to roll over and not feel the warmth of Jess's body next to her. She wished Jess would call...just to hear her voice. She missed the laughter they had shared, the small touches, and the passion Jess had rekindled inside her. The bailiff's booming voice brought her back to the present.

"All rise! The court is back in session. The Honorable Howard Landers presiding."

"Be seated," Landers intoned as he adjusted his robe. "Mr. Lassiter, are you prepared to call your next witness?"

"The people call Louise Harmon," Lassiter said.

Glancing at the witness list in front of her, Harriett stood immediately. "Objection! This individual is not on the witness list, and the defense hasn't had an opportunity to prepare its cross-examination."

Harriett felt Sharon's hand grab her arm. "You can't let her testify," she whispered. For the first time Harriett thought she saw fear in Sharon's eyes.

"Ms. Harmon was only brought to the people's attention late last night, your Honor. The prosecution is willing to grant the defense sufficient time to consult with her client regarding the testimony of this witness," Lassiter offered.

"Ms. Markham," Landers said. "I'll grant you a one hour recess to confer with your client."

"Thank you, your Honor," Harriett said, glancing down at Sharon.

Harriett and Nick watched as Sharon paced back and forth in front of them.

"Please sit down, Sharon," Harriett finally said.

Shaking her head as she continued to pace, Sharon said, "You can't let her testify."

"Why? What does she know that can hurt your case?"

"She knows I did it."

"We already know Jan did it, Sharon."

Raising an eyebrow, Sharon smiled slightly. "No, counselor. Lou knows *I* did it," she said stabbing her chest with her index finger. "How the fuck did they find her anyway?" she said almost to herself as she resumed pacing. Glaring at Harriett, Sharon walked to the table and, placing her hands flat, leaned closer to Harriett. "Have you breached our attorney-client privilege?"

"That's absurd," Harriett said. "If we knew Ms. Harmon was your friend, surely others did as well. If the woman knows about Jan, there's nothing she can say that will hurt your case. In fact, it could help."

Turning her gaze to Nick, Sharon asked, "Could I have a moment alone with Ms. Markham, please?"

"Of course," Nick nodded as he stood. Placing a hand on Harriett's shoulder, he said softly, "I'll let you know when they're ready to reconvene."

As she watched her client, virtually seeing her mind working furiously, Harriett gave Nick a nod and settled back in the hard wooden chair. Obviously, Sharon was struggling with whatever it was she needed to say, but Harriett decided to let her client make the first move.

"What do you know about Lou Harmon?" Sharon asked a few moments later.

"Just what you and my investigator have told me. She is or was your best friend, your daughter's godmother, and a reporter for a Dallas newspaper. What else do I need to know?"

Staring out the small window of the conference room, Sharon didn't turn to face Harriett as she spoke. "Lou is my best friend. I love her very much. I just didn't love her well enough, but I can't believe she would betray me."

"Do you have any idea what she will say under direct questioning?"

"The truth," Sharon shrugged. "It's not in her nature to lie, unlike most people I know."

"What is the truth?"

"I killed those people. I, Sharon Collins Taggart, did those things. I planned to do them, and I carried out my plan. I didn't plan for it to be so many." Finally turning toward her attorney, her lips hinted at a smile. "It became...I don't know...addictive. I wanted someone to suffer besides me, I suppose. For just those few seconds, I held all the cards. I was in control of something."

"And Jan?"

"Ah, yes. Well, Jan wasn't as strong as she thought she was after all. I had to kill her, too."

"Did she ever really exist?"

"When I needed her to. I don't need her any more now."

"What can I do to help you, Sharon?"

"Probably nothing. But I'm going to finally get the one thing I've always wanted. Perhaps the only thing I've ever wanted."

As Harriett looked at her, the unasked question in her eyes, Sharon smiled contentedly. "Peace," she said so softly that Harriett could barely make out the word.

Harriett sat quietly as Sharon returned her attention to the world outside the window. She didn't know any more about Louise Harmon than she did before, but she knew much more about Sharon Taggart. Or at least she thought she did. When Nick tapped at the conference room door a few minutes later, Harriett escorted her client back into the courtroom. She was still her defense attorney.

Shortly afterward, Harriett settled in her chair and watched as Louise Harmon stepped into the witness box and swore to tell the truth. As Lou adjusted her body in the witness chair, seeking a comfortable position, Sean Lassiter rose from his chair.

"Your Honor, this witness is here as a reluctant witness and was escorted to court by an officer from the Dallas Police Department to ensure her presence. I ask permission to treat her as a potentially hostile witness."

"Granted," Landers said, glancing at the witness. He had never seen so many hostile witnesses in one trial in all his years on the bench.

"Ms. Harmon, you are a friend of the defendant's, are you not?"

"Yes."

"How long have you known Sharon Taggart?"

"Since before she was Sharon Taggart."

"Since before her marriage?"

"Yes."

"How old was she when you met her for the first time?"

"Mid-twenties."

Harriett rested her head on her hand and stared down at her legal pad, suppressing a grin. Lou Harmon was planning to say nothing more than she had to as her way of protesting being forced to testify. Although she couldn't remember for sure, she seemed to remember from Wayne's preliminary report that Lou Harmon was about her own age, forty-five. Her hair was short and casual, as was her attire for court. She appeared to be relaxed, which Harriett took as a positive sign.

"How did you meet Mrs. Taggart?" Lassiter continued.

"She was a summer intern for the Dallas newspaper where I am employed. I oversaw her internship."

"So you were her boss?"

"More or less."

Lassiter picked up a folder from the prosecution table and opened it, looking at the contents for a moment before proceeding. "Are you familiar with a manuscript entitled *An Accidental Death*?"

"Relevance, your Honor?" Harriett asked.

"To establish intent, your Honor."

"Of what? The intent to read a book?" A smattering of laughter followed Harriett's retort.

"If it pleases the court, the people request that this partial manuscript, the beginning of a novel written by Ms. Harmon, be marked as People's Exhibit Number Nineteen at this time. The relevance will become clear."

"Objection overruled," Landers said as he motioned Lassiter forward. "I mark it People's Exhibit Nineteen," Landers said before handing the folder back to the prosecutor.

"Did you write this manuscript, Ms. Harmon?"

"Yes."

"Have you submitted it for publication?"

"It was never completed, so the answer would be no," Lou chafed at the direction of the questioning.

"Have you allowed other people to read what you have written thus far?"

"Yes."

"And was one of those people the defendant, Sharon Taggart?"

"Possibly," Lou answered as her eyes darted toward the defense table. Harriett felt a little sorry for Lou Harmon.

Changing his tactic slightly, Lassiter continued. "How long have you and Mrs. Taggart been friends?"

"Objection," Harriett interrupted. "Asked and answered."

"Sustained."

"Isn't it true, Ms. Harmon, that you and the defendant are more than just close friends? In fact, weren't you once lovers?"

Lou's eyes shifted to where Sharon was sitting before she answered. Out of the corner of her eye Harriett saw her client nod almost imperceptibly.

"Yes," Lou responded calmly.

"And was it during the time that you and she were lovers that you began writing *An Accidental Death*?"

"It might have been. I don't remember the date I started the piece."

"Did you ever discuss the premise of this story with Mrs. Taggart?" Lassiter asked as he held out the folder for the jury to see.

"We might have. It was a long time ago," Lou said.

"Did you ever discuss ways to commit a perfect murder with Mrs. Taggart?"

"I might have."

"When the killings on the freeways in Dallas began, didn't you think it was a little strange that they mirrored what you had written?"

"Those were reported as accidents, Mr. Lassiter, and there is nothing strange or unusual about traffic accidents on the Dallas freeways."

"You know," Lassiter said, shaking his head slowly, "I've read this partial manuscript, and it is amazing how similar it is to both the freeway killings and the actions of the defendant."

"Objection," Harriett said. "Is there a question somewhere in that book review?"

"Sustained. Move along, Mr. Lassiter," Landers instructed.

"What is the name of the main character in your manuscript, Ms. Harmon?"

"Janet Rutherford."

"And as is common practice, she is usually called by a shortened version of Janet, isn't she?"

"Yes."

"And what would that be?"

Frowning slightly, Lou once again looked at Sharon, as if asking forgiveness in advance. "Jan," she finally answered in defeat.

For the next half hour, Lassiter had Lou read portions of the manuscript he had marked aloud to the jury. No one could have missed the similarities with the case. When Lassiter completed his questions, he turned to Judge Landers. "Your Honor, the prosecution requests that People's Exhibit Number Nineteen be admitted into evidence."

"So ordered," Landers intoned.

"The prosecution has no further questions for this witness, your Honor."

As Lassiter turned the witness over to Harriett, she wasn't sure there was anything she could do to rehabilitate the succinct testimony. As she cleared her throat to ask her first question, Sharon leaned closer and whispered, "Don't hurt her. I've already done that."

Patting Sharon's hand, Harriett turned back toward the witness. "Ms. Harmon, how did you feel when Mrs. Taggart told you she was getting married?"

"I was hurt, but I understood why Sharon did it," Lou answered, the hurt apparent in her eyes. She clearly still loved Sharon.

"Did my client confide anything about her childhood to you?"

Seeming to brighten somewhat, Lou leaned forward as she answered. "She told me she had been abused as a child by her brother. It was difficult for her to talk about."

"Do you know Mrs. Taggart's parents and her husband?"

"Unfortunately, I do."

"Why unfortunately?"

"I got along fine with Mr. Collins, but Sharon's mother is a real piece of work. There was no way in hell anyone could have lived up to her standards. I knew I couldn't and didn't even try, but Sharon...," she paused. "Sharon lived in fear all the time that she would disappoint Clarissa. Nothing she seemed to do was ever good enough for that bi...biddy."

"And Mr. Taggart?"

"I never liked him. It wasn't simply because I was jealous, although I admit that I was. Even if I wasn't the one she chose, she deserved so much more than Frank Taggart. Only good thing he ever did was help create two kids." Lou blushed slightly, glancing at the jury. "Sharon told me each one took about thirty seconds and four or five drinks on her part to accomplish."

"How does Sharon feel about her children?"

"I think she thought they would be someone who would love her and never hurt her."

"Studies show that abused children often become abusive parents. Do you know whether or not she ever hurt her own children?"

Shaking her head, Lou answered firmly. "No, she would never hurt them. There were a couple of times when I know she wanted to, though, and that frightened her."

"What did she do when that happened?"

"She locked herself in the bathroom until the feeling passed except once. That time she called me in a panic and asked me to take her to a clinic for help."

"And did you?"

"As quick as I could get to her house. They didn't do anything for her, though, and she seemed to get over whatever had triggered her anger."

"Was she always like that, angry?"

"Not much until after Laurel was born. Then Sharon's emotions would be up and down, almost manic."

"Objection," Lassiter said. "The witness is not an expert in psychiatry."

"Neither was your other witness, *Mister* Stevenson," Harriett shot back, reminding the jurors of the earlier testimony.

"Objection sustained," Landers frowned. "The jury will disregard the witness's statement. Move on, Ms. Markham."

"No matter what, Sharon wouldn't hurt anyone in her family," Lou volunteered.

"Do you think, based on your intimate relationship, that Sharon would hurt anyone else?"

Pausing for a moment and looking at Sharon, Lou said, "I don't know."

Chapter
Forty-Seven

HARRIETT PULLED HER glasses off and tossed them on her desk, leaning back in her well-worn leather chair and pushing her hair over her head. "This case is giving me a headache," she said as she pinched the bridge of her nose.

Nick chuckled, "Well, at least it will soon be over. What do you think the jurors are thinking right now?"

"That we're all freakin' nuts," she laughed.

"Lassiter got you pretty good with Lou Harmon. I'd still like to know what led them to her."

"So would I," Harriett said, puffing out her cheeks as she exhaled. "So would I. But it wasn't all bad. She made Sharon look sympathetic, if not a little crazy."

"Why do you think she did it? Kill those people, I mean?"

"She didn't kill anyone, remember?" Harriett smiled. "They just overreacted and killed themselves."

"Maybe there was something to what Lou Harmon said. Maybe they were just substitutes for the ones who really hurt her."

"So what the hell does that make me? Her avenging angel?"

Nick shrugged. "Maybe that was all she was looking for, her own kind of justice for everyone who had hurt her. After everything you brought out during the trial, Senator Collins's career is pretty much over. He probably won't be getting either married or re-elected. Mrs. Collins should drop in esteem in social circles, and I'd volunteer to be Sharon's divorce attorney. Frank Taggart has been branded as a wife beater and a probable rapist. And Alexis Dunne's reputation was certainly damaged as well. They all hurt her in one way or another, either physically or emotionally, and she found a way to get even."

"And you think she was willing to go to prison or worse for that?"

"I still think she's crazy, Harriett, but you're not going to be able to convince the jury that she's insane. Not after Lou Harmon's testimony."

"I know," she said, slipping her glasses back on. "But maybe I can still save her life."

Nick looked at his watch as he flipped another page on his legal pad. "It's getting close to dinner time. Why don't you call Jess and see if she'll pick something up for us? Then we can work through and get out of here at a reasonable time."

"I can call someplace that delivers," Harriett said. "What would you like?"

Setting his pad down on the coffee table, Nick watched Harriett as she leaned her head on her hand and continued working on her closing statement. "Come to think of it," he observed, "I haven't seen Jess around in a few days."

"She has a job, you know. Probably got behind when she was babysitting me," Harriett said, hoping she sounded nonchalant enough. She wanted to pick up her phone and call Jess but wasn't sure what kind of reception she would receive. She had spoken to Helen briefly the night before about the way they had parted and her reaction to being touched. Even though she had wanted Jess to touch her, her mind wouldn't allow it. She wasn't sure it ever would, but she resolved to call her as soon as Sharon's case was sent to the jury.

"LADIES AND GENTLEMEN, you have sat through an emotionally draining case, and my client and I appreciate the attention you've paid to the evidence and testimony presented. Sharon Taggart is a woman who has endured a lifetime of abuse at the hands of those closest to her, people she should have been able to trust to protect her. But they all failed her. I have presented you with expert testimony that Sharon Taggart suffers from a treatable mental illness, which rendered her incapable of making sound decisions. Unable to strike out at those who hurt her, she instead chose to hurt other people. Rather than hurt those who deserved to be hurt in return for their actions against her, she chose to put them all on trial here, along with herself. You cannot render a verdict against those who knowingly harmed her, but you must decide her fate. What Sharon Taggart did was wrong. We know she shot at those vehicles, which resulted in four deaths and serious injury to others. A witness testified that she saw her do it. Experts testified that it was a weapon readily available to her and that she purchased the ammunition used to commit the crimes.

"Mr. Lassiter will tell you that she planned to shoot at those vehicles by bringing up the testimony that she patterned the crimes after something she had read. I suppose that's possible. However, Sharon Taggart had no way of knowing when her husband would rape her, when her daughter would accidentally be injured, when she would have to have her pet euthanized, or when her lover would unexpectedly end their relationship. Mr. Lassiter would like for you to believe that Sharon Taggart read something and then filed it away to be used at a later date, just in case something or someone hurt her. I submit that we all do things that we have read about." Smiling and briefly catching the eye of each juror, she continued, "I once read that during the Second World War, the military included a bar of chocolate in every soldier's rations on the battlefield because the sugar gave them energy when they were tired. Using Mr. Lassiter's line of reasoning, the only reason I reach for a Hershey bar when I'm feeling tired is because I read in a history book that it would increase my energy level.

"None of us can be sure when we will finally reach the end of an intolerable circumstance or how we will react to it. Sharon Taggart managed to hover at the edge of stability longer than anyone could have expected only to slip over the edge and into severe postpartum depression brought about by the birth of her second child. A depression so deep that she couldn't find her way out without help, and then was turned away by medical professionals who could have helped her. Even though she pulled the trigger, the deaths of four innocent people and the injuries to three others were assured twenty-five years earlier when the defendant's brother, a sadistic sexual predator, began molesting her and allowed others to hurt her while he profited from her suffering. Through a second personality, Jan, Sharon Taggart protected herself until even Jan could stand the pain no longer."

Taking a deep breath, Harriett lowered her voice slightly for effect. "We all have a dark side, ladies and gentlemen. Some hidden part of ourselves we hope will never surface, never be let loose. But, rest assured, if sufficiently provoked, that darkness will surface into the light of day and it will strike out, just as Sharon Taggart's did. Thank you."

As Harriett listened to Sean Lassiter's closing arguments, she hoped the jurors would remember what she had said. She had no doubt that Sharon was mentally disturbed. Relatively few people were just plain evil like Jared Wilkes had been. He had never been mistreated by anyone, had everything he wanted with good and loving parents, and yet he had become an indescribable evil. She thought it had been a miracle that Sharon had maintained her stability as long as she had.

THE JURY BEGAN its deliberations in the afternoon session after hearing the charge to the jury by Judge Landers. Their choices seemed simple enough. Either the defendant had a mental defect or she didn't. If she did, a mental institution awaited her. If she didn't, she was guilty of murder in the first degree and could receive either the death penalty or life in prison without the possibility of parole. Somehow, Harriett couldn't believe that imprisonment would upset Sharon very much. It would finally give her what she had probably been longing for her entire life. The chance to be away from everyone who had hurt her, left alone in peace with only her own thoughts.

Once the jury began its deliberations there was nothing to do but wait. It was impossible to concentrate on other work. Finally dropping her pen on her desk, Harriett picked up her phone and punched in a familiar number.

"Sex Offenders, Davidson," a deep male voice answered mechanically.

"Jess Raines, please," Harriett said.

"Detective Raines isn't in the office right now. Can I help you or take a message?"

"This is Harriett Markham. Would you ask her to call me when she returns? She has my number," Harriett said.

"I'll leave a message, ma'am, but it might be a while before she gets back to you. She took a leave of absence."

"Did she say when she would be returning?"

"No, ma'am, she didn't. Sorry."

As soon as she disconnected, Harriett punched in the numbers for Jess's cell phone. *I can always be reached at this number*, Jess had told her. But after four rings, Harriett was instructed to leave a message by an automated answering device.

TWO DAYS PASSED and Harriett was beginning to feel hopeful. "The bailiff said they have sent out notes asking to see evidence or clarification four times," she said, joining Nick in the office kitchen for a snack. "What do you think?"

"Well," Nick said as he slid his glasses onto the top of his head, "it could mean anything. Maybe they're looking for a way to justify the lesser charge."

"I was surprised the charge gave them that out. I wasn't expecting it, and I don't think Lassiter was either." Taking a diet tea from the refrigerator, Harriett sighed slightly. "Where do you think Lassiter got Lou Harmon's name?"

"Maybe from a family member."

Frowning to herself, she said softly, "I think Wayne leaked it."

"Why would he do that? He works for you."

Joining her partner at the table, Harriett shrugged. "He's always thought Sharon was faking. Lassiter's people found everything about her that we did. Except that one piece that drew it all together."

"Have you asked him about it?"

"No, and I don't plan to," she said as she nibbled at a cracker.

"Ms. Markham?" Phyllis said from the kitchen doorway. "You have a call on line two. Mr. Lassiter."

Harriett and Nick looked at one another for a moment before responding. "Thank you, Phyllis," Harriett said as she got to her feet. Nick followed her to her office and waited while she took the call.

"What did he want?" he asked as she replaced the receiver on its cradle.

"A meeting. In an hour."

"Maybe he's worried about it taking the jury so long to reach a decision."

"Guess we'll find out in an hour."

NICK SAT AT the conference table in a room on the second floor of the Travis County Courthouse while Harriett paced in front of a window overlooking the street below, periodically glancing at the clock on the far wall. She was startled when Lassiter walked into the room.

"Ms. Markham. Mr. Lazslo," Lassiter nodded as he pulled out a chair and set his briefcase on the table.

"Ms. Markham," Lassiter said, clearing his throat, "I can honestly say that the things I have heard during the course of this trial have both disgusted and angered me. However, even though I have enormous empathy for what your client has endured, I cannot, in good conscience, hold her blameless for the deaths of those four people, but..."

"But you're concerned that the jury might find her insane," Harriett finished for him.

"It's a possibility that I would rather not face. While I don't believe Mrs. Taggart suffers from the disorder she is claiming, I have no doubt that she is mentally disturbed." Taking a deep breath, Lassiter said, "Therefore, after conferring with the Dallas County District Attorney, we are willing to offer a plea and make a sentencing recommendation that would allow Mrs. Taggart to receive psychiatric help."

"What are you offering?" Nick asked.

"Second degree murder, twenty-five to life with the possibility of parole after she serves the minimum," Lassiter stated. "Non-negotiable."

"I see," Harriett said. "I'll have to confer with my client, of course."

"Of course," Lassiter nodded.

HARRIETT WAS WAITING in a small interview room when Sharon was brought in. She looked tired. When they were alone, Harriett said, "The DA has offered to make a deal, Sharon."

"Why?" Sharon asked.

"They're afraid the jury will rule in your favor, but I'm just as afraid that they won't. Or it could still go either way. I think this is the best deal you're going to get."

Sharon frowned, "What are they offering?"

"Second degree murder with a sentencing recommendation that will allow for parole eventually if you agree to receive psychiatric help while in prison."

"I see. And you think I should accept this generosity?" Sharon asked as she folded her arms across her chest.

"Yes, I do."

"When do I have to decide?"

"As soon as possible. The jury could come back with a verdict at any time. The judge will have to be notified that we have agreed or declined to take the offer."

Sharon walked to the window and stared out. "How long before I would be eligible for parole?"

"They're recommending twenty-five to life," Harriett said. "Fifteen years minimum served, possibly less with good behavior."

Sharon turned and smiled at Harriett. "And this is a good deal?"

"You're guilty, Sharon. You know it and I know it. There was never a Jan, but you did a damn fine job of fooling everyone."

Sharon laughed, "Fooled you, didn't I? And those idiot shrinks who examined me."

"You need help, Sharon. Maybe you didn't think those people would die, but they did and for what? So you could drag your family and husband through court?"

"I might win."

"You might, but if you do and get out, what will you do the next time someone hurts you?" Moving closer to Sharon, Harriett said, "Who will you hurt the next time, Sharon?"

"Has anyone ever hurt you, Harriett? Hurt you so badly you didn't think could get over it?"

"Yes."

"Have you gotten over it yet?"

"I'm working on it," Harriett admitted.

"So I don't suppose I'll be seeing you after this," Sharon smiled.

"No, you won't."

"You did the best you could," Sharon grinned, the look in her eyes unnerving. "Maybe this way I'll get a chance to see whoever told them about Lou Harmon through my rifle sight someday."

Chapter
Forty-Eight

SHE HAD BEEN driving through an unexpected gray rain that seemed to be following her for nearly a hundred miles before the truck finally popped out into bright sunlight that glared up from the road. Rolling the driver's side window down, she rested her elbow on the window frame, allowing the spring air to blow her hair wildly. The rain dripping from the roof occasionally found its way against her face. She ignored it. For the first time in months, she felt strangely free. The air smelled fresh as she took in deep breaths. She wasn't in a particular hurry, but hoped to make it into the silence and safety of the cabin before the rain could pursue her any further. She had loved the rain as a child. Thoughts of soaking rains cooling the dusty soil around her parents' house had soothed her and carried her off into a dreamless, peaceful sleep. She hadn't experienced that feeling in a long time, and she needed it now more than she ever had before.

Without any real need to, she flipped the turn signal and turned the steering wheel, guiding the truck onto an unpaved road toward the lake. By morning, the narrow road would be too muddy to navigate, but that was fine, she thought. She wouldn't be going anywhere for a while anyway. She couldn't wait for the solitude ahead of her and realizing how much she wanted it, needed it, she accelerated toward it, covering the final two miles quickly. Bringing the truck to a stop next to the cabin, she lifted her duffel bag from behind the truck seat and slung it over her shoulder. Wayne had promised that no one would know where she was, she thought as she walked slowly up the front steps, glancing over her shoulder at the small whitecaps that were beginning to form in the cove. The rain would be there soon.

Unlocking the cabin door, she stepped into her past and was momentarily flooded with memories. The air smelled slightly stale as she looked around. She smiled at her mind's sight of her father attempting to flip pancakes in an old skillet, making yet another snack on the floor for his dog instead of breakfast for his hungry, laughing daughter. Moving across the front room, she paused in front of the cold fireplace, seeing herself in Alex's arms, warm and contented at the time. Blinking the memory away, she shook her head slightly and walked into the master bedroom and tossed her bag on the bed.

As she carried three bags of groceries into the kitchen, she set them on the counter and opened the refrigerator door. She was surprised to see a familiar looking bottle of wine lying on the bottom shelf and picked it up. "It can't be," she said aloud. It was Alex's favorite wine. "Surely Wayne has cleaned out this damned refrigerator at least once in the last twelve years."

Searching through the kitchen drawers, she found a corkscrew and peeled the silver, metallic wrapper from the cork. Slowly extracting the cork she sniffed the contents and shrugged as she opened another cabinet and took down a wine glass. "What the hell?" she shrugged, pouring the glass half full. After a cautious sip, she smiled. It had aged better than she had. When everything was put away, she carried the glass into the front room and reclined on the couch, propping her feet on the coffee table. Staring out the front window, she watched the gathering storm move across the lake toward her, took a deep breath, and closed her eyes.

A flash of lightning and the sound of low rolling thunder woke her. It was almost dark, but she couldn't tell if the darkness was from night falling or the storm that had claimed the area. Forcing her body up, she placed an armful of logs in the fireplace grate and built a small tent of tinder. As the fire began to take hold and creep up the sides of the larger pieces of wood, she refilled her glass and dragged a pillow onto the floor, watching the sparks from the fire as they drifted slowly upward until they were sucked into the updraft of the chimney. It had grown completely dark outside, but she preferred to sit in the dark, the room illuminated only by the flickering fire and an occasional streak of lightning. She had no idea what time it was and didn't really care. She had left her watch in the truck, as usual.

Gradually the storm passed, leaving in its wake a soft, soaking rain and the wonderful smell of freshness. She was suddenly incredibly tired and banked the fire before wandered into the bedroom. Lifting the duffel bag off the bed, she slipped her shoes off and stretched out on the bed, feeling her body sink into it. The pillow smelled freshly laundered, and its scent conjured up memories of the sheets her mother always sun-dried. To soak up the sunshine and bring it into their bedrooms, Irene had told her children. A smile tugged at Harriett's lips as sleep pulled her further down into the bed.

A SHAFT OF sunlight across her face woke her the next morning. Holding her hand over her eyes to block the light, Harriett rolled away from it, but didn't fall back to sleep. Reaching out, she let her hand run over the empty coolness of the other side of the bed. It shouldn't be this way, she thought. She shouldn't be alone. Like so many things lately though, that hadn't been her decision. She felt her eyes mist over, but blinked it away. Sitting up and leaning back on her elbows, she waited a few minutes before swinging her legs over the side of the bed. She pushed hair over her head with both hands as she made her way into the kitchen.

She was surprised at the lingering coolness the rain had left behind when she carried a steaming cup of coffee onto the porch, sipping it cautiously. Sitting on the top step, she squinted at the light sparkling off the water in the cove and wondered if Wayne had left any fishing gear in the cabin. After a good rain, she was sure she would be able to coax a few earthworms from their hiding places. Swallowing the last of her coffee, she set the cup on the porch and made her way toward the fishing pier. She didn't have a plan. She wanted to be alone to think, to decide what she wanted to do. She had never thought about it before. She had always known what she wanted, had always gone after it, and had always caught it. Did she now, at forty-five, still want what she had wanted when she was twenty-five, or had she outgrown it?

If she never worked again, she was sure she had invested well and saved enough to stop working. Looking mentally through her personal dossier, however, she discovered that it was empty. She had a few good friends but otherwise was alone. Lacey would be leaving in a couple of months for college to pursue her own dreams and hopefully catch them. She could spend her time doing charity work, maybe join the Junior League and spend her time at book readings and fund-raisers for worthwhile organizations. Harriett threw her head back and laughed out loud. No matter how hard she tried she couldn't imagine herself doing any of those things. She didn't have any hobbies to occupy her time and, although she donated generously to charitable causes, it wasn't something she'd want to do full-time. She was an attorney. It was all she'd ever wanted, all she'd ever been happy doing. She loved the competition of it, the jousting back and forth in court, fighting the good fight or at least letting the other guy know he had been in a fight. Maybe Nick was right. She could become a visiting lecturer for young attorneys. She could write that book on the disparity of legal representation between the rich and the poor she had been thinking about. She could accept nothing but pro bono cases. Hell, she could join the public defender's office. But she liked seeing her name on the front door of her practice every morning when she walked through those gracious beveled glass doors that announced the entrance to Markham and Lazslo. But no matter what decision she ultimately made, she would still be alone.

Shaking her head vigorously, she decided she had had enough deep thinking for one day. Maybe just a few minutes of serious thought each day would make it easier. She didn't have to make a decision that day, that moment. The world wouldn't implode into itself if Harriett Markham didn't make an instant decision.

THE AFTERNOON OF what she thought was her fourth day of solitude she dragged her body up from the couch, which was becoming much too comfortable. Slipping a bookmark into the paperback in her hand, she walked toward the bathroom, stripping out of her clothes as she walked. She stepped into the shower a few minutes later and felt the water pelt her skin. Reaching up, she twisted the nozzle of the showerhead anticipating the water that would change from a mere pelting into a deep pounding. Moving under the water as it beat against her, she began to feel the muscles across her shoulders and down her back relax under the massaging stream. Bracing herself against the shower wall, she was surprised and angry when she felt warm tears run down her face, joining the water from the shower. Why the hell was she crying? Whom was she crying for? Turning the showerhead back to normal, she let the clean water wash the tears away.

She had just finished preparing a small salad to accompany the salmon she was planning to grill for dinner when she glanced out the kitchen window. Dark clouds spread across the horizon and appeared to be moving toward her. "Probably an hour or so away," she muttered to herself. There would still be plenty of time to get the salmon fillet on and off the grill before the rain swept across the lake. The wind was beginning to pick up slightly as she placed the rack over the coals and closed the lid of the grill. Brushing her blowing hair away from her face, she smelled the scent of rain. Every few minutes, she basted the fillet with butter and freshly squeezed lemon juice. When she saw the skin around the edges of the fish begin to blacken, she removed the rack from the grill and emptied the fish onto a platter.

The wind battered rain against the front windows of the cabin in waves as she set the salmon and salad on the coffee table. Returning from the kitchen a minute later, she flipped the small stereo on to keep her company while she ate dinner. Darkness fell quickly around her, and while she loved the rain, early spring storms worried her. One never knew when something more ominous would be spawned from the dark clouds.

The sound of banging on the door of the cabin moments later startled her. No one in their right mind would be caught outside after dark in this kind of weather, she thought, uncertain of whether to open the door. It was probably an idiot fisherman who thought he had enough time to escape before the storm hit. Wiping her mouth, she looked out the window next to the front door, but could see nothing more than a hunched figure, soaking wet, standing on the porch. Not willing to take a chance by opening the door to a stranger unarmed, she picked up the fireplace poker and held it as she pulled the door open.

The figure turned toward her, hair plastered to her scalp, water streaming down her face and glasses.

"Jess?" Harriett asked.

"Can I please come in? It's a little...damp out here," Jess said, trying to wipe rain away from her face.

"Oh, my God, of course. Let me get you a towel."

As Harriett quickly disappeared, Jess stepped through the door, trying not to drip in too large an area. Just as quickly as she had left, Harriett returned with a large bathroom towel.

"Thank you," Jess said as she ran the towel over her head and clothing. "Sorry if I made a mess. I'll clean it up."

"Don't worry. You can't hurt this floor," Harriett smiled.

"Wayne said the fishing here sucked, and now I know why. Too damned much rain," Jess mumbled.

"Let me get you a cup of coffee or some hot tea. You must be freezing."

Handing the towel back to Harriett, Jess cleared her throat. "I won't be staying. I just needed to tell you that I'm sorry I couldn't protect you, Harriett. That I couldn't keep my promise. You're not the first person I've let down, but I hope someday you can forgive me for not being there when you needed me the most. I'm so sorry."

"There's nothing to forgive, Jess," Harriett said softly.

"Sorry I made a mess," Jess said glancing down at the floor, "of everything." Looking at Harriett for a moment, she turned and walked out into the rain again.

Jess had jogged halfway to her Durango by the time Harriett reached her again. Trying to brush away the rain dripping down her face, Harriett said loudly over the thunder, "You...you didn't say goodbye."

"I don't like goodbyes," Jess said just as loudly, rivulets of water running down her forehead and cheeks. "It sounds too much like the end of something. Go back inside. You shouldn't be out in this mess."

Shaking her head, sending water flying, Harriett asked, "Why didn't you tell me you were going away? It was because of me, wasn't it? Because of what I said? I didn't mean any of it, Jess. You have to believe that. Please. I...I don't want to lose you."

Slowly, Jess moved closer and pulled Harriett into her arms and held her tightly. "Have you had enough time to think?" she asked softly, bringing her mouth close to Harriett's ear.

"About us, you mean?" Harriett asked as she pressed her head against Jess's shoulder.

Releasing Harriett from her arms and looking down at her, Jess nodded, "And other things."

Harriett shivered slightly, from Jess's touch as much as the rain. "Can we at least get out of the rain and warm up before we have the rest of this conversation?"

Jess nodded as she wrapped her arm around Harriett's shoulders and turned back toward the cabin.

More Brenda Adcock titles:

Pipeline

What do you do when the mistakes you made in the past come back to slap you in the face with a vengeance? Joanna Carlisle, a fifty-seven year old photojournalist, has only begun to adjust to retirement on her small ranch outside Kerrville, Texas, when she finds herself unwillingly sucked into an investigation of illegal aliens being smuggled into the United States to fill the ranks of cheap labor needed to increase corporate profits.

Joanna is a woman who has always lived life her way and on her own terms, enjoying a career that had given her everything she thought she ever wanted or needed. An unexpected visit by her former lover, Cate Hammond, and the attempted murder of their son, forces Jo to finally face what she had given up. Although she hasn't seen Cate or their son for fifteen years, she finds that the feelings she had for Cate had only been dormant, but had never died. No matter how much she fights her attraction to Cate, Jo cannot help but wonder whether she had made the right decision when she chose career and independence over love.

Jo comes to understand the true meaning of friendship and love only when her investigation endangers not only her life, but also the lives of the people around her.

ISBN 1-932300-64-3
978-1-932300-64-2

Reiko's Garden

Hatred...like love...knows no boundaries.

How much impact can one person have on a life?

When sixty-five-year old Callie Owen returns to her rural childhood home in Eastern Tennessee to attend the funeral of a woman she hasn't seen in twenty years, she's forced to face the fears, heartache, and turbulent events that scarred both her body and her mind. Drawing strength from Jean, her partner of thirty years, and from their two grown children, Callie stays in the valley longer than she had anticipated and relives the years that changed her life forever.

In 1949, Japanese war bride Reiko Sanders came to Frost Valley, Tennessee with her soldier husband and infant son. Callie Owen was an inquisitive ten-year-old whose curiosity about the stranger drove her to disobey her father for just one peek at the woman who had become the subject of so much speculation. Despite Callie's fears, she soon finds that the exotic-looking woman is kind and caring, and the two forge a tentative, but secret friendship.

When Callie and her five brothers and sisters were left orphaned, Reiko provided emotional support to Callie. The bond between them continued to grow stronger until Callie left Frost Valley as a teenager, emotionally and physically scarred, vowing never to return and never to forgive.

It's not until Callie goes "home" that she allows herself to remember how Reiko influenced her life. Once and for all, can she face the terrible events of her past? Or will they come back to destroy all that she loves?

ISBN 978-1-932300-77-2
1-932300-77-5

Available at booksellers everywhere.

FORTHCOMING TITLES

published by
Quest Books

In the Blood
by Rick R. Reed

By day, Elise draws and paints, spilling out the horrific visions of her tortured mind. By night, she walks the streets, selling her body to the highest bidder.

And then they come into her life, a trio of impossibly beautiful vampires: Terence, Maria, and Edward. When they encounter Elise, they set an explosive triangle in motion. Terence wants to drain her blood. Maria just wants Elise...as lover and partner through eternity. And Edward, the most recently converted, wants to prevent her from making the same mistake he made as a young abstract expressionist artist in 1950s Greenwich Village: sacrificing his artistic vision for immortal life. He is the only one of them still human enough to realize what an unholy trade this is.

In the Blood is a novel that will grip you in a vise of suspense that won't let go, forcing you to stay up long past midnight, turning page after page, until the very last moment, when a surprising turn of events changes everything and demonstrates, truly, what love and sacrifice are all about.

Available September 2007

Face of the Enemy
by Sandra Barret

Helena 'Dray' Draybeck is a military brat finishing her final year of fighter pilot training at a Terran Military space station. She's cocky about everything except her dismal track record with women. Dray is driven to be a top pilot like her mother, but someone at the space station does not want Dray to succeed.

Jordan Bowers is the daughter of a high-ranking ambassador. She wants a career as far away from politics as possible. As one of the best cadets in the fighter pilot program, Jordan captures Dray's attention in more ways than one. But Jordan won't let anyone get close to her. She hides a terrible secret that could end her own career and turn Dray against her.

When an explosion on their training station turns into a full-fledged attack, Dray and Jordan are put on the fast track to active military duty. But Dray's enemy sabotages her assignment and her chances with Jordan.

The threat of war pits Dray and Jordan against family, questionable allies, and an enemy neither is prepared for. Can they build something more than friendship, or will war and family secrets tear these two women apart?

Face of the Enemy is a stand alone novel set in the Terra/Nova universe, where chip implants and DNA manipulation are commonplace, and bigotry drives an interstellar superpower.

Available November 2007

OTHER QUEST PUBLICATIONS

About the Author:

A product of the Appalachian region of Eastern Tennessee, Brenda now lives in Central Texas, near Austin. She began writing in junior high school where she wrote an admittedly hokey western serial to entertain her friends. Completing her graduate studies in Eastern European history in 1971, she worked as a graphic artist, a public relations specialist for the military and a display advertising specialist until she finally had to admit that her mother might have been right and earned her teaching certification. For the last twenty-plus years she has taught world history and political science. Brenda and her partner of ten years, Cheryl, are the parents of three grown children and one still in high school, as well as two grandchildren. Rounding out their home are four temperamental cats, May-May, Bitsey, Harley, and Tootie, as well as a brand new puppy named Tipper. When she is not writing Brenda creates stained glass and shoots pool at her favorite bar. She may be contacted at adcockb10@yahoo.com_and welcomes all comments, good or bad.

VISIT US ONLINE AT
www.regalcrest.biz

At the Regal Crest Website You'll Find

- The latest news about forthcoming titles and new releases

- Our complete backlist of romance, mystery, thriller and adventure titles

- Information about your favorite authors

- Current bestsellers

- Media tearsheets to print and take with you when you shop

Regal Crest titles are available from all progressive booksellers and online at StarCrossed Productions, (www.scp-inc.biz), or at www.amazon.com, www.bamm.com, www.barnesandnoble.com, and many others.

Lightning Source UK Ltd.
Milton Keynes UK
10 March 2010

151220UK00002B/18/A